ACTS OF CONSCIENCE

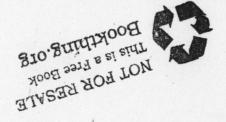

WILLIAM BARTON

ACTS OF CONSCIENCE

ASPECT®

WARNER BOOKS

A Time Warner Company

Aspect name and logo are registered trademarks of Warner Books, Inc.

Warner Books, Inc., 1271 Avenue of the Americas, New York, NY 10020

Visit our Web site at
http://pathfinder.com/twep

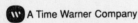 A Time Warner Company

Printed in the United States of America

First Printing: January 1997

10 9 8 7 6 5 4 3 2 1

Library of Congress Cataloging-in-Publication Data

Barton, William
     Acts of conscience / William Barton.
         p.   cm.
     ISBN 0-446-67251-3
     I. Title.
PS3552.A778A64   1997
813'.54—dc20   96-3004
                                                            CIP

Book design by H. Roberts
Cover design by Don Puckey
Cover illustration by Wayne Barlowe

to
H. Beam Piper
fuzzy logic of a sort

ACTS OF
CONSCIENCE

If a man hasn't discovered something that
he will die for, he isn't fit to live.

—Martin Luther King, Jr.
23 June 1963

1

I have . . . always loved the stars.

When I was a boy, in a time almost thirty years ago, when my life was hardly begun, I loved to wander the remoter parts of Martyred Sasha's Wilderness, to lie on my back on a favorite hillside in the night. Lie there for hours, looking up at the sky, soft wind in my face, on my bare skin, in my hair, full of wonder.

There on my hillside, I could look out over the whole world, beyond my feet the long slope of a dark lawn, daylight's green grass hardly illuminated by the wan light of the faraway stars, the dim, splotchy shadows of the trees, beyond them the black outlines of the recreational center's lightless buildings. Other buildings farther away, equally dark, were the unlit entryways to the underground, to the human-dense warrens of the Meadows of Dan, and the black plains of Volterra's dusty floor beyond, flooded by the hard light of a sun so bright it was like a hole in the sky.

I remember lying there at midnight, when the darkness was already a week old, cool, very cool breeze on the bare skin of my chest, making me wonder if Maintenance had screwed up the temperature coupling on the city's eutropic atmosphere shield.

Irrelevant to a boy looking up at thousands of hard dots, like motionless, steely pinpricks in the flat black background of the sky, most of them empty white, a few tinged with some pastel hue or another.

Bright, colorless Polaris hanging in the heavens, just above the top of my head, always high because crater Volterra and the Meadows of Dan lie just shy of sixty degrees north, not so terribly far from the north pole of the Moon. Pale blue Regulus off to my left. Yellow-tinted Procyon suspended over my belly button. Orangish Aldebaran just off the sky's centerline, to one side of the Milky Way's pale, irregular starry road.

I'd lie and stare at some sky feature or another, look at the jewel box of the Pleiades, staring and staring, waiting for just one more pale violet star to pop out of the absorbent background, waiting for the cluster's nebulosity to take on its famous, rarely seen streaky appearance . . .

"Du Cheyne." Sharp. Snapping me back to the here and now. Rossignol's voice: "You going to put your stuff on or not?"

Me, hanging weightless in the air in my undershorts, holding on to the open door of my locker, half-naked men and women bobbing all around, soaring back and forth as they got ready for change of shift. "Sorry." Me, grinning a grin that, for some reason I could never quite understand, seemed to make people angry.

Rossignol, holding a corner of the locker bank, gold line-supervisor's belt in the other hand, shaking it at me, mouth set in a characteristically crooked smile. "I swear, Gaetan. Sometimes . . . well." A shrug. "I sure as hell am glad you don't pull that shit when we're outside. You looked like you were in some kind of trance."

I reached into my locker and unhooked my soft gray suitliner coverall, started pulling it on, making sure the footies were straight, that my fingers went all the way down to the tips of the gloves, before zipping up the front. "Sure. The job's the job."

Rossignol's smile fading. Dark brown eyes looking me over. He said, "Yeah." Eyes measuring me. "Gae, I'd like you to step in on the D-1 prime mover Jimmy Haas's been working. There's something fishy about the power screen."

"You let a Nine work on a drive modulus connected to a live field well converter?"

A quick look around. "Jimmy's a Nine step Twelve. He'll have enough points to make Ten Step Zero in a few weeks."

"He will if you don't fuck him up, Ross. And don't call me Gae."

"Sure. Sorry."

"Are there bonus points on this?"

A slightly sour look. "Standard seven."

Seven. Thirty more and I could jump to Wage Grade Ten step Nine and a few more livres in my paycheck. Thirteen hundred more and I could have Rossignol's gold belt for the asking. Ten thousand more and I could apply for a white belt and conversion from wage to salary grade. "Make it ten."

Mouth set in a flat line. "Okay, Gaetan. Ten." He turned away, and I went back to putting on my suit.

Suit pants, made of something that looked like a fine, chrome-plated chain mail of mirror-bright links, cinched in tight. Tunic of the same stuff. Helmet like a balaclava hat, covering everything but my eyes. Thin black boots made of something like flexible plastic, coming up to mid-calf. Black plastic gauntlets covering my already-gloved hands. Blue belt around my waist, the blue of our shop and trade, Outside Machinists and Spatial Machinery Mechanics.

Muffled by the helmet, coming from the other side of the locker bank, I heard an angry mutter: "God damn it, Ross, why the hell did you assign the D-1 to *that* asshole?"

I slipped into the equilibrimotor harness and started hooking it up. Wrapped my toolbelt around that. Clipped on the inertially heavy battery pack. Rossignol, that same shushing tone in his voice, said, "It needs to be done right, Todd. Jimmy—"

Todd Sanchez said, "Why the fuck *him?* Why not me? Jimmy and I could—"

"I'm sorry, Todd. I . . . Hell, you're a good mechanic. But du Cheyne . . ."

I slid the comlink diadem over the outside of the helmet, settled it carefully around my temples, and thought, Netlink on. Autocheck.

The suit thought, All systems nominal.

Sanchez said, "I've been in this business just as long as du Cheyne, Ross. I'm *better* than any damn shithead who—"

Rossignol: "And you're still only a Ten step Four, Todd."

Long silence.

Sanchez said, "You're a fucking asshole too."

Another long silence, then a sigh: "Let's get outside, Todd. The job's waiting."

I flooded the suit's limbs with power and life, watched my pale shadow, cast on the front of the locker bank, fill up with pastel sparkles, with tiny moving rainbows. Felt the suit harden against my body, molding itself to my form. Felt it fill up with its own awareness, felt it flutter against my chest, like the beating of some distant, impersonal heart. Outside then. Outside with all the others, slipping through the shop's airscreen, metadynamic force field reaching through the suit to tickle on my skin, a soft feather touch.

They call this place Stardock, romantic name, I've heard, from some old story. Prosaically: Alpha-Five Shipyard, Chromo-electric Starship Division of the Eighth Ray Scientific-Industrial Enterprise. ERSIE-5 to her intimates.

I like Stardock better.

Stardock stretching away in all directions, a regular, three-dimensional array of pale yellow girders, dotted here and there with little buildings, habitats, work centers, many-armed cranes crawling about like so many spiders, vast spiders, spiders the size of small asteroids.

I could look out in any direction. See square after yellow-lined square, each smaller one set within the larger square that surrounded it. Some squares blocked by broken-down, half-dismantled ships. Others empty. Empty right through to . . .

black sky. Stars blotted out by the brilliant lights of the work teams. By the light of the cranes. By the light of the brilliant sun, Old Sol hanging right over there . . . the suit whispered, 134,702,092.8 kilometers, in my head. In the other direction, one-tenth as far away, Earth was a tiny, bright blue-white circle, Luna a much smaller, very much dimmer reddish gray spot by its side, almost invisible.

I couldn't really see well enough to know, but from her position relative to Earth it might be nighttime over the farside, darkness long fallen over crater Volterra and the Meadows of Dan. Maybe some little boy was lying on a hillside, cool wind ruffling his uncombed hair, looking up at the stars.

I can't have been the only one.

Rossignol, like a ghost in my head, ghost in everyone's head just now: "Let's go, boys and girls. Clock's ticking."

I let the suit read my mind, let it pass my wishes on to the equilibrimotor's little brain, felt that distant pulse start to throb against my chest, harder and harder, like the strengthening beat of powerful wings, wings of fire, sculpted from impalpable lines of force, and we began to move out into space, out into a maze of struts and girders and broken-down ships, hanging between Earth and Sun, hanging in a void that surely pervades all of Creation.

Almost noon. Jimmy Haas squirming beside me, while the two of us floated on air down in the D-1's propulsion segment, ship's guts hanging open before us.

When you look down into a live field well converter, it feels like the thing wants to pull your eyes out. No sense of the energies contained there. No feeling that if this thing got away from you, Stardock would be vaporized in an instant, the $L_1(SE)$ industrial complex blown to bits a fraction of a second later by an expanding fireball far, far brighter than the Sun.

Funny to think of it that way. I could reach in with my tools, pop the safeties on this thing. Somewhere in Work Control, alarms would start to scream, but, of course, it'd be much too late. Vidnet would link to my suit, start shutting down my tools, command my suit limbs to freeze solid. Too late. By then I'd've opened the converter's artificial event horizon, the accumulator core would wake up, surprised, and make a run for freedom.

Down on Earth, the pale, wonderful, impossibly lovely blue skies would flicker and rich men would look up, surprised, at a momentarily violet Sun, wondering, *What the fuck . . .*

Jimmy fidgeted and said, "Five till, Gae."

Little shit's been calling me that all morning. I glanced at him, then looked back down into the well. Hardly anything there at all. A hollow plastic shell, composite osmiridium and berylodiamond whiskers holding a net of weak boron filaments. Almost-invisible lines of turquoise light, streaking through a dusty-looking mist, aiming down to some infinitesimal center.

The suit'd been nagging me all morning about the way the engineering space around us was flooded with hard X-rays. Someone was going to have to come in here later and clean up after us, cost the Eighth Ray Scientific-Industrial Enterprise a certain amount of money and . . . fuck it. Let Temporary Services deal with the matter. It's their job.

Down in there, where my eyes couldn't see, something not at all like a black hole was gathering vacuum energy, skimming it right off the surface of the plenum, adding to the store its manufacturers had given it in the first place. Somewhere down there a region of Planck sockets, charged with Kaluza-Klein entities of a specific configuration, kept a little bit of the universe sequestered, kept increasing its imaginary mass . . .

"Gaetan."

The suit whispered, Eleven fifty-eight, in my head.

"Sure, Jimmy. Let's just slide the cover back on and get out of here."

Jimmy said, "What about our tools?"

I put mine in *park* and unhooked the belt, complete with power pack, from my harness, letting it float free, bobbing gently beside the open mouth of the converter. "They'll be all right without us."

My suit whispered, Mr. Haas' hardware matrix respectfully submits that it is the property of ERSIE-5. Mr. Haas is holding a personal responsibility marker in the core memory of the tool dispensary.

Right. These are *my* tools. If something happens to them, it's between me and the insurance underwriters of the Metal Founders, Machinists, and Aerospace Workers Interplanetary. Jimmy loses the tools he's borrowed from Stardock and they'll dock him a thousand points, bust him all the way back to Wage Grade Eight.

I said, "Noted and logged. I'll pull your dispensary marker onto my tab. Go get lunch, Jimmy." A long, dark stare, then he was gone. Shit. Little bastard didn't even slide the cover back on.

I slid up through the long access tunnel from the propulsion segment to the command module, slipping through the hatch into a small, cool dark room, control boards lit by a twinkle of amber lights. I floated up over the backs of the seats, turning feet first, let myself slide down into the command pilot's seat. Maybe flight engineer would've been more appropriate, but still . . . I put my hand on the throttle and just sat there. Sat. Waited.

How is it that this longing still grips my heart, after all these hollow years? I said, "Is the navigation subsystem up?"

My suit whispered, The software is still loaded and processing. Command subsystem uplink revision won't be started until after propulsion and power are done.

"Is it locked?"

Not locked.

"Monitored?"

Not monitored.

Hmh. Sloppy. Very, very sloppy. "Will you tell on me?"

The suit said, This particular hardware matrix does not have a rule sieve cluster to that effect.

What a nice little spacesuit you are. Better not ask if it wants to go for a little joyride. "Bring up nav displays please."

The whole undersurface of the display dome flickered, very

dim yellowish light, letting me know the subsystems were very badly in need of renormalization, nothing to worry about, not my job, then the stars came out.

It was as if we were floating free in space. This way the Sun, that way Earth and Moon. There. Red fleck Mars. White spark Venus. Yellow dot Mercury. Bright, orangish Jupiter. Yellow-white Saturn. Pale blue Uranus. Royal blue Neptune. Picked out like rich jewels, strung along the necklace of the ecliptic.

A little swarm of dust motes, a flattened ring reaching around the whole sky. Piazzi's Belt between Mars and Jupiter. A thicker, more diffuse swarm out beyond Uranus, beginning to fill the sky beyond Neptune, Kuiper's Belt, Pluto-Charon a fat double-dot out there, no more than first among its kin.

Hundreds of little green wedges all around the sky, concentrated along the ecliptic plane. Interplanetary shipping in transit, as reported by Space Traffic Control. The suit whispered, Vidnet link is down. This display is more than three weeks old.

I could feel the throttle under my hand.

Light the field modulus device then. Pale blue fire flickering around this half-dismantled D-1 prime mover. Work Control calling over the link, *What the hell do you think you're playing at?*

Shove the throttle forward. Ship sliding from its berth, falling down into the planetary deeps.

Reasonable, I suppose. This ship's main purpose is to haul heavy cargoes around the solar system. They gave it big, strong legs with which to do that job, but I could use them to run, faster, faster than any conceivable wind, fiery wind from the Sun, out beyond the Oort, out to the fixed stars. Out where the big ships go.

Of course, I'd starve to death and/or suffocate in just a couple of weeks, but what the hell.

1220.

Better go get a little snack now, while I've got the chance.

Shop mess hall. A three-tiered, mezzanine-style dining room under about one-tenth standard gee. Just enough so you can sit and eat, not enough to stop you from flying an equilibrimotor. Self-service. Food just sitting in steam table piles. Most of it already gone. Caesar salad, wilted and slimy under its dressing, croutons getting soft. A cold bottle of grape-tinged ice tea. I looked at the big bowl of banana pudding, cookies crumbled, bananas turning dark, custard starting to weep some kind of clear stuff.

I flew up to the table where I usually sit, set my tray down, unhooked my equilibrimotor harness and leaned it against the wall, near some others. Sat down with the people I usually sit with. Looked at the crap in my tray. Why did I think I was going to eat this shit?

Across and diagonal from me, Layla Garstang looked up from her tray. "Hey, Gaetan, you still coming with us next week? We need to know for sure. Zell's got to sign out the camping permits tonight."

I lifted off my diadem, pulled the space helmet from my head, dropped them beside my tray. "Sure. Already turned in my vacation voucher."

Garstang grinning, a nondescript woman with an open, boxy face. Blue eyes. Pale pink lips. Freckles on light, neutral Caucasian skin. "All right, that makes six."

Zell Benson, tall, heavily built, bullet-headed, dark brown face more or less empty, said "Okay. You and Phil. Me and Millie. Rua Mater . . . and du Cheyne."

I used to wonder about these people. I always thought they didn't want me here, but then . . . Hell, before she took up with Phil Hendrickx, I even fucked Garstang a few times. Maybe enough times to think we'd gotten something . . . started. How long's it been? Six years? Something like that. Maybe I fucked her five or six times, and it seemed all right to me. Worth continuing, anyway. Not worth it to her, apparently. I still have a distinct memory of things from those few nights. The way she smelled. The way she felt, on my fingers, on my prick.

She said, "I'm glad you're coming along this time, Gaetan." Blue eyes on me. Curious, perhaps. What does *she* remember about those few times we were together, way back when? Maybe those mysterious feelings that made her decide we weren't *right* for each other?

"Yeah. Sure. It'll be fun."

She smiled, then looked down toward the other end of the table, where Rua Mater, small and dark, face shadowed by her long black hair, was sitting. No lunch. Just sitting there, eyes closed, readerclip stuck in her hair like a child's barrette.

End of shift. Go on home. Home to my little hole-in-the-wall dorm room. Trudge up the half-gee corridor with a faceless horde of nameless gray men and women, close the door on a murmur of tired voices. Sprawl in my favorite gray recliner, sit back. Stare.

Plenty of stuff in the refrigerator. I could winkle a steak, maybe. Too much trouble? Go down to the plaza level then, get some gourmet ethnic crap . . . definitely too much trouble. I glanced at the vidnet link monitor over the door, felt it reach out for my thoughts. Not that the apartment appliances could make up my mind for me . . . at least the monitor might guess.

I heard the bartender go through its setting-up routines. I pictured myself swilling a black Russian, then a second, maybe a third, heard the ice tinkle and the nozzles hiss. Shit. Now I'll have to get up and reach for the glass. Whatever idiot laid out this apartment . . . maybe I should just move all my furniture over to the breakfast nook.

By the time I got back to my seat the infolink was up, colors swirling over half the room . . . falling away, as if the walls were turning to vapor . . . node-popping through my standard-interest filter . . . thirty channels of precanned news, each with its own political slant, a couple of dozen relatively specialized "educational" channels, fluff, mostly, but . . . I stopped it on *Planets and Animals and You.*

Long shot across some craggy gray and brown badlands, tumbled rocks and towering cliffs shot through with streaks of dark vermilion and bright jade green. Sullen red-orange sky, through which peered a fat brown sun, cloudscape around it brightly backlit. Flat, murky, gray-brown sea reaching out toward the far horizon. Near the edge of the world, between cliffscape and sea, a dun-colored forest, narrow, towering trees, brought closer now by a telephoto zoom. In the distance, projecting above the horizon, the smoky gray cone of an active volcano.

We jumped into the forest, came face-to-face with something that looked like a cross between a centipede and the sorts of monsters little kids like to make with their Tinkertoy robots. The monster roared and snarled and reared, showing serrated, bright yellow fangs.

A dinosaur show for the kiddies. Monsters from deep space, educating them, you see, all about the faraway world of God, Delta Pavonis 2, just a little more than eighteen-point-six light-years from our safe, tame solar system. God, called home by a few hundred thousand human colonists. Home that was, by fast starship, almost twenty years' travel from Earth and Moon and Mars and all the other little places where all but the tiniest fraction of humanity lived.

I let the monitor move on. *Other Worlds, Other Cultures.* A more recent favorite, sort of an extraterrestrial archaeology presentation. Little domes under a sullen, blue-black sky. Little white fleck of a faraway sun peering down, barely illuminating a pristine white snowscape; snow broken here and there by crags of white ice, long lines of blue escarpment.

A tiny world named Snow. Ancient ruins, more or less intact. Things built by nobody knew who or what, a long, long time ago, on the fourth ice-moon of a huge, red-orange, pale-ringed gas giant. Yes, there it was, bisecting the horizon, rings sticking up in the sky, obscured by the ice-moon's thin blue clouds, gas giant sixth out from a low-K star named Groombridge 1618, just shy of fifteen-point-three light-years from Sol.

Move on. News shows. Union bullshit. Legislative bullshit. Commercial bullshit. Corporate bullshit. A voice-over was saying, ". . . therefore, representatives of Berens-Vataro Enterprises Interplanetary were permitted to land their experimental spacecraft, *Torus X-1*, at a private spaceport servicing the Board of Trade Regency Building in Kiev, where a special plenipotentiary hearing was called into session, expected to meet shortly with members of this so-called Kentish embassy . . ."

Long shot across a half-empty plain dotted with old ruins, undemolished buildings from a few centuries back, when Earth's population was topping out close to forty billion, buildings left standing, I suppose, because of their "historical significance."

Odd-looking disk-shaped spacecraft, falling out of the pale blue sky, surrounded by a nimbus of opalescent light, decelerating hard, just before it hit the ground, settling in a cloud of dust.

Close-up shot. Hatch opening in the saucer's ventral surface, metallic ramp extruding to the ground, men and women walking down, looking around. Some of them dressed in pretty much standard solar system fashions, others wearing rather baggy, colorful outfits. Costumes I'd seen before. Similar to, though not identical with, the sort of clothing you saw in newsreels from Kent, the big, old colony on Alpha Centauri A4.

Cold lump forming in the pit of my stomach. Once upon a time I bought 120 shares of Berens-Vataro stock for my little portfolio, money I've been piddling with on and off ever since my income grew big enough that I had money to waste. The last time I'd checked, months ago, I think, the B-VEI stock was worth just shy of two hundred livres, a little more than twice what I'd paid for it.

It'd been a very nice little spec-tech company, headquartered on Callisto, a start-up venture whose prospectus discussed raising capital for the investigation of technologies leading to fully inertialess spacecraft. Included were a couple of research papers, published stuff of course, no trade secrets, detailing the work of the company's founders, physicists Roald Berens and Ntanë Vataro.

Hell. ERSIE has had the market in space drives sewed up for close to five hundred years. Still, I knew enough about the matter, working with the technology every day, to know they had a shot at it. A hundred livres? That's just the size of the pay voucher ERSIE downloads into my account every month. Just about a tenth of my portfolio, these days.

Then the announcer said, "Spokesmen for the Eighth Ray Scientific-Industrial Enterprise state categorically that faster-than-light travel is technically impossible, violating physical laws established more than six hundred years ago. ERSIE representatives on the Board of Trade Regents have called for a full investigation of what they suggest is a 'cruel hoax,' possibly intended to divert investors from the failure of Berens-Vataro researchers to develop a commercially viable non-CESD space drive."

Not much more detail in the news. Shots of the little ship, under guard at the BTR landing field outside Kiev. The fact that the flight crew of *Torus X-1* had been placed under arrest, along with the supposed embassy . . . Then a shot of baffled-looking members of the regular Kentish trade legation to Earth showing up at the prison, identifying the men and women in colorful, baggy costumes as actual, prominent Kentish citizens, including an infuriated man who was supposed to be the Kentish minister for interstellar trade.

I took direct control of the monitor and hustled off to the stock-trading nexus, quickly looked up my B-VEI accounts. I don't know what the hell I was expecting. Maybe they'd be zeroed out already. Or maybe, with enough suckers falling for the hoax, which appeared to be very well planned indeed, I might be able to scoop a few thousand livres out of the mess and . . .

My, my, what a busy little bee that stock-trading AI had been. Just looking at the numbers made me reach for that third drink. Dividends traded out, bought back in, rolled over by the auto-reinvestor routine. Doubled. Split. Doubled again. Scraps. Margins. All sorts of odd slang terms I'd never seen before. Just now, my account appeared to hold twelve thousand shares of Berens-Vataro Enterprises Interplanetary.

Value?

Zero.

Big red flag flapping from the node: *Trading in B-VEI stock issues has been suspended.* By the Board of Trade Regents of the Earth and Solar Space.

A little side note popped up, generated by my tracking module. At original investment value, the stock would be worth something like twenty thousand livres. Conservative estimate. About what I'd make with sixteen years' paychecks. Other estimates, based on what'd already gone down, assuming the immediate resumption of programmed trading, showed a wild array of higher values, some of them just shy of a million livres.

For Christ's sake.

Right now, though, the official value of the stock was nothing. And, apparently, warrants were being sought for the arrest of the company's principal officers.

I let it pop back to the news. Sat and stared. Ordered up a fourth drink, feeling myself start to grow dizzy as the alcohol rolled through my system, started diffusing into my brain.

What the fuck would it be like to be worth a million livres? That's a hell of a lot of money, isn't it? I could buy myself an interplanetary yacht. Or a mansion on Mars. Hell, I could afford a nice little dacha down on Earth. Maybe even a cabin in the Adirondacks, if prices hadn't gone up too much . . .

With my attention directed elsewhere, the monitor started to node-pop again, going, very slowly, through the various newsnodes, stopping for extra-long pauses at the various financial channels, being careful to service my most recently exhibited interests, gradually speeding up and widening its airplay.

I found myself watching one of my favorite pornodes, an hour-long show called *Crotchmate of the Day*, on a channel that did nothing but show that same hour, over and over again, all day and all night. Maybe today's crotchmate would help defuse the anger I could feel sputtering away beneath a drunken buzz. Faster-than-light travel. God damn it. Maybe the oh-so-nice little quasi-imaginary girl would help.

*   *   *

New day. New shift. New tasks to perform. Black of space filling half the sky. The repair and refit of starship *Aardwolf,* leasehold of Harmattan Transport, was almost complete, vast cylindrical body, close to a kilometer long, floating free in Stardock's exobay six, hull patches closed at last, turrets in place, radiator vanes for the field modulus device a shiny black star aft.

Floating next to me, anonymous in his glitter-sparkly silver spacesuit, Phil Hendrickx, who'd stolen Garstang's sleek ass right out from under me all those years ago, said, "Hey, du Cheyne. You see that shit about the FTL hoax last night?"

"Sure."

"What d'you think?"

Garstang was hanging in space beyond him, one hand on his arm, body well outlined by the form-fitting silver links of her suit. I could remember touching those breasts anytime I wanted to. I shrugged, staring at *Aardwolf.* Rossignol, floating behind me, said, "What if it were *true?*"

What if? In only a few more days we'd be done with *Aardwolf.* Her crew would come back from rest and recreation, climb aboard. Start the machinery. Put her through local paces in the space around Stardock and the L_1(SE) space station complex. Take her out on space trials, out to Pluto and back maybe. Inspectors would declare her fit for deep space.

From close beside me, Rua Mater's soft voice said, "God. That'd change *everything.*"

Everything? What would change? The fact that rich men and their rich cargoes could go back and forth between the stars in a hurry? *Aardwolf* here would be heading out in a few months, headed for Mimir's Well, Eta Cassiopeiae A4ii, the farthest shore of the long-halted interstellar colonization movement, a round-trip that would consume forty years' worth of stay-at-homes' time, though the crew would show up here again one day just a couple of years older.

Would I still be here then? Sure I would. Probably wearing a white belt, maybe even be the poor bastard who had to sign off on her next repair and refit, personally responsible if anything should happen to her after the fact.

Still. Wouldn't it be something if . . . Cold hand in my chest. Sure. It'd be cool. But my B-VEI accounts were locked up and set to zero value already. Policemen were looking for Doctors Berens and Vataro. I'd be lucky to get back my original hundred livres.

Finally, Rossignol sighed and said, "Well, let's get to it, boys and girls. The work's waiting."

Someone snickered and said, "Yeah, right. The job is the job."

Is the job is the job. One day and another, and week and a month and a year and a decade and century and a lifetime. Better than nothing? Sure it is.

We stooped, en masse, and fell upon the starship out of a flat, Stygian sky, leaving our dreams behind.

2

When you come down out of the Virginia hills, riding a tramway suspended above the bed of some old turn-of-the-millennium superhighway, you can see the well-preserved remains of Washington DeeCee, once upon a time the national capital of Earth's last great federative superpower.

You can see that little cluster of shining white buildings from a long way off. The faux-Egyptian obelisk of George Washington's Monument, the vertically exaggerated white dome of the U.S. Capitol Building, ridiculously tiny statue on top, old square buildings with their Greco-Roman columns. A few featureless Postfunctionalist boxes, left in place because they once meant something to someone.

We hadn't planned to spend much time in Washington, just stop by to see the old buildings because it was so close by the spaceport, because we had to come here to Union Station anyway and get our tram to the campground. Just stop for a few hours. Go up the famous Monument. Stand at the feet of Lincoln's statue and read his famous words.

I talked them into a trip to the zoo. Talked them into it, though Zell and Millie had already been and hated it, though Phil and Garstang didn't have the slightest interest, because Rua

17

Mater said, "Yes, let's. That'd be interesting." I saw Garstang poke Millie in the ribs, saw them look sharply at Phil and Zell. Phil rolled his eyes and grimaced. Zell let out an exasperated sigh, and we went.

The zoo, the Greater North American Zoological Garden, was set up in a part of the old city called Anacostia in the early twenty-second century. It was divided into segments representing the various continents of Earth, various parklands labeled Africa and Asia and the like. Eventually, they started bringing in things from other star systems, exhibits supposedly representing the habitats of interesting animals and certain plant-like things that more or less acted like animals. They say it's degenerated since then, and so the place eventually began taking on some of the characteristics of a second millennium zoo. Things in cages.

Zell and Millie dropped out first, stopping at an outdoor café in the European Pavilion, telling us to come back and get them when we were done, they'd seen it all before, ho-hum. Then Phil and Garstang decided they'd sit in some big park we found, a green hillside looking out over something called the Serengeti, a pale grassland sparsely dotted with grazing herbivores and slinky predators. We left them lying under a tree, arms around each other, nuzzling and cooing.

Rua Mater followed me on and on, silent, looking at whatever I looked at, dark eyes conveying nothing, a pair of glassy brown sponges, soaking up the world's light.

Alpha Centauri A4. Kent. First colony. Pretty much like Earth, a big surprise to the planetologists, a fully habitable world, ready for humanity to move right in, most interesting because it was right at the termination point of its geochemical cycle. In twenty million years, its ecology would be gone. Not much native life on land. Some interesting things like big arthropods. A thing like a crab made of molten gold, sitting on a flat red rock, looking at us through a hundred molten silver eyes, droplets of shiny metal on the end of long stalks.

A section on the iceworms of Sundown, Epsilon Indi 1,

which mostly did nothing but sit there, looking like so many piles of steaming black refuse.

We came to the Green Heaven pavilion, representing the habitable planet of Tau Ceti. When I was a teenager, I went through a phase where I was crazy about this stuff. A time when I was particularly interested in Green Heaven itself. I can remember thinking about what it would be like to be living in the open cities of Green Heaven, just like the now-extinct cities of Old Earth. I used to imagine myself walking the streets of places with names like Midori'iro and Azraq Azará and Relàmpago. Used to see myself trekking the yellow sand ergs of the Adrianis Desert, climbing the craggy immensity of the Pÿramis Range, wandering through the dank, dark Mistibos Forest.

Ultimately, before I gave it up, I settled on a fantasy of myself as a great white hunter, ranging the tawny grasslands of the wide Koperveldt wilderness, the magically named Plains of Brass, of going on up into the cloudy antarctic highlands of the Koudloft where I would exterminate dangerous packs of white wolfen, Green Heaven's splendidly weird, intelligent predators.

And, because I was just the right age for that sort of thing, I saw myself taking parties of rich terrestrial tourists into the vast green outback of the Opveldt, taking them out on hunting safaris where we could bring down those mightiest of Greenie herbivores, the great brown womfrogs.

Bang-bang. Heavy rifles kicking against our shoulders. Womfrogs howling in agony, falling like thunder on the ground.

And, because I was just the right age for that sort of thing, I saw tourist women coming to me in the tropical night, drawn, fascinated, by my incredible masculinity. As time went on, the fantasies stopped being about the slaughter of animals; became pleasant masturbation exercises in which I saw myself mainly as the fucker of rich tourist ladies.

Oh, Gaetan, they'd whisper. Oh, Gaetan.

Christ.

Rua Mater and I were standing in front of a plain, unadorned cage. No natural habitat exhibit here. Just a square box, concrete in back, with a little square hole of a door, open on three sides with plain metal bars. Letting you know, I suppose, how *really* Earth-like Green Heaven was.

The thing inside sat on its haunches like a dog, facing us, motionless but for a soft pulse of breathing, muscles moving its fat sides in and out. A massive, squashed-looking thing, maybe a couple of hundred kilograms in mass, like some sort of huge, flattened-out fairy-tale wolf, covered with shaggy white hair, almost like a polar bear, these superficial resemblances I suppose giving rise to its common name, white wolfen. The travel guides said there were red wolfen and black wolfen and even rare green wolfen as well.

Not really like a wolf though. Flat head like an alligator, with heavy triangular white teeth that were visible at all times. Squatty build, a bit like an ancient amphibian carnivore I once saw on some paleontology node. *Eryops.* That's the one. Six legs, each ending in a fat round paw. A lot of toes. Ten, maybe, on each foot.

As I watched, one paw clenched, extending slender retractile claws. Long. Curved. White. Translucent like ice.

When I looked up, the white wolfen was looking at me, close-together mottled gray eyes giving it fine binocular vision, letting it seem to look right into my eyes.

Rua Mater took hold of my arm. Seemed to shiver slightly. Maybe it seemed to be looking into her eyes too, Mona Lisa–like.

It leaned forward, face coming close to the bars, closer to us, and made a whispery sort of mutter, a succession of guttural noises that sounded like, *Wooroowah. Werrawaghroo wahgh-waooghaahhh* . . . trailing off in a breathy snort. There was a faintly sweet odor, a bit like caramel, coming from it as it spoke.

We turned away, and Rua Mater abruptly jumped and squeaked, grabbing on to me, bumping into my side, trying to get behind me by going right through me. I felt a hard pang myself, though not enough to completely mask the feel of her breasts mashing against me, the bony thud of her hip on my side.

Things standing behind us, looking past us at the animal in the cage.

Imagine one of those pale brown walking stick-bugs children on the Moon like to keep for pets. Imagine it crossbred with the praying mantis your mother wouldn't let you buy at the pet store. The one that was advertised as being able to clear your warren of roaches and spiders and flies, clear it completely clean, in just a couple of months.

Now imagine it being two meters tall.

Rua Mater gasped, "Oh God. I thought the animals were loose!"

One of the things unclipped a box from its harness, poked at some buttons. Held it up beside its head, shook it a bit. Poked it again. Then held it against the side of its chest. Sharp, high, raspy sound: "Greekeegreekee greekeegreekeegreekee!"

The box said, "I'm terribly sorry. We didn't mean to startle you."

Tourists from Arous, Sigma Draconis 3, just under eighteen-point-three light-years from the Sun. I'd heard there were increasing numbers of them traveling to the solar system, parties of students sponsored by Mace Electrodynamics, the big interstellar conglomerate that owns the patents on the field well converter technology and controls access to the Sigma Draconis star system. A couple of years ago there was an incident in which an Arousian wandered off from its tour group on the Moon, wound up lost in one of the deep underwarrens of Eratosthenes City. Some kids running one of the down-deep "parks" came across this poor bastard, thought it was something from a vidnet horror show come to life, and killed it.

Turned out that not one of those little boys and girls had heard there were *real* starships, real extraterrestrial beings, real anything beyond the underwarrens of the Moon and some myth about an aboriginal human homeland called Earth. Kept babbling about their favorite episodes of *Star Battlers* and how they'd just shot themselves a real, live Swoogenbork killranger.

I smiled at the Arousians, wondering if a smile meant any-thing to them. Probably not, but the translator box made faint *greekeegreekee* noises as we walked on. Probably telling them all about it.

Another cage, great big brown thing inside, some guy in a park ranger suit unloading what looked like cubic-meter blocks of frozen spinach from a floating forklift onto the ground before it.

Rua Mater, hand gentle on my arm, said, *"Womfrog."*

Yes, indeed. The fearsome womfrogs of Green Heaven, womfrogs that I'd killed and killed as a teenage boy. Killed and killed, so pretty, wealthy women my mother's general age and appearance would come to my tent in the middle of the night and suck my dick.

It was about the size of a schoolbus, covered with long, shag-gy brown hair. Six legs, the rearmost two of which were outsized and facing the wrong direction, like the hopping legs of a crick-et. High-domed head that looked a lot like a mammoth's head if you thought about it. Bulging eyes the size of basketballs, set close together in front, defying the received wisdom that only predators get to have binocular vision.

Human-like mouth with big, yellow, flat-crowned buck teeth. Long, elephantine trunks on the sides of its head, where a ter-restrial animal's ears would have been. Trunks ending in bony, fist-like knobs, each adorned with little pink pads of what appeared to be scar tissue . . .

I looked over at the guy unloading frozen fodder. "Hey, buddy."

He straightened up. Took off his cap. Wiped sweat from his brow with the sleeve of his tunic. "Yeah?"

"What the hell happened to its fingers?"

He looked at the womfrog. Looked back at me. Shrugged. "Son of a bitch kept figuring out how to work the combination lock, kept guessing the right numbers and getting out of its cage. So we cut 'em off."

Animal standing right behind the bars, looking down at

him, flexing its trunks, staring. No real expression in those big, pitted-looking, orangish eyes. I glanced down at Rua Mater. Staring at the womfrog. Nothing written in her face. We walked on.

Once upon a time, there was a little island at the mouth of Henry Hudson's useless river, property of the Manahatta tribesmen. Once upon a not quite so long ago time, there was a great city here. Towers of stone and metal and glass. Layers of gray-brown smog. Streets full of taxicabs like so many big, shiny yellow bugs. A few million people, maybe ten to a toilet. They call what's left of Old New York *Manhattan Interpretive Park.* Close beside me, Garstang put her hand on the tram platform's guard rail, and said, "That's quite a sight."

Quite. Not really a lone and level plain, of course. Huge island, bracketed by narrow rivers, cloaked in dense green jungle, pretty much like all the wilderness we'd passed over, coming up the east coast of North America. Here, though, the shattered stumps of old buildings jutted from the forest, some coated with vines, others bare and ragged in the hazy noonday sun. Toward the north end of the island, just about on the horizon, you could see the ruins of taller buildings, more intact-looking somehow.

Rua Mater put her hand on my arm, pointing, "Are those the lakes?"

Through the screen of trees, not all that far from the tramway terminus, you could see a shine of water. "I think so."

Millie said, "Let's get going. If we're any later we won't get a waterfront campsite."

Once upon a time, the United States of America was the biggest, richest, most powerful nation of the world, New York its premier city. By the middle of the twenty-first century, all the other great federative superpowers of the world had come apart, the Union of Soviet Socialist Republics breaking up into its fifteen constituent states, trying to maintain the fiction of something called the CIS. Siberia breaking free of the Russian

Federation, then collapsing into six smaller nations. Sinkiang and Tibet and Mongolia breaking free of the Chinese Republic, then China itself vanishing, Tang south sundered from Han north.

For a little while, this America ruled the Earth, pretty much did as it pleased, her leaders angry and proud. *America locuta, causa finita.* One fine spring morning, just about 8:15 A.M., on August 6 of the year 2045, a small party from one of her more disgruntled client states showed up in Manhattan bearing five egg-crates in their luggage. Spotted them on five street corners in the area between SoHo and the Trumpville slums. Said their prayers. Stooped and pushed five buttons.

There were five bright flashes of light, five loud bangs, five little mushroom clouds, five kilotons apiece.

Five kilotons is not much of a nuclear explosion, about enough to blow up a conventional twenty-first-century city block. So a few hundred buildings were knocked down. Maybe a half million people killed. A similar number badly injured. And the other eight million or so living and working on Manhattan island just had to move away.

City services stayed intact for the other boroughs, of course, and there was talk of restoring the heart of New York, but it never happened. Over the course of the next generation, seventy percent of the thirty million people who'd inhabited Greater New York found reason to go elsewhere.

We pitched our tents beside the clear, placid waters of a 550-year-old bomb crater, stowed our luggage, built a cooking fire in the campsite's metal and stone hibachi using firewood from the little pile the park service provided as part of the ten-livre camping fee. Cooked our sausages and meat patties, watched our neighbors swim while the sun went down, watched the stars come out as the sky turned dark.

If you look sharp, you can sort of see a faint spiderwork of monorail lines on the face of the Moon. The lights on the night-side show up like bright, steady, misplaced stars.

*   *   *

Much later. Fire dying down to embers, soft breeze rustling the leaves of the trees, making a sound not so different from what you hear by the seaside, soft rush of water during an ebb tide. Stars glittering overhead. Twinkling's the word Earthpeople use, I think.

I sat dressed only in my shorts, back pressed to some smooth-barked tree, still sun-warm to the touch, bare feet combed into the turf and leaf litter, looking out over Lake A71K's flat black water, lake named, I think, after the serial number of the bomb that dug the hole. There were stars reflected in the lake, light coming to me from stars hanging over the low treeline beyond the lake, stars sitting over the centuries-old remains of broken buildings.

I thought about the prayer my parents'd made me say every night when I was a little boy. *Now I lay me down to sleep* . . . Remembered arguing with my friend Shelly, whose own version of the prayer began with *soon* instead of *now.*

If I should die before I wake . . . I used to have nightmares about waking up in the emergency room resuscitation unit, empty inside, emptied of feeling, hardly like a human being at all . . . Well, Doc, the Lord came and took my soul while I was dead. What am I supposed to do *now?*

Soft rustling from the campsite nearby, from inside the nearest tent, the one pitched beside mine. Phil and Garstang. I heard them murmuring, whispering together. No words I could make out, only words I could imagine. Something like a giggle. Rustle of cloth. Sleeping bag zippers.

Long, trenchant silence. Then the soft shadow of a sigh. Garstang used to make that same sigh for me. I sat, still as a mouse, quiet as a worm, paying careful attention to the sounds.

Dark shadow suddenly looming over me in the night. Rua Mater coming back from the showerhouse, wrapped in a flimsy robe, dark blue I think, looking down at me, dark hair, dark eyes buried in shadow, no more than a hint of liquid glitter. Standing there with the robe clutched tight around herself, a curved outline of hip and breast superimposed against the lesser shadows of night.

I heard her make an intake of breath through her nose, short and sharp, and she opened her mouth, about to speak.

Garstang groaned, "Oh, Phil. Yes."

Rua's mouth hanging open, startled, words halted.

From inside the tent, rhythmic sounds started up, mostly the sound of cloth rubbing on cloth. Phil's knees pushing the air mattress around, Garstang's back moving on the sleeping bag maybe.

Rua whispered, "Are you . . ."

Am I what? Am I going to get my dick out and masturbate while my old girlfriend takes it up the middle? Well, yes, I was thinking about it before you came along.

Rua Mater standing there, staring at me, while, inside the tent, Garstang's breath started coming in short gasps. Rua whispered, "Jesus, Gaetan . . ."

You could hear Phil's breathing now, deeper sounds, longer gasps. Rua stood over me, suddenly reached out with one hand, halfway toward me, stopped, stood stock-still, arm outstretched.

What now, Rua Mater of the dark hair and eyes and omnipresent vidnet clip? Feeling sorry for me, are you? Pity, then? Or contempt? No way for me to know. Or guess what was going to happen next. Women have their own agendas, driven by a very different sort of reproductive psychology. She might reach for my crotch now, or just kick me in the nuts.

Rua whispered, "Good night, Gae." Turned and walk away, stooped down and crawled through the fly of her own tent.

I called out, "Good night!"

The sounds from the tent suddenly stilled.

The next day, we went for a long hike, northward through the forested, ruined streets of New York, on up toward the tangled jungle where Central Park had been. Gloomy trails, old, broken asphalt. Tall trees and fallen buildings. Openings in the ground, the dark mouths of caves, leading down into the ancient, flooded subway system.

Zell and Millie were in the lead, pretty far ahead, tiny fig-ures dressed in safari gear, white pith helmets, boots laced up their calves, passing from sunlight into shadow and back again. Phil and Garstang were much closer, walking just ahead of me, walking close together, holding hands. Rua . . . Walking some-where behind me. Watching *my* rear end? Hard to imagine, though I've heard any number of women swear that's what they like best about men's figures. Probably just looking past me, watching Phil and envying Garstang.

I looked back over my shoulder at her and smiled, watched her eyes brighten and her step quicken.

We came out into a bright clearing, a place of knee-high brown grass surrounding some kind of marble sculpture. A wide, flat basin, full of trash and muck, statuary in the middle, a conglomeration of leaping fish, their mouths gaping open.

Zell said, "Well. This seems like as good a place as any to stop for lunch. Rest of you hungry?"

I looked down at Rua, who smiled up at me and said, "Sure."

Phil and Garstang opened their packs and started spreading blankets on a patch of flattened-out grass near the fountain, while Zell and Millie started assembling the lunch. Rua Mater and I stood there like idiots, staring at each other, half-paralyzed, having forgotten that we were carrying the beer.

Phil said, "For Christ's sake."

Garstang, harsh, insistent: *"Shh."*

Into the silence, a rhythmic rumble, a vibration in the ground, breaking up into a sedentary *klop-klop-klop* . . . From the trailhead opening into the forest on the far side of the fountain there came a man in a pale blue uniform, riding a shining white horse.

Zell Benson on his feet, staring, open-mouthed, "Park ser-vice?" Such an odd sight. You see it in vidnet historical dramas, of course, but a human being sitting astride a live, half-ton animal? It was making the oddest damned sounds. Fantastical heavy breathing, little snorts and grunts as it walked toward us.

I said, "Those are Range Police." Range Police, the planetary security service set up some three centuries ago, after they'd kicked us common scum off-planet, sent us to work beyond their precious, pale blue sky. Set up to protect the property and interests of the rich and super-rich from the bushwhackers and swagmen left behind, hiding among the ruins.

Behind the leader there were more horses, empty horses, carrying no one, burdened by small black backpacks. Cargo horses? In the distance, back in the woods, you could see another blue-uniformed Range Policeman, sitting astride a blotchy brown and white mount. Phil took a step forward, smiling, waving at the two men. Stopped short, stiffened. Made an odd sound. Beside him, Garstang gasped and said, "What the fuck are *those* things?"

Not saddlebags on the riderless horses at all. Shiny, wet-looking black baggy things the size of hassocks sitting right on the horses' bare backs. Things that looked rather like huge, partly inflated ticks.

Rua Mater cried out, "My God! *Kapellmeisters!*"

Correct. Coming closer now, you could see all those famous details. Eyestalks sticking out of the middle of pulpy, leathery backs, eyes on top of them like so many colored tennis balls, seven per Kapellmeister, orange on this one, blue on that one, a lovely teal green over there . . . Millie stood up and whispered, "Holy *shit.*"

The lead policeman slid a late-model military weapon, a nice, shiny new electric rifle, out of some kind of saddle holster, pointed the long, thin, silvery stick of it in our general direction. "Stay where you are please." I found myself, briefly, imagining the thing fired, imagined hearing the sharp, sizzling *zzzzzzip!* of the barrel's magnetic-induction catapult, the dull thup-*whack* of the bullet flying through the air and hitting someone. Dumdum? Poison? Or would I see gobbets of meat flying from an explosive load?

Phil lifted his hands halfway, as if trying to put them over his head. Twit.

I called out, "No problem, Officer. What're they doing here?"

The nearest Kapellmeister lifted one of its chelae, something like a long, narrow lobster's claw, but colored and textured like it was made from polished brass, made a sharp, insistent noise, a loud, metallic *chatterclinkchitter*. A little box hanging from the policeman's belt muttered something indistinct. He glanced at the alien, picked up the box, said something I couldn't quite make out, and the box made little rattling noises in return.

He said, "Same thing as you, buddy. Just sit tight and we'll be on our way. Please don't try to follow us." Horsemen—horsethings as well—riding on, hooves lifting dust out of the grass as they headed for the opposite side of the clearing, disappearing into the shadows one by one. Policemen keeping those guns sort of loosely pointed at us.

Zell said, "Man. Those things are *weird!*"

No harness gear on their horses. No saddles. No nothing. When one of the Kapellmeisters passed close by, I could see its eight skinny legs, segmented like bugs' legs, stretching out from under its fat body, clutching the horse tight enough to dimple its flesh. And it had what looked like a third arm coming out of the middle front, ending not in a lobster claw but something like a wet gray octopus, or maybe a squid, slimy-looking tentacles anyway, pressed into the middle of the horse's back.

Interesting. The eyes of the policemen's horses were rolling in their sockets, trying to get a look at us as they passed by. The Kapellmeister's horses' eyes were . . . glassy. Still. Staring out at odd angles. Up at the sky. Down at the ground. Straight out to the side. Like they were drugged or something, though the horses walked quite well, walked with pretty much the same gait as the policemen's horses.

Rua Mater put her hand on my forearm and said, "No. Not weird at all. Pretty neat, in fact."

Pretty neat? Yes. When human civilization started spreading through interstellar space, a little more than four hundred years

ago, I guess we fully expected to run into other sentient species.
We weren't disappointed, of course. The Arousians, with tools
and things that were enough like cities we could think of them
as *people*. Other beings, not as smart as us, but . . . brighter than
various species of extinct ape perhaps. The womfrogs on Green
Heaven are a prime example.

Bit by bit we got farther afield, until one day a squadron of
starship explorers sailed into the planetary system of 82 Eridani,
a *very* nice G5V star just a little more than twenty light-years
from Earth. Planet number three turned out to be inhabitable,
a lot *like* Earth. And inhabited already.

Our little fleet found itself hailed on assorted radio frequen-
cies as it decelerated toward 82 Eridani, then met by a pair of
armed warships that escorted them to what appeared to be a
large industrial site circling one of the star's larger gas giants.
Ultimately, they were welcomed on Salieri itself, and now these
most interesting Kapellmeisters have an embassy on Earth.

People have noticed that the Kapellmeisters' technology is
at least the equal of our own, their technical civilization of
unknown antiquity, apparently somewhat older than our own,
and have wondered why they didn't go starfaring. Wondered
why they didn't show up on Earth a long time ago.

It's been suggested that they simply thought it not worth the
effort. And, of course, the usual pack of idiots started digging
up old flying saucer stories. Back then, the Face on Mars still
had currency, though the supposed Monument itself was gone,
having been carried off bit by bit by souvenir hunters. Back
then, it took no great effort to start reinterpreting something
called the Zeta Reticuli Map.

The Kapellmeisters of Salieri swore it hadn't been them.
And, after a while, people stopped asking just *why* they had a little fleet of very nasty warships. Paranoia, that's all. Maybe.

The last policeman disappeared into the woods and was
gone. Garstang said, "Shit. Let's eat." So we sat and ate. Rua
Mater, bubbling over with excitement, wanted to talk about
aliens. Nobody else did, other than me.

* * *

Sunset. Overhead, the sky was a layered palimpsest of flat red and orange clouds, backed by a fuzzy, translucent vermilion through which one or two bright stars were visible. Almost, I thought, like the heavens have been painted over, the paint weathered now and starting to peel.

I stood by the edge of the lake, looking at other campers, in the middle distance, farther away. A very tall, angular-looking woman with very dark skin, standing up to her thighs in the lake over there, fishing, motionless, with a long, thin pole.

Some children at the rowboat dock on the other side of the lake, running, leaping into the air, screaming just before they hit the water. Swimming ashore with a splashy, inefficient stroke. Getting up on the dock, laughing, doing it all again.

I wonder where they're from? Merely the Moon? Mars? Somewhere in the outer system? The tall woman? Someone like me, on a quick vacation? Or a rich tourist from one of the interstellar colonies, making a once-in-a-lifetime pilgrimage to Manhome?

Nearby . . .

I stood still. Stood and watched Phil and Garstang, down by the edge of the water, shuck their sweaty clothing. Going swimming, of course. I guess I thought maybe I'd stand there, watch Garstang get undressed. Stand there and look at familiar sights, familiar things and places, body parts I thought I'd cherished . . .

Pale horror, deep down inside.

I'm obsessing about this.

I wonder why?

It's been six *years*, for God's sake.

Phil and Garstang holding hands, wading out into the water.

Someone tugging on my arm.

Rua Mater, of course, looking up at me, eyes wide. Almost frightened looking. Afraid of what? Me? Or . . .

She said, "You want to go in?"

In . . . where? Oh. The water of course. "Sure."

Another moment of standing still, then, despite the shadows

of dusk, I saw her blush deeply as it occurred to her what I might be waiting for. A little trickle of irritation. We're . . . adults, for Christ's sake. What does she expect?

I saw her decide, blush deepening for just a moment, turning into a flush of anticipation. She put her hands to the front of her blouse, undoing the buttons from top to bottom, cloth falling open, bit by bit, exposing her chest. One of the subtle differences between real-world women in the here and now. Rua Mater could get by without a bra when she wanted to, unlike heavier-breasted Garstang.

Rua Mater stepping out of a rubble of cloth, watching me look at her. Gray-shadowed face. Dark eyes. Tits. Little black swatch of pubic hair. Legs. Feet. Female, all right.

She stepped closer to me, close enough I could smell the faint soap-scent of her hair, reached up, started unbuttoning my shirt. Pulled it off over my back. Put her hands on my chest, sort of feeling the long, almost silky black hair growing there. Looking up at me. Eyes wide. Unfathomable.

Much later. Sky dark black overhead, freckled with bits of white light where it was clear, featureless and empty where there were clouds.

Rua Mater and I lying side by side on the soft grass, rolled slightly toward one another, naked, waters of Lake A71K lapping gently, not far away. I could hear a soft breeze blowing in the trees, rustling the leaves against each other. A soft chatter somewhere. Some kind of little animal, perhaps. Distant voice, people conversing by their dying campfires.

The soft, intermittent gasp of Rua Mater's breathing, breathing right in my face. Kissing her then, feeling the soft, formless flex and twist of her tongue in my mouth. This way and that, stroking my tongue, moving around my teeth, as if counting them, withdrawing, coming back in, the taste of her rather sweet to me.

The feel of her pressed tight against me, breasts pressing against my chest, flattening. Her leg sort of doubled over me, foot tucked behind the angle of my knees. Rua's hand alternately resting on my hip, cupping my scrotum, finger fumbling now and then with the flabby softness of my prick. First one place, then another, then back again, making the stations of the crotch upon my body. I could feel a hard tightness form up in my chest, anxiety building, slowly, very slowly, but inexorably. Tightness as well down between my legs, where nothing at all seemed to be happening.

Finally, Rua pulled back, trying to look into my eyes, foiled by the depth of nighttime's shadows. She said, "What's . . . wrong?" I could almost hear her thoughts. Is it me? I thought Garstang said . . .

"No. Nothing. I . . ."

I let go of her, lay back on the grass, staring up at the stars, where they showed between the clouds. Nothing. Nothing's wrong at all, dear little Rua Mater.

You know what to do now, Gaetan du Cheyne, Master Mechanic. Start doing all the things you know how to do. Maybe it'll be all right. Maybe, after you're down there awhile, as she closes in on some kind of crescendo, you'll be infected by her passion. Maybe . . . while I lay looking up at the stars, thinking my thoughts, deciding what to do, Rua Mater got up and went away, disappearing into the darkness, heading in the direction of her tent.

It occurred to me to get up off the grass and go after her, but I did not.

A night, then the better part of another day, and we were in a room full of chairs, waiting for our flight out of Dulles, going back home. Me standing by the observation window, looking out at a field of spaceships, Rua Mater sitting not far away, vidnet clip hanging in her hair, eyes closed, gone . . . wherever she goes. The others . . . I don't know. Somewhere behind me.

It hadn't been a bad night, really. I lay out under the half-occluded stars, looking up at my friends, naming them individually, imagining what they were really like. Alnilam up there, blazing in Orion's belt. Wolf-Rayet star. Sometimes I still think about what it'd be like to visit some such hellish star system. Imagine.

I'd fallen asleep out on the grass beside the lake, Rua Mater and my uncooperative dick forgotten, blinking awake naked in the gray light of an overcast dawn, Garstang, dressed only in a pair of bright, silky, sky blue underpants, nudging me in the side with a blunt big toe, frowning.

She'd said, "What happened?" An off-side glance, as if in the direction of Rua Mater's tent.

"I don't know. Nothing."

You could see her think, *Nothing?*

I'd gotten up, gathered my dew-damp clothing, put it in my tent, found my robe and gone off to the showers, and stood quietly, warm water pouring over my head and shoulders, splattering on the bumpy tile floor, listening to Garstang humming in an adjacent stall.

Garstang finished first and I'd waited for her to be gone before turning off the water and getting out of my own stall. When I did, Rua Mater was there, standing there, just looking at me, dark eyes fathomless, expressionless, beyond my reading. When I tried to say something about being sorry, she'd just shrugged and said something about it not mattering, had gotten into a stall and turned on the water.

Voice in the here and now, recalling me to Dulles. Garstang's voice: *"Gaetan."* Flat. Imperative. When I turned, the rest of them were sitting in a row of chairs by an active-access multinode vidnet terminal, Garstang using the machine, Millie leaning over her shoulder, getting inside the nerve induction field. Zell and Phil were sitting beside them, apparently uninterested.

Garstang motioning to me. Come here. I went over and sat beside her, leaning close, almost putting my head on her shoulder to get it inside the field. There was a low, curving horizon formed of rounded, black-ice hills, darkened by night, looking like the far side of the Moon, but obviously not the Moon. Black sky overhead, leached of stars by the fat, bright, slightly squashed-looking ball of a full Jupiter. Callisto, I thought. Possibly Ganymede, but . . . right. Jupiter looks too small.

In the foreground, under the barely detectable glimmer of a very high energy eutropic shield, was a broad expanse of what looked like white concrete. Probably that ferrocrete stuff they make from Trojan asteroidal debris, rather than the sintered, dark gray lunocrete common throughout the inner solar system. A big landing field, surrounded by low buildings, surmounted by a couple of dozen spaceships, much like the spaceships standing outside the Dulles Cosmodrome terminal building, here on Earth.

Voice-over: ". . . although Eighth Ray lawyers have now acknowledged the apparent validity of Berens-Vataro claims of having developed a faster-than-light space drive, in depositions before the Board of Trade Regents, ERSIE has laid claim to B-VEI patents, insisting that the new drive is based entirely on physical principles developed by ERSIE founder Dominique Kerechenko more than four hundred years ago and currently owned by her heirs in simple trust for the stockholders of ERSIE.

"CEO Maslett Gilhoolie, in a statement from Trade Regency headquarters in Kiev, further held that since the interstellar drive systems of *Torus X-1* and its sister ships were built entirely from components manufactured by Eighth Ray, under the principle of intellectual property rights, those drives are in fact the property of Eighth Ray.

"Meanwhile, in a related development, representatives of Berens-Vataro revealed that additional colonial embassies have arrived at the B-VEI facility on Callisto and are awaiting transport to Earth, following guarantees that no legal action will be taken against them or the officers of the Berens-Vataro Enterprises, pending resolution of the case by a formal vote of the Board of Trade Regents.

"During an interview, earlier today, B-VEI chairman Roald Berens stated that his new ships, capable of what he deems 'pseudo-velocities some four hundred times the speed of light in a vacuum,' will open a vast new frontier to the human realm, whose volume of space has remained almost static at the thirty-five-light-year mark since . . ."

Heart knocking quite steadily in my chest. Garstang twisted in her chair, staring at me, beady-eyed.

Millie Ai-chang's voice was very soft, almost a whisper. "It's . . . real."

Garstang said, "You . . . own a few shares of Berens-Vataro, don't you, Gaetan?" Eyelids slitted, she looked at me. Glanced over at Rua Mater. Seemed to hesitate. Looked over at Phil Hendrickx, apparently asleep, then looked back at me.

I shifted in the chair, pulling my head out of the nerve induction field. Sat and stared at Rua Mater, Rua still embedded in whatever dreamworld had claimed her. Twelve thousand shares. Trading suspended. Value zeroed out, pending . . .

I tried to imagine what those shares might be worth, if, by some miracle, the Board of Trade Regents should decide that B-VEI *did* own its patents. That . . . No. That can't possibly be right. Just shy of four *days* to Alpha Centauri? Little calculator clicking away in my head, some piece of toolbelt software that had made itself at home there long ago. Ninety-four hours, ten minutes, twelve seconds.

I forgot about Rua Mater, forgot about Garstang, forgot, for just a moment, about my God-damned prick, and tucked my head back into the induction field. The ruddy-complexioned board chairman of the Eighth Ray Scientific-Industrial Enterprise was standing before the Forum of the Board of Trade Regents of the Earth and Solar Space, waving his arms, shouting, a very fiery speech indeed.

The roving pickup suddenly tilted up and started panning across the spectator gallery. Newshog types mostly. There. The moon-faced president of the Ancient and Benevolent Brotherhood of Metal Founders, Machinists, and Aerospace Workers Interplanetary. Arms folded across his chest. Right next to him the well-known, gaunt and bony face of Mrs. Cartairs, head of the One Universe Social Justice Party, commonly known as Aus-Gyp. Both of them grinning. Grinning like hell.

My heart started leaping again.

Home again now, the appliances awake to my wants, glass of gin and tonic in one hand, lovely juniper smell in my nose, rising into my head, reminding me of the Manhattan wilderness, gin and fizzy sugar water sharp, bitter on my tongue . . .

The news was full of this business of the Berens-Vataro Interstellar Drive, media hounds in full-throated pursuit, the Big Story, you see, broken, exploded, splashed to every corner of the net, while I'd been wandering around in the woods, rubbing my pecker on poor, downcast Rua Mater, hoping it'd wake up and . . . hell. It was awake enough right now, making me want to dump the newsnet crap and run for the nearest pornode.

When I checked the stock ticker, nothing much had changed. The Regents' lock was still on B-VEI trading, zero-value flag still flapping away. A couple of stickynotes had appeared, one from the stock exchange operating system, an annotation to the effect that all common stock owners tracking B-VEI had been threaded together, for the convenience of . . .

A soft prickle of alarm. There's not supposed to be any Big Brother watching what private citizens do with their money. Local governments levy point-of-sale taxes. The Regency levies an infinitesimal VAT. But . . .

A second note was tagged to a general broadcast from Aus-Gyp, protesting this egregious violation of private citizens' rights, not just all the nameless peons playing penny-ante stocks like B-VEI, but the indicted corporate officers as well. In fact . . .

I looked at the AI's scrolling tables. Still doing its job. Um. Even though there's no job for it to do? What then? I looked down rows and columns, back into the 3D subtables beyond. How odd. My stock manager had continued to place buy/sell orders on B-VEI and some related stocks, manufacturers of components that, apparently, went into the making of those little starships. Including ERSIE.

There was a long list of futures options here. We'll buy this with the proceeds, should B-VEI stock come unfrozen. Sell here. Buy more B-VEI on thus and such a day, when it's anticipated value equals . . .

And then a very, *very* hard pang of alarm.

This God-damned thing is preparing a *lawsuit.* Totting up a bill of how much money we *could* have made, had the Board of Trade Regents not voted to close down B-VEI stock. If it stayed closed, if ERSIE won and the officers of B-VEI went to jail . . . well. Nothing lost but a little processor time.

And if the Regents' vote went with B-VEI? If the stocks came unglued? Who did the AI think was going to pay me for my hypothetical losses? Where did it think I was going to send the bill? This file here . . .

Jesus Christ. The form for making a private petition before the Inducements Committee of the Board of Trade Regents. ERSIE, of course, held a full seat on the Board, but, by inducing the Regents to suspend trading in B-VEI stock, it had acted as a private lobbyist in its own behalf. Chapter and verse on that. And over here was a citation on a legal precedent dating back more than three hundred years, suggesting that political lobbyists could be held liable for monetary losses incurred by their actions, provided that the Board of Trade Regents ultimately reversed some earlier decision induced by said lobbyist.

Various pangs and prickles were merging in my head, dissolving into the gin. And the next file in the stack? The proper formulas for filing a class-action suit in the name of every other *ab initio* holder of original-issue B-VEI stock, each holding amounting to no more than 0.1 percent of said issue. Here were several hundred pro forma date stamps, representing the interests of other people's AI trade managers.

So what the fuck does it think it's going to achieve, other than maybe getting me in a lot of hot water? Christ, I'll have to pay point-of-sale taxes on every fucking transaction, complete with late filing fees and . . . A gentle touch in the back of my mind, like being brushed all over by infinitely soft feathers, then the household composite whispered, You have a visitor, Mr. du Cheyne.

Visitor. Not a familiar word, I . . . The apartment said, Mr. Hoseah Rothman, representing the $L_1(SE)$ legal offices for the Eighth Ray Scientific-Industrial Enterprise. He wishes to discuss a personal matter with you.

Personal. Oh, fuck. There are no *really* secure channel locks on the vidnet. Not for the likes of me and thee, dear stock-trading algorithm. I finished my drink and ordered up another, listing to the icemaker tinkle. Took a sip from my fresh, cold glass, and croaked, "Show him in."

The door slid open, admitting a moment of corridor bustle. Slid closed again. Waiting right *outside*, for Christ's sake! Rothman stood there, a quiet thing in a pale gray jumpsuit, very handsome, black of skin, black of eyes, with a tight skullcap of curly black hair and an expression on his face like he was in the presence of a bad smell.

He said, "How do you do, Mr. du Cheyne."

I think I managed some kind of fatuous grin or another. "Want a drink?" Rattling my glass of ice and fizz up at him.

Rothman's stinkface twisted a little tighter. "No thank you."

"Sit down then."

A long, snotty look around at my apartment. Neat as a pin, the household saw to that. Nothing wrong but my shoes in the middle of the floor, half-buried in vidnet imagery . . .

When did the AI start channel surfing? Did it shut off my stock options when this little shit came through the door? What's playing now? An old episode of *Planets for Man*. The one about the terraforming project on Mimir's Well, Eta Cassiopiae A4ii, some nineteen-point . . .

He said, "I'll get right to the point, Mr. du Cheyne."

I felt a hard moment of freezing dread, imagining God knows what, but I smirked and said, "Please do."

A quirk of distaste on his lips. "Mr. du Cheyne, I am empowered to offer you a par trade in ERSIE Prime stock for your static options on Berens-Vataro Enterprises."

Par. A little stab of annoyance now, fueled, I suppose, by the gin, as I put down the fourth empty glass. "A hundred twenty shares? Man, you can just take a flying . . ."

Voice very sharp: "Static at closure."

Twelve thousand. I popped open a little window and checked. Felt a slight shock. ERSIE stock was being steadily traded up by the current furor and . . . "Eight hundred thousand livres?" My voice sounded a lot higher than normal.

"Correct."

Blink. "Is this because of my . . ." A wave at the little window.

A chopped look of contempt. "Your little suit hasn't got the proverbial snowball's chance, du Cheyne. In fact, if you lodge it, you run the risk of being slapped with a frivolous legal action fine."

"Then why . . ."

Look of contempt deepening. "If you can't figure that out . . ." A slow head shake. "Just take the offer, boy."

I sat staring at him, looking at that arrogant little asshole law clerk face of his, face sneering at me, face full of superiority, feeling my anger sizzle. Because I *can* figure it out, you see. Shithead. Sooner or later, the Trade Regents will vote. If ERSIE wins, it owns B-VEI. If B-VEI wins . . . ERSIE will want to hold a big enough chunk of stock options to claim a seat on the B-VEI board of directors and . . .

I said, "I don't know, Mr. Rothman. I . . . I'd like to think it over."

He smiled. "Go ahead. Take as long as you want. Just remember: The Board vote will not be announced beforehand. They'll just vote and that will be that."

And, if the vote goes against B-VEI, I've got nothing.

He said, "I've left my mailtag with the apartment datastore. You just post me your authorization and I'll make the transaction." He turned, the door opened and closed, and he was gone.

I sat and stared. Ordered another drink and felt my sweat start up afresh. Glanced in the little window and saw with a start that the value of ERSIE stock had gone up another six mills while we'd been talking.

3

By mid-morning of the next day, Jimmy Haas and I had the D-1 prime mover buttoned up and ready to go. He'd been working on it in my absence, working mostly under Rossignol's direction, though with a bit of help from Todd Sanchez, and seemed a little nonplussed when I came back and more or less took over the final stage of operations. Watched me. Did what I said as I ran systems checks on the work that'd been done in my absence, made little changes here and there.

I didn't say anything when I discovered someone had failed to set the throat diameter on the plasma exhaust. Didn't comment on the fact that the work record was unsigned, in clear defiance of regs.

But I did open the comparison table to the section on plasma channels and ran the simulator to see what would've happened if the ship's engines had been started with the settings as is. No explosions. Nothing flashy. Just a major overheat, components fusing, safeties running a too late shutdown.

The exhaust system on a relatively small field modulus device like this one isn't too expensive, maybe in the range of fourteen thousand livres. I didn't say anything. But I knew he'd be seeing. "Okay, Jimmy. Let's go up front and see if it works."

He started silently disconnecting the monitor system while I reeled in my tools and stood down the engine's internal operating system. Finally, he said, "Gaetan, I was the one who was responsible for seeing to the throat settings."

So. I was wondering if he'd just let it slide. Maybe be pissed at me for seeing it, even though . . . "Jimmy, did Rossignol *tell* you you were responsible?"

Silence. Then, "Um, no. He just took a quick peek before Todd and I shut the casing."

Well. Todd Sanchez knew I'd be coming back to finish her up. And he knew I'd be the one to sign off on the whole job. Have to have a nice chat with Ross, maybe during afternoon break. I said, "Don't worry about it. Thanks for telling me."

With our appendages pulled in, we backed out of the exhaust bay and started moving up the outside of the ship's hull, toward the forward airlock pressure curtain, where the others would be waiting. I wouldn't be surprised if asshole Sanchez was trying to slip one by me. Rossignol? Damned sloppy is all. He knew I'd be coming back to the job. Knew Goddamned well I'd be thorough, would catch any mistakes.

So he just fucking let it slide.

I could imagine what he'd say when I brought it up: I'm sorry, Gaetan. Jesus, we've just been so damn *busy* . . . Sometimes. Yeah. Right.

Going home already, the end-of-work conversation with Rossignol already fading. No more than shadowed memories of taking him by the shirtfront as we floated in a dark, empty, private corner of the locker room, bracing myself with feet and free hand, swinging him around my center of gravity, hauling his face close.

I think he was pretty surprised. I'm bigger and stronger than most of the mechanics at ERSIE-5, I guess, but it never matters. I haven't gotten in a brawl the whole time I've worked here. Haven't hit another person in anger since . . . well. Kids. You know.

Rossignol's eyes popping with astonishment as I held him close and told him what a lazy fucking shit I thought he'd become. Pitching my voice probably lower than I ought to have, I told him he'd have to have a chat with Todd Sanchez if he wanted to keep the peace on his crew and . . . I'd let him go, told him to fuck it, kicked off from the front of a nearby locker bank, making the flexible plastic boom, sailing away from him, toward the door, going on home.

How many times have I come here like this, come in and slumped in my chair, staring at an empty wall, waiting . . . Not waiting for anything. The appliances know what I want, listen to my thoughts, anticipate my needs . . . like servants in some old movie, some movie from before the days of vidnet, before the days of . . . anything at all. Image of silent men and women dressed in black and white, silent men and women standing in the shadows, reaching out silent hands for the rich man's coat and velvet top hat . . .

Slim silent woman in black dress and white apron, polishing silver and wood and . . . Rich man's eyes on her slim, starved back, eyeing a curve of hip, the hidden length of thigh and . . .

Somewhere now, the icemaker tinkled, making me whatever the bartender software thought I wanted, knew I might be needing just now, while the vidnet display swirled, turning the far wall to a wilderness of mist and color. What would I see next? A cooked-up script about those far-gone days? I can just imagine. Now I'll see some skinny, famished maid, some *charwoman* bending over her silver-polishing job, bending over, back of her too-short black dress rising up . . .

Here and now, a pulsing yellow light of warning, superimposed over the landscape of my stock exchange access node. Somewhere in my head, a soft whisper, whisper from the apartment sentience: Important message from the trade controller AI, Mr. du Cheyne. Important message . . .

Go ahead.

Jesus, I can't make these decisions. Call up the ERSIE lawyers and tell them I'll take the eight hundred thousand? Or sit tight and wait for the resumption of trade you think is coming? Another whisper, in a subtly different inner voice: Cusp of decision axis may come with insufficient lead time for you to participate effectively in procedural processes, Mr. du Cheyne. Rule sieves suggest you grant this software per diem power of attorney. Meaning it thought it was going to have to jump fast when the time came.

Uh. "Granted." Said aloud, seeming to echo eerily in the empty apartment, though the walls were as acoustically perfect as cheap consumer technology permitted. A quick look. Okay. So nothing's really happened since last night. B-VEI still flagged and frozen. Board of Trade Regents now in closed session. At the stock ticker . . . the transitional value of twelve thousand shares of ERSIE stock was valued at 817,468 livres. Okay. So it's gone up a little bit.

What does it *mean?* Does it mean the bidders believe ERSIE will win the legal battle going on in Kiev just now? Does it mean I should sell? Eight hundred seventeen thousand livres, for Christ's sake . . .

But what if they're wrong? What if my software knows what it's doing? How much is that B-VEI stock going to be worth tomorrow if . . . if . . . Then that familiar soft touch from the apartment: You have a visitor, Mr. du Cheyne. That wretched Mr. Rothman, come to sneer at my things and offer me more money? Or brandish ever scarier threats?

The AI said, A Miss Tallentyre, representing client services for Berens-Vataro Enterprises. A small, hard clenching inside, filling me up with nameless dread. Next act.

Much later, I sat in the darkness, staring at an empty wall. The household kept trying to read my thoughts, trying to bring up the vidnet link and do what it was supposed to do . . . a faint blush of dawn forming on the far wall, hesitating, then going dark again.

Miss Tallentyre's visit wasn't so different from the previous night's meeting with the ERSIE lawyer. A round of meaningless chatter, then getting down to business, telling me historical bullshit I already knew, her company's opinion of what might happen, again, just a rehash of news reports. Asked me how much the lawyer offered me for the stock options and didn't seem surprised at the answer. Asked if she could look at my stock ticker.

I'm not sure why I let her do it. A slim, pretty, blond woman, quiet and serious, with pale blue eyes that didn't seem to be seeing anything when they looked at me. A typical modern woman's slim, trim figure outlined under a tan linen suit. Not as sturdy-looking as a working girl, I guess.

I was wondering what it might be like to be . . . involved with such a woman, wondering as well how much B-VEI was paying her . . . two, three, maybe four times my mechanic's salary . . . she'd surfaced suddenly from the AI's composition tables and, without preamble, offered to buy back all my options at the program's estimated parity value.

Cool, empty blue eyes, pale blue eyes, staring into mine.

Well, Mr. du Cheyne?

What I said then was the same thing I'd told the ERSIE guy. And got the same little speech in reply. Is this realistic? Is it? I don't know. I'm not the only one holding a chunk of B-VEI stock, after all. There are dozens of Miss Tallentyres out tonight, visiting little shnooks around the solar system, making similar offers to . . . Why the hell would they do it, if they thought ERSIE was going to win?

Because ERSIE's made them a very nice offer for *their* stock holdings? Sure. If ERSIE wins, it gets everything. If it loses, maybe it will have bought up B-VEI at a steep discount. Just like that. And if the B-VEI people think ERSIE has a good chance of winning, it's certainly to their advantage to sell.

Shit. No matter what happens, somebody is going to have to continue working the B-VEI technology. If ERSIE wins its case before the Board of Trade Regents, Doctors Berens and Vataro will probably be offered vice presidencies with ERSIE, maybe directoral seats, maybe . . .

On the wall, the AIs had finally managed to overrule my will that the net link stay dark. Light and motion and a swirling depth of detail . . . A moment of confusion, followed by a moment of recognition. This was an old drama, made in the middle of the twenty-second century, just a generation or so after the first interstellar crossing, in the days when starships were new and wonderful and strange. *Into the Stardust.* About the development of the first faster-than-light vessel, about its voyage to the galactic core . . .

They thought it would happen soon, didn't they? Space travel begun in the middle of the twentieth century. Space colonization in the middle of the twenty-first. Interstellar expeditions opening up the twenty-second. All this wonderful new science, medicine, physics and engineering, *starships*, for God's sake!

All right, so it took five hundred years, but . . .

Cold chill of realization.

It's happening *now.*

At lunch the next day, I sat with all my usual friends, Garstang and Phil sitting together, diagonal from me. Millie Aichang and Zell Benson with their heads pressed together, bent low over a placard display of travel brochures, bright pictures throwing moving blue shadows on their faces, travelogue an animated whisper I couldn't quite make out. Rua Mater down the other end of the table, node clip hanging in her hair, eating with her eyes closed.

Empty chair opposite me. Empty chair opposite her.

An alternate history suggests itself. Passion rising in the night by the shores of Lake A71K, soft wind stirring across my back as I lay on her in the faux-wilderness of Manhattan Island. Rua Mater whispering under me. Oh, Gaetan. Oh, my God.

The feel of her innards clutching my prick.

The spasm of my orgasm. The clenching of hers.

Lying together, pleasantly sweaty in the night, holding each other, satisfaction rather than desperation settling in, making itself at home. *And so they lived happily ever after.* But I was looking at an empty chair, not at her. And she was lost in whatever ersatz dream she'd provoked from the net.

A shadow on the table then, falling over our food, Garstang looking up with a start, seeming to recoil against Phil Hendrickx's side, surprise, fear, visible in her eyes, the set of her jaw. There were two beefy guys from corporate security standing at the end of the table, looking us over. Two guys with a look of the gymnasium, a look of athletic drugs about them, stun rods dangling from their brown belts.

Looking us over, eyes almost amiable. Then looking right at me, one of them said, "Gaetan du Cheyne?"

"Uh, sure."

"You're wanted in the shop supervisory office."

Albacore? Maybe Ross hadn't taken as well as I thought to . . . "I'm off the clock now," gesturing at my lunch. "Why the hell didn't they just send a netmemo?"

Garstang's voice, a little shaky: "Gaetan . . ." Unstated: *These are security guys!*

The one who was doing the talking put his thumbs through his belt, heel of one hand bumping the stun rod, making it swing a little. He said, "You're wanted in the shop supervisory office. Right now."

Rua Mater's voice from the other end of the table: "Gaetan, you want me to call the shop steward for you?"

Rua Mater maybe not so disinterested after all. Maybe I *should* have climbed in the shower with her, brief jolt of memory even now a slight pang somewhere in the neighborhood of my prostate gland. I eased back my chair and stood. "No. I guess not."

The security asshole smiled and glanced at his chum. "Smarter than he looks."

So what did these little bully boys think was going on? Were they looking forward to zapping me in front of a whole roomful of workers? Probably dumber than they looked.

Garstang said, "What's this about, Gaetan?"

I shrugged. Why tell . . . But then I said, "Probably about my

Berens-Vataro stock options. They've been trying to get me to sell them."

Garstang's eyes wide. *"Sell?"*

I turned away, walking beside the two security guys, walking away from the table, grabbing my equilibrimotor from the wall rack and . . . Voice inside: What do you think? Are those livre signs in her eyes? Nice big £'s waking up her libido?

So what am I imagining? Am I imagining once she finds out how much money is at stake here, I'll get her back from Phil Hendrickx after all these years? She must *care*, you know. That business with Rua Mater . . . She was still staring at me from across the room when the elevator door slid shut, closing us off from one another.

Then, I sat in a supervisory office, somewhere deep inside the main ERSIE-5 administrative complex, sat in an antique wooden chair across a wooden desk from a woman in a creaky leather chair, woman dressed in a fine azure suit of soft, watered silk, no one I'd ever seen before. She smiled and reached out her hand for me to shake. "How're you doing, Mr. du Cheyne?"

The name on the door. "Miss Yoshida?"

She nodded, still smiling. "Do you have any idea why you're here?"

All I could do was shrug, try to smile back. You're not in trouble. No trouble at all. Nothing's at stake but a decision on whether to hold out for the most money you can possibly . . . "Well. If there's no trouble with the *Albacore* decommissioning project . . ."

The net node embedded in her desktop was flickering, displaying images for her eyes only. Maybe Rossignol *did* send in a report. They could bust me a whole step for grabbing him like that. On the other hand, they'd find out just what happened. Maybe I'd be getting a bonus. Maybe Ross would be losing his gold belt, sitting in another office somewhere nearby, sweating your proverbial bullets.

I said, "I'm guessing this is about the stock options thing."

The smile slowly faded. "Du Cheyne, I don't *know* what this is really all about. I got a router instruction this morning . . . waiting for me here when I logged on. I . . ." A long hesitation. An odd look. What had all the smiling been about? Maybe she figured I'd let her in on the secret before . . . She said, "Look, this is nothing personal. I've got a router instruction in my pad and a job to do. You understand?"

A sudden, intense alarm. Why the hell wasn't I facing a company law clerk, that ridiculous Mr. What's-his-name? Something not right here.

She said, "Line one of the router instruction tells me to offer you, in exchange for a parity quitclaim on your B-VEI stock options, the sum of one million livres and advancement to Wage Grade Eleven step Zero."

I could feel my mouth suddenly hang open.

I stammered. Tried to get some words out. Failed. Stammered again.

She said, "You have to make the decision right now, Mr. du Cheyne."

"I . . . can't . . ."

She looked back down, looking deep into the desk's imagery. "Line two of the router instruction requires me to tell you that this is the company's final offer."

I shrugged, suddenly found my voice. "They must know I've had a counteroffer. Berens-Vataro will be—"

She spread her hands. "This has nothing to do with me. All they want to hear is, Yes or no?"

Something. Something she's not telling me. I can see it in her eyes.

I said, "No. I'm sorry, I—"

She said, "Now that you've made your decision, line three of the router instruction requires me to tell you that your employment contract with the Eighth Ray Scientific-Industrial Enterprise is terminated."

Long moment of silence.

Almost stupidly: *"What?"*

She let out a long sigh, sounding somehow relieved, and said, "Sorry."

I found myself standing, mouth open, eyes wide. *Fired?* I said, "You can't fucking get away with this. The machinists' union . . . the steward . . . I . . ."

She motioned at something in her desk display and the office door whispered open, two beefy security guys standing out in the hall. Then she said, "Mr. du Cheyne is no longer employed here. Please escort him from the company premises."

Security guys stepping in, hands raised, as if reaching for me.

I said, "Now wait just a *second* here . . ."

She folded her arms across her chest and said, "Look, I'm sorry, Mr. du Cheyne. There's nothing *I* can do. I'll have the shop steward gather your personal tools and bring them to your apartment." A glance downward. "I guess the equilibrimotor belongs to us. You can leave it here."

No more words left inside.

All I could do was nod.

Nod and be led away.

Somehow, I got back to my apartment and sat down in my favorite chair, facing the vidnet wall, still wrapped in my space-suit, spacesuit curious, for it'd never been to my apartment before. What the hell am I going to do with my tool packs when they get here? They're not going to be happy, just lying around.

Orange pulsing now. Apartment AI clamoring for my attention. Mr. du Cheyne! *Please*, Mr. du Cheyne, you've got to . . .

Shut the fuck up.

AI quite puzzled.

But Mr. du Cheyne . . .

Shut up, damn you.

I heard the drink mixer rattle forlornly, off in the kitchen, ice cubes clinking softly, glasses shifting back and forth, waiting for me to want them.

Just sitting here. Staring. Waiting. Empty. I keep thinking there's something I ought to be able to *do* about this.

The apartment said, Mr. du Cheyne, *please*. . .

Communicating a great sense of anxiety to me, as if I didn't have enough trouble. Jesus. Maybe I can call them up in the morning, call that nice Miz Yoshida and tell her I changed my mind. Call that fucking lawyeroid asshole and . . .

Something chattering away in the background. My suit. Talking very fast, not to me. Talking to the apartment. Suit's a lot damn smarter than the household appliances' AI, even without its ERSIE-5 processor link. I . . .

God damn, I *want* my job.

I *liked* going there every day.

My friends.

The ships.

The machinery.

The . . . *doing.* I . . .

The suit said, Mr. du Cheyne? I'm sorry, sir, but I'm forced to override your last order to the apartment.

Boggling. *Override?* Like this was some kind of hardware rule sieve emergency? I . . .

The vidnet wall lit up with a flash, and there was the Board of Trade Regents meeting hall, down in good old Kiev, down on the black-earth plains of the world we left behind. Ringed tiers of men and women, sitting quietly at their stations, as if . . .

One man, furious somehow, standing up, shouting, shaking his fist at the rest of them, storming away up the long flight of red-carpeted stairs and out the heavy black teak door, door inlaid with bright silver and some kind of clear crystal. People up in the spectator gallery, yelling, cheering, hugging each other, and I could hear the excited voice of the announcer, ". . . bringing you this historic event, *live* from the floor of the Trade Regency in Kiev . . ."

Historic event?

But, God damn it, I've just been *fired*, you see, and . . .

Voice-over: ". . . secret ballot of the assembled Regents voting to break up an industrial monopoly that has endured for more than five hundred years . . ."

Those two men hugging each other, teetering on the gallery's edge, in danger of toppling over the guardrail and falling down on the Speaker's dais. Those would be Drs. Roald Berens and Ntanë Vataro then, wouldn't they? Cold, dispassionate voice starting to speak inside of me just then. They've taken the vote then, have they? Well, then . . .

The stock-trading AI popped up over the vidnet display, excited, waving fistfuls of displays, including the automatic renewal date stamp on my power of attorney. A great feeling of triumph, the joyous surge of a job well done. The happiness of a tool employed.

Trading in stock options for Berens-Vataro Enterprises Interplanetary has been resumed. Option values currently held by trading license #0A61C-84, in the name of solar citizen Gaetan du Cheyne, occupation none, resident at L_1 (SE) workerhostel #67, room 472: £3,207,968.

Three million, two hundred seven thousand, nine hundred and sixty-eight livres. The calculator chattered inanely: Just about what I'd see in my ERSIE pay voucher over the next . . . oh, call it the next twenty-five hundred years or so. I . . .

My heart, just then, seemed to come to a complete stop.

4

I awoke the next morning, still sitting in my chair, still dressed in my spacesuit, feeling fine, in the bland, gray light of my empty apartment. Okay, du Cheyne. Time to groan and yawn. Time to get up. Time to go to work.

Long moment of nothing at all.

Fragments of memories.

Memories of sitting here, listening to the drink mixer rattle and hum, of sitting here, watching the vidnet, having one each of all my favorites, drinking far into the night. Staring at the news. Watching my stock ticker. Useless.

I'd let it scan and found myself watching bits of old movies. I think I was watching a twenty-fourth-century 3vee re-creation of a prehistoric drama called *The Philadelphia Story* when Rossignol showed up with my toolbox and ancillary belt hardware. Rossignol and the shop steward, I think.

Rossignol bending over me, recoiling from my breath. Jesus Christ, Gaetan, are you all right?

I think I said something about wishing there were pornode viddies starring Katharine Hepburn, but maybe it was before her time, Rossignol looking over his shoulder at the display, bewildered.

The shop steward said, I don't know. I guess you could program the system to—

Rossignol: Shut the fuck up, Jessie.

Jessie the Steward rolling his eyes.

Sometime later, I realized the spacesuit must have picked up on what I'd said, giving instructions to the house AI, blending the re-creation of Philadelphia with something called *Bringing Up Baby*, where dear old Kate gets it on with Cary Grant after all, I can't give you anything but love, Mr. Bone . . .

And now I was awake, clear-headed, empty-headed, sitting alone in my apartment, wondering what to do. Inside my toolbox something stirred, restless.

Finally, I took off the suit and hung it in the closet, feeling it go to sleep as I undid the seams, a twinge of regret from the apartment. Went and got cleaned up, standing for a long time under the shower head, hot recycler water running down my body, splashing around my feet, swirling down the drain, through the filter, back up the pipe and down on my shoulders again. Got dressed. Went out. Don't know where the hell I intended to go. Sometimes you just have to get the fuck out.

Down in the lobby I was headed for the entrance to the common tunnel to which all these buildings were docked, hostels and shopping malls and whatnot, when someone came out of the business office, a young woman, maybe someone I've noticed from time to time, name unknown: "Mr. du Cheyne?"

I stopped, turned, not even wondering, and waited for her to come over.

She said, "Mr. du Cheyne, we've been informed that you are presently . . . unemployed." Her gray-green eyes rather bleak under neatly trimmed reddish brown bangs.

I said, "So?"

"Well . . ." fidgeting a bit. "Mr. du Cheyne, this is a *worker*hostel, you understand?"

"So what?"

"Well. We cater to a *worker* clientele, employees of $L_1(SE)$

industrial concerns, mostly ERSIE. Not unemployed transients. You understand?"

I stared at her. "No. I don't think I do."

Exasperation in her eyes then. *Why are you making this so difficult, Mr. du Cheyne?* She said, "I'm sorry. We'll have to terminate your lease at the end of this month. Six days."

I think by then my mouth was hanging open. "But I can pay my rent."

"I'm sorry, Mr. du Cheyne. Management regulations. You understand."

A sizzle of anger starting up. "How about if I pay my rent for a full year in advance?" A full year? Hell, that's only a hundred twenty fucking livres.

A startled look in her eyes. "I . . . I don't think so, but . . . I'll check for you." She said, "Look, if you're *retired* . . . there's a *very* nice retirement hostel just down the tube. Mostly people who've retired from ERSIE, I think. I could have your things transferred this afternoon and . . ."

Eyes nonplussed. "I'm sorry, Mr. du Cheyne. Look, if you have a new job by next Tuesday, let us know. Otherwise . . ."

Great. Fucking great. I turned away and headed out, heading down the tube, blending in with a light crowd of industrious walkers, folks with places to go, people to see, and found myself, eventually, at the bus terminal.

No places to go. No people to see. Nothing to do. That's me.

Back in my apartment with four days to go, spacesuit hanging silently in the closet, tools stirring softly in their box. House AI flashing things on the wall, stock ticker clamoring for my attention, let's do this, let's do that.

When I move, the house AI stays here, part of the appliance operating system, an extension of the hostel's net segment. Will you miss me, apartment mine? Nothing. Silence. Can't answer that. Don't know how. But I know it'll miss the stock ticker software, which belongs to me and will have to be moved off the local node. And, of course, it'll miss its new friend the spacesuit.

Drink mixer rattled forlornly from the kitchen. Ah, yes. What if the new occupant is some kind of teetotaler? What then? I told it to mix me . . . what? What do I feel like? The drink mixer whined and, when I got the drink, it was a Manhattan, rather on the sweet side.

Funny to think of someone else coming and living here after all these years. Sitting in my chair, drinking from my spigot, eating from my stove and refrigerator, fucking in my bed or even just sleeping there . . . I never gave a thought to all the people who lived here before me. This hostel is two, maybe three hundred years old. I never thought to ask.

Sitting there, as always, sipping my drink, watching the vidnet wall, logged on to a pornode, offered a menu of choices, as if the house AI couldn't quite figure out what I wanted. My standard selections? Why do I always like to watch women masturbating, all by themselves? I hardly ever call up things with two women together, much less long, luxurious scenes of heterosexual couples doing the old Adam delved/Eve span thing.

A slight sense of something like impatience from the house. As if to say, *What the fuck do you want?* Sorry. Sorry I'm such an asshole, dear old house. The pornode menu was displaced by classified listings, by phone book pages. Live shows, at theaters in the habitat parts of L_1(SE). Sure, that'd be cool. I haven't done that in a long time. Private shows in booths. All right. That too.

Flip the page.

Long, long listings of whorehouses, all kinds of whorehouses, fancy ones and cheap ones, houses for general trade and specialty spots. We can suck it for you here, whatever it is, for a price . . .

Call girls, much more expensive, available by the hour for such and such a price, grouped by the districts they worked. Girls from houses who'd come to you wherever, at a somewhat higher price. And then, of course, the private contractors.

I had the menu re-sort itself by price and looked at the top of the list. Camilla Seldane. Whole nights only. Five hundred livres—discounts for longer engagements. No groups . . . What the hell could a woman possibly do for me, in a single night, that might be worth five hundred livres? A couple of days ago, I'd've called that just shy of five months pay.

Before I knew what was happening, I found that I'd loaded my credit code and address and made myself a date. Then I sat back in my chair and held tight to my drink and felt an attack of the willies come on. My God.

When the house AI whispered, You have a visitor, Mr. du Cheyne, I felt my asshole clench. Tell her to go back . . . tell her to go away . . . tell her . . . I was on my feet, walking across the room, empty glass still clutched tight in my hand, when the door slid open, admitting harsh, institutional light from the hall.

A man and a woman. Woman slim, pale-haired, with dark blue, fathomless eyes, standing closer, closer than the man, man somehow lost in shadow. She turned to him and said, "All right, John. You can pick me up in the morning, at the usual time."

Emerging from the shadows. "I . . . think I'll wait for you, for just a while, down in the lobby . . ." Looking at me, mean-faced, scowling, big, thick-necked man with a handgun holstered at his hip, not a stungun, something deadly, ID patch on his shoulder, branding him with the name of a licensed security agency.

She stepped across the threshold and the door slid shut behind her.

Silence.

Then a slow grin, secretive, letting me in on the secret, the grin of a friend. A very close friend, someone I'd known, perhaps, for . . .

She stepped closer, no more than a meter from me now, taking those deep blue eyes off mine, looking around at the apartment, then looking back, locking me in again. "So, Mr. du Cheyne. Someone die and leave you a bit of money did they?"

I swallowed past a long dry spot in my throat, tried to lift my empty glass toward my lips, forced myself to let it dangle. "Um. Sort of."

"Sort of . . ." She swept past me, into the rest of the apartment, turning round, looking at . . . things. Pirouetting. For me? I . . .

Not an astonishingly beautiful woman. That pale neutral-color silk dress, clinging just so to the curve of breast and hip and buttock . . . very flattering, supremely flattering, a thousand-livre dress, but . . . Garstang would've looked better in it, I . . .

Something about the scent of her as she brushed by me. As if she'd . . . touched me somehow. Not perfume, no. Nothing I could put my finger on, you see. Just . . .

She stepped closer, smiling into my eyes, looking at me. Only at me. As if there were nothing else, no one else, right now, in the entire universe, but me. Nothing in the universe but me, right now, maybe for ever. Nothing but me, until the end of time . . . That tremor in my chest must be the beating of my heart.

She took the empty glass out of my hand, brought it to her nose, sniffed delicately, smiled and made a *tsk-tsk* sound, put it aside, though there was nowhere to set it down, empty glass bouncing noiselessly on the carpet, rolling into a corner, forgotten.

Looking into my eyes. Looking into them as if she could . . .

Stepping closer, reaching out with one hand, touching me lightly on the chest. My God. Something about her breath, washing lightly over my face. Camilla. I remembered her name was Camilla.

She said, "It's all right for you to be in a hurry."

In a hurry. Desperation. That sense of tightness between my legs. Just like . . . just like . . . Oh, God. Nothing down there now. Tightness in my chest, a building sense of familiar horror. What if . . . what if . . .

Say something. Just say something.

Hard to swallow right now, throat so very dry. Christ, I need a drink, I . . . In the background, the drink mixer started to rattle . . . a flicker in Camilla's eyes, a moment of distraction. The machinery suddenly fell silent.

Odd. As if the whole apartment had suddenly gone away.
As if she'd . . . commanded all of creation to leave us alone.
I whispered, "I . . . I . . ."

Blue eyes deepening, drawing me right in, her hand reaching up, feeling the paperiness of my cheek, fingers along the line of my jaw, a powerful tingle of . . . Oh, Christ. Of nothing. Nothing at all. Eyes telling me, It's all right. Tell me. I said, "I'm sorry. I'm . . . sort of impotent. Sometimes."

She smiled, sighed, warm exhalation on me, in me, the scent of her somehow coming right into my heart, and said, "I think not, Mr. du Cheyne." She kissed me, standing on tiptoe . . . no, that's not right, it . . . Our mouths welded together, her tongue extruding, seeming to fill my entire head.

And my erection deployed like a hydraulic ram at her command.

She pulled back, just a little, still breathing in my face, her teeth glittering, white and moist, so close to me, tongue visible, small pink creature, flexing behind her teeth, as if . . . She said, "You see, Mr. du Cheyne? It's *all right* for you to be in a hurry."

She kissed me again, any thought I might have had, might have wanted to have, disintegrating under the impact of her touch, arms around me, pulling me close, massaging the back of my neck, sweeping down the long panel of my back muscles, caressing the curve of my buttocks . . .

Somehow, we were on the floor, the front of that no-color silk dress pulled up, my trousers undone, slid halfway down, down around my knees perhaps, no sense at all of where they'd gone or how, Camilla still holding me with her lips, me on top of her, her body miraculously ready, hot and wet, the hard grip of her inner muscles as she took me in . . .

Delirium. Like I was having some grand hallucination.
And it was done.
Somehow.

Lying on my back on the floor beside her, gasping for breath. My God. I had forgotten, so completely forgotten, what it could be like. Lying there with my lips swollen, my teeth feeling like they were starting from their sockets. Like my nose, somehow, had gotten bigger, was subsiding now. Wet prick draping itself across the top of my thigh. Conditioned apartment air cool on damp pubic hair.

Yes. Those *are* the realities, aren't they?

But the magic. The magic that preceded this pleasantly icky aftermath . . .

Shadow falling over me. Camilla standing now, stretching, clutching my eyes with the splendid curve of her back, arms reaching up, crossing over, drawing the expensive no-color silk dress off over her head in one long, fantastically liquid motion, leaving her naked.

Not the most beautiful girl I ever saw. Not by a long shot. Not even the most beautiful girl I ever screwed, though by not so very long a shot. Better than average, that's all. She turned, stood still while I looked at her, smiling down at me, eyes so deep and blue and . . .

I looked away for a minute, catching my breath, then looked back, careful to stay focused on her body. So. Belly. Breasts. Hips. Inner sides of long thighs shining wet with the residue of me. Lightly furred blond snatch, standard-issue mons and standard vulval divide.

Nothing I hadn't seen a thousand times before.

How many women in my lifetime? Real ones, real in my bed, for me to touch and taste and fuck? Not so many. A couple of dozen, maybe. Enough.

I looked at her face, at the eyes behind that rich, inviting, friend's smile, felt those eyes reach out and start fingering the stuff of my soul. Jesus. She was coming closer, standing beside me, and I could smell my scent on her, her own far richer, magical scent beyond that, demanding, demanding . . .

I swallowed past renewed dryness, and said, "How're you doing this?"

Her head cocked to one side, a momentary *intent* look, as if she were puzzling something out. "You really want to know?"

Then a long look around, at certain things in the apartment, the spacesuit hanging in the open closet, the toolbox in the corner, which, come to think of it, had stopped its ceaseless, restless stirrings the moment she . . . A smile, looking at me again. "I guess maybe you do."

She sat down on the carpet beside me. "Some of it's relatively simple, of course. Enhanced biochemistry. Special receptors attached to my vomeronasal organ so I can sample your pheromones. Modifications to my salivary and apocrine glands so I can manufacture pheromones of my own, specially tailored to . . . affect you. And my vagina's been fixed to make a number of interesting hormones too."

Easy to guess, if I'd been able to think. They make fuck dolls that work just that way. I could have bought one for the price of two nights with Miss Camilla Seldane here.

She said, "That's not the half of it, of course. You know how your suit and appliances know what you're thinking? How they can . . . talk to you?"

Ignorant people, technically unsophisticated folk call it "machine telepathy," like something from an old fantasy story. Nothing magical about it. Human bodies are infused with nanometer-scale medical symbiotes, things which have augmented and in some sense displaced the natural systems evolution gave us. Artificial infusions, symbiotes injected centuries ago, now a natural part of us, passed on from generation to generation, carried in the germ plasm of the female line, as much a part of us as, say, our mitochondria.

AI machinery uses magnetic induction to read the whereabouts of these artificial organs in our blood, our bodies, uses them to detect the firing of our neurons, read what's going on in our bodies and brains, and uses a rule sieve, the nature of the human soul long ago worked out, to figure out what we're thinking. To, quite literally, *read* our minds.

And those same AIs can then induce electrical fields in the symbiotes, command them to move hither and yon, cause blood to flow, cause our neurons to fire, cause new connections to be made, can, in fact, cause our brains to think new thoughts. As simple as that.

She said, "I've got a headreader wired into my nervous system." A gesture at my spacesuit. "About as good as that one, I guess." A friendly smile, a sly grin, letting me in on the secret. "I tried to get a police-grade unit, what they call a lie detector. Couldn't."

Christ. Knowing eyes on me. Knowing what I was thinking, even now. A sudden feeling of warmth. A drawing toward this woman. Something very much the way I imagine true love must feel, I . . .

Her grin broadened. Eyes on me.

I said, "You could do a lot more than be a call girl with a setup like that."

She said, "Superintendent of Whores would pull my license. They'd take my rig away and I'd be spreading my legs for dismes again."

Right. And she was probably still paying off the surgical fees and hardware loans too.

She laughed, stood up, straddled me and let me look up at her for a minute, let me look up at her face, at her crotch, both in a line somehow, dominating my field of view. Was she expecting . . . yes. Of course. I said, "I . . . don't think I can . . ." Well, no. Erection already established and waiting, down at the bottom of my belly.

She laughed, merry, witty, inviting, happy somehow. Kneeled, took my solid prick in her hand and guided it inside, slid down the length of me until she was sitting on my pubis bone, massaging me with ridiculously supple internal muscles.

She said, "We've got all night, you know?"

I nodded. Helpless.

Soft laughter. "By the time I'm through with you, Mr. du Cheyne, you'll be frisky for weeks."

I woke up, sometime the next afternoon, sitting naked in my chair, legs splayed out, bare heels on the carpet, head thrown back, mouth hanging open, in the silence of my empty apartment. Throat so very dry. Thirsty as hell. Atmosphere in here almost . . . steamy. Air still full of pheromones the apartment would have a struggle filtering out.

Something stirred, very softly, in my toolbox. One delicate clink, as of ice, from the drink mixer. Right. Aloud, in a rusty-sounding voice, I said, "Sure. I'd like a nice, tall, cold glass of orange juice, please."

A moment of silence; the apartment stunned? What could it be thinking? Does it visualize Gaetan the Drunken Slob, somehow revitalized, somehow redeemed, by one great big hearty dose of superenhanced almighty goddam technopussy? Talk about amazing grace . . . Fucking God, am I *thirsty*, though!

Rosy-fingered dawn blushed on the far wall, then the vidnet connection swirled out into the room, house AI already threading its way, oh so carefully, down my usual roads, surfing past this scene and that, no sign at all, mind you, of the pornode.

Headline News Service.

Familiar scene of the B-VEI landing field, somewhere on Callisto, orange Jupiter hanging in a matte black sky over a bright ice horizon, ice bright only by contrast to the black sky. Vacuum-sealed buildings in the foreground, insulated landing stage, spacecraft here and there, designs familiar and strange.

Close-up, one of those little B-VEI disk-ships, this one clustered round by emergency vehicles, surrounded by hundreds of men and women in sparkly silver spacesuits, the familiar suits of technical workers, just like the suit hanging silent in my closet.

My God, look at that.

Flying saucer, once featureless, silvery, like something from a Medieval dream, now twisted, skin broken open here and there, riven by long, lightning-bolt cracks, skin dented in, blackened . . .

The voice-over: ". . . experimental faster-than-light spacecraft *Torus X-4*, just returned from a test flight to the prominent blue-white star Regulus, some eighty-three light-years from Earth, a round-trip voyage of approximately twenty weeks, reports having been attacked by a spacecraft of unknown design and origin . . ."

Blue Regulus flaring out there, like an infinitely deep white hole poked through the flat black sky, letting the energies of deSitter space in to consume us, dry voice of *X-4*'s captain narrating the vid for us, Regulus without a regular planetary system, surrounded by a fine planetesimal field, like an immense Kuiper Belt, rich, so very rich, you see, in metals and minerals of every sort, including a number of unusual . . .

Then the voice of some other crewman: *Captain? Captain? I'm getting a reading on the mass proximity indicator. No. No sir, it's not an asteroid. Sir, it's vectoring toward us at nearly point-three cee! It's* . . .

Something crossing the exterior view, transiting the camera field at high velocity, an eight-armed starfish trailing a sparkly silver plasma cone, background stars whipping behind it as the camera struggled to track it across the sky.

Captain screaming, *What the fucking hell* . . .

Starfish going flash-flicker-flash, just before it disappeared, exterior scene dissolving in purple fire . . .

Captain! Jesus, Captain, it's coming back!

Flash-flicker-flash.

Switch to an interior scene. Someone standing in the middle of a wrecked control room, man in a nice-looking company uniform. Man on fire, dancing and screaming and dancing as the flames licked around his face and crawled in his hair . . . Ship's fire extinguishers going on, blanketing the room in airless fog, captain blowing out in a puff of black smoke, falling down into the fog like a toppling corpse . . .

". . . engineering officer Michiko Landry reports the ship's AI system was able to make the transition to hyperspace and escape the attack by making a short-range jump to the other side of Regulus. The ship was apparently detected there by the assailant, which pursued in normal spacetime, giving the ship's navigation systems the few minutes they needed to calculate an escape trajectory toward Earth . . ."

Trajectory toward Earth? Then won't they know where we

live? No. No, don't be stupid. Hyperspace navigation wouldn't be like cross-Einsteinian geodesic pathways, for Christ's sake . . .

Voice-over: "Captain Hamilton died from his burns en route and is now in Cedars Sinai Hospital on Earth, undergoing full resurrection. Though a complete physical recovery is expected within days, medical technicians doubt a full memory-association chain can be established. Trade Regency representatives are expected to begin questioning Hamilton as soon as he can be awakened . . ."

I could feel my heart pounding. Jesus. Changes *are* coming. All this tawdry, ordinary bullshit going on here and now . . . while the whole universe comes down around our fucking ears. Meanwhile, I've got three days to find a new job, or else find a new place to live. Fucking Christ. I got up, started getting ready to go. Knowing, suddenly, just where I wanted to be.

It takes about nine hours to get from L_1(SE) to Callisto, much of that time spent making your connections. At the corporate offices of Berens-Vataro Enterprises Interplanetary, cooling my heels, I listened to a nice young man, a receptionist, I suppose, say things along the lines of, ". . . I'm sorry, Mr. du Cheyne, we just hadn't expected anyone to . . ." and ". . . yes, I appreciate that you own twelve thousand shares of B-VEI stock . . ." A keen look then, right in the eye: "You *do* understand the current stock issue exceeds three million shares?"

Who did I want to talk to? And why? Now that I'd gotten here, it was hard to put into words. A tour? Well, sure, I'd like that, but . . . Finally, they found my name in their records and I sat in a crummy little office, looking across a cheap desk at the same young woman who'd come by my office a few days ago, looking to buy my stock. Miss Tallentyre.

"Xenia," she said. "Call me Xenia." Looking at me, quite puzzled. "I have to tell you, Mr. du Cheyne—"

"Gaetan." Smiling at her, eying that sleek form speculatively, but remembering Camilla Seldane, who'd given me . . . something, at least.

She shrugged "I have to tell you, we no longer have any interest in reacquiring your stock. B-VEI managed to secure an absolute majority share, with ERSIE taking most of the rest, other than a very few small holdouts like yourself. Now, you *can* sell it at parity on the open market, or ERSIE may still offer you a small premium . . ."

"That's not why I'm here."

Puzzled. "Then . . . Mr. du Cheyne, if you'd like a tour of the facility, I'm sure we could come up with something, but—"

I said, "What I'd like is a job."

Startled look, eyebrows going up. Then she laughed, skin around her pretty eyes crinkling. "Whatever *for?* Mr. du Cheyne, you're a rich man by anyone's standard. Sell the stock. Then find something to *do.*"

"I'd like to work on the new starships. I, uh . . ."

She reached forward and touched the top of her desk, then squinted down at whatever image was forming in its depths, out of my line of sight. "I see." She looked up at me. "Look, I'm sorry ERSIE fired you, Mr. du Cheyne. You did us a good turn by at least holding on to your shares when there was no certainty that . . ." A shrug. "I sympathize but . . ."

Sympathize. Isn't that what they all say?

She said, "We're not hiring just yet. We—"

"But you'll need good people. Soon. I've got training, class Ten certification and twenty years' experience as a metadynamic engineering technician. You—"

She nodded. "Sure. But right now, we don't even have a personnel office. Up to this point, we've been hiring on the specific recommendation of existing employees. Friends of friends."

"But . . ."

She looked at me impatiently. "Mr. du Cheyne, Berens-Vataro hyperdrive engineering is *very* different from chromo-electronics. Now, we *will* be establishing an apprenticeship program and—"

"I'd like to apply for that."

"All right. The first three apprentice classes will be filled by recommendation from our existing mechanics, so we can sort of get a running start. If you want to come back in four years and take the entrance examination we'll likely have worked out by then—"

Four years. I said, "If I haven't found another job by then, I'll have had to have my tools put to sleep. They'll never be the same after that."

A blank look. "So? Sell your tools and buy new ones in three years. You'll need a major upgrade anyway."

"Miss Tallentyre . . . Um, Xenia. You ever have a pet?"

She said, "No." Long silence. Then she smiled and said, "Look, I'm sorry Mr. du Cheyne, but that's just the way things are. I really do feel badly for you, but there's nothing I can do. Let me take you on a nice tour of the facility, introduce you to a few people . . . You really *do* have the qualifications we need. Maybe in a year . . . two . . ."

Not much of a place, really. Insulating platforms under heavy-duty eutropic shields, keeping the Callistan environment at bay. A few admin centers. A landing stage with a variety of commercial spacecraft. Machine shops. A couple of medium-sized cranes. A lot of it clearly antique equipment bought from a discounter.

If I didn't know the story, I'd turn my nose up at this place. Me? Work *here?* You've got to be kidding. I'd just as soon work at the bus depot. But over there sat the cracked and blackened remains of *Torus X-4*, surrounded by what looked like armed guards. Company cops? Rental forces?

Seeing me stare, Miss Tallentyre said, "Those are Regents Security. We've been having a, um, little trouble with the media."

Closer to us, *Torus X-1* was a bright disk, shiny and new, hull patches opened, swarmed over by workingmen and -women. Look at that. Toolpacks and testrigs. All the right stuff. I tried to peer inside, past strings of temporary lighting, into . . .

Tallentyre said, "Mr. du Cheyne, this is Gordon Lassiter, shift supervisor for the turnaround refit on *X-1*. She'll be going to Salieri next week, carrying the embassy team home with the news."

Tall, skinny man, smiling at me, offering his hand. Wary eyes, probing, looking me up and down. I said, "Hi." He took my hand in his, gave it a quick shake.

Tallentyre said, "Mr. du Cheyne is one of our small stockholders, Gordy, he . . ."

He said, "You sure don't *look* like a richbitch, Mr. du Cheyne."

So.

Tallentyre laughed, and said, "Gordy! He's a class Ten mechanic. Formerly with ERSIE."

"Yeah? Me too. But I've been with B-VEI for almost ten years now."

"Mr. du Cheyne would like to come work with us. I've explained to him about the time line on the apprenticeship program."

Silence. Watching me stare at the bustling workers. Finally, Lassiter said, "So what do you think of our little ships?"

I said, "They're . . . very nice. Could I go aboard?"

A quick look between the two, then Tallentyre said, "We have pretty strong regulations against that, Mr. du Cheyne. Sorry."

Lassiter said, "If you make the grade, you'll see soon enough. I can't *wait* to get started on the big new ships! I . . ." Sudden halt, *oops* forming in his eyes. "Well, I guess I better get back to work. Nice meeting you, du Cheyne."

Nothing more than a quickly receding back, a sense of *loose lips sink ships*. Tallentyre said, "Shall we go?"

I stood still, quietly watching them work. "I expected you'd begin commercialization as soon as you could. When? If it's all right for me to know. As a stockholder."

She said, "It's not really a secret, Mr. du Cheyne. We begin construction on the new shipbuilding ways next week. We'll begin with a line of interstellar luxury liners and class A manifest cargo carriers, for which we already have some tentative commitments. We expect to have the first deliverables in about six years."

Six years. "That's a long time."

"Yes. And we can't legally issue contracts until the new ways are completed and we have a certain amount of new financing in place. It's a pinch."

"Do you mind telling me how much those ships will be going for?"

She put one hand thoughtfully to her chin, a very pretty gesture, eyes far away. "Um. I guess, since we'll be publicizing in just a few more days . . . well, market analysis and preliminary customer contact indicates we can get about twenty-three million livres for the luxury liners. Maybe two-thirds that for a stripped-down freighter."

So. No matter how rich you *are* . . . "That's a fuck of a lot of money. Not many companies going to be able to scrape together that much cash."

She said, "They will if they want to stay competitive, Mr. du Cheyne."

"I wonder what'll happen to the stock market?" Wondering just what my AI could do with the 3.2 million I've got already. Not that, for sure. What the fuck am I dreaming about this for? Twenty million livres? Why the hell don't I just buy a fucking ERSIE slowboat and go crawling slug-like off into the cosmos?

She said, "Look at it this way. In a few years, if you decide you *don't* want to work for us, you'll be able to plan on some *very* nice vacation tours."

Vacation tours. Right. I said, "So what happens to these little ones? Going to keep sending them out?"

Silence. Then she said, "I shouldn't be telling you this, but . . . Mr. du Cheyne, the company is quite strapped for cash right now. We've shut down the experimental production facility and we'll be selling these ships for whatever we can get. Regents Security has logged a preemptive bid for the hulk of *X-4;* we'll be advertising the other three in about a month."

I thought about that. *Surely* a company in B-VEI's position would be able to float just about any loan it wanted. Wouldn't it? Or maybe some big bad wolf was floating out there in the economic void, stopping . . . What the hell. Can't hurt to ask. All she can do is laugh. Then you'll go your merry way, get ready to move. Think about what you want to fucking *do* for the next few years. I said, "What would you take for *X-3* here?"

Long, long silence. Then she said, "Um. Mr. du Cheyne? I think maybe we'd better go chat with Dr. Vataro."

Vataro. As in Berens-Vataro. "What for?"

She said, "Um. The company's in a tighter squeeze than I may have suggested, Mr. du Cheyne. Dr. Vataro will be meeting with some investment bankers in a little less than one hour, trying to arrange a small cash infusion so we can make it through to our first contract signing without selling any more of our company-held stock. He'll be signing one of those eighteen percent notes."

Interesting.

She said, "After that we'll be able to get the usual fully secured four percent commercial loans, but . . . we need the money *now* and it's going to cost us."

"So? What does this have to do with . . ."

She beamed at me, a flash of pretty eyes and a sexually suggestive smile, most likely all in my imagination. "I was thinking you might be able to help us out here. The company holds precisely 50.07 percent of the voting stock. What we were thinking of borrowing was something on the order of three million livres."

It took me a minute to realize just what the hell she was talking about.

5

I opened my eyes and looked at the ceiling, naked, pressed to my narrow bed by Callisto's absurd point-oh-five gee, dorm room air cool on slightly night-sweaty skin and . . . Wind of cold wonder striking my back just then, smarmy cramp of unresolvable horniness abruptly forgotten. *I'm here.*

When my feet hit the thin, velvety carpet, I heard the shower start up, dorm AI setting it for the temperature it knew I liked, numbers picked from my memory, I suppose, or maybe even cross-loaded from L_1(SE). A friendly voice, a familiar feel to the thing. A lot like the old apartment AI. Flatter affect, of course, it not having had time to grow accustomed to my ways . . .

Chatter from the stock ticker, already comfortable in its new compspace, updating me on how it was handling the measly 278,413 livres of my diminished account. Angry at me, little one? Is that possible? Probability table spawning, showing me the very low likelihood it would ever be able to build me another three-million-livre fortune . . .

After breakfast, full orange Jupiter high in a black, moon-pocked sky, Sun somewhere below Callisto's dark gray horizon, Gordy Lassiter had the sense to be quiet while I stood on the edge of the drydock platform and looked at my ship.

Torus X-3.

Well. No. I . . . I'll think of something when the time comes. Finally: "Might as well go inside, Gae."

I turned and looked at him. No urge to tell him my name wasn't *Gae?* No. I could see the fire of naked envy in his eyes. *My ship.* I smiled and said, "I guess so."

Nothing before us now but a shining silver disk, the mirror brightness of chrome rather than the duller burnish of real silver. A flattish silver disk with the cross section of a spiral galaxy, complete with spherical hub. At a guess, I thought the thing measured a hundred meters across the plane of the disk, maybe twenty meters through the central bulge. For a starship, an itty-bitty thing. As we walked closer, I could see the silver finish was faintly tarnished here and there, irregular blotches of faint bronze, gold, bits of rainbow glimmer. Tarnished by the energies of hyperspace? I don't know.

We went under the rim, into shadow, where four stubby landing legs, unfolded from pods attached to the southern hemisphere of the ship's central bulge stood spraddle-legged on the pavement. Lassiter said, "We haven't really started pulling her down yet, so when we get inside, you won't see much at first besides her public face." We walked around the curve of the hull to where a long ramp of stairs had dropped down on two curved supports from its recess against the underside of the disk, leading up to an open door in the side of the sphere.

He said, "Central bulge is all pressurized habitable space, control rooms, staterooms, whatnot." A gesture overhead. "Since our modified gravity polarizer and the new hyperdrive components had to be toroidal, we built the life support system into the doughnut hole, then hung the rest of the flight hardware, avionics and whatnot, around the rim. This is the main gangway, of course, and there's an airlock door on the bottom, between the landing legs, an escape trunk hatch on top, mounted in the upper bulkhead of the control room . . ."

Listening, of course, listening to his blather, as I put my

hand on the gangway railing, put my feet on the risers, which some idiot had engineered for one-gee . . . Even on Earth, I'd've taken them two at a time, I think. As it was . . .

"Watch your head," said Lassiter.

Me, powering up the stairs, toes barely touching, mainly just hauling myself up the handrail, excitement a tight nervousness in my chest, touched by a matching flutter of joy from the spacesuit.

Then school days. Taking me back, I suppose, to my mother's useless architectural school on Luna, much more to Syrtis Major, which I chose for myself and loved after a fashion. Strange way to look at it. Loved? I suppose so. If it's true that I actually . . .

These new friends were a mixed bag, the first class made up for the in-house apprentice school of B-VEI, expected to be much like the apprentice schools at other industrial concerns, teaching those special things that companies need their technical personnel to know. I'd had to spend a few weeks at the ERSIE apprentice school—*just so you'll know the ropes*—but those years at Syrtis Major, my years of prior experience . . .

Different here.

Classes taught by our predecessors on the line—*this is the way we do things here*—startling to find Roald Berens himself teaching theory, Ntanë Vataro showing us the guts of the machines, showing us how things *really* worked.

Do I remember things like that from before? No. The president of the Eighth Ray Scientific-Industrial Enterprise is a red-faced politician. Saw him on the vidnet only days ago . . .

So how *does* the Berens-Vataro faster-than-light overdrive really work, Dr. Berens? Small, Nordic sort of man with pale blue eyes, what they call mulberry eyes, and thin, flat, mouse-brown hair. Small man with a secretive smile and a rather hapless shrug.

You'll have to ask Dr. Vataro about that. Me, I only figured out a way it *could* work. That little smile and shrug again. Most of you came out of the ERSIE apprentice school—a gesture at me—Mr. du Cheyne, I believe, went to good old Syrtis Major . . .

Anyway, you were taught how Kerechenko and her team worked out the basic principles of the field well converter, using Mace Electrodynamics money; how they then separated themselves from the company and got government loans to extend this technology to the field of gravity control, among other things . . .

At Syrtis Major the history-of-technology course spent some time on the way ERSIE, Mace and the government of the Mitteleuropa went round and round over who owned the patents on antigravity. Gravity control is one of those magical technologies that simply changes everything. Like agriculture, like writing, like steam, nuclear energy . . . hyperdrive too, I suppose.

Dr. Berens: "For my scholar magistral dialogue at Pantech, I did an exhaustive numerical run on the mathematics of Kerechenko Analysis. You know, it's funny. I would've thought Madame Kerechenko would've done that herself, right at the outset, but . . ."

Some woman in the back of the room, a pretty dark-haired girl with a long nose and oddly colored tan skin, sort of a funny sallow-brick hue, said, "Didn't have the computing power in those days."

Berens squinted at her and shrugged. "Right. Ms. . . . Strachan is it? They didn't do it because they couldn't, and in the ensuing centuries, as Kerechenko's discoveries turned into money, money and more money . . . Anyway, it looked like a good project to me, so I ran the arrays through TPI's Skylark analogue-numerical sieve, then started doing a statistical analysis. All sorts of interesting bullshit came popping out, graduate school research topics for a thousand years to come." He laughed. "I considered taking out a loan right then and there, so I could go into business as a professional thesis adviser. That would've been fun . . ."

Long silence, while we watched him reminisce about his

own good old days. Then, in a pale, faraway voice: "So you put a field well converter inside the system event horizon of a gravity polarizer, link to a power load, charge up the well, run the polarizer to full throttle and head out. That was the theory behind the starships we've been using for so many years." Another silence, then: "What do you suppose happens if you open the loaded well's event horizon just then?"

Leah Strachan said, *"Bang."*

"You're a pilot, aren't you, Ms. Strachan? Always a good idea for a pilot to know how her machinery works, isn't it?"

She said, "You never know what might happen."

"I suppose not. That's why I went into mathematics, Ms. Strachan. I wanted to *know* what would happen."

Then: "You know what? After I linked up with Ntanë, we had a hell of a time getting permission to test our experimental apparatus. It was so damned little, we figured we could fire it off in one of the desert wastelands on the farside of Crater. Hell, it's just like the Moon was in the early days, when there were hardly any colonists . . ."

Only sort of like the Moon of course. Maybe halfway between the Moon and Mars? But colder than both.

He said, "We figured it'd just be a *little* bang, you know? Fifty, maybe sixty kilotons . . . Guy in charge of authorizing potentially destructive experiments made me read up on something called *Castle Bravo*, the first test of a lithium-deuteride-fueled thermonuclear bomb, back in the 1950s. Seems the scientists who put that one together didn't know about the lithium-6 reaction. Maybe they knew about it and just failed to take it into account. Scientists are always forgetting crucial numbers. That's why they call them *experiments* . . . Anyway, they were surprised as hell when their nice little five-megaton bomb made a fifteen-megaton bang."

He said, "They made us do a space test, which of course led us to build a much bigger test apparatus. Our engineering test models suggested we develop a prototype toroidal gravity polarizer, one that could fly the ship as well as test my suspicions about event horizon canceling in a massively accelerated inertial reference frame. People thought we were nuts.

"You know, those paranoid bastards not only made us test the ship in the outer system, they made us go to a point in space that placed 61 Cygni A in the line of sight between our test site and Earth. I guess they were afraid if we made a big enough bang, somebody might notice and come asking questions.

"Made us wait till Crater itself was behind 61 Cygni C relative to our position as well. Paranoid. Silly. . . we went to our appointed position, ran it up to full throttle, accelerating directly toward 61 Cygni A—"

Strachan said, "What the hell for?"

"Funny you should ask that. I wanted to accelerate away from the system's barycenter. Just in case, you know?" He shrugged. "Ntanë insisted we aim for something that could catch our debris cone, if worse came to worst . . .

"So we fired the test apparatus and discovered ourselves on the opposite node of our orbit around 61 Cygni, at the center of an expanding energy shell that appeared to have originated in the experimental device, basically a soft gamma ray burst in the few-hundred-megaton range. As if the ship had exploded or something."

As if. Or something. His calm amusement wasn't the way I was imagining the scene.

"You know, if we'd done it my way, pointed the damned thing straight up, the apparatus would have carried us to a point . . . oh, I think we calculated it was something like 219,000 parsecs from here in the direction of the classical constellation of Cygnus, as seen from Earth."

Empty space, but . . .

"As it happens, zero time passes for the passengers on a Berens-Vataro starship, even a primitive one like our test apparatus, so we'd've popped out, instantaneously to us, somewhere in intergalactic space. Think how surprised we'd've been when we figured out where. And, of course, when. It turned out the test apparatus moved us at something like fifteen cee . . ."

The calculator in my head chattered softly. Fourteen thousand six hundred years? I said, "It would've been interesting if you'd gotten home sometime around the year 30,000 . . ." Imagine that. Will things be different then? Or, trapped in our own corner of space with no Berens-Vataro drive . . .

That same smile and hapless shrug. "Well, no, Mr. du Cheyne. In order to run a reverse geodesic, conditions at our emergence point would have had to mirror those at our departure point. They wouldn't be, of course . . ."

No, of course not. Stupid.

He said, "No, we would've wandered around the universe, hopping here, hopping there, completely at random, until the end of time. Or until our supplies ran out. Whichever came first."

Silence.

Then someone in the back of the room murmured, "Well, *shit.*"

Berens said, "We were damned lucky. As it was, TPI confiscated our research notes and nondirigible faster-than-light starship, placed us under house arrest . . ."

No surprise there.

He said, "Campus police didn't *have* a good mechanism for holding on to us and Crater doesn't *have* a government, so we got away, hopped a freighter, came here, and you know the rest, I guess . . ." A final shrug, and he said, "First thing we did after we got *Torus X-1* flying was lift a team of lawyers to Crater. Turns out the administration diverted most of TPI's resources to developing control systems for the test apparatus, but no one could figure out my math. Now, of course . . ."

Sometime later, walking back toward my dorm room, it occurred to me to wonder what my life would've been like had FTL ships been introduced twenty years ago, not long after I'd finished up at Syrtis Major College of Industrial Arts.

Now I lay sprawled through the guts of *Torus X-3*'s hyperdrive machinery, angular lumps and bumps on my back, spine twisted at an odd angle, one arm reaching, the other compressed against my side, rainbow sparkles from the worksuit's live integument reflected in my face from the flat, gray-green surface of the nearest drive-horizon interface discharge array. Knowing.

Comfortable. Familiar. Warm happiness. Belonging.

Even these new machines, these unknown machines, are my friends, entities I *will* know, friends who'll never betray my trust, even if I grow careless to the point where they kill me.

I can hear them whisper, when I'm among them: *Do thus, and we'll do such. Always. Forever. You can trust us.*

Dark shadow moving toward me, throwing sparkles against the inner curve of the hull, a few meters away. Sleek woman shape in a glittering worksuit, slithering through the hardware, this way and that, muscular hips oozing through a hole just a touch too small, hardware giving birth to even, bright blue eyes, eyes looking at me through the eyeholes of the helmet. Leah Strachan. Leah the Pilot.

Expressionless? Or is it true that eyes are just spheres of transparent tissue, white parts and colored, little red veins, colored iris muscle, dark hole of pupil, casting light down into the dark soul beyond . . .

Christ. Turning into a fucking mooncalf here . . .

She said, "I thought you'd be in here, du Cheyne." Lying beside me then, twisting until she was lying on her back across the access coverplate of a big heat exchanger pump, looking up at the discharge array. "This is really something, isn't it?"

Really something.

I reached out and grabbed the array's sensor-control throughput waveguide, tugged it from its socket, pulled the woven metal/glass snake across my chest and looked into the plug socket. Collared male connector, forty-seven little golden prongs of some exotic composite whose name I'd remember if I thought about it for a while.

Pitting in there, down where the connectors were seated into their mounts. Something going on that some engineer hadn't thought about beforehand. Maybe not a problem now, but when this ship had been flying for thirty years or so. What was I imagining? Some catastrophic failure? Some horrific crash, all fire and flames and bits of bodies? No. Imagining myself, someday, stuck in the space between the stars. Hyperdrive dead. Gravity polarizer dead. Calling for help on some old-fashioned maser device, hoping someone was listening at my target star. Hoping they'd come get me, someday, somehow.

"Hmh." Futile. Stupid.

Leah's head was pressed close to mine, our helmets more or less touching, looking down into the plug. She said, "I bet that's what they call exotunneling."

Particles, apparently, have the power to decide they don't *really* exist, switch from orbiting a real chaotic attractor to orbiting an imaginary one. "I bet you're right."

Blue eyes on my face then. No. Not my face. Blue eyes on my eyes, all that's visible through the eyeholes of my helmet. See anything in there? She said, "What the hell are you going to do with this thing?"

My ship? I shrugged. "Travel, I guess."

Remote whisper from my suit, engaged in conversation with hers, a rapid, incomprehensible exchange of data. If I asked nicely, would it get her suit to read her mind and then tell me what she was thinking? Brief electronic silence in my head, as if the two suits were considering the question, then the faraway whispers resumed.

She said, "Right. And here I thought you were going to start an amusement park ride for all the kiddies of Mercury."

Feeble sarcasm. As if she weren't used to being one of the gang. Another shrug from me. "I'll see what there is to see. What little there is to see, I guess. Not that many colony worlds."

She said, "You got the money to just wander forever?"

I shook my head. "I don't know that I've got the temperament to just . . . explore, I guess. Maybe . . ." Maybe nothing. Maybe I just don't know what I . . . maybe they call this cold feet? Christ, am I *afraid* of what comes next?

Maybe so.

She said, "Then what? And *why?*"

How many shrugs does it take to constitute a definitive answer? "I'm . . . hoping I'll find out, I guess."

She said, "Hmh."

Then silence.

But she didn't leave, either, lying there quietly beside me.

A gradual creeping sense of consciousness between my legs, just forward of my asshole? Is that what this is all about? Is that what's going to happen? Is that what I *want* to have happen? Christ. Finally, I said, "I guess I've been thinking about flying passengers and cargo, once I've gotten used to . . ."

"Prosaic," she said.

Ordinary. Mundane. Boring.

Gaetan du Cheyne, hero of the spaceways, vanishing in a puff of . . . dullness. Leah Strachan's loose, moist vagina drying up on me, closing up, going away, I laughed. "Guess having my own damn starship is exotic enough for now."

Her head cocked to one side and I thought I could see those blue eyes brighten, making my nuts tighten up, like hopeful idiot dogs. "I guess so." More silence, as if considering, then: "*Torus X-3*'s not much of a name for humanity's first faster-than-light interstellar yacht."

No. I . . . "I've been thinking about changing it, I guess."

"Any ideas?"

I said, "I dunno. *Random Walk*, maybe."

She twisted around, resting the back of her head on my shoulder for a second, touching me the way workers always end up touching when they labor together in these confined spaces, reaching up to twiddle her fingers in the mechanical complexity hanging over us. "That's pretty good."

Whisper from the suit's operating system then: She's had her gear for a long time, to the point where its AI is well integrated, very much interested in looking after her interests and privacy. But it seems as though she may be interested in you.

Small, crystalline particle of surprise. Does the spacesuit actually have some grasp of the needs of my dick? Does it care?

Machinery all around me now, *Do thus and we will do such. Always and forever.* Machines doing as we made them to do. Maybe we are better gods than the older gods who made us. Our creatures betray us only as we instruct them to. Kill us only when we wish, on some level, to die.

Comforting thought.

I said, "Time for a break. You want to go for coffee?"

She said, "Sure."

Time passes, and we pass within it, swept along by evolving entropy's immaterial stream. School, work, tearing down *Torus X-3*, rebuilding her as *Random Walk*. A few things that might be called dates with Leah Strachan, lots of friendly talk but nothing that got me any closer to her pussy than I'd been as we sprawled alone together in the starship's technology-clogged guts. Other men and women that I got to know during those few brief weeks, weeks evolving to a couple of months, no one worth remembering, worth carrying forward into that unknowable future that I . . .

Three weeks along, cutting through the external caisson storage bay in the rear of the toolcrib dome, I came out of the shadows to find Leah with her arms around Gordy Lassiter, their faces pressed together, eyes shut . . . she had one leg raised, cocked over his hip. If they'd had nothing on, it would've been easy for him to . . .

Backed into the shadows, went to my destination a different way.

Soft shrug to myself. What the fuck? If it meant something to me, anything at all you see, I'd be more proactive about it.

Sure. Right.

Three weeks after that, I was back in the vicinity of Earth, sitting in one of the tourist observation decks of a huge old LEO platform, looking downward through empty space at the world, blue-white-red-brown Earth, turning slowly below. Dull blue-green Atlantic just now, evolving into the dark deserts of north-west Africa. That must be Morocco down there, those dry-looking wrinkles the Atlas Mountains.

Seething with anger, remembering voices.

I'm sorry, Mr. du Cheyne. This office can issue you a registration certificate for your ship, what is it, Registry FTL000001? Congratulations, sir! But we can't issue you a permit to move it anywhere in the solar system. You have to have a commercial FTL pilot's license for that.

Well, sir, I know you plan to leave the solar system with it, but you have to move *through* the solar system to leave and . . .

Could I hire a harbor pilot, just to see me off?

Don't know. Why don't you go down to the Union Hall and see?

Ah, yes. And so off to the Interplanetary Space Transport Association, the pilots' guild.

Well, sir, as it happens there are no registered harbor pilots rated to guide an FTL-equipped starship out of the system.

We wouldn't be leaving the system exactly. I'd have to light the hyperdrive at some predetermined point inside the Sun's gravity well and . . .

Be that as it may, there are none. We do have a few applicants who've applied for an FTL endorsement on their commercial licenses, regular pilots, most of them with quite a bit of interstellar flight experience already. Of course, you'd have to hire one of those as command pilot for your ship and . . .

No sir, we can't issue you a pilot's license. You'd have to go through the ISTA apprenticeship program, then take the regular Trade Regency licensing examinations. Takes about six years.

Yes, sir. That's true, sir. Have a nice day, sir.

Back to Callisto then, with no solution in hand other than the one in the old joke. Interesting how the folks in our apprentice class have paired off so quickly. Boys and girls together, with the usual scattering of boys and boys, girls and girls. And a couple of sulky old peckerheads like me.

A lot of them will be staying on at B-VEI, of course, going to work as new mechanics under Gordy Lassiter's direction, settling into the new shipbuilding ways, from which the great liners and fast freighters will flow.

Leah Strachan?

Mostly things were just the same. Every now and again I'd see the two of them walking together, hand in hand, heads pressed together, or grappling in some dark corner, as if they couldn't wait till off-shift, as if they didn't have damn-all forever to get sick of each other.

Working together then, alone in some odd corner of *Random Walk*'s now wonderfully familiar insides, crammed into some small space together. Me head down in the work, Leah pointing the other way, up by where we'd parked our tool arrays, practically straddling my face.

Work getting done, I guess. Me imagining all sorts of idiocy in various fleeting instants. "Leah? What're you going to do when the program's over?"

Working down there, talking, with her practically sitting on my face, thinking endlessly, caught in some inescapable loop, about . . . Tried to ask her for it once. One day when I ran into her back in the recesses of the half-built ways, found her sitting in a bubble, helmet off, odd, flushed look on her face, trying to sort out a toolbelt array that'd gotten tangled somehow . . .

Me popping my question/suggestion, bringing up an odd, ugly glint in her eyes. Gae, I was fucking Gordy less than an hour ago. Did you think this would be a good time to slip one in? Like there was some kind of lingering . . .

Me shrugging, making my little excuses. Hell, did you think I could *tell*? Sorry.

She seemed to forget about it, move on to the evolving business at hand. I've known a lot of women who just let it slide like that. Maybe those are the ones for whom it's a constant part of life's background stench. Something like that.

Now . . .

"I don't know, Gae. I've got a contract with Nomiura Transport, and they've got dibs on the first five production-run freighters here. I'm supposed to go back and start teaching maintenance blocks to our front-line techies. That's starting to seem a little . . . dull. You know?"

So. Gordon Lassiter doing his endless, adventureless job right here on Callisto. Leah gone back to wherever Nomiura has its roundhouse. Probably out in one of the Kuiper densities. Will they visit back and forth? Of course not. Casual encounters no more than static in the greater void of modern life.

Come on. All you have to do is lean forward, nuzzle your face into the soft space between her legs. Its just a dozen centimeters or so. She'll get the message and . . .

I leaned back, got as far away from her as I could in the confining hollow of our little workspace. Took my hands out of the machinery I'd been buttoning up. Folded my hands across my chest, quelling a nervousness so idiotic I couldn't imagine where it was coming from. Open your mouth. Speak, God damn it.

Silence.

Then Leah said, "Is something wrong, Gae?"

Something in her voice? Does she imagine I'm down here smelling her, maybe smelling some remnant Lassiter's left behind? In another minute will I open my mouth and ask for her pussy again?

I told her about my visit to ISTA then.

Another silence, then, "Jesus, Gae, I could have told you that! Somebody should have."

Sure, but nobody did.

"What're you going to do?"

I said, "Hire a pilot, I guess."

She said, "Oh. That's . . . not what you wanted, is it?"

"No."

Longer silence.

"I could recommen—"

Abrupt halt.

Obviously pregnant silence.

My turn? Apparently. I said, "Would you be interested in the job?"

I could feel her tighten up, maybe move a little closer to me. "I don't know. Jesus, Gae. I'll have to think."

"No hurry. Three more weeks till the program ends and I have to start paying storage fees." Out of what little I've got left.

Stillness and silence.

"You know, I'd have to charge you union scale."

Has the pilots' union already decided on an FTL fee schedule? Most likely. Mouth dry, I said, "Sure."

Fucking heart pounding away in here, making me sway in the low gee. Tension twisting up so tight it was making me feel nauseous. I said, "I guess we better get this done. It's almost lunchtime."

Lassiter would be waiting for her of course, and they'd disappear for their usual noontide tryst. But if I've got her with me, out among the fixed stars, you see . . .

Graduation day comes and then the day after, and then I'm sitting in *Random Walk*'s command-pilot chair, up in the propulsion control room under the top of the central bulge, hands resting on smooth, plasticky controls, looking out through video display segments that mimicked real windows, down the silvery expanse of hull, across white concrete, twirling orange light on a little pole nearby, warning people away, across white concrete to the flat black-ice landscapes of Callisto, low, rolling hills beyond, barely silhouetted against a flat black sky.

Punch these buttons, flip a few switches, middle finger on the appropriate slider and . . .

Leah came up from below, dropping the hatch shut behind her, came and stood behind me, one hand on my shoulder. Finally, "It's about time to go, Gae. We'd better switch seats now." Pause. Then, "Sorry."

Sorry. Yep. Leah with my three-thousand-livre fee already in her bank account, fifteen hundred livres repatriation deposit in escrow with ISTA, in case our contract broke and she had to walk home.

I bounced out of her seat, settling in at the flight engineer's station, lighting up my panels, looking the hardware over, making sure I'd done everything right. No problems, except . . . my ship. Her seat. Childish annoyance bottled up inside me. A hard-bitten feeling that once, just this once maybe, I'd like to have things all my own way.

A brief vision of all the helplessly enslaved billions glaring at me from all their little social and economic and psychological traps. *Just this once?* Fucking asshole, they'd say. People with bad jobs, menial jobs, demeaning jobs, hell, no jobs at all, eyes brimming over with jealousy and hate for a man who's had a decent life poured all over him like so much maple syrup. Rich man now, bitter because he can't play with his rich man's toy right away.

Leah muttering to her suit, suit muttering to the ship, ship muttering to the B-VEI control tower, B-VEI's AIs dancing down through the net to Jovian System Central, getting the necessary permissions, filing our flight plan with Space Traffic Control, *Random Walk*, Leah Strachan, command pilot, Regency license number so-and-so, Callisto to Luna, four hours, fourteen minutes in transit.

She moved her hands over my controls, eyes bright, full of fire, and we lifted, no sense of motion at all, surface of Callisto merely dropping sharply, tilting under us, abruptly curving, whirling round us, turning to a sunlit crescent, suddenly pasted on the flat black sky, right next to crescent orange Jupiter, the two of them in matched phase turning to full, bright disks, almost the same size now, as our trajectory twisted insystem. Shrinking away to brilliant little balls and . . .

Sharp, tingling realization that, despite everything, everything I'd seen and done over the years, I'd never seen a planetary liftoff like that. Never watched from a control room seat, numbers spinning and rolling in my eyes.

The universe before me then, touched by the fragile hands of beauty.

Looking up at the Earth from the nearside surface of the Moon, good old Tranquillity Cosmodrome, where ships have been coming and going for 635 years, I could see that it must be late afternoon in the ruins of New York City, the fuzzy terminator already lying across the tip of Cape Cod, deep dusk coloring the ocean around the eastern end of Long Island.

Mr. Jenkins-Lafferty from the All Worlds Travel Agency shook my hand, standing in front of his little group of tourists. My tourists now. Passengers. Shook my hand, grinning a pasted-on grin. Pleased to meet you, Captain du Cheyne.

I stood looking over his shoulder at them, feeling odd. Not Captain, you see. Master and Owner. Twenty rich little earthlings, as alike as so many peas in a dinnerpack despite their colorful rich folks' clothing . . . Not really rich. Not rich at all; merely well-to-do. Folks able to pay All Worlds a fee that came to something like twice my old annual salary apiece for an FTL ride out to one of the colony worlds, much, *much* better, you see, than some old vidnet tour.

A trip to Green Heaven, three months vacation, with me getting fifteen hundred livres a head to ferry them over, a deal I'd worked out with a glitter-eyed rep from the travel agency. Yes sir, Mr. du Cheyne. Yessiree! Rubbing his hands together . . .

So. That makes thirty-six thousand livres gross from the agency, which will make whatever it makes for itself. Now, it will cost me 26,250 livres, give or take a few, to operate *Random Walk* for the round-trip to Tau Ceti. And, of course, there's the 4,500 livres for the privilege of having Leah, plus the gating fees at Luna and Green Heaven . . . Slim. And once the big liners start coming on line, my profit margins will go down to nothing and I'll have to think of something else. Doing something wrong here, but I don't know what.

Leah nudged me in the side, "Time and tide, Boss . . ."

Boss. Right. But I am staring at the passengers, one young-looking woman in particular, very thin black-haired woman with small, yet somehow prominent breasts, woman seeming to look me right in the eye with an impossibly private grin.

I glanced at Leah, who seemed to roll her eyes. "If we don't get moving," she said, "I'll have to reset the countdown clock and renegotiate our place in the ramping schedule."

At the maximum Regency-legal transit velocity, it took us forty-nine hours plus to reach the calculated jump-point for Tau Ceti, boosting in the direction of Boötes, a spot in the outer reaches of the Kuiper disk, some seventeen light-hours from Sol in a patch of sky just opposite Cetus, making a long, high-velocity turn back toward the Sun, accelerating back in toward the jump-point.

Now I sat in the flight-engineer's seat, heart running a little fast, alternately watching Leah fly my ship and monitoring my instruments. Concentration in her face, jaw set just so, as we accelerated at just under eight hundred gees, feeling nothing, maybe the occasional odd kinesthetic tug, maybe not, compensators working almost perfectly, a testament to my newly polished skills as a drive mechanic.

Theory says we hit 0.866502 cee just as we cross the calculated jump-point, drop the ship's event horizon structure, and go. Honest. It's been done several hundred times already, you know that.

Even though we'd set the panels for "natural view," the stars in the direction of flight were starting to look a little blue; twisting my head to look over my shoulder, I could imagine those other stars might be stained slightly red. Maybe not, I . . .

Leah said, "I didn't think much of the way you acted during dinner last night."

A quick glance at my instruments, before looking up at her. Three minutes, forty seconds and counting, 0.6774 cee. "What're you talking about?"

"Look, just cut the bullshit, Gae. These are your paying customers. Mine too, after a fashion. If they lodge a complaint with ISTA, it'll be against me too."

So. Sitting at the "captain's table," maybe getting a little bit farther in my cups than I'd intended, leering at some sweet thing or another, making some peculiarly pointed remark or another, pretty girl glancing at a frowning pretty boy and rolling her eyes . . .

I shrugged. Little tug inside my head there. Looking at numbers. Hmh. Let's adjust compensator a5a-67β. Numbers scrolling as the ship's command circuits went in the direction I indicated. "I don't think it did any harm, Leah, besides—"

Irritation. "For Christ's sake . . ."

You could hear the word *asshole* in her voice, of course. You always can. They've perfected that methodology, they have, or evolution, in its infinite wisdom, has perfected it for them. "Look, I'm sorry, Leah. But I haven't gotten—"

"Whose fault is that?"

Blinking, looking down at my console. I'd intended to say she couldn't blame me for wanting to *try*, and what the hell harm would it do to . . . right. 0.77948 cee.

Leah turned toward the intercom. "This is the captain speaking. Interstellar jump will be in ninety seconds." Dry, flat, somehow friendly voice. This is your omnicompetent captain speaking . . . She said, "Safety regulations require that you take a seat in the observation lounge." So you'll be warm and comfy if we go *boom*? "This should be quite a show, ladies and gentlemen."

Quite a show. Aren't you the least little bit excited, Leah superwoman Strachan? When you've seen one hyperdrive jump, you've seen them all, so why get excited about the first time?

When I glanced up, she was looking over at me, grinning. Thumbs up. "Ready? Here we go, Gae . . ."

Down below, my little gaggle of paying passengers would be getting in their seats, looking out at vaguely colored stars. We are just not going fast enough to create that fabled starbow effect, and I could imagine that journalist jerkoff, what was his name? Luigi Montoni, I think, grumbling about it, just the way he'd grumbled about our not having serving staff aboard *Random Walk*. Imagine, having to retrieve your own tray from the servitron and . . .

Time on target.

I looked at the Berens-Vataro Drive monitor and thought, *Now.*

The monitor blinked assent.

Some almighty cold ghost reached right up my asshole and grabbed me by the heart.

The universe outside flashed a pure, brilliant, sparkling turquoise, then the stars came back, stars against a flat black sky, seemingly unchanged.

Leah gasped, "Holy *shit!*"

My face was covered with a warm, smarmy sweat, an odd smell rising like fog from my armpits. A feeling that I'd somehow become . . . greasy all over. Swiftly drying now, sensations fading . . .

Leah said, "We're climbing against a much weaker gravity well than the one at Sol."

At . . . *Sol.* Right. That's still Cetus I'm looking at. With one star missing. One minor star. And back over my shoulder, there would be Boötes, you see, with one extra . . .

Instruments. Yes. Safe and sound. *Random Walk* at the center of its expanding spherical shell, soft gamma pulse spreading in all directions at the speed of light. "Well." Some historical words to say? No. "I guess we better start getting turned around then." That bright spot back there, one of *two* extra stars in Boötes . . .

Leah glanced at the intercom and said, "Ladies and gentlemen, welcome to the Tau Ceti star system. You are now more than eleven light-years from home."

We made a long, slow turn through the outer reaches of the Tau Ceti system, killing velocity as we went, spooling kinetic energy back into spacetime, dumping the equivalent waste heat down the field well converter's event horizon, watching the starfield turn around us, watching that bright star turn to a sun as we dropped into the system, twisting around to a prograde ecliptic orbit.

Leah had gotten out of her pilot's chair, was standing at the big manual circuit control panel at the rear of the cockpit, leaning on her arms, looking out at a bright Milky Way streaming behind us, beside us, all around the sky.

I was sitting on the back of my seat then, leaning in the point-oh-nine gee internal field we'd settled on as best for our earthborn passengers. A little less than Earth's surface gravity, so they'd be feeling light and airy now, a little more than Green Heaven's, so they'd feel lighter still when we arrived.

Sitting, watching Leah watch the stars, a million suns visible beyond the long, lean shape of her back, the compelling dark waves of her hair. What, I wonder, draws my eyes to her? The seductive, reproductive shape of her hips, understandable, long, dark hair, falling just so . . .

She said, "Where do you think we'll wind up, Gae? What's it like out . . ." A gesture at the fat part of the Milky Way, where it cut through Sagittarius, in the direction of the galactic core. *Out there.* Way out there.

Where'll *we* wind up? You and I, dear Leah? No. That's not what you mean, no matter how much I wish . . . I said, "Long trip." Thirty thousand light-years? "I guess it'd take *Random Walk* about seventy-five years to reach the Core Spindle."

"That'd be a hell of a thing to see, wouldn't it?" Voice so terribly wistful now, full of longing.

I walked up behind her, visualizing what we'd see, down by the Core. Big black hole, tiny, invisible, mantled by its glowing disk of infalling star stuff, great jets of energy to north and south, reaching for the intergalactic wasteland . . . Hell. Seventy-five years? That'd be . . . doable.

I put my hands on her shoulders, looking out over the top of her head at a star-cluttered universe. If you looked closely, you could see between the stars, look deep into black space and . . . here and there, little oblong smudges of light, other galaxies, so far away, what they used to call "island universes."

Andromeda then, M-31, a hand's breadth and more of remote, misty white light. Two-point-eight million light-years? At four hundred times the speed of light, it'd take us seven thousand years to . . . My God! *Not* seven thousand years . . . no time at all! We could go, Leah, you and I, go see all the universe has to offer, jumping forward through time, and never come home again. We . . .

Leah turned in my arms, looking up at me, eyes soft, and said, "This isn't what I want, Gae. Please . . ."

I tried to pull her closer, felt her hand against my chest, shoving me away. "Leah . . ."

She broke free, went over to her pilot's chair and turned, facing me. "Look, Gae, I'm sorry you're having a hard time, but . . ."

All sorts of vignettes, things I've said, things I've done. What harm would it do? I could ask. It'll only take a few minutes, hell, maybe you'll enjoy it too! Even if you don't, you can take a nice, hot shower afterward, and forget it ever . . . no. Hell. Come on, be a sport, Leah! Do a good deed.

What I said was, "You know, I've still got a lot of money left, Leah. I could . . ."

Saw her face harden right up, cold eyes looking into mine, asking some question I couldn't quite fathom. Right. Fucking boob. You just asked if you could pay for the brief use of her cunt, didn't you?

She said, "Um. No. Sorry." Went down the cockpit hatch, down into passenger country.

I went back to look at the stars, alone now, suddenly quite numb. What the hell good does it do me to try? Why *don't* I just stick with whores, who give an honest fuck for an honest livre? Is there something I want *other* than a periodic dose of pussy on my prick? Is there something I want that I don't even fucking *know* about?

Green Heaven began in our sky as a blue spark, a rather dim star, swiftly brightening, that made me wonder why they'd called it Green Heaven. Much bluer than the Earth itself looks from deep space, with kind of an off-center shine to it.

Little voice inside, me as a child chattering away to myself: Shallow, deep blue ocean almost worldwide, covering more than eighty percent of the surface. Nice, even, water-mediated climate, no arctic icecap, antarctic limited to some high plateau country with winter snow and a few broad, permanent mountain glaciers. Land limited to that one antarctic continent, Panviridia, total area about the size of Eurasia, with Australia stuck on somewhere for good measure . . .

Sitting in my flight engineer's seat, watching the numbers whirl and change, while Green Heaven the world bloomed against the starry sky, a brilliant blue leftward-facing crescent from our angle of attack, Leah silent, piloting, staring out the window.

Does it feel odd to her? Odd and new? Or has she done these things so many times . . . Well. I got to look in her ISTA service record when I hired her. She's been here five times before. Five times in two hundred years.

We were decelerating heavily and I knew the ship's drive would be a pale, pastel blue-white glow to anyone looking up into Green Heaven's nighttime sky. Do starships come here often? A familiar sight perhaps. Radar and mass proximeter data told me there was quite a lot of crap in planetary orbit, the world a fat, respectable globe before us now. Lots of little shit, metsats and the like. Six or seven big hunks of metal. Freighters, most likely dealing with in-system mining operations, bringing home the steel, you see. But one or two of them would be interstellar haulers.

What happens to those ships and crews now? Sit and wait? Or do they take the slow road home, home or to wherever they'd been going next, sliding out of some other black sky to another world, another time, five, ten, twenty years on?

Leah said, "Ladies and gentlemen, this is the captain speaking. We are approaching Green Heaven landfall, please take your seats in the observation lounge . . ."

Somehow, the thing in our sky, almost too large now to see as a whole object, was more breathtaking than Earth had ever been. Brilliant blue ocean under a banded layering of sharp white clouds. Antarctic continent coming at us now, sliding over the horizon, two long ranges of tall, white-capped mountains, mountains so tall you could *see* them sticking up, reaching for the tropopause and the tenuous beginnings of outer space.

Islands surrounding little bays at the coast. Broad amber plains. The lesser one would be Koperveldt, the Plains of Brass; greater one Opveldt, land of the Vrij Veldteboeren folk. That snow-colored landscape between them, that would be the Koudloft, frozen hill country surrounding the south pole. Long, silvery lightning bolt of the Somber River right there, flowing through the Opveldt, then on down through a dark, somehow electric green patch of landscape that must be the Mistibos forest . . .

There on our left now, a big peninsula stretching out into the sea beyond the Himalaya-class Pÿramis Range, the gray gravel bleds and blinding, waterless white gypsum erglands of the Adrianis Desert, home to the fabled Hinterling nomads, I . . .

All the sexy-romantic places I dreamed about as a child, as an adolescent, suddenly become a whole world, a real world, incomprehensibly vast . . . Outside, the sky lit up hot, fiery pink as *Random Walk* skidded into Green Heaven's ionosphere.

Finally, I stood at the foot of *Random Walk*'s debarkation ramp, light on my feet in the local point-eight-four gee, nodding kind of absently as my passengers got off and walked away, across the concrete to the cosmodrome's terminal building . . . I can't remember the name of this place, if I ever knew it. Not much to see here, broad expanse of conventional cement, with various antique spacecraft sitting around, mostly lighters from the orbiting freighters, terminal building looking like a concrete tent.

Flat land here, of course, and I could see buildings, few of them more than a dozen stories high, sticking up in all directions. That would be the western suburbs of Orikhalkos, where the All Worlds Travel Agency had its local offices. There'd be somebody in the terminal, bored, manning a desk, not expecting anyone, much less *my* passengers, but knowing when a ship touched down someone might come toddling out, baffled by an alien sun, looking for the All Worlds agent you see and . . .

Hard to miss that alien sun, hanging up there in the metallic blue-green vault of Green Heaven's sky, cloudless hereabouts, today. Looking up, I felt a sudden crawling inside. Big. Big sky, with a huge, sunsetty-looking sun, pendulous orb, not quite halfway between horizon and zenith, blanketing the runway with some kind of warm, golden light.

Maybe they called it Green Heaven because of the sky? Child voice, almost the voice my suit used when talking to me, commenting that the original colonists, twenty-second-century research personnel from the Planetary Commerce Institute, had called it Kalyx, after their ship. Did I know, even as a child, that a calyx is that whorl of leaves, usually green, that surrounds a flower while it's still in the bud? I must have, since I know it now, another green word for a world seeming greener with each passing minute.

Passengers gone now, me standing alone at the foot of the ramp, looking around at nothing much. If it weren't for the warm sky and that fat sun . . . another quick glance. Rather more than twice as wide in this sky than Sol seen from Earth, maybe? What does that mean? Something like eighteen times as much surface area to shed that golden light on us?

The rest of it, though . . . dirty concrete, small buildings, shoddy old spaceships, as if this were the recovery ramp of some twenty-fourth-century terrestrial junkyard rather than the premier spaceport of a civilized world.

Movement in the distance, catching my eye. People? No. Small chatter of alarm, curiosity inside. Not people at all, a group of . . . things? Animals. Well, sort of. Familiar sight from the zoo, from the Green Heaven pavilion, but not in the cages. A party of Arousian stick-bug people walking together, heading in toward the terminal building from one of the other little ships.

Footsteps on the ramp coming out of the ship. Leah, standing in front of me, small valise dangling from one hand, looking at me, face expressionless. So. I said, "Well, we've got four months to hang around before we have to take them back. Maybe you and I could . . ." a feeble gesture toward the terminal building.

A look of surprise seeming to crystallize on her face. "You can't possibly be that stupid, Gae. I'm quitting now. You understand?"

"Quitting?" I reached out a hand toward her, felt a slight sting on my skin as she slapped it away.

"What, is there a fucking echo out here? *Christ.*" Shaking her head, turning away, striding away toward the terminal building, back narrow and straight, hips moving in her trim black slacks so . . .

Just standing there, watching her go, wanting to call out, something, anything. Coming up with nothing worth the effort. What will you do now, Leah? Where will you go?

Well, of course you know. Four months from now you'll find some way to take those passengers back home, and ISTA will want to know what became of command pilot Leah Strachan, and you'll tell them. Goodbye fifteen-hundred-livre repatriation fee, at least.

And Leah will . . . know people here. Five visits over two hundred years? She'll know families, over generations. She'll visit lovers grown elderly, sleep with the sons of nice young men she dandled on her knee the last time she was here . . . Go home somehow, by slow boat, or wait for an FTL ship to happen by, I . . .

I put my hands in my pockets and started walking toward the Orikhalkos terminal, where landfall paperwork would be waiting. I'm not really a fish out of water here, or anywhere else. It's just that . . . sometimes things get away from you.

Passengers secured, paperwork done, ramp rental fee paid for months in advance . . . Converting from the local currency, *drakhmai,* surprised, only one livre, fifty dismes a month? My God. Distant glimpse of Leah standing at a counter, talking to some young man. Yes, that's the ISTA representative, manning his lonely cosmodrome kiosk. I expected them both to turn suddenly, turn and see me walking in the distance across the sparsely populated main concourse floor, but . . .

Not the center of my own little drama, I guess. A bit player even in my own universe.

I went back out to button up *Random Walk,* buoyed by a bit of good news. Green Heaven, you see, as you should have seen all along, *has* no central government. Vrij Veldteboeren don't care what you do with your starship. Hinterlings don't care. French Islanders won't give it a thought . . . And as for the local jurisdictions of the Seven Cities of the Compact . . .

Well, Mr. du Cheyne, so long as you pay your ramp fees and pay for anything you happen to damage . . . So, what then? There's a whole star system here. Won't cost me much to fly her around, go sightseeing and . . . Well. Whole world here too.

I packed a small case with clothes, casual stuff, all I'd happened to bring with me anyway, my . . . regular clothes, not expecting I'd be going to any fancy dress . . . Christ. Old imaginings.

Up in the control room, I took off my spacesuit and reassembled it empty, draped it across the back of the flight engineer's chair, powered up and hooked into the ship's operating system. Look after things while I'm gone, old friend. I'll be back in a while and we'll see what we can think of to do next. Meanwhile . . .

As I turned away, the little pang of gratitude I'd felt from the hardware matrix was already fading, masked by a rising rumble of conversation between my suit and the various AI nodes that made *Random Walk* a living thing.

Not really necessary to leave any of it turned on of course. Shut down the ship. Take the suit apart, fold it up and put it in a drawer until I need it again. I . . .

Hell. How would you feel if it was you being put to sleep, unneeded?

6

Parked by the curb outside the cosmodrome terminal building were a few yellow ground cars, bench seats inside, each with a lone pilot at its controls. *Taxi.* I've seen them in hundreds of old films. But old films, whether colorized or in the original grayscale, don't show you the dirt. Not like this. I walked over to the nearest one, opened the rear door of the cabin the way I knew was proper from the movies, and got in.

The pilot, a swarthy, sweaty-looking fellow with uncombed hair and a bristling moustache, turned, grinning, showing the most peculiar stuff, like green algae, clinging to his teeth, and said a long sentence in what sounded exactly like Spanish, but wasn't, not a single recognizable word.

Great. "I don't suppose you speak English?"

He seemed taken aback. *"Adrianikoi?* You, ah . . ." scratching his head, "Reggie *në* Robbie?" Look on his face like a man smelling a particularly unusual fart, half disgust, half amusement.

I pointed at the sky and said, "Earth." Whatever the hell it'd be in Greek. *Kosmopolis? Gaia?*

Sunny brightening. "Oh! I, ah . . ." A helpless shrug. *"Nihon-go?"* Brief wait, then, "No? *'Arabiyyah?"*

"Nope." I opened my suitcase on the back seat and started rummaging around in it, the cabbie, if I was remembering the right word, looking suddenly impatient, drumming his fingers on a black box with a sideways metal flag on it. There. Picked up the comclip and slid the barrette into my hair, just above my left ear, as close to Wernicke's area as I could manage.

The look on the cabbie's face . . . nervous? I wonder why? I thought, Open ship to shore.

The spacesuit's voice whispered in my head: Channel open. Ready.

Link to library AI. Standard spool. Languages and literature.

Linking. Spool 45, maximum transmission rate secured.

Why the hell didn't I put this thing on back at the ship? I looked at the cabbie, who was silent and wide-eyed. What the hell does he think is going on here? "Come on, pal. You have to *say* something to get it started."

Puzzled look, followed by a quick, bubbly phrase in Pseudospanish.

The library's soft, gender-neutral voice said, *Romaïkos*, descended from the post-Helladian *demotikí* of southeastern Cyprus, late twenty-second century.

A quick echo, as if the cabbie had spoken again: "Look, if you're not going to go someplace, get the fuck out of my cab, you fucking jerkoff!" A little aftershock as well, deep connection being made, as a part of my brain automatically memorized the translation of *vrea malaka* as "you fucking jerkoff."

I opened my mouth to speak, felt the AI take possession of the verbal stream content as it passed through my arcuate fasciculus, felt it operate Broca's area, felt the muscles of my mouth tighten up strangely, lips pursing . . . A cascade of nonsense words came out, apparently meaning, "Take it easy, buddy. I need for you to find me a good hotel."

Suspicious then: "I thought you couldn't speak Greek."

"I can't." I tapped the barrette. "Nobody ever show you a translator before?" I pulled the thing out of my hair, leaned forward and stuck it behind his ear, hoping I had the right side, since I hadn't noticed whether he was right- or left-handed. "What d'you think?"

Startled look, snatching it out of his hair, turning it over in his fingers, muttering something incomprehensible. When I got it back on, the library AI told me he'd said something like, "Unbelievable," noting that the word he'd used conveyed a bit of superstitious dread.

I learned how to speak Spanish with a clip like this, hooked to the school library, when I lived on Mars. It kept telling me what to say, until I didn't need it anymore. I said, "Sure. Weird as hell. Let's get going, huh?"

The hotel, located somewhere near the center of Orikhalkos, was a seven- or eight-story concrete tower, a tall tan box with more window than wall, whose two-word name the translator kept insisting was something like "A Really Good Hotel." Something about the form of the name kept being snatched away by the translation process, and when I moved the barrette around to the back of my head so it could do a visual filter, all I could see was that the name on the front of the building was some foreign phrase transliterated into Greek letters.

Pay the cabbie, pay the hotel bill for a few days in advance, up the elevator and into my room . . .

Bed. Primitive bathroom. Antique holodeck table. No kitchen devices whatsoever. Warm green-gold light flooding in through the big window, Tau Ceti now sliding along the far horizon, outlining the black silhouettes of buildings, dipping behind distant mountains . . .

Sun sets in the west, by definition. If a planet rotates backward, it must be upside down. Venus, for example. I slid the glass doors open, warm air with an odd . . . scent, almost like chemicals flooding in, wiping away the slightly stale smell of the room, stepped outside into the golden light. Stood leaning into the wind, eyes half shut, hands on the railing.

That odor. That's the faint aftertaste of ground car exhaust

I'm smelling. Eighty million people in an entire world? They can run internal combustion engines, burn all the fossil fuels they want.

Cityscape below. Lots of featureless boxy buildings, most of them smaller than the Really Good Hotel, windows here and there lighting up now, glass in buildings at certain angles reflecting the light of Tau Ceti like pools of molten metal caught in their walls.

Parks here and there, vegetation maybe green, maybe not, darkened by shadows, looking blue-gray-brown, larger park in the distance with small irregular lakes, a little bit of Old New York clipped from history, plunked down here . . . Maybe Edith Wharton once stood on such a balcony and saw a cityscape like this one.

Past the city, I could see that the sun had gotten beyond the mountains, was bisected by a flat horizon now, rays reddening as they swept across a flat, glossy, glistening surface that I knew must be the sea. When I leaned out over the railing, craning my neck, peering toward the north, I could see more of it, going on forever, right over the edge of the world.

All right. This is it. Here you are where you longed to be, Gaetan du Cheyne. Now what? Now nothing. Go back inside, put on the holodeck, let the drink mixer anticipate your . . . no. Have to think of everything myself, call . . . room service, I guess, tell them what to send up. I . . .

Pale spark of emotion: anger, resentment, self-pity, something like that, all of them mixing together in the shadows beneath my heart. What did you expect, Gaetan du Cheyne? That woman down in the lobby, sitting with luggage piled round her feet, looking the part of a maiden all forlorn, is she one of your safari ladies? Will she come to you in the night, unbidden, strip for you and dance for you and suck your dick for you until your walls fall down and the passion they know you possess is somehow provoked?

As I watched, the sky turned a burnished red-gold, Tau Ceti disappearing behind the sea, leaving, for a while, a band of pale green light shining over the horizon, then it got dark, the sky turning black, the stars coming out.

Maybe the most interesting sunset I ever saw, sun going so far south, so very slowly, before being extinguished by the edge of the world. I glanced into the library, exiting the language spool, going to the factoid elicitor. Orikhalkos, it told me, lies on the northwest-facing shore of a large peninsula, at approximately fifty-four degrees south latitude.

The library whispered, Green Heaven is a literal translation of the Groentans word *Groentehemmel*. The word *groente* would be better translated into English as "greens," as in "spinach and kale," and is most usually seen in the word *groenteboer*, meaning "greengrocer."

I pulled the barrette out of my hair and dropped it on the nightstand beside the lamp and a little box that appeared to be a vidicom transceiver.

So here I am lying in the bed with a hard-on in my pants, nowhere to go and nothing to do, embedded in the land of my dreams. What was it the cabbie had called me? *Vrea malaka*, you fucking jerkoff . . .

Here I am on Salad Heaven, doubtless having my salad days.

After a while, I must have fallen asleep.

When the morning sunshine floods your eyes, it's a new day and anything seems possible. I got up early, Tau Ceti in the far southeast, scraping along behind the low buildings of the inner city's skyline, got myself washed and dressed and got going, down the elevator and out the door, concierge giving me an odd look as I crossed the lobby and went out the doors.

Walking along a deserted street under a vast, cloudless sky of turquoise tinted with pale gold. Not a soul out here. Soft breeze. A little cool. Greenies late risers are they, not starting the day until . . .

Library whispering inside my head, whispering in the spacesuit's familiar voice now: It's late spring in the southern hemisphere of Tau Ceti 2 just now. Green Heaven rotates on its axis in 150,120 seconds, compared to a standard terrestrial day of 86,400 seconds.

Some part of my brain, used to doing rudimentary calculations translating that to a more usable 41.7 hours . . .

Vague visual image forming in my imagination, the barrette reaching out for my visual cortex, near the limits of what it could do from its perch over my left temporal lobe. Planet here, sun there, axial tilt, Orikhalkos here, sunrise . . . So I'm doing the equivalent of walking down the street at three A.M. Typical.

By the time the sun was relatively high in the sky, maybe two-thirds of the way to what the library pointed out was its forty-degree zenith, the streets were full of Greenies, dark-haired men and women in rustic-looking costume, lots of blue denim and leather, babbling to each other in their ancient Greek, words and phrases snatched out of context by the translator and stuck into my head.

Going places. Doing things.

Why the hell do these people have so many dogs? They're common enough on Mars and Luna, popular anyplace you can have a pet less tidy than a cat, but . . .

Standing at a street corner, waiting for the light to change, watching bolder souls make broken-field runs through traffic, dodging cars, automobile pilots making loud blatting noises with their signaling devices . . .

". . . what the fuck is wrong with you, you fucking *putz*, get the fuck out of the fucking *street* . . ."

Library commenting quietly that Orikhalkoïné seemed to have adopted a certain pejorative, meaning *penis*, from the once widespread *Jüdische* dialect of Middle High German, possibly by way of the English that had once been the official language of the original PCI bases on Kalyx, still spoken by the Hinterling nomads of the . . .

Running man grabbing himself by the throat, holding his left elbow in his right hand, making a wigwag motion at the driver who cursed him, calling him a "pitiful little snakeling" as he ran . . . Filthy city, full of cars and trash, pedestrians not seeming to notice as they stepped around and over all the neat little piles of dogshit.

I found a place to have my lunch in a restaurant atop the highest building anywhere around, sitting alone at a table near a railing, barrette transferred to the back of my head so the translator could have a stab a reading the menu. I wouldn't need to do that much longer; I was already starting to learn the Greek letters, relearn most of them from childhood astronomy lessons, with new *romaïka* names, ahl-fah, beetah, ghummah, dheel-tah . . .

When they brought the lunch the library told me to order, it proved to be hollow disks of bread, stuffed with raw vegetables, some of it, bok choy and sweet red peppers, recognizable, other withered green things like nothing I'd ever seen before, drenched in a peppery white sauce that made me choke as I tried to swallow.

Christ. Tried to put the fire out with the alcoholic beverage I'd ordered, a soapy wine that tasted like it'd been mixed with some of the asphalt they used to pave the streets of Orikhalkos. Useless. Waiter looked at me like I was an idiot when I asked for water, finally brought me a glass of lukewarm tea, a fully saturated sugar solution apparently, which appeared to do the job.

Sitting alone then, almost alone in the restaurant, Greenie lunch hour long since ended, drinking my too-sweet tea and working on a flaky almond-flavored pastry, looking out at the still cloudless deep blue-green sky, sun slowly declining in the west as I dawdled, too slowly, the only natural days I'd ever gotten used to being the Earth-like days of Mars.

Brilliant spark of light, pale behind the blue of the sky, but bright nonetheless, sliding rapidly along, west to east, on the northern horizon, far out over the sea . . .

Green Heaven's inner moon, Hope, running the racetrack of its prograde equatorial orbit, some eighteen thousand kilometers out, circling the world three times in a "day," best use the local word *iméra*, the way the Martians always said *sol*.

Background chatter from the library made me look toward

the west, out over the ocean, spread out like a blanket of cold, dark steel from this height. A small, pale crescent, yellowish, pastel, hanging over the sea, far, far away. The outer moon Wan, said the library. Four million kilometers away, slightly larger than Mars, with a thin atmosphere all its own, all carbon dioxide and nitrogen, a few shallow seas, no life of its own, other than a bit of terragenic contamination.

In the early days, it was thought people would settle on Wan as well, but . . . what would the point have been?

I stood, putting my hands on the railing, looking out over the city, empty of . . . pretty much everything. To the east, where the sky was a deeper blue, between the city and those vast, far-away white mountains, Thisbÿs Bergketen, said the library, unasked, was a broad, almost featureless yellow-brown-gold landscape, flat, humped up here and there with low, rolling hills, an occasional metallic glint shimmering, there and gone again in the blink of an eye.

Koperveldt, the Plains of Brass, whose name alone had been sufficient to provoke my dreams, not so terribly long ago. What's out there now? Anything at all from those dreams, or will it simply be more . . . A look down at the dirty city. More of this.

If I go out there, I risk having those dreams ground away to nothing. And dreams are all I have. All I've ever had.

I went back to my hotel room for a little while, late in the afternoon, sitting on the edge of my bed, watching the sky turn brassy as the sun went down, feeling useless, worthless, whatever. Feeling the way I'd felt for the past thousand years, it seemed, wishing for . . . something.

What *are* you wishing for, peckerhead? Just wishing for your apartment and job, your vidnet and drink mixer and all those old, familiar comforts of home? Wishing, somehow, that you'd been given the grace to win a Garstang for yourself, all those years ago? Or . . . Well, there won't be a Camilla Seldane out here in the colonies, but there might be . . .

I picked up the barrette and shoved it in my hair, heading

for the door, maybe an idea in my head, maybe not, maybe nothing, maybe just more dreams, I . . . Whisper in my head, the voice of the suit, Wait. Gaetan. Image forming in the back of my head, faint and full of shadows. Ah, yes. The little dartgun I'd taken out of *Random Walk*'s small arms locker, almost on an impulse, thrown in my suitcase before heading into town. This is Green Heaven. Green Heaven. World of all your dreams. Men are dangerous here. Men carry guns here . . .

Dangerous men. Women love dangerous men. Only dangerous men. Men who carry guns. Not little putzes who spend their lives playing with mechanical toys, I . . . The suit AI whispered, Please, Gaetan. Put the gun in your pocket. Very earnest, sincere, ethereal fingers reaching into my head, stirring thought into action. All right. Little thing hardly big enough to cover my palm, not even making a bulge in my jacket pocket as I went out the door.

Walking in the darkness, bright stars pocking the sky overhead, growing in number as I walked away from the bright heart of the big city, walking into a darker landscape of shadowy buildings, passing by dark doorways, the hollow entrances of forbidding alleyways, a landscape of nightmares, more than mere dreams.

Nobody here. An occasional black, irregular shadow, the outline of a human form, always fleeing. Fetid smells, sewer smells, fresh toilet smells from every beckoning alley. I imagined myself sliding along through the darkness, eyes wide, gun in hand like some adventure hero, some . . . *private eye*. What would I find?

Rotting garbage and dead cats, perhaps.

Who do I want to be, right now? Travis McGee, following the hot trail of fresh, steaming gold and impossible, honey-scented women? Wrong landscape. Somebody else belongs here. Some sullen Chandler hero, some broken-spirited Hammett man, functioning still because functionality is all he has left.

I turned down a street full of lights, lights and people, tall fellow on the corner, black, curly hair shining in the streetlight, as if freshly oiled, dark eyes on me, watching me pass on by. Hunger a soft twist in my stomach now.

A storefront that had once had windows, glass still in place, covered from the inside by what looked like big sheets of paper, heavy paper that might once have been white, was stained yellow-brown now by airborne dust, by the rays of Green Heaven's golden sun. Something had been drawn on the paper, once upon a time, very well drawn, in fact, in delicate charcoal shadings. The image of a child's doll, doll stripped naked. If you looked closely, you could see it had been a very detailed doll, a girl doll, with tiny nipples, a belly button, a little slit of baby vulva.

The eyes though. Just a doll. Obviously a doll, not a real child at all. Not even a fancy robot, the sort of thing a certain kind of man . . .

The door next to the window popped open, banging against the wall by the frame, disgorging a staggering man, a puff of odd-scented air. Peculiar smell, indefinable smell, so quickly come and gone I couldn't even begin to sketch its . . . parameters. Just the sense that the hair on the back of my neck began to prickle.

The man reeled in the doorway, staggered down the steps, door closing itself behind him with a muted hiss. Stood there on the sidewalk, dark face upturned, eyes fixed on the sky. Heaved a heavy breath, sucking in the night air.

Rubbed a hand across the back of his neck, hand coming away shiny, wet with sweat. "Jesus!" Muttered, but quite loud enough. "Fucking *dollies*. My God . . ."

Glancing at me then, eyes rolling, as if terrified, then turning, walking swiftly away into the darkness at the end of the street, tall man on the corner watching him go, nodding slowly, seeming . . . Maybe that's a smile on his lips. Maybe a sneer. Maybe something else.

I looked back at the drawing of the doll again, wondering

what drama I might be missing, what glimpse into other men's dirty dreams, then walked on, compelled by a simpler hunger.

Barroom, neon sign with what the library told me was a rather archaic form of the Greek word for a male cat, underneath it a little placard, *All Girl Staff, Private Counseling Available.* But there was a distinct *food* smell coming from somewhere inside, so I went in, took a booth by the rear wall, waited for the all-girls to come.

Comfortable place of warm, deep, secretive shadows, a place where you could huddle if you needed to huddle, by yourself, reduced to nothing more than eyes. Round tables packing the floor between the wall booths and the low stage, a bar with stools and rail off to one side, men lining the bar, bearded bartender tapping beer, so much for the all-girl staff, I . . .

Young woman in tight shorts and halter top, cloth so tight you could make out the location of her nipples, maybe imagine the architecture of her vulva . . . eyes on me. Waiting. She said, "Want a menu?"

Defining moment: "Sure."

She put it in front of me, a flat, laminated sheet with a couple of dozen items, went away without a backward glance.

Plenty of people in here, men at the bar, one woman sitting on a corner stool, sloppy-looking woman with big tits inside a loose blouse, sitting turned away from the bar, away from the men, looking toward the stage. People sitting around the tables, clustered toward the stage, mostly men, some women. Shadows of people visible in the other booths.

The waitress passed by again, let me order a nameless beer and something the translator insisted would be a chef salad.

This is a familiar place, warmth flooding out of the walls, getting inside me somehow. Not a clean place. Not well lighted. Familiar. I feel like I know these people.

Skinny man, young, sweaty-looking, hair plastered flat on his scalp, came out on the stage and went to a drum kit set up in the corner, sat down behind it, started fiddling around, people at stageside tables turning so they could face the lights, men at the bar turning round, leaning their elbows on the Formica, grinning, muttering to one another.

Waitress brought my bottle and bowl, fork and a few squares of paper towel, waited while I produced bits of local currency, paper money I'd picked up at the hotel desk because the library AI told me it'd be a good idea. *Tip*, whispered the voice of the suit. She's waiting for a tip.

Waitress's dark eyes on me, unsmiling. I gave her thirty percent and watched her eyes brighten, a little smile as she turned away, a bit of a nod. Maybe she'll come back later to see if I want anything else? What will I want?

A sip of beer. Too fizzy. Too sweet. Almost flavorless, but for that faint nip of alcohol, that little scent of tar. Forkful of salad. Peppery dressing. Bits of crumbled, stinky cheese. Black olives.

Drummer on the stage banging a single thump, stamping his foot on a pedal, *bump*. Roomful of people, mostly men, some women, looking up, room transforming itself, somehow, into a sea of eyes, my eyes among them. Thump, silence, no ". . .laydees an' gennulmunn . . ."

Bump-bump-a-bump-bump-a . . .

Half-naked woman sliding out on stage, gliding on blue-slippered feet, muscular woman all sleek white skin and long, wavy brown hair, hair cascading down her back all the way to her ass, whirling, clingy blue underpants, silky blue bra . . .

Not much for a stripper to take off.

Dancing, dancing around, seeming to linger before the few tables that had women, women among the men.

Women at the tables all eyes, all attention, men with them reaching out to stroke their necks, lean toward them, as if waiting to smell their rising heat. Stripper dancing, taking off what little she had on, breasts bouncing as the bra fell away, red nipples immense, sticking out like dowel rods of flesh, then the little panties, kicked out over the audience's heads, falling on the floor in the middle of nowhere, lying there, a lifeless scrap . . .

Trite drum bumping away in its corner while the naked

woman danced, drum supposed to speed up our hearts, make us want to . . .

Watching a man and a woman close by the stage, woman arching her neck under the man's hand, woman at the table watching the naked woman dance . . . Man? Eyes on *his* woman, not the creature on the stage.

Would I want to be that man? No. Any of the people here? Be like the women whose ardor was aroused watching another woman spread her legs for men to see? How about the men leaning on the bar? Look closely. Grinning men, drinking beer, erections ignored.

No.

Behind the bar, the barkeep was taking glasses out of some crude dishwashing robot, wiping smudges away with a clean white cloth, putting the glasses on a shelf until they were needed. Barkeep blasé, chewing a toothpick, ignoring the naked dancer, ignoring the drums.

There was a momentary irrational pang, something like jealousy, then I turned back to the stage, watched the dancer writhe and play with herself as I ate my wretched salad and drank my tasteless beer.

Outside again in the now-fresh-seeming midnight air. Black sky still overhead, not so full of stars because the streetlights here were too bright, but I knew they were there. Sense of fullness under my breastbone, not so much from the little salad as from swallowed beer fizz trying to get out.

The man with the dark curls was still down at the corner, leaning on a lamppost now, looking my way. Maybe that's a man with a job too? Standing guard? Or is he just a certain kind of whore? I started walking toward him, thinking maybe now that I'd seen what the tomcats were up to I could investigate the goings-on in the dollhouse.

Sharp memory of that other man, staggering out the door, drinking deep drafts of night air. *Dollies.* What could he have meant by that? Somewhere in the back of my head I could feel the library AI's unease at being unable to answer my question. *Should* it expect to know everything about Green Heaven, everything about all the faraway worlds of the Tau Ceti system?

Biff.

Soft, meaty sound, almost wet sound, coming out of an alleyway. Man at the lamppost not so far away unmoving, as if he'd heard nothing.

Soft yip of a man's voice, touched with pain. *Biff.* Then a soft gabble of Greek. Translator: ". . .little son of a bitch fucking *bit* me!" Metallic chatter, like scissors being snapped, over and over again, then *biff.* "Fucking asshole . . ."

I can't imagine what force impelled me into the mouth of the dark alleyway just then. Maybe no force at all, merely the absence of fear, of any force keeping me away. Sliding through the darkness then, smelling the alley's shit smells, slinking like a thief around some big metal box reeking of discarded food, eyes straining, listening to *biff* and *boff* and the scuffling of leather shoes on asphalt pavement.

A chattering of scissors and "Ow! Fuck!" and *biff.*

Don't know what I was expecting to see as I peered round the edge of the Dumpster, keeping my body back in the shadows as much as I could. Danger here. You know there's danger here . . . heart pounding like mad, making me feel afraid and excited all at once.

Making me feel like I was, for once, really part of a vidnet show.

Prickling at the back of my neck. Sometimes, in your better sort of vidnet show, you see the hero slink forward, peering into the night, facing the pickup remote, so you see not what he sees, but the view over his shoulder, the shadow of an upraised arm, the looming club about to strike . . .

Christ.

Chatter. Scuffle. *"Shit!"*

And . . . *biff.*

Three slim men, no more than shadows in the dark alleyway, sort of dancing around each other. Fighting? No. Kicking.

Kicking something small, a black outline no bigger than a medium-sized dog, something with the outline of a well-upholstered hassock.

Something like a lobster's claw coming up in black silhouette, claw snapping at the nearest leg, making a sound like sharp metal, like whetstone and iron, *"Yi!"* skinny man dancing back, then *biff!* Black hassock rolling over and over from the kick.

Gabble of Greek, curses untranslated, translator AI muttering about unrecorded slang, derived from foreign loan words, Russian perhaps or—

Spacesuit's voice a frantic whisper: Get out of there, Gaetan! This is none of your business! Get back out to the street; leave well enough alone . . . Tingle of fear in my head, impelling me to shrink back, but . . . The barrette's reach wasn't enough, ethereal fingers unable to reach deep enough into my limbic system, traverse my brain stem and . . .

Chitter. Chatter. Clink. *Snap.*

Thing on the ground among stamping feet and kicking legs, desperately trying to defend itself.

Defend itself and live.

No impulse.

No nothing.

Just me watching. Impassive. Watching. Waiting. I . . .

I stepped forward, stepped around the side of the Dumpster, out of the shadows into the alleyway's lesser darkness. Stood still. My mouth opened, reaching round the spacesuit's anguish to grab the translator's attention. Nothing. Frantic urgings to . . . *"Hey!"*

Three men freezing, spinning round. Shadow hassock with waving claws backing up, getting itself into the corner made by two dark brick walls. Three men staring at me, looking beyond me, fathoming the night, then one of them said a single word, several syllables long.

Well? Translator?

Whispered. Please, Gaetan. Then, resignation. It means, "Fucking asshole."

Not a policeman, you see. Not someone who fucking matters. Just a fucking asshole. He took a step forward, teeth visible,
white in the shadows of his face, just below the liquid shine of
his eyes. Grinning.

I took the little dartgun out of my pocket and held it up so
they could see.

One of the other men said, "What the fuck is that?"

I aimed it in his direction and pulled the trigger. Com-
pressed-air *thup*. Man jumping from the *spock* of the glass dart
shattering on the wall beside his head, astringent anesthetic
smell filling the air.

Untranslated word, sudden realization that I'd learned *skatá*
must mean "shit" in Greek.

All three of them stepping forward as one, three angular
shadows, grinning, reaching out for me. I shot the nearest one
in the belly, watched him jump back, "Fuck . . ." reaching for
the little dart, where it stuck out of his shirt. "Fuck, I . . .. hub-
bahubbahubbahubba . . ." Dropping to his knees, falling on his
face, little tinkle of the dart being crushed.

Two angular shadows stock-still, then, *"Demos?"*

The third man, silent until now, said, "Is . . . he dead?"

"No. Asleep." I motioned with the gun and, incredibly, they
understood. Stooped, took their friend by shoulders and knees,
picked him up, carried him away into the deeper shadows.
Maybe this alley had another end. Maybe there was an open
door. Maybe . . .

I wonder how long it'll be before they realize it's a permanent anesthetic, that he's not going to wake up without some
medical help? I wonder if the doctors on Green Heaven will
know what to do?

Hassock thing still cowering in its corner. Soft chitter, chitter from its claws. Soft, rough sound, like desperate breathing.

I came closer, stood looking down. Watched one eyestalk
rise from its back, hard to discern in the dim light, blue maybe
or some shade of pale green. Chitter, chitter. Claw reaching out
for something nearby, a small box, perhaps.

I picked it up, turning it over in my hands. Once upon a time it had been a very sophisticated, self-contained translation computer, orders of magnitude better than anything I could ever have afforded to buy, even with the wealth that'd given me *Random Walk.* Just now, it was stepped-on junk.

I reached out and touched the . . . being, felt it flinch away from me, shuddering, felt some thick, sticky stuff on my fingers. Christ. I stood, looking down, and whispered, "Well, Mr. Kapellmeister, you are in deep shit, I'd say."

One claw came up, chitter-chitter-*snap.*

Decisive agreement.

Waking up in my hotel room, sitting on the edge of my old-fashioned bed, golden sunlight streaming in through the window. Almost midday. Long night full of . . . interesting deeds? You could call them that.

Image of myself gone numb, unfeeling in the darkness, facing three bold bravos, brave men satisfied to be kicking around something the size of a dog, kicking it, killing it, laughing together in celebration of their courage.

Image of the dart appearing like magic, a bit of glassy glitter in the darkness, decorating the front of surprised Demos' shirt, man clutching at himself, gabbling softly, falling down like a dead rag doll.

Competence is a transient thing, deserting those men, flooding into me, men afraid to face my little weapon, afraid to take their chances and rush me. If they'd acted, I would most likely have fallen before their blows. Would I be dead now? Perhaps.

Numb feeling inside that it wouldn't have mattered.

Competence pervades much of my life, you see. I can fix anything, from a wrecked starship to a broken safety pin. No mysteries before the magic of the godhead, you see, just . . .

Well, violence is a form of competence as well, those two men cowering under my gun. I'd been secure in the knowledge that they wouldn't throw themselves on me, that they somehow *knew* I'd just shoot them down and turn away, full of a hero's contempt for the weak, the fearful.

Not even the first time, you see, because competence is everything, transcends fear, replaces courage. Why would you need courage, when you *know* you can win?

I got up from the edge of the bed, stretching, feeling odd. Not lousy, not ill. Machinery in my blood sees to it that I always feel well. Why doesn't it see to it that I *feel* well then?

Someone once told me that the inability to develop a competent seduction strategy comes from a misplaced respect for women. Woman a sacred thing, you see, the object of heart's desire, but then you want them to kneel in the dirt before you, suck your dick and swallow your scum, rub their face on your belly and worship you, lie on their backs and spread their legs for you with adoring, uncomplaining eyes.

That same someone looking at me then, with amused, smirking eyes. Tell us something about your mother, Gaetan du Cheyne.

I showered, got dressed, and got the hell out, going nowhere.

Hours later, with Tau Ceti heading for the western horizon, far from the city center, I sat on a wooden bench in an empty park, facing eastward, where the sky would soon grow dark, where the first stars would pop out. Bright sky there now, visible over the low rooflines of these little wooden houses, wooden houses painted yellow and blue and pink, identical but for color, under identical layers of black, overlapping shinglework.

Nobody walking the streets out here. Nobody but me, sitting on my bench surrounded by empty playground equipment, warm breeze ruffling my hair, seeming inappropriate. It ought to be cold, damp, gray.

Over the line of roofs, I could see the distant mountains, lower slopes colored blue with the Rayleigh scattering of distance, upper slopes bright with snow, peaks a stark and steely gray where the mountains protruded above the tropopause. I've got to get out of here, whatever the risk to my dreams. Why else did I come, for God's sake?

Just so I could play dirty little hero boy in some filthy alleyway? I could've stayed on Luna for that, prowling the underwarrens until I fucked up and got myself killed. Wouldn't my parents have been surprised to inherit all that fucking money?

Brief memory of trying to carry the wheezing, bleeding, clattering Kapellmeister, all spindly crablegs and gooey, sticky bag of a body. Finally giving up, rummaging in the Dumpster until I found a plastic bag of some sort, emptying out the reeking garbage that filled it, rolling the alien inside, carrying him off like I was Santa Claus bearing gifts and toys, lumps of coal and punitive carrots.

Didn't take long to find a hospital, and I'd enjoyed the excitement when I dumped my cargo out on the check-in desk, receptionist leaping to his feet, rearing back and screaming, *What the fuck is* that *thing*?

Patiently explaining to him that it was a sentient nonhuman being, denizen of the planet Salieri, 82 Eridani 3, you see, a species with whom humanity had *formal* relations, you see, and hadn't they better get busy seeing if it was still alive?

One eyestalk bearing a featureless sky blue Ping-Pong ball of an eye, presumably looking at me, claws making a feeble *chitter-clack*, third hand, hand made of boneless tentacles reaching out to make a juicy slapping noise on the desktop.

Thanks, pal?

Who knows.

Maybe warning me that Gort would soon be on the march, that I'd better be about my *Klaatu-barada-niktoing*, if I knew what was good for me.

7

Next day, on my way. On my way to something the travel
agent had called the Vrouwvenarts Bandwinkel, Greek
woman looking up at me oddly when I framed my question, gesturing at her crude network display terminal, snapping
romaïka that the translation algorithm claimed meant something like, "How the hell should *I* know what it means?"

Library AI nodes arguing with each other then, Groentans
not a *formal* language, you see, full of unrecorded slang, and no
it can't *possibly* be a gynecological supplies store . . . then how *do*
you say "dude ranch" in Orikhalkoïné?

But it made me feel warm inside somehow, hearing them
bicker like that. Warm just the way the bus made me feel when I
saw it. Warm the way I felt just now, riding along a dusty road on
the bus's open upper deck, open to the wind, warm wind in my
hair under a clear, empty, *immense* blue sky, Tau Ceti hanging,
like some huge, golden, impossibly bright Christmas ornament,
low on the northern horizon as we drove more or less southward across the Plains of Brass, low skyline of the city sinking
away behind us, disappearing below the horizon as if swallowed
up by the ground.

In the distance, in the direction of our travel, there were

low, white mountains, more like rolling hills, barely clearing the tan-gold-gray grassiness covering this almost flat world. Koudloft then, still very far away, surmounted by pale, silvery, sunlit ghost clouds. Whisper in my head, soft, familiar voice, *kowt-lufft,* meaning "cold attic," the high, glaciated plateau country of approximately two million square kilometers surrounding Green Heaven's south pole, separating the Koperveldt plains from the much larger Opveldt country of the eastern hemisphere . . .

Bus rocking gently under me as I lay back, closed my eyes, let the warm, slanting rays of an already familiar sun warm my face, soft, indefinite smells of Brass in my nostrils, fighting to overcome the burnt organics of the engine's exhaust.

Soft growl of the engine in my ears, mechanical marvel. If you'd asked me, a year ago, if I thought there might be a functioning gas turbine drive anywhere in the known universe, I might have said no. Or, perhaps, guessed that some museum or another might possess one.

Now this. Were gas turbine drives still in use four centuries ago, when humans first set foot on Tau Ceti 2? I don't think so. Reinventing the wheel, as the saying goes, because . . . No. Reinventing something else. Gas turbine growling as it drove big ducted fans, puffing up the air cushion's rubbery skirt, bus sweeping along a dusty Koperveldt trail, hardly track enough to be called a road, blowing up dust, old dirt, dry grass, a faint odor of what must almost certainly be dried herbivore dung.

"Look, Joop! There. Look at the sons of bitches."

Two tall, ruddy-cheeked, heavyset men with hay-colored hair sharing the bench seat directly in front of me. Men dressed in rustic garb, what must be a workingman's costume, blue serge pants, heavy brown boots coming just above the ankle, brown suede vests over what appeared to be canvas shirts . . . Sitting up now, bolt-upright, looking into the distance with their identical cornflower eyes, shading their eyes against the sun, pointing.

I looked, looked that way, keeping my head lolled back

against the seat's headrest, rolling my head to the side, as if drowsy. Low hills that way, superimposed against remote, craggy mountains, the same mountains I'd stared at from my hotel room in Orikhalkos.

Something loping along there, something white or perhaps pale gray, almost invisible against the snowy slopes of the mountains. Can't quite make them out. Like shaggy Shetland ponies, perhaps? Maybe a pack of enormous dogs or . . . useless. No way to get at my luggage, stored below, get out those expensive antique binoculars I'd bought in the safari shop next to the travel agency.

Joop, speaking in his thick, spitty-sounding Groentans dialect, said, *"Ja,* Gerrit. Fucking white wolfen . . ." Squinting at them, shaking his head.

Distant memory, ancient memory, standing in the zoo, looking at an alien animal, silent animal, motionless but for soft breathing, animal staring back at me with unreadable alien eyes, eyes like bits of mottled marble . . . What are you doing just now, Rua Mater? Has your luck changed?

Gerrit laughed and said, "Hell, if we had some decent rifles along we could pick them off from here."

Silence, the three of us watching the wolfen run. Decent rifles. I wonder if the wolfen know?

Joop said, *"De smartinaass blank-wolfens in beslag gedoopt en in de oven gebakken."*

Another laugh: *"Ja, en toost met gesmolten kaas!"*

Sure thing, Gerrit. They'd be real good with toast and melted cheese, wouldn't they . . . I looked back at the horizon, but the white wolfen were gone. Maybe they'd been listening too.

Our destination lay in a broad, flat, vaguely wok-shaped valley, hardly more than a dent in the endless, rippling Plains of Brass, an unplanned-looking hodgepodge of low buildings, extended log cabins under dry thatch roofing beside a small, silver-watered lake, lake itself hardly more than a pond. The bus parked, settling with a breathy wheeze of dying compressors in a billow of pale dust beside an unfinished wooden sign, gray lumber into which had been burned the legend *Vrouwvenarts Bandwinkel, Hansel en Gretel Blondinkruis, Eigenaars.*

Listening to the AIs chatter, I had to wonder at the translation depth setting. Our proprietors, Hansel and Gretel, with the flavor of blondness about them? Hell, if I wondered about it hard enough, some subroutine or another would pop up and offer me a translation of *du Cheyne,* no doubt.

Only a few passengers got off the bus, stolid pilot retrieving our luggage, making a row of sturdy bundles on the ground by the sign, a handful of Greek-speakers from Orikhalkos, atwitter with excitement, gawking at the little lake, at the rambling, rustic buildings; a swarthy, pretty young couple, small, thin folk, heads close together, whispering to each other in a nasal Romance language the library identified as French. Joop and Gerrit stayed aboard, then the bus pilot went up, door chuffing shut behind him. A soft, grinding whine as the turbines wound up, air cushion inflating, blowing dust and loose grass over us, then the bus was on its way, sliding up the hill, back up to the road on the Koperveldt and gone.

The woman had been there by the sign all along I suppose, tall, slim, blond as her name, with bright blue eyes and an improbably friendly smile, white teeth exposed, a little rim of pink gum, arms folded across her chest, beginning, "Welcome, friends, to Blondinkruis Boerderij . . ."

Not looking at her face, not looking at the muscular forearms exposed by sleeves rolled up to the elbow, crossed over obvious breasts. Looking at the front of her blue jeans, startlingly suggestive.

Beside me, the two dark French people were whispering, mostly the man, translator making a double echo as it revealed their words, a reprise of Gretel Blondinkruis' speech, translator pointing out his mistakes, translating *eigenaar* not as *propriétaire,* which, the precise words of the library informed me, had come to mean "a well-behaved little girl" in Les Iles des Français, but as *propraetrix.* A female lieutenant-general? Or merely an assistant governess?

Frenchman, I note, addressing Frenchwoman by a word that had once meant sister. Does it still? Eyes distracted from Gretel's presumably blond crotch to dark-haired girl's slim, equally suggestive hips.

Gretel Blondinkruis finished her speech and turned, leading us up the flagstone walkway and through the main entrance of her inn. All I could see, of course, walking in a shadow of my own making, was the moving, muscular swell of her buttocks.

In the morning, Tau Ceti was an enormous red-orange ball rising through a layer of low-hanging mist. *Juvrouw* Blondinkruis and her staff took the guests out for their first ride. *Juvrouw* rather than *vrouw*, an unmarried woman, you see. Hadn't taken long for that to come out, as we'd gathered at the long table in a room with a big, crackling firehearth, shadows leaping from the flames.

And where is *mijnheer* Blondinkruis, this Hansel fellow?

Ah, my brother has taken an *omganger* hunting party up into the mountains and won't be back from almost two weeks. Sorry you'll have missed him.

I couldn't take my eyes off her all during dinner, eating steadily, unaware of what the hell I was putting in my mouth, watching her eat and talk, knowing from her occasional amused glance that she was aware of my rapt attention.

Christ. I must have been staring like a zombie, other guests giving me troubled, sidelong looks as fair Gretel laughed and told them all about this word *omganger*, twinkle in her eyes as she explained that in Old Groentans, *omgang* usually referred to *trade, business,* what have you, *Omgangers*, you see, being the traders and businessmen Groenteboeren had to deal with, and, generally speaking, all the folk who'd come to inhabit the Seven Cities of the Compact in centuries past.

Traders, then. Except *omgang* had also come to refer, in a pleasant, slangy sort of way, to the act of sexual intercourse. General laughter, men and women tittering. Calling us *fuckers*? How droll, Miss Blondinkruis!

Frenchwoman's dark eyes so very serious, little Évie asking, through handsome little Claude, translator having figured out *les Français* said brother and sister when they meant husband and wife, "Even *us?*"

Even you Frankenvolk—over time, an *omganger* was everyone not of the Groenteboer kind. Then, glittering eyes on me. Every one of you here's a fucker except *mijnheer* du Cheyne.

Tart little pang, down low in my belly, wondering if she knew how that would sound to *me*. A little mean streak in you, then, my fair lady?

Mr. du Cheyne, you see, is what we call a *vreemdeling*.

Translator whispering, It only means "foreigner," but . . .

Yes?

Vreemd: Strange. Odd. Queer.

Paranoic imaginings creating threads between cultures that cannot possibly exist. I found voice enough to ask, "And what would you call a sentient nonhuman being? A Salieran Kapellmeister, say?"

Startled astonishment in her eyes. "That's very good, Mr. du Cheyne. Perhaps you will speak in Greek, so the others may understand?"

I hadn't even been aware the translator made me speak in Groentans.

She said, "We say *smartinaass*, Mr. du Cheyne."

Lunch, Tau Ceti as high as it would ever get in that clear blue-green sky, trail leading us now into scrubby woodland country a dozen kilometers from the boerderij, Miss Blondinkruis, sliding a slim rifle from her saddle holster, swinging it quickly, hardly seeming to aim, zzzip-*pop!* Spindly gray-green-brown thing the size of a big dog falling from one of the low, shrub-like trees, struggling briefly on the ground, making a soft, agonized sort of a coo, then still.

Gretel said, "We call this thing a *hoekker*. They're pretty good eating."

Thing on the ground like a fat, hairy monkey, with wide-open, brilliant green eyes staring at us, panicky *oh-no!* expression frozen on its dead, humanoid face, translator whispering in my head that *hoekker* meant "scavenger," but was also cognate with a common Medieval English expression for whore.

It sizzled over the open fire she built, hair burning away in a puff of sweet-smelling blue smoke, scent of roasted peanuts filling the air, liquid fat popping out on its now-naked flesh like so much sweat, face retaining its comically terrified look until the green eyes burst and ran like clarified butter.

We rode on through the afternoon, making camp on toward dusk, setting up our little tents in a copse of trees around some kind of natural spring, clear, slightly sulfur-smelling water welling up from a little pile of rocks, forming a little pool where it evidently soaked back into the ground, back down to the water table, since there was no evidence of a stream flowing away.

Gretel and her assistant, called DenArrie I think, pale-skinned, more or less bald, who'd been in the background all day, went out together, came back a while later with a dead brown hexapod thing not much smaller than a grown man, something they called a *fokkbok*, butchered it in front of us, throwing the entrails back into the woods a way, cut it up, cooked it over the open fire, served us steaks that tasted rather too much like chocolate.

Somehow, that had never been part of my dreams. Maybe it would have distracted me from my dreams of matronly cunt, had the educational vidnet producers thought to tell us the flesh of Green Heaven's herbivores tasted like candy. Maybe I'd've dreamed about eating and grown up to be a fat man.

After dinner, I went away for a long walk, escaping into the woodland alone. Not looking out for their guests, not caring for us properly? Hell, maybe there's nothing around here that could or would hurt me? No way to know. Certainly not represented in the land of my dreams, hm?

Walking then, uselessly, aimlessly, under a clear black sky peppered with white stars, the familiar glossy stream of the Milky Way, black trees and far horizon no more than empty places where the stars were not, glow of the campfire always visible somewhere behind me, puddle of red light a beacon to guide me home when I finally got sick of reviling myself.

On the way back, sleepy, ready for my tent, I heard soft noises, crept through the trees then, silent, curious, parting underbrush stealthily so I could see . . .

Once again, I can't imagine what I was expecting to see.

A little clearing, the black trunk of a fallen tree. Slim Évie sitting on the tree, skirt pulled up. That white scrap I see in her hand must be her underpants then. Évie sitting on the tree trunk, slim Claude kneeling between her legs, head thrust forward into her crotch, rocking back and forth. I hear little gobbling sounds, I think. Évie's head is thrown back, face lit up white by the wan light of Wan, mouth open, a dark oval.

Oh. Oh, Claude. Little white hand on his soft black hair, guiding his movements, urging him on. Her voice, a high whisper, making sounds straight out of all those old dreams. How *did* they get to be dreams again? Real women once made those sounds for me. Now . . .

Hand on my shoulder, making me jerk, turn . . .

Gretel Blondinkruis holding me, grinning, shining eyes on my face. Soft whisper in my ear, face so close I can feel her breath on my skin, smell some sweet lingering residue of dinner. "Oh, Mr. du Cheyne. I don't think you should be spying on them like this."

Me silent, staring at her, intensely conscious of the way the front of my pants must be poking out, though she never once glanced down, eyes fixed on my face. Finally, she made a little snort through her nose, as of amusement, and said, "You seem like a nice enough fellow, Mr. du Cheyne, but . . . Well, I make a policy of never fucking with my paying guests, you see. Sorry."

Letting me go then, turning away. What the hell *was* I expecting? Probably, no more than to not be quite so ridiculously transparent.

In the morning, something a little bit like a double-decker bus came by, bench seats for passengers in the open upper deck, stalls for our ponies down below. Though clean, this bus retained a faint, apparently permanent smell of horseshit, and we went rumbling and whining away over the plains, in the direction of the white Koudloft mountains.

Just before noon, the transporter set us down at a much-used campsite in lightly forested hill country, maybe two hundred kilometers from the boerderij, Gretel's people leading the ponies down the cargo ramp, putting on the saddles for us.

Gretel herself chattered merrily away, unloading the boxes of guns, telling us stuff we'd never remember, no matter how hard we tried, stuff about the forest country here, where the Koperveldt gave way to the foothills of the Koudloft, where the wildlife was still pretty much intact despite centuries of human depredation, though, of course, the vast herds of womfrogs that'd once roamed these plains were *somewhat* reduced . . .

When she handed me my rifle, I felt a familiar spark ignite, flood me with welcome warmth, spacesuit's long-silent voice suddenly alive in my head, whispering specifications, suggesting a range of tools. Stock unclips from the gun mechanism just *so*, you see, and then you unseat the power pack from its plug at the back of the magnetic induction catapult mount . . . look at that. Copper *wire*. Incredible. All right, the trigger mechanism, just a dummy for a somewhat antique solid-state switch *here*, comes off the control box like *this*, then you . . .

Gretel's voice, at my shoulder, in my ear: "You seem rather familiar with our hunting rifles, Mr. du Cheyne."

I looked up and was startled to see everyone else had stopped talking, stopped doing whatever they'd been doing, that I was surrounded by a silent, staring circle, people watching me dissect the silly thing. "Well, no. I never saw one before, but . . ."

Narrowed eyes, a funny sort of grin. "That's a little hard to believe, Mr. du Cheyne. I've seen professional gunsmiths with clumsier hands than yours."

Not very good gunsmiths then. I shrugged. "What can I say? It's just a piece of machinery, I guess. Not very complicated."

A long, measuring, still-suspicious look. "What did you do, back on Earth?"

Back on Earth, back on the Land, *de Aarde* their word for Sol System, because they still thought in terms of *worlds*, these colonials. "Do? Um." Didn't she believe I was just some nice, idle billionaire, touring all the worlds? "Take things apart. Put them back together."

"Some kind of repairman?"

"Sort of."

She said, "Can you put it back together?"

Starting to believe me? Maybe understanding anyone can take something apart until it's just a pile of loose, unfamiliar-looking parts. I looked down at the box lid where I'd laid the dismantled hunting rifle. Sixteen major parts, some wires and plugs, a miscellany of connectors, mostly clips and thumb-screws, simple machinery designed by some kind of idiot.

Too many parts. Too easy to lose.

"I guess so. I . . ."

She sneered, and said, "Well, maybe I'd better . . ." Sort of reaching out now.

I picked up the MIC core, cold metal in my hand like the thunderbolts of Jove, unfinished, not quite ready for the god. Grinned at her, feeling a little wobbly on my feet for some reason, but . . . Sure. This here. That there. Snap. Click. Screw the screws. Clip the clips. Plug in the plugs. Fumble with the stock until you get it lined up . . .

I thumbed the igniter safety switch and felt the gun vibrate, listened to the soft whine of the condenser cascade charging up. "Um. Where are the ammunition clips?"

Gretel Blondinkruis standing there, hands on hips, looking

at me, face expressionless, eyes in shadow. "Over in the green box, Mr. du Cheyne. There's a belt for each of you."

Behind me, I heard Évie whisper in French, presumably to Claude, and the translator echoed in my head: "There's something rather *odd* about that man."

Claude said, *"Pas merdez, Soeuriée . . ."*

I think, after a while, I started to get the hang of riding a live animal, convincing myself that the horse was a *being*, rather than some kind of machine. The problem, more or less, was expecting it to be like a spacesuit or toolbelt, responsive to my needs as soon as they surfaced, anticipating them when it could. I kept trying to *think* of what I wanted it to do, not quite able to grasp what I was supposed to do with a crude control mechanism consisting of leather ropes, connected to a studded cylinder laid across the poor fucker's tongue, of issuing commands with subtle movements of my hands and feet.

The countryside around us was changing slowly, subtly, as we rode down the trail, trail that ever so slowly grew forested, riding through hills that slowly grew steeper, so that, more often than not, we could look out over the tops of the trees in whatever direction happened to be downhill. Outcroppings of rock now, gray slopes of granite, white knife-edges of quartz here and there, poking out of the dirt.

Finally, a long, distant view, out over the rolling hill country, facing southward, Tau Ceti now an orange-gold ball in the west, sliding toward some far horizon. The Koudloft looked a bit like an aerial view of the Himalayas I'd once seen, jumbled white mountains, but mountains with gentle, non-Alpine slopes, mountains more like hills in the nearer distance, rimed with white snow, shrouded in pale mist, mist hanging above dark valleys where . . .

Movement above, catching the corner of my eye. When I turned my head to look, upslope, in the direction of our local hill's bald dome of pale gray stone . . . Something looking down at us, gray-white, motionless against the rusted blue of a late afternoon sky . . . Again, that view from the zoo, that memory, fat white wolfen staring at me out of its cage, whispering a soft *werroowahh* . . . Not words. Not even a little bit like words . . .

Zzzippp!

Sharp, loud-in-my-ear noise right beside me, making me jump, animal vanishing from the hilltop, then a little flash of light, remote *pop!* maybe ten meters from where it had been . . . Some fat Orikhalkisto whose name I'd not bothered to learn, astride his horse beside me, rifle still leveled, grinning. "Almost *got* the little bastard!"

Gretel then, a glint of anger in her eye: "Mr. Pandazides. Unless you want to alert the womfrogs we're following, please keep your rifle in its holster till I tell you to take it out."

He lowered the thing, resentful of the reprimand. "How d'you know there're womfrogs nearby?"

I snickered, looking at Gretel, feeling a crawl in my belly knowing I was, somehow, craving her approval. "Unless I miss my guess, those mossy-looking piles the horses keep stepping over are relatively fresh womfrog dung."

Pandazides gave me a slightly sour look, *asshole* in his eyes.

Gretel smiled. "You continue to surprise me, Mr. du Cheyne."

A couple of hours later, just as Tau Ceti was starting to scrape the horizon, downslope to the west, out beyond the Plains of Brass, we caught up with them.

We were riding along under a darkling sky, streamers of vermilion and red overwhelming the blue-green, purple looming in the east, presaging nightfall. And, quite suddenly, one of Gretel's men, a plump, rat-faced fellow with whispy silver-blond hair and eyes so pale they looked almost white, reined in his horse, nose in the air, hand raised.

Évie said, *"Qu'est-ce que . . . ?"*

Breath of sound from motionless Gretel Blondinkruis, watching her man: "Shh."

Silence.

Well, hell. If there's silence, they're listening for something. Images from old movies, Indian scout with his ear pressed to the ground. *Hear-um pounding hoofbeat in distance, Kemo-Sabe . . .*

The library AI took that as a cue and started cataloging the sounds it was getting, using my ears as a remote pickup. Sure. The wind in the heidensaard trees, a whisper we'd been listening to all day, to the point where it'd become soothing white noise. The faint, periodic *hooop* of a common segmented arthropod, something like a centipede, with the pleasantly illogical name *hoepslang . . .*

Horses breathing, moving, little snorts and clops and belly gurgles no training could suppress. Maybe one horse breathing a little louder than the others. Gretel whispered, "All right. They know we're here. Don't know we've heard them."

Heard *what*, for . . . Oh. People breathing. Horses breathing. Something else breathing. I muttered, "Are you telling us they're *hiding* somewhere nearby?" Image of the thing in the zoo, fingerless, staring down at me. Where, here, would you hide one or more giant elephant-crickets the size of school buses?

She said, "Yes. Keep your voices down. Get off your horses, take your guns."

We made a great deal of noise, despite attempts at caution, the library AI telling me the unaccounted-for breathing had become rather softer, become intermittent. They, whatever, wherever, tightening up with fear, holding their breaths? Shhh. They're coming. Be still . . .

We crept up the rocky path, hardly a trail anymore, though *something* regularly passed this way, Pandazides cursing softly, angrily, as he stepped on one of the mossy piles, breaking through its crisp integument, getting some kind of green-black goo on his boot, liberating a smell like rich licorice, tainted with nutmeg.

Gretel, "Shhh . . ."

Somehow, I was right behind her, walking in her footsteps, my shadow falling on her back. Is it wise to approach whatever from up-sun at dusk? Won't they see us and . . . She stopped and I bumped into her gently, Gretel crouching before me, bent over. She looked over her shoulder, eyes more or less expressionless, motioned with her head for me to creep around her and look.

All right. The underbrush, rather moister here than it had been down on the plains, seemed to cooperate with my attempts at silence, falling to my knees on ground covered with broad, soft, wet, leaf-like things, crawling forward to what appeared to be the edge of a . . .

My head poked out of the underbrush. A rocky gorge, maybe six meters across, more trees on the other side, gloom down below, glint of ruddy evening light on shallow water and glittering, wet eyes. Sensation of my heart clamping, high up, almost in my throat, my own breathing stopped.

Looming below us like shadows, motionless, silent, legs folded close to their bodies, as if crouching. Yes, certainly crouching, making themselves as small as possible. Just the way a spider freezes when you look at it. Crouching just so. Ready to spring, watching you . . . Counting shadows. Six? Maybe seven if that little dark patch over there was a calf.

I watched the nearest womfrog's eyes turn, tracking together, until they were looking up at me. Cold crawling on the back of my neck. Mottled, unearthly eyes looking right into mine. Seeing me. *Knowing* . . .

It sprang, earth crunching loud under its hooves, reaching up the face of the muddy cliff, twin trunks curling forward, black-tentacled hands reaching for my face . . . I recoiled, pulling back into the underbrush, stumbling against Gretel, for Christ's sake I . . . Arm and hand slapping on the ground where I'd been, clutching a basketful of leaves, fingers like so many fat snakes, each one big enough to squeeze me like a movie python, I . . .

Gretel laughing, rising to her feet, the sharp whine of her rifle's condenser drowned by her shout of, *"Tally-HO!"*

Gretel Blondinkruis stepping over me, stepping right on

that big black hand, stamping down hard on boneless fingers, some vast human voice, voice deeper than orchestral bass, bellowing, *"ArArArAr!"*

Gretel like a goddess in denim and khaki, aiming her gun down into the defile, *zzzip-POP!*

Agonized scream, as of a giant's dog, hand snatched away just as Gretel raised her foot and let it go, and *zzzip-POP!* Something thrashing down below. More sounds from the defile, womfrog's voices like so many panicking cellos, *ururur* . . .

Crunch.

Shadow flying over us, vast, black against the sky, shadow with the merits of a flying elephant, the shape of a leaping frog.

Gretel: *"DenArrie* . . . "

One of the others: *zzzip!* Fire forming on the elephant-frog's dark flank, *POP!* Shadow shape tumbling suddenly, seeming to fall down into the trees, hard crackle of breaking trunks and a dense shiver of moving earth.

Others coming forward, my excited comrades-in-arms, Pandazides, with his candyshit-flavored boot stumbling over me, seeming to aim a deliberate kick before stepping to the precipice, people aiming their guns, condensers snarling, and *zzzip! zzzip! zzzip!*

Sound of opera singers howling from the shadowy defile, interrupted by the heavy popping of explosive loads. I got up, stepped forward to stand beside Pandazides, fat man standing with his gun held high, recoiling in his hands as it sizzled away. Flashes of light down below, bullets bursting among the trapped womfrogs, womfrogs boiling around each other, big ones trampling the little ones, screaming, trying to leap away, falling back as the bullets tore them open.

Zzzip. Zzzip.

Pop.

Almost silence down below.

Soft rustling, less and less and . . .

A deep voice, choking on phlegm, whispered, *"Ooooohhhh* . . . "

Then nothing.

Gretel clicked off her rifle, listened to the gentle static susurrus of the condenser discharging back into the battery. "Well, that's it then."

Dark, motionless, hulking shadows down below.

Pandazides, rifle tucked under one arm, turned to grin at me. "Hey, you little shit, did you even—*uk!*"

Eyes bugging out, dropping his rifle in the mud as I planted a quick kick in his crotch. *"Oooh!"* Soft whistle of Pandazides trying to catch his breath, astonished. Grabbed him by the shirtfront, gave him a hard shove, watched as he toppled, flailing, shouting, and fell down into the ravine, falling right on the carcass of the nearest womfrog.

Gretel Blondinkruis said, "God damn. If one of them is still alive . . ."

I shrugged. "Well, that'd be something."

Long stare. Shadow of a grin. "You are a peculiar fellow, du Cheyne. You know?"

All I could do was stare at her and wonder why she would think I might not know I was a little odd.

Somehow, by the time full night had fallen, familiar stars blazing overhead, hard and wintry-looking, we'd divided into two groups, some people gone back down the trail to where we'd left the horses, going with DenArrie to unpack the tents, start the cooking fires, visible now as a ruddy glow through the trees, generally set up the camp. I stayed with the second group, standing on the rim of the defile to watch the butchering of the womfrogs.

Down in the little valley, hardly more than a giant gully I suppose, Gretel Blondinkruis gathered her tourists around her, taking out her big *boeie* knife, chromed blade glinting like a mirror by the shifting light of twin moons Wan and Hope, showing them what to do, Mr. Pandazides an attentive pupil, watching her closely, keeping his back to me.

I could feel a smile tugging at my lips as I watched him, remembered the way he rose, hunched over, clutching his genitals with both hands, angry, blustering, staggering up the hill, slipping and falling on his face in the mud.

Claude and Évie were standing on the edge of the little cliff beside me now, preferring, I suppose, to watch, clean and dry, rather than go down and participate in the . . . meat cutting. Talking to each other in French:

She said, "This is a disgusting business. I wish we hadn't come."

A sigh from Claude. "I suppose so. These are disgusting people."

Évie: "Especially that wretched Mr. Pandazides. I'm glad Mr. du Cheyne did what he did."

A nod from her slim, handsome dark husband: "I too. Nice to see such an unpleasant bully get what's coming to him." Turning to me then, smiling, in heavily accented Greek he said, "He thought you were a coward, this Pandazides. The look on face when you threw him down the hill . . ."

The fear in his eyes when he looked back up the hill, saw me waiting with my hands dangling most capably by my sides, wishing to kill me, knowing what would happen to him if he tried. I shrugged, looking at the admiration evident in pretty little Évie's dark eyes, and said, "It's a common enough mistake."

More common than I care to remember. This du Cheyne, you see, unresponsive and . . . afraid? It must seem so. Seem so until they act, until I . . . react. It makes them angry, but . . . courage is a figment of men's imaginations. Most bold men are merely unafraid, which is a different thing entirely.

Évie, astonished: "You speak French?"

I said, "So it seems."

Small, slim Claude, suddenly looking at his wife, nervous, seeing her look at me. What is he thinking? Is he wondering if she got wet between her legs, watching me kick Pandazides' nuts and then throw him down the hill? Is he imagining her in my tent tonight, invisible in the darkness, sighing to me, sighing in French, *Oh. Oh, Gaetan. Que j'aime le soleil et les belle fleures . . .*

I grinned and shook my head, trying not to imagine what

poor little Claude was making of my smile. The truth? Somewhere inside of me, on the other side of the adolescent idiot who still dreams of women throwing themselves upon him, there dwells a still larger idiot, making fun of the whole damned business.

Below, Gretel's knife slid down the length of a dead womfrog's belly, making a long, soft *wheep!* like an old-fashioned metal zipper, hairy, leathery hide parting like magic, glistening yellow fat showing through. Stroke. Stroke. Stroke again. The fat and muscles and fascia burst open and the womfrog's guts came tumbling out, along with an overpowering stench of hot apple pie.

Évie said, *"Mon dieu, Claude!"*

Back at the campsite, I sat in a folding chair in front of my little tent, while the others milled around the fires, helping with camp chores, watching, smelling, laughing and talking, while bits of womfrog cooked, sliced steaks frying in little plastic pans, chunks of leg, haunches, calves, roasting as they turned on the mechanic spit this useful Mr. DenArrie had put together. Amazing what you can carry in the saddlebags of horses. Even with Green Heaven's antique technology, camping equipment folds up small.

Gretel standing over there, leaning against a tree, arms folded across her breast, watching everything at once, more the goddess than ever. When I look at her, all I see is the angular, yet rounded outline of her classic shape, tilt of hips, length of thigh . . .

Mr. Pandazides sitting on a big rock away from the fire, still sullen.

Claude and Évie standing together, small and slim, hardly more than shadowy outlines by the fire, he with his arm around her shoulders, she leaning in close. *Mate-guarding behavior,* I remember the phrase from some old book.

Mr. DenArrie tending the fire, laughing and talking now, the center of tourist attention, it seems. Maybe he doesn't follow quite the same rule as his boss. Maybe the women will come to his tent tonight and sigh and sigh and . . .

That little plump woman who'd seemed to be eying me earlier in the evening, the one whose name I can't quite remember, hanging around DenArrie now . . . Abrupt memory of her riding on the bus, sitting with Mr. Pandazides, the two of them chatting merrily away.

Well. Sorry, old boy. Sorry I threw your ass down the hill and made you look like such a putz. No pussy for you tonight, eh?

I found myself imagining the two of them together, perhaps for the first time, plump woman stripped down, confronting him with her nakedness, Mr. Pandazides with an erection perhaps, confronting her with his. There's always a tension in that moment, when you watch them looking at you, paying so much attention to their reaction you hardly have time to appreciate what you're seeing.

Brief memory of Jayanne in my bedroom on Mars, that first night we were together, standing there naked in the half light, dorm room in gloom, campus outdoor lighting shining through the blinds, painting us with little yellow-white stripes. Jayanne's dark eyes, not quite in shadow, obviously afraid. Afraid of what? I couldn't imagine.

I'd looked at her then, taking my eyes off her face, looking at her small, round breasts with their prominent pink nipples, gently domed belly telling me she wasn't getting quite enough exercise, but then no one did at Syrtis Major, my own belly rather slack in those days, because we were all so busy studying and . . .

Long, lingering look at the rust-colored hair of her crotch, eyes trying to penetrate the deeper shadows, wishing I could make her lie back on the bed, turn on the little reading lamp, push her legs apart, lean in close and look and touch, probe with my fingers, smell her and taste her until I knew her as well as a man can ever know . . .

When I'd looked back at her face, what I saw there was stark terror.

I'd had the wit then to say, Oh Jayanne. You are so incredibly . . . lovely.

Jayanne closing her eyes, swallowing softly, breath exhaled gently, an astonishing sigh of relief.

Memory of our little life together, relationship passing in a fleeting kaleidoscope that seemed over in an instant, resolving on the image of our last night together, memories collapsing in on one another like so many imploding stars.

The day before, making my decision with a feeling of . . . horror. Well, yes, Jayanne. I will marry you.

Jayanne's eyes on me, full of doubt.

Me, wandering around for the better part of a Martian sol, feeling lost, full of regret, imagining myself husband and father and . . . oh, you know the rest. That *trapped* story as old as humankind. This is the way that the world ends, etc. I'm sure I did more than my share of whimpering, that day.

And the next night?

Jayanne in my bed, naked, but strangely distant, avoiding my touch.

Come on. What's wrong?

Urging myself on her, already erect, ready to just climb in the saddle and get it the hell over with. Damn it, Jayanne . . .

Then, eyes on me, eyes in shadow, full of . . . something, she'd said, Well, Gaetan, I went to the clinic this afternoon and got rid of it.

What? *Why?* I thought we agreed . . .

Already, in that moment, even as I spoke my lines, I could feel a terrible flood of *relief.*

She'd shrugged and said, I just . . . don't think you're what I want for a husband. Afterward, she went away, and I never saw her again.

Didn't really mind, because I hadn't really even *liked* her, you see, until a couple of days later, when I woke up one morning, alone.

I looked away from the leaping shapes inside the cooking fire, looked across the camp clearing at the tree where Gretel

Blondinkruis had been standing. Not there anymore. Pandazides still on his rock, brooding into the fire. Hell, we must have looked like twins. Claude and Évie. DenArrie and the little plump woman . . .

I got up and walked off, away into the dark.

Up near the top of a steep hill, I found an exposed ledge, dry gray rock, and sat looking out across the nighttime world, cool wind blowing over me, hugging my knees to my chest. The stars filled the black sky, so bright and hard and untwinkling they seemed close, seemed to bring the sky down to hang right overhead, Milky Way a river of remote golden dust beyond the stars, Hope long set, Wan a pale crescent hanging over the northern horizon, seeming much larger than I knew it really was.

After a while I lay back, staring upward at nothing in particular.

Why the hell am I here?

Is it really because I have nowhere else to go?

I'm not so stupid that I imagined my childhood dreams had any validity. They never do. Maybe I just wanted to *see*. But it's so stupid to just sit up here, crushed by a shallow, pointless malaise, wishing for . . . wishing for . . . Hell, that thing in your pants is getting hard again. You know what *it* wants. You know how to get what it wants. Go back down to Orikhalkos, where money will buy whatever there is to be had.

Then get aboard your ship and go back home.

Sell that asinine conglomeration of metal, plastic and dreams.

Three million livres?

Christ Almighty, that will buy six thousand nights with the likes of Camilla Seldane.

I tried to picture that.

Is *that* what you want, Gaetan du Cheyne?

Why the fuck don't you *know*?

Just then, Gretel's voice said, "Nice night, hm?"

I didn't jump, didn't react, no pang in my chest or anything like that. It felt almost as though I'd been expecting her. Maybe those old dreams run deeper than I know.

She stood still for a while, facing away from me, looking out over the dark, empty lowlands, down into the Plains of Brass, while I stared, idiotically, at the shape of her rear end, wishing and wishing, saying nothing, fantasies growing more foolish with every passing second. The machines are telepathic. Why aren't we?

The voice of the spacesuit whispered, I'd help you if I could, but she's not logged on anywhere that I can detect.

I had a momentary spark of wondering just what the AIs made of all my obsessions and useless dreams. They've never said, merely done what they could, with the vidnet, negotiating with other people's AIs, with . . . Brief memory of Rua Mater, always logged on, always sunk in dreams of her own. They could've . . . done something there. I wonder why not. I . . .

Gretel turned and looked down at me, smiled, turned again and sank down gracefully beside me. You know she must be able to see you've got a nice little erection bulging down there in the front of your pants. Does she expect me to . . . do something? Or should I just wait and see?

Silence in my head.

Wait and see, of course.

She said, "What's it like out there?"

Out there? Gretel Blondinkruis gesturing at the sky.

I fumbled for words, wanting to tell her how it *felt*, but nothing would come. What then? Tell her lies? Make something up? Recount whatever I could remember from all the viddies I'd seen, all those old movies and books and . . . I said, "It's different."

Silence. Then a sigh, almost like the women sighing in my dreams. *"Different."*

I felt my heart go bump in my chest, suddenly understanding what I'd heard in her voice. This is, I told myself, an open door. Rouse yourself. Walk on through. I actually had my mouth open, formulating lies, getting my story ready. But there was something else in there as well, something reluctant, holding me back. A little voice, so far away and weak: If you buy her with the coin of your dreams, then she's *bought.* Just that and nothing more. And you *know* how that feels.

Sure do.

Why the hell does it matter?

Then it was too late. Gretel Blondinkruis got to her feet, dusting off her shapely backside, looking down at me, smiling. She said, "I'd like to get away from Green Heaven someday. Get out there and . . . see what there is to see."

An invitation. For God's sake, make up your mind, asshole. Say something. Tell her who and what you are. Tell her about *Random Walk.* Tell her . . . tell her you'll take her to the stars! She'll make a deal with you. You know she will.

Wasn't that one of your oldest dreams, recurring in endless variation? The dream in which you had a little ship, sometimes a sailboat with which to cruise the South Seas. Sometimes a systemic yacht, cruising the moons of Saturn, the Piazzi, the Kuiper, the Oort, the . . .

Always. There was always a girl. A pretty girl. An innocent girl. A girl who was willing to . . . do whatever you wanted. Gaetan. Oh, Gaetan . . .

Idiot.

She said, "Well. We'd better get back down to camp. Mr. DenArrie will start to worry."

8

Somehow, I got through the rest of the trip, simply by not thinking about it anymore perhaps, and went on back to my little hotel room in Orikhalkos, where I could watch the sun rise over a squalid cityscape through the convenient frame of my sliding glass door.

One night, I found something interesting to do. I'd been exploring down by the dockyards, Orikhalkos being a coastal city, and really having a pretty good time. There are probably still ships on the Earth's oceans, but nothing like these. Big ships of steel and composite, some of them propelled by giant versions of the automobiles' gas turbine drives, others running on nuclear-thermal steam.

Something I hadn't noticed before was that all the Compact Cities of Green Heaven, with the sole exception of Vapaa, a small city at the headwaters of the Somber River, lie on the ocean. Over the centuries a sea trade has grown up, sea trade, tourism, island hopping in the remote northern hemisphere— I'd heard of Les Iles des Français, but there were others . . .

I found myself standing in the darkness atop a narrow caisson wall, my back toward the quietly slopping seawater, looking down into a concrete drydock lit by long, dim strings of

145

electric bulbs. The ship, resting on heavy keelblocks, was a dark shadow, rounded, looking at first glance like some old-fashioned spaceship. I could imagine I was on Earth, maybe five hundred years ago, in the days before interstellar travel perhaps. Down there, just maybe, those men and women were repairing a freighter that would one day be bound for red Mars, or faraway Jupiter, where the first volatiles plants were even now being set up.

I could see them down there, little mannequin shadows moving about, backlit by the blue flare of carbon arc torches. Hear distant voices, snatches of Greek words, too indistinct for the translator to pick up. Probably talking about the work. *Careful with that coverplate, Basil. Line's still pressurized and . . .*

I walked away into the darkness, hungry, and went to a little restaurant not far from the dockyard, sat and ate among tired workingmen and -women, and thought about it. I could stay here. I could be part of this.

Or go somewhere else. Somewhere where I'm needed. Hell, there are starship yards on Kent. I could do my familiar work, work among funny double shadows cast by Alpha Centauri's twin suns, hanging, brilliant, in the sky. That'd be interesting, wouldn't it?

The library said, In time, the FTL ships will come.

So they will. And I'm trained for that work as well. Should I just go home then? What's going to happen, when people can get out among the worlds and come home again, to the same world, all the same people that they left behind? Will it make a difference?

I finished my meal, got up and walked on in the darkness, cutting through a very dark, empty-looking part of town, on my way back to the brightly lit city center, glow on the sky beckoning me back to my hotel. Found myself standing in front of a building that looked like a warehouse.

People coming here, by ones and twos and little groups. Drunken men and women. Laughing men and women. The same sort of men and women who'd decorated my other life.

The same sort of men and women I'd left behind me at the midnight diner, at the graveyard shift of the dockyard.

Inside, the place was brightly lit and full of people, concentric tiers of level floors descending to a dirt-lined pit, ceiling high overhead not domed, but rather unfinished girders from which electric lights hung in a mess of wiring. More or less, I thought, like the commonplace small sports stadia you see on Luna, places where you see *sumo* and *pelota*, or maybe the little illicit *pugildromes* of Mars.

Something like that here? Maybe, though the tiered floors were lined with café tables rather than inward-facing seats. Dinner theater in the round? Maybe I can get a nice dessert here while I watch Aristophanes in the quasi original. Something about the crowd . . . unlikely as all hell these boys and girls are here to see *Frogs*.

I walked down a narrow flight of stairs, cutting through tier-arcs to the lowest level, standing at a brass rail, looking down onto the dirt-covered . . . well, *ring* is the only appropriate word. Not really common dirt either. More a nice, absorbent sand, like high-class kitty litter. Little doors in the side wall, low and wide. A man would have to stoop to get out, maybe even crawl.

"Kali mera!"

Soft female voice at my elbow, making me jump a bit, making me look. She was small and thin, dark eyes set in a dark, narrow face framed with shiny black curls that fell almost to her shoulders. Narrow smile, no more than a rim of even white teeth, smiling up at me.

I smiled back. "Is it morning already?"

She started to glance at some kind of chronometer strapped to her wrist—yet another reminder of just how antique this world, remote in time and space, could be—when a tall, heavy-set, beady-eyed man standing behind her said, "Sunup's in just under two hours . . ."

Short nights here.

He held out his hand, took mine firmly, and said, "My name's Telektasos . . ." translator whispering softly under the words, This may be a nickname, *telektasos* means "dilator" in Greek. "My co-workers at Porphyrion Iron Works, Melîna . . ." a nod at the small woman who'd spoken to me first, then, putting his arm around a short, broad woman at his side, "and my girl-friend, Mira."

Melîna said, "We noticed you standing on the caisson wall at Porphyrion, just as we were coming off shift."

"And again later, eating by yourself at Spartákili," said Mira.

Telektasos motioned with a broad hand. "We've got a table here. Want to join us?" Grinning, Mira elbowing him in the ribs, translator speculating that he'd made some crude double entendre or another.

I said, "Uh. Sure."

I told them my name and we sat down. pulling our chairs around to one side of the table, so we were all facing the dirt arena, Mira sitting close beside Telektasos, Melîna squeezing in next to me, her thigh pressed against mine. I could feel my heart starting to go thump in my chest, a little prickle of antic-ipation in the back of my neck, but . . . A soft sigh, my own, well concealed. Starting to come out the other side, are we? Maybe so.

Melîna said, "Du Cheyne . . . You don't look French. More like some kind of Koromalisto. They all have that pale skin and dark hair. And your eyes are such a light brown they're almost yellow."

Right. Especially in certain kinds of spectrum-limited artifi-cial lighting, I look like some kind of spook. People have been telling me that all my life.

Mira said, "We could tell you were some kind of foreigner. The way you were eating."

"What do you mean?"

Melîna said, "Keeping your fork in your left hand and knife in your right like that. People here only do that to cut up meat, then we put down the knife and hold the fork in our right hands."

The waiter came then and took our orders, drinks only just now, and I was pleased to realize I'd been here long enough that I knew the brand names of several rather nasty beers. I ordered a *retsîna* instead.

Telektasos, once the drinks had been served and sipped: "So, where *are* you from, Gaetan?" His pronunciation made it sound a bit like *hhay-tawn.*

I sat blinking for a moment, wondering what to tell them, even where to begin, as if it were complicated, but . . . why not the simple truth? So I said it.

Moment of silence, then Melîna leaned in close, looking right into my face, and said, "Earth? You mean, *the* Earth?" Wide-eyed astonishment, as if I'd said I was from some other galaxy or something.

Then Telektasos, voice rather gruff, said, "So. What is it you do for a living, Mr. du Cheyne?"

Mr. du Cheyne. Right. "I'm a mechanic. Same as you."

"Not the same as me, brother. Hell, I can't even afford a vacation in the islands!"

And here I am, come all the way from some glittery paradise among the stars, huh? I said, "Well, a spaceship mechanic. I'm sort of retired."

Melîna whispered, "*Spaceship* mechanic . . ."

Mira: "When the day comes that I'm good enough, if it comes, I'd like to work at the Géricault-Boeing Aerospaceworks on Malakandra . . ." translator reminding me Malakandra was the next planet out, Tau Ceti 3, an abiotic juvenile terrestrial icehouse of a world, where, apparently, the Cetian in-system spacecraft were built.

Telektasos said, "I guess every technical worker has that dream." A long look, then, "Why the hell are you *here*, Gaetan?"

Good, back to Gaetan again. No pause this time, no dissembling thoughts. This is . . . yet another open door. So I told them a little bit about those childhood dreams, watched their interested, understanding eyes. And I said, "I was . . . thinking of settling here."

Melîna said, "But you've got a round-trip ticket home, don't you?"

I hadn't gotten around to telling them the rest of it yet, so . . .
I said, "Sure." Leave it at that. Plenty of time later to . . .

Telektasos said, "You show up down at the Porphyrion personnel office, they'll probably put you in charge."

"Or," said Mira with palpable envy, "you could go right to
Malakandra." As if I could elect to ascend straight to God in
Heaven, no Purgatory in between. What will these people think
when the *real* starships come?

The waiter came again and took our food orders and, as we
ate and talked, the lights slowly went down, all but the bright
lights lining the inner walls of the little dirt arena, which I'd
almost forgotten. Now, in the gloom, Melîna was tight against
my side. I could hear her soft breathing, feel the in-out movement of her ribs, sense the rapid beating of her heart.

Well. That being so, doubtless my own pounding pulse . . .

My left hand, done with its fork-wielding duties, had slipped
off the table, was resting on Melîna's thigh. Not bare skin. She
was dressed in a short, pleated black skirt over some kind of
opaque hose, tights maybe, possibly even a body stocking. Is this
what these women wear to work?

Telektasos, leaning back in his chair, had his arm round
Mira's shoulders now, was talking almost nonstop, mostly about
the world, his work, and the place of one in the other. A commonplace memory, these rough-hewn philosophers of hard
work. I've known a thousand like him.

Melîna now was leaning against me, head almost down on
my shoulder, silent, her right hand having slipped around the
back of my waist, resting on my opposite hip, thumb tucked
through one of my belt loops. All right, I know this game, and if
what's happening down in my pants is any indication, perhaps
I'm ready to resume . . . all the rest of my life, at last.

Cold wash of blessèd relief, a little bit like religious ecstasy.
Just maybe, I haven't made a mistake after all. I let my hand
slide up her thigh, under her skirt, and felt her other leg move
out of my way. Smooth muscle under tight hose. That nice ten-
don, like a guideway, leading my fingers in to the flat place

between her legs. Melîna scrunching down a little bit in her chair, so she could rock her hips back . . .

I could just feel the outline of her vulva, a soft indentation, a place of slightly greater heat, through the stretchy cloth. Her face rolled against my shoulder, and I could feel her nip at me, a tiny bite of small teeth through my shirt.

Well then. I let my hand go up on her belly and found the waistband of her tights, felt a twist of relief that it wasn't a body stocking after all, pulled it down a bit and put my fingers inside. Soft skin, smooth over tight muscle, short, crisp, dense hair, wiry, like the hair of a man's beard. Fingers running down into the hair, smoothing it apart, parting a soft double-dome of flesh, finding her already wet and slick and . . .

She grabbed at my hand, pulled it away, pulled it out of her pants, shoving it back between her legs as she smoothed her skirt into place, whispering in my ear, ". . . *é khrístoi*, Gaetan, take it easy! We'll go to my apartment later on."

Heart pounding horribly in my chest, like someone giving me CPR. I think I must have been about two minutes from throwing her on the floor and . . . She slid her hand between my legs, palpating the front of my pants, encircling what she found there with thumb and forefinger, giving it a little shake, a soft giggle, and, ". . .if you *can* wait! Anyway, the show's about to start . . ."

As if on her cue a spotlight blinked on, shining not down into the pit but onto a man standing on a little platform above its rim, short, fat guy in what looked like a twentieth-century tuxedo, outfit seen in so many of those reconstituted old movies. Shouting now, "Ladies and gentlemen, for our first contest . . ." Stirring throughout the big room, a scraping of chair legs as people turned away from their tables, turning to face the pit. The man said, "Prince Juggernaut of Hemmelmans, a white, victor by kill in seven contests, by withdrawal in fourteen, never defeated, never withdrawn . . ."

Mira said, "Well. That's a pretty high card for a first event."

The man said, ". . .versus Terror Incendiary of Koelhartz, a green, victor by withdrawal in three prior contests."

Telektasos said, "Oh, for Christ's sake! Greens are no fucking good!"

Not a clue. All right, boxers seldom kill one another. Even in the old days, back when . . . memories of ancient Rome, of Byzantium. These are *Greeks* after all. Greens and whites and the chariot races, gladiatorial schools for the blues and reds . . . Mira said, "I don't see why the hell they just don't pit whites against whites and leave it at that."

Melîna: "You know, if they accidentally got two from the same tribe, they'd be able to talk to each other, maybe cook something up and . . ."

Talk to each other?

Telektasos: "Well, grays are pretty good too, and there're plenty of them over in the western Opveldt. If they'd just fucking forget about the God-damned greens and reds, not to mention those useless, fat fucking browns . . ."

One of the doors down below slid open with a rough, raw scrape of wood on stone, and the crowd grew silent, something of a hush falling over the chamber. I think I leaned forward in my seat, trying to peer down through the bright light, penetrate the darkness beyond the door frame.

A . . . glimmer? As of light from two big eyes. It came out then, very slowly, craning its neck, looking around, obviously frightened, and Telektasos said, "Look at that, for Christ's sake." Withering contempt in his voice.

Melîna said, "Well, the second and third events will be better." Hand still resting between my legs, not far from my balls, warm on the inside of my thigh.

The thing down below was fully exposed now, slinking along the base of the wall, looking up at us, pressed belly-down in the sand, as if trying to make itself look small. Trying to hide, I thought. Other than that murky green fur, it wasn't very different from the wolfen I'd seen in the zoo back on Earth. Or the ones I'd glimpsed in the distance earlier this week.

So. Green wolfen. Memories of my childhood vidnet dramas, memories of my dreams, telling me this was a denizen of the dank Mistibos Forest, beyond the Opveldt in the area just south of the equator, where the Somber River flowed down to the sea.

Up and down the aisles between the tables now, men and women were walking back and forth, "Bets? Place your bets! Two minutes, ladies and gentlemen! Place your bets!"

Two minutes to what?

Don't have to be a genius to figure that out.

In all sorts of old dramas, you see things like this. Read about it in old books. Maybe it makes you mad if you're the sort who . . . Something very different when it's *real* I guess. I . . .

The other door slid open.

Melîna breathing, "Now . . ."

When the white wolfen sprang out onto the sand, huge, fur bristling, mottled orange eyes seeming to bug from its head, I felt Melîna tense with excitement. And, down below, the green seemed to shrivel, cowering, looking around.

Nowhere to go, its own door long closed, door through which the white had come already scraping shut. Faraway throb of a growl from the white. Then a whisper from the green, high and soft, *ah-werroowaahhhh* . . . trailing away to nothing.

White wolfen motionless, looking at the green. It seems as if they're looking into each other's eyes, but, with that mottled effect, no visible pupil, no differentiated iris. The white grunted, once, twice, each an abrupt sound, green flinching with each . . . word?

Telektasos said, "Oh, hell . . ."

And the white sprang, one, two, three bounds, all the way across the ring, sand flying from beneath its heavy paws, green jerking, trying to get out of the way . . . Useless. Green flattened under the white's weight, crying out, I could imagine a frightened man's voice, wailing, *Oh, God! Oh, God!* If you listen closely, you can hear that piquant horror.

Remember watching all those old films? Nature, the narrator says, red in tooth and claw. The lion grabs the antelope in its jaws, antelope's eyes wide, stark with terror, bleating with agony as long white fangs stab inward and the blood begins to flow. Surely. Surely divine Providence has seen fit to make it, somehow, painless, somehow . . . Or does the antelope experience all the horrors of hell in its last long, terrible moments?

Ask this green wolfen now, wolfen torn open, sprawling in the sand, internal organs spilling out through that vast rip, spilling out on the sand in a wet, yellow-brown stain . . . Green wolfen looking up at us, gasping, *Ohhhh, ohhhh . . .* Soft words, full of dread.

Then the white wolfen stood over the dead green, silent, sitting on its haunches, one big paw on its victim's motionless head, looking up at us, looking round the room, as if . . . The announcer said, "Prince Juggernaut of Hemmelmans, victor by a kill!"

When its door slid open, the white walked away into the darkness without a backward glance. When the green's door slid open, three stooping men came out, two of them dragging Terror Incendiary of Koelhartz away, the third setting to work, smoothing the bloody sand with a short rake, turning it over, covering up the mess.

Mira said, "Well! That was better than I expected!"

Telektasos: "Yeah, there's something to be said for a quick kill."

Melîna: "What did you think, Gaetan? You ever see anything like that before?"

Slowly, "I went to a bullfight on Mars once. It was . . . a little like this." No sense in telling them it was a Mexican format contest, where they don't kill the bull.

Mira said, "That so? Isn't a bull some kind of cow? Doesn't seem like that'd be very . . ."

I reached down and pulled Melîna's hand out of my lap, stood up slowly. She looked up at me, puzzled. "Something the matter?"

I said, "I've got to pee. I'll right back."

A sharp grin. "Want me to order you another drink?"

"Sure."

I walked away, headed for where I thought the rest rooms would be. Walked away into the gloom and right out the door.

Outside in the cold, I stood leaning against the metal wall of the building, feeling my heart, still pounding in my chest. For Christ's sake, they're just *animals!* What difference does it make? Get back in there and watch the rest of it. Let her take you home. Remember the way her pussy felt under your fingers? Remember how *ready* you were?

Hand on my chest now, not damp anymore of course, but . . . that lingering, residual scent of . . . I got off the wall, made one step back toward the door, then turned and ran, away into the darkness.

I found myself, after what seemed like no more time than it takes a star to move its own breadth, walking up a familiar-looking street, coming into an area of brightly lit stores, restaurants and shops and whatnot. Familiar, perhaps, because I'm . . . wandering around in a finite space, night after night after . . .

I stopped in front of a barroom, looking in through a poorly cleaned window, clear glass rimed with white grime. Men and women at the bar, sucking from bottles of beer, men and women at tables, pouring from bottles, drinking from glasses, laughing, talking . . .

I could use a drink.

Go on in.

Turning away then, stomach churning briefly. Too many dinners, drinks, too much . . . Face covered with cold, unpleasant sweat, a sweat as of sickness. Go on home. No, not home. Go on back to your hotel room, at least. Go to sleep. In the morning you'll . . . think of something.

Walking on down the street a ways, heading out of the light, back into the darkness. You know the way. At the end of the street, on the corner, opposite a big parking lot full of dark, empty ground cars, three women stood together, talking, idle, merely . . .

The women saw me coming, looked at each other, nonverbal communication in swift cascade. Right. Yours. See ya. The designated hitter came sauntering over, smiling, making those come-fuck-me moves, hips rolling just so, pelvis tilted, back arched, tits sticking out, cloth of her bandeau stretched tight, long legs, long hair, dark and oh-so-hollow eyes . . .

Somewhere in my head a little voice, my own almost certainly, screamed, What the fuck is *wrong* with you?

She came up to me, still smiling, teeth fine and white, eyes a wet glitter under her brows, not hesitant at all. Reached up and touched the side of my face, as if . . . jerked her hand away just a bit, feeling my cold sweat on her fingertips. Small trace of frown then. A problem here?

She said, "You okay, brother?"

I nodded slowly, looking down at her. Something of a scent in the air, overpowering the complex street smell. Pheromones? Something like that. I nodded slowly, feeling an urge to just . . .

Her smile came back, a little more tentative than before. She reached up again, smoothing her hand across my cheek, accepting the sweat, no sign of revulsion. What would you expect? Think of what she *does*, idiot. Her hand went on, fingers running up into my dank hair, stopping when they came to the barrette.

"What's this?" Honestly puzzled.

Well, of course. Men don't wear jewelry here. I thought of just telling her I was a fag, preparatory to running for it again, feeling like a still bigger idiot . . . the translator told me it'd have to use a term that meant, roughly, a boy who likes to have sexual intercourse with the assholes of tender, young piglets and . . . Great. Forget it.

I shrugged, and said, "How much?"

She rolled her eyes, definite sense of *good grief* conveyed. "Half-drack."

Half a *drakhma.* At the apparent exchange rate generated by my letter of credit, we're talking two seconds of prime-time vid-net service charge here. "Okay."

A little look of surprise, as if she'd expected me to haggle, then she took my big, hard, blunt-fingered hand in her small, warm, soft one, led me away toward the mouth of a black alley-way. Pang of fear, of unease, at least? Nonsense. You've got that little gun in your pocket, remember?

Then we were standing in the greater darkness, in the deep shadow behind one of those big metal Dumpsters that seemed to inhabit every alley in Orikhalkos. As my eyes adjusted, I saw first the white of her teeth, then the glint of her eyes, finally the rest of her coming out in fine shades of gray.

She said, "Do you mind doing it standing up?" A gesture round, at the filthy pavement, where who knows what had been spilled and never cleaned up.

I shrugged. "Fine."

She leaned back against the wall, her chosen patch of bricks perhaps, cleaned by daylight, planting her feet just so, pretty far apart, knees slightly bent, pelvis cocked, weight mainly on her shoulders, position assumed in a single, fluid, practiced movement. Pulled up the front of her little skirt, no underwear, no hair, pussy shaved clean. There you go, pal.

Not bad-looking, even in this pale gray light, with her arms and legs, face and hair and everything vanished from my consciousness for a moment, just that flat white belly, shining by starlight, little shadows cast by the edges of her hip bones, raised ever so slightly above the surrounding topography, the dim crease of her vulval slit. I . . .

Well. I kneeled in front of her, looking up into the shadows of her face. No expression there. "Do you . . . mind?"

Voice neutral: "Help yourself."

Christ. How the hell could she *mind*? Think of what her life must be like, peckerhead. I leaned forward, eyes closed, slid my face across her smooth belly. Stuck out my tongue and tasted her, tasted a tang I imagined must be other men, soft, slick on my cheeks, hardly a hint of stubble.

Then I was standing again, standing close to her, my pants undone, fallen a bit, just enough, my hands behind and under her, little round ass cheeks cupped in my palms, lifting her up, prick pointing in more or less the right direction, probing, probing . . .

That faint, familiar dread.

What if . . .

I felt her take it in her hand, aim it just so, guiding my thrust.

I slid in, into the hot and wet of her, felt the muscular stricture of her introitus go past the end of my glans, down along less sensitive but more . . . *feeling* skin, down as far as it could go.

Felt her settle herself just right against the wall, feet off the ground, knees beyond the sides of my thighs, feet down on the backs of my legs, head tucked up onto my shoulder. Whisper in my ear, hardly audible, like a sigh, *"Okay, brother."*

OK.

It's OK.

Really it is.

I withdrew, as far as I could without falling out of her, hearing my own faint gasp at the sensation. Hasn't been that long. Hasn't been that long. Remember Camilla? Remember what that was like?

But it seems like forever.

Seems like . . .

I slid back into her, out again without pausing, then in, finding an old, old, too-familiar rhythm, nameless street girl snugged up against me, smooth face pressed tight and warm against my cheek, my face in her hair, which was full of some flowery sent, lilac maybe, or lavender.

Just now, I want this to go on forever.

Just now, I feel like I'm in love.

Feel like this . . . woman . . . I . . .

Felt my dick suddenly swell, felt the girl clutch me tight with her arms and cunt, slid in as far as I could go, one hard crackle of regret as I felt a surge that . . . what do they call it in all the silly books? *Rising tide of inevitability.* That's it.

Felt the ring of muscle at the base of my pelvis clench hard, once, twice, like dry heaves when you're sick and empty, then the first thready sear of semen on its way, then . . .

Hollow ache of pleasure, deep in my belly.

Warmth in my face, a flush of warmth, not at all like a blush, brief, tingling thrill running right up my spine, up into the base of my skull, flooding my eyes with . . . I relaxed against her, pressing her against the wall, feeling a flood of relief, a slight scald of nausea. That's it then.

The girl took her legs from around me, rocked her pelvis back so my wet, quickly softening dick popped out, flapping against the top of my thigh, smoothed down the front of her skirt, looking up at me, watching as I pulled up my pants, buttoning, zipping, buckling . . .

Well.

I turned and started to walk away . . .

Angry voice: "Wait!"

Turning back.

Angry girl, hand outstretched, palm up. "Asshole!"

Oh. I took out my money clip, handed her a thousand-*drakhmai* note, and walked away, quickly, before she could react.

I awoke the next morning, sprawled naked on my hotel room bed in a warm pool of butter yellow sunshine, looking down the length of my torso at a nice, fat, solidly erect prick, and grinning. Hell, maybe I'd been grinning in my sleep too.

Whisper from an inner voice, Is that all it takes, you little shit?

A quick glance at the table. The transceiver barrette was lying there, next to the dusty television remote, so the voice was only me. I reached down and curled my fingers around it, warm palm on warm dick, Cetian infrared a pleasure on my face, and wondered. *Is* it?

Maybe.

Anything *really* wrong with that?

Maybe.

But all I wanted to do, just then, was send for that nameless, faceless, neatly shaven whore, throw her naked in my bed, lay her across this wonderful patch of sunshine and screw the hell out of her, until I'd forgotten all about the last few weeks, the months before that, then all the years, all the . . .

Forget about Rua Mater, lost in dreams. Forget about Leah Strachan, about Garstang, about Jayanne and her discarded baby. Forget about Lara Nobisky, who'd been mine only in the short-lived realization of a boy's fantasy, even before concerned adults had had her . . . cured.

The head of my dick was turning purple, skin shiny and tight, from the strangle hold I had on it.

I let the damned thing go and lay back on the bed, hands behind my head, staring at the ceiling, and thought, There aren't many people who would not laugh at me now, laugh at the notion that a man's spirit could be so elevated by a paid-for fuck that lasted all of two minutes. Maybe it doesn't matter.

After a while, when answers, the will to action, failed to emerge from the ceiling, I picked up the remote and hit the power button. There was a sizzle of static, a smell of dusty burning, and the instrument in the corner came to life, shimmering color image leaning forward out of the glass screen. Great. Three-hundred-year-old holodeck technology . . .

Fuck. I sat up in bed, heart pounding, staring at a view from the spaceport, view of the landing field, in the middle of which sat the silver disk of *Random Walk*, surrounded by what looked like armed, uniformed police, hatches open, people coming down the ramp, while a deep-voiced announcer babbled in rapid, fluid Greek from which I could pick out nothing but the few conjunctions I'd subconsciously memorized.

I grabbed for the barrette and shoved it into my hair. Almost panicky: Ship? Suit? What the hell . . . The library AI's voice whispered, Here, Gaetan. All is well.

Well? What the hell are those people doing in my ship? Jesus fucking . . .

The suit's voice whispered, No one's in here, Gaetan. *Ran-*

dom Walk is secure. A second FTL ship landed during the night—we've been waiting for you to log on.

Library: We were seriously considering attempting to ring your hotel phone through the InfoNet gateway we've established. It's late and we were worried.

Announcer's voice, translated now: ". . .this ship, *Torus X-2*, which carried a special legation from Orikhalkos to Earth several months ago, under the corporate aegis of Berens-Vataro Enterprises, has now returned that delegation. As we mentioned earlier, the ship now appears to be under the command of the Earth's Board of Trade Regents, who have sent a delegation of their own to Green Heaven. The *basileïos* of Orikhalkos has arranged for a special conference call to the mayors of the other Compact Cities, with the object of creating a planetary agency for dealing with these new developments . . ."

A sigh of relief, then. Nothing really the matter. Just . . . the beginning of the next phase. I . . . The library whispered, Gaetan, there's something else you should know.

The holodeck image began to pan away from *Torus X-2*, making a longer shot across the concrete wasteland of the cosmodrome, where dozens of ships, large and small, of endlessly varied design, lay waiting, until it focused on yet another small, shiny silver disk.

Uh-oh.

That's what we wanted to tell you, said the ship.

The announcer's small, monkey-like face came up, floating disembodied in the upper right-hand corner of the image. "When *Torus X-2* landed last night, with great fanfare, we sent crews to cover the event. And we began to wonder: to whom does *this* ship, so obviously of the same design, belong?"

Fucking great.

"When we attempted to approach, we were turned away by spaceport security. Authorities would only tell us that the ship landed a few weeks ago and discharged its passengers, tourists apparently. The crew then paid for a slip rental of three months and disappeared."

The man's face enlarged, so the audience could see how serious his expression was, face wreathed in a wrinkling frown, eyes dark and flashing. "This reporter is *outraged* to find that a faster-than-light ship can appear in our star system, land at our largest spaceport unannounced, and sit there for *weeks*, apparently unnoticed!"

I flopped back on the bed, warm sunshine spoiled, erection gone wherever the hell it is erections go when they're gone, and thought, Great. What next? And what the hell happens when I try to go get my ship?

On the holodeck, the image had shifted away from *Random Walk*, was now focused on a scene of the dark-faced reporter, who was posing angry questions to a slim, neatly dressed bald fellow, under whom floated a luminous placard that said, *Zeïos Keimannon, Spaceport Manager.* Just now, he was saying, "You understand me correctly, Mr. Demókissas. So long as the landing fees are paid, it's none of our *business* who these ships belong to, *or* where they come from!"

I found myself wondering, briefly, what he'd say if the starfish-shaped warship *X-4*'d met at Regulus turned up, wanting to rent out a landing slip.

Washed and dressed, hair combed and teeth brushed, I walked across the hotel lobby, headed for the sunshine-flooded street, thinking I might get breakfast while I tried to figure out what I might want to do next. Go to the spaceport and try to sneak aboard my ship? Unlikely, with these media dogs watching and . . . right, Leah Strachan will have seen this too, will be coming in to contact the crew of *X-2*, looking to cash her repatriation ticket.

Maybe, somewhere deep down, I was figuring she'd come crawling back to me, looking for a ride home so she could take up her contract with Nomiura. Maybe I was imagining what I'd do then.

The library AI said, Right now, if you can get aboard *Random Walk*, the spaceport authorities of Orikhalkos will let you go. It seems unlikely, of course, that any laws will change in the *immediate* future, but . . .

So. And did you have any ideas about *where* I should go, dear starship persona? I mean . . .

"Mr. du Cheyne?"

Greek voice in translation, pulling me up short, making me look around. A woman's voice, after all . . . Young woman, standing behind the concierge's desk in the corner of the lobby, looking at me, hand raised.

"Mr. du Cheyne, you have a message waiting for you."

Leah Strachan, perhaps? There was an inappropriate, icy dread. I've got the starship. There are more worlds than this one. More than just Earth. What could happen that . . .

Library AI: You can refuel anywhere there's a cosmodrome, but the ship will need repairs, refitting every now and again. Shipyards with that capacity are to be found on Earth and Kent, where you'll need some sort of legitimate pilot's licence. Not to mention the economics of the thing. I keep avoiding that. Just don't think about it. Maybe the whole business will go away?

The message she handed me was written by some sort of stylus on a little paper message pad, technology so old I almost didn't know what it was, at first. Greek letters in blue on pink paper. I stared, puzzled, waiting . . . finally shifted the barrette to the back of my head so it could rest over my visual cortex. Watched with interest as the letters squirmed, changed from Greek to Roman, Watched as the words rearranged themselves, watched as they changed from transliterated Greek to colloquial English.

Gaetan du Cheyne: I have a business proposition for you. I will have a luncheon table at Kalikanzáros, 1330 this afternoon, if you're interested. Santos Delakroë.

Hmh. Business? No prickle of foreboding. No sense of . . . shit. What do my *feelings* have to do with reality? Nothing, of course. I thanked the concierge, who smiled like a pretty girl, turned and headed for the street.

*   *   *

Kalikanzáros turned out to be a classic-style Greek restaurant, like the ones you'd find somewhere in a big orbital mall, back in the Solar System, at the interface between the main downtown business complex and the waterfront warehouse district where I'd done so much of my recent wandering. A lot of stuff down here. Plenty of deserted blocks, big, empty buildings where an enterprise can be . . . enterprising, I guess.

Inside the frosted glass doors, I told the maître d' I was joining a Mr. Delakroë, was led to a table near the back wall of a big, gloomy dining room with slowly wheeling paddle fans on the ceiling, feeling ever more intensely like a character in some cheap vidnet show. Maybe that's what atmosphere is all about, feedback between life's original archetype and the simplified ectypes of fiction.

Santos Delakroë was a tall, thin man, extraordinarily pale-skinned despite his dark eyes, with a long, narrow face under salt-and-pepper hair, gray-streaked goatee framing lips that looked almost white in this light. He stood, and took my hand, "Mr. du Cheyne?" Gestured to another man, sitting at the table. "My associate, Andrész van Rijn."

This one was short and fat, with dark, shiny skin and long, oily-looking black hair that fell in sticky ringlets down the sides of his flabby neck. When he shook my hand, murmuring, "Duquesne . . ." I noticed he had a heavy ring on every thick finger, gold and silver intermingled, some with gemstones, red, green, yellow, the rings on his thumbs plain, like old-fashioned wedding bands.

As I sat, Delakroë muttered, "Du Cheyne."

Van Rijn said, "Mph. Of course."

They let me order a drink, one of those resinous beers is what I asked for, let it come and watched me take a long pull before starting in. Delakroë said, "Mr. du Cheyne, we'd, um . . . like to discuss a charter with you. *Random Walk* will be here for another ten weeks before your passengers go on to their next destination, wherever—"

A little pang at that, but . . . I held up my hand. "How did you—"

Van Rijn: "We do, um, a *lot* of business at the cosmodrome, Mr. du Cheyne. Your ship was noticed and, um . . . well it was a simple matter to get into All Worlds' office computer system and . . ." His wide, thin leer showed small, widely spaced yellow teeth.

A quirk of irritation on Delakroë's face. "Andrész, *please.*" Then he said, "Mr. du Cheyne. Gaetan. The fact is, we know more or less everything about your visit to Green Heaven. We've . . . talked to Captain Strachan as well and . . ."

I had a sense of cringing inside, imagining the sort of thing she might have said, but, well, these are men here. Mere men. I imagined myself taking Santos Delakroë by his long, spindly neck. Smacking him face first into the side of van Rijn's nice, round head. I put my hands together on the table, fingers neatly interlaced, and said, "I wouldn't be here if I wasn't interested in hearing about your . . . proposal."

Men glancing at each other, maybe a little taken aback, probably not. Delakroë said, "All right. Simple enough. We'd like you to carry a cargo from here to Epimetheus. With your ship, we think we can get a good price for our . . . product. And we can pay a prime rate for the haul."

Epimetheus. Interesting. 40 Eridani A2i, 9.72 light-years from Tau Ceti, closer than any colony world except Shayol at Epsilon Eridani, 5.25 light-years. And Prometheus, of course, 40 Eridani A2. You don't see much about Prometheus and Epimetheus on the vidnet back home. Creepy, unsavory places that . . .

The library AI whispered, We did what checking we could. Santos Delakroë appears to be a legitimate businessman, president of the Keravnos export-import service, dealing mostly in interstellar luxury trade futures. Mr. van Rijn, though, has a police record and appears to be some kind of smuggler, though of what we couldn't find out. It's difficult to say what the two of them have in common.

I snorted softly. Failure of imagination is a common failing of artificial minds, just as it is with your natural sort. I said, "So. What's this illegal cargo you want me to risk my license for?"

Delakroë blinked and sat back in his chair, obviously surprised. Van Rijn glanced at him, then back at me, that unpleasantly toothy grin spreading his fat cheeks again. "Oh, Mr. du Cheyne. *You* don't have a license."

Delakroë, recovering: "Or a pilot."

I cracked my knuckles and shrugged. "I do know how to fly my ship."

Van Rijn snickered, "We were sort of hoping you did."

Delakroë: "What would you say if I told you we could get you a pilot's license that would be acceptable to the authorities on Kent?"

Kent, Alpha Centauri A4, where there are any number of decent shipyards. I said, "*Legitimately* acceptable to the Kentish Space Command?"

Van Rijn laughed. "If you take your license to the portmaster of astronautics at Bakunin Cosmodrome, People's Republic of the Vardon River Valley Project on Kent, he will see to it that you receive a valid solar system flight endorsement."

The expression on my face must have been enlightening.

Delakroë smiled and slid a white cardboard square across the table to me, green letter embossing the Orikhalkan address for something called Club Gámoi. He said, "You come here tonight at midnight and give this card to the doorman. We'll . . . show you the prospective cargo and talk over the details."

Club Gámoi was in a section of town down by the oldest, shabbiest part of the waterfront, a section so deserted it made me a little nervous. Walking through, I didn't see a soul, though I did once stand in the shadows of an empty alleyway while a police car cruised slowly past, console radio muttering softly to the car's two officers, a reedy voice filtered by window glass.

Quiet in the alleyway. No rustle of rats, or whatever passed for rats in a Cetian night. The library AI whispered, Rats descended from early laboratory animals, now interbred with other strains brought in on poorly packaged S.A. cargo pallets. They are a nuisance in the cities, but apparently cannot survive in the wild, where they are outcompeted by native scavengers and subject to severe predation.

Unlike some other terrestrial life forms we all know and love.

No smell in the alleyway either, just a faint, stale tang, like old, sterile dirt. No rats because no garbage because no one lives here anymore. The little gun became a comfortable bump in my pocket, protecting me from nothing.

The club doorman, a skinny, homely young man chewing your classic toothpick, seemed to sneer through his grin as I approached. "What can I *do* for you, ska'fai?"

The translator whispered, *Ska'fai*—possibly a contraction of *skatá*, excrement, and *fai*, an emphatic form of eat. I silently handed him the business card. He frowned, then said, "Oh. I took you for a new scumbag. Sorry." He handed it back. "Go on in and sit down, Mr. du Cheyne. I'll let the boss know you're here."

Inside, Gámoi was the usual big room, a half-amphitheater rather than in the round like the wolfen pit, tables on tiers not quite so steep, arrayed around a small proscenium stage, dark now, room filled, I noticed with a slightly stark pang of . . .

God damn, I feel . . . strange. Like my hair's about to stand on end, like . . . Nothing but men here. Men at every table, some in groups, laughing and talking, others alone, silent and staring. Where is it you don't find women? Homosexual clubs? Oh, there are always a few fag hags hanging round. Strip joints always have women in the audience too, as well as up on the stage, slumming lesbians and curious "tourists," the inevitable I'll-do-whatever-you-want girlfriends of domineering men.

I took a table off to one side, away from what I perceived as excessively crowded tables, sat and . . . Creepy. God damn it I feel . . . I took a deep breath and wondered just why the hell I was getting so sweaty. I . . . There's a smell in here. Something I can't quite put my . . . finger on. I . . .

The house lights fell away and what little noise there was hushed, leaving us in near darkness, darkness filled with an uncanny prickle of anticipation. Anticipation and that smell. Stage lights rising, ever so slightly, putting a rosy flush on the curtain and . . .

What the hell is . . . that? Someone already on the stage. A little girl, perhaps, dressed in a white cowgirl outfit. Little girl with long, pale, golden brown hair, white cowgirl outfit just touched with brown as well, maybe the tips of all those fine little tassles streaked with golden brown, moving as she swayed, swayed when she walked . . .

The faint, tingling pang I'd felt when I first came in here turned to a distinct dread at what I imagined I was going to see next. Hell. This sort of thing's illegal in the solar system. Illegal and one of damned few things actually persecuted by the authorities. Persecuted and prosecuted. Now we're going to see that little girl, size such that she must be no more than eight or nine years old, take off that elaborate, obscuring costume, show us her naked flesh and . . . I realized with a horrid little shock that the little fat man at the next table was lolling back in his chair, muttering softly to himself, that he'd gotten his dick out and was already masturbating. Christ, was just the *idea* of the little girl on the stage enough to . . .

Now there were two little girls on the stage, dressed in identical, weird-looking little cowgirl costumes. Two forlorn little . . . Well, no, you can't tell just *how* forlorn those little girls are. Three little girls now, with some kind of mask covering their little faces. Animal masks, making them look like some kind of little white teddy bear cowgirls, with big, sad eyes that . . .

Memory of watching pornography, just once, with Garstang, so long ago. We'd watched a movie together, gotten aroused, made love on the floor, wallowing right into the misty depths of the vidnet display, had spent ourselves, and were lying back, still watching, as the actors and actresses went on and on, though we ourselves could not.

She'd said, I always thought part of the attraction of pornography was seeing the sad look in the people's eyes. Ineradicable sadness, no matter how they grimace and posture and . . . The very word *pornography*, with its deep Latin roots. *Stories about whores*. Sad-eyed whores, presumably.

As opposed to what? Erotica? Is *erotica* really stories about Eros and love? What about *romance* then? Garstang had laughed, and said, Yeah? What about it?

Four little girls now, fat man at the next table still muttering as he mopped up his mess with a napkin. What a waste of time. What will you do *now?* Now that you've spent your . . . Five little girls dancing in a chain, dancing across the stage to a little flight of stairs, stairs leading down toward the audience, men in the darkness stirring now, filling the room with an electricity of anticipation. Electricity and that . . . smell.

Something so God-damned very *odd* about those little girls. I . . . Oh, Jesus. Why do I have an erection? I'm not . . . Little girls conga dancing toward us, dancing down the stairs.

Dancing now between the tables, men muttering and moving, soft moans here and there, my fat neighbor . . . for Christ's sake, erect again, jerking off again. Somebody with pretty solid hormones, maybe on some kind of special vitamin regimen, or with his system adjusted to . . . Why the hell would anybody do that? It's bad enough having to be just *ordinarily* horny, I . . . Note that hard-on, straining at your pants? Like something out of *Alice*, screaming *eat me* and . . .

Someone moving through the deeper shadows along the wall, a tall black figure walking along, paralleling the girl's dancing, moving its arms as if directing an orchestra. See. The little girls are watching that figure and . . . Fat man holding his swollen dick in one hand, waving a fat handful of Orikhalkan *drakhmai* in the other. Dark figure by the wall snapping the fingers of a raised hand. *Click. Click.* And pointing. One of the little girls broke away and began dancing over to the fat man, getting closer and closer and . . .

I don't want to see this, but . . . right. Not looking away.

Little girl in cowgirl costume dancing up to the fat man. I

could feel my hair sort of standing on end, sweat trickling
under my shirt like thin, cold, crawling snakes. Little girl rubbing herself on him, tickling him with the strands of her costume.

Any minute now, she'll start to take it off, I . . .

Instead, she just crawled up in his lap, straddled him, fat
man squealing faintly, like a faraway pig in the clutches of the
butcher, little girl straddling his lap, already moving in some
ineffably coital rhythm.

Look at the men, watching her.

Look at yourself watching her.

Almost a cheat, for the rest of us. Why is she still wearing
that costume? Why can't we *see*? The little girl straddling the fat
man's lap, so obviously impaled on his dick, turned and briefly
looked at me, her animal mask . . . Dark eyes, wide open, looking at me. Muzzle, wet black nose of a little dog over a dog's
cleft lip, mouth agape, panting, little teeth plainly visible.

Not a mask at all.

A living face.

What the hell am I seeing here?

Long, empty silence in my head as I watched the fat man
convulse, watched the . . . thing get off his lap, take his money,
dab briefly at its crotch with his napkin, then dance away, rejoin-
ing the conga line of teddy bear cowgirls. Over on the other
side of the room, another man was holding up money, and that
unidentifiable smell was like mist in the air.

The spacesuit's voice whispered, We can find nothing in the
Orikhalkan InfoNet on this.

I heard the fat man whisper, "Oh. Oh my *God* . . ."

Then a voice in my ear, black shadow leaning over me: "Mr.
du Cheyne? If you'll come with me please."

My erection persisted, even after I left the room of the dancing . . . things, as I followed an unknown man down an
unknown hall. When I came into the office where van Rijn and
Delakroë were waiting, they saw it, saw the front of my pants

poking out, and van Rijn laughed. "I guess you liked our little dollies, huh?"

Dollies. I felt scattered memories linking up, falling into place. I sat down, mopping my brow with a slightly less damp palm. "Jesus. I thought they were little girls at first."

Delakroë looked pained; van Rijn gave a vidshow-class bellow of coarse amusement. "I guess that's part of it," he said.

Part of it. My God.

Delakroë said, "I suppose you've guessed the rest of it then?"

I nodded slowly.

Van Rijn said, "We've got a cargo of fifty dollies that will be ready for, ah . . . shipment. Yes. Ready for shipment to Epimetheus in about four weeks. We normally ship them frozen as S.A. cargo, um, mixed in with . . . other commodities, accompanied by a factor who . . . rides as a passenger, you see, and—"

"And you'll get a higher price if there's an unexpected shipment?"

Delakroë: "No one will be expecting us. And the dollies will be in . . . much better shape if they're not frozen."

I can imagine. "How high?"

"I beg your pardon?"

"How much will you get for the . . . dollies?"

Silence. Then van Rijn, eyes narrow, said, "That's none of your business, Mr. du Cheyne."

I looked at him for a long moment. "Sure. How were you expecting me to handle and store fifty live . . . um. Animals?"

Van Rijn: "We'll provide appropriate . . . handlers. And we've looked at your ship. We know you can land in pretty rugged territory."

I nodded. They wouldn't be expecting to transship their goodies at the cosmodrome.

Delakroë: "We're offering you a hundred thousand livres to do the job."

I felt a little spark of surprise at the figure, but . . . Well. There's a shadow of the truth in their eyes. "Not enough."

Silence. Then Delakroë folded his hands on the top of the desk, fingers neatly interlaced, and smiled. "Well, I'm sure we can work this out, Mr. du Cheyne. It's . . . always a pleasure to do business with an honest man."

Right. It only took a few minutes, and I'd run them up to 225,000 livres before van Rijn balked and wouldn't budge. Wouldn't budge although I could tell I hadn't made much of a dent in their profit margin. As for me, I'd be pulling close to eight times what I'd gotten to haul passengers, and . . . "The license."

Van Rijn grinned a grin I was already quite sick of, reached into the front of his tunic and pulled out a thick white envelope, tossing it on the desk between us. "There's a hundred thousand livres in there, Mr. du Cheyne, along with a document for the authorities on Epimetheus. Consider it your down payment. When we get to our destination . . ."

"We?"

The smile broadened. "I've never been to another planet, Mr. du Cheyne. I'm looking forward to this trip." When we stood, shaking hands, van Rijn looked down at the hump in the front of my pants, and laughed. "You ought to do something about that, Mr. du Cheyne. Why don't you go on out and enjoy the rest of the show?"

On the way out of the building I went into the rest room, intending to jerk off and be rid of the damned thing, but the stalls were already full of gasping men, including one fellow furtively crouching over the sink.

Outside, the night air was cool and, as I walked through the darkness, I started to feel a little better. Glad, perhaps, that they *hadn't* been little girls.

9

Another bright and sunshiny morning, all the stacks and program counters of my soul reset by a good night's sleep. Sometimes, I wonder if we're truly the same person from one day to the next, or whether yesterday's man isn't gone, a new one formed from nothingness to live for today. Death and resurrection. *Metempsychosis*. Something like that.

Just now, I followed a rental agent whose name I kept forgetting across a macadam parking lot on the outskirts of Orikhalkos, fresh yellow stripes stark against newly sealed blacktop, Tau Ceti hanging like some great Medusan eye in the turquoise void, turning the landscape of distant mountains over low wooden buildings to impressionist stone.

Four weeks to kill. Four weeks before it's time to start . . . my new job. Sharp prickle in the back of my head at the sound of that. It isn't a job. Not really, but the sense of . . . something. Something . . . *real* that I've got to do . . .

The rental agent said, "I think this is exactly the sort of thing you'll be wanting, Mr. du Cheyne." He looked at me, eyes searching, looking for something . . . "Um. We call this a pop-up."

A fairly substantial vehicle sitting before me, roughly nine meters stem to stern, by two meters abeam. Nice bubble canopy in the front, two bucket seats and a boxy control panel visible through clean Plexiglas, behind that a flat, vented compartment of some sort under two long, bronze-colored whip antennas, then a larger box, faceted with joint lines, the whole finished off in shiny, lemon yellow enamel.

The rental agent was saying, ". . . and there's a gun rack behind the cockpit seats, pre-equipped with a standard zipgun, a sparkler and a compression rifle. We'll remove them, of course, if you want to substitute your own—"

"They'll be fine." I walked back along the machine, trailing my hands across the finish. Some kind of acrylic, soft enough to take fingerprints. "Power plant under here?"

"Power . . . oh. You mean the motor and batteries. I suppose so, I . . ."

There was a legend printed in black near the line of large, flush-set metal screws securing the bonnet, and I suddenly realized I'd learned the Greek alphabet well enough to subvocalize the words. The translator whispered, *No User Serviceable Components Inside. Warranty Void If Seal Is Tampered With.* Is it grammatically incorrect in Romaic as well? The translator admitted it was.

The rental agent was saying, ". . . and if you hit the pop-up button over there on the driver's left, the living compartment will expand to a full seventeen square meters, easily enough for two adults to camp out in comfort."

No doubt. I fished out my shiny new All Worlds credit card, and said, "Fine. I'll take it."

He inspected the thing, seeming to puzzle out the embossed words with interest. "You some kind of travel agent?"

"Something like that."

"Must be interesting work."

"I suppose so."

I'd given the All Worlds staff a few difficult moments this morning when I'd showed up with a hundred thousand livres cash in the form of Compact Reserve Notes drawn on Delakroë's bank, fine, untraceable money of a sort that hadn't been used in the solar system for hundreds of years. At first they told me they *couldn't* suffix it to my letter of credit, that I'd have to convert it to commodities if I wanted to take it off planet with me when I left. Then, once they admitted it could be done, they wanted a ten percent commission for the privilege of doing it. And when I asked for them to arrange a debit service . . .

I finally talked them down to a five percent commission on the whole thing and left it at that, took my shiny new credit card and left the office staff to contemplate their cut of the dollies' misfortune.

I'd loaded my gear into the pop-up, toolbox in the cargo bay under the living compartment, and set up my transponder unit on the passenger's seat, plugging waveguides into console jacks the rental agent told me he hadn't known were there. "I guess I thought the antennas were just for TV and telephone service . . ."

With the box in place, the bandwidth back to the ship was expanded hundreds of times, solving most of the problems I'd been having. So long as I stayed line-of-sight to the camper. I'd had an easy time getting the stuff I needed out of *Random Walk*, driving unchallenged across the landing field, parking in the shadows under her hull, the Orikhalkan media, apparently, having forgotten all about me.

Toolbox, with the toolbelt inside awakening, full of joy at my touch. You could tell the spacesuit wanted to come along, *You'll be safer if you're inside me, Gaetan.* I left it draped over the seat, still plugged into the ship's subsystems, running my hand just once over its substance, whispering, "I need you here. Sorry."

Felt its flush of pleasure at my use of the word *need.*

The pop-up had lifted off in a whirl of dust and turbine whine, making me think of the rental agent's ignorance: "Well, no, it doesn't need refueling. All electric and . . . what? No, sir, I don't know if the batteries ever need recharging. Sorry I can't be more help, but . . ."

Now I was running smoothly over the plains, feeling the seat surge under me every time we went up a little rise, surge and then settle, bobbing slightly, digital meter on the control panel reading *75* and no more whenever the thumb-throttle was set higher than thirty percent, vehicle scraping along less than a meter above the ground no matter how I lifted on the stick.

After about an hour, I shut down and landed, out on the empty plains, got out and stood looking back at Orikhalkos, still visible like a collection of child's blocks on the horizon, sunlight from Tau Ceti shining on white clouds hanging over the sea. Orikhalkos and all its grimy millions, still less than a hundred kilometers away.

I went back and got my toolbox, set it on the ground and opened the lid, plugged the toolbelt into the transponder box and stood back. All set?

The spacesuit whispered, Boot track liftoff. Autodiagnostics. Warming up . . . The belt's main sensor head rose like a snake out of the box, and I could feel it make contact with me through the barrette. I directed it to the middle compartment of the camper. The screwdriver head snaked out, *bingbingbing,* pannier catching screws as they fell, and the bonnet opened, lifted by internal springs that must have put considerable stress on the fasteners. Poor design.

I stepped forward and looked in. Electric turbine, probably derived from twenty-second-century airliner engines I remembered studying in my history of technology class. A set of hefty accumulators rigged to a series of AC-cycler batteries, for Christ's sake. Ingenious stone-age crap, all right, and . . .

Hmh. Whole mess wired up to the longer of the two whip antennas, only the shorter one going forward to the comdeck in the cockpit. Which means, I suppose, there's a powersat up in the sky somewhere. Cellular broadcast towers here and there? I didn't remember seeing any, but that didn't mean they weren't around.

All right, so why don't they use this system for *all* their cars? No answer. I sighed, and said, "All right, let's disconnect the God-damned governors and get the fuck out of here."

With the governor modules unplugged, the camper was

another sort of vehicle entirely, electric turbine driving the big fan with enough power to lift the underside of the chassis twelve meters or so off the ground, and when I fed in the juice, the two axial flow syphonjets would accelerate her, slowly it was true, but continuously, until, a little above two hundred, the body's laminar flow surfaces started detaching, making her wallow like a fat duck, and I had to throttle back.

Good enough. I settled back in my seat and powered southwest, toward the distant glow of the Koudloft, watching the metallic yellow grasses of the Koperveldt whip by below, easily clearing the occasional clump of shiny, blue-green trees, skirting clusters of low farmhouses when I saw them in time, just once, because I wasn't paying attention, having to yank hard on the control yoke to avoid running into some kind of wooden windmill . . .

Please be careful, Gaetan, the spacesuit's alarmed whisper.

I ran a quick diagnostic and found a second jack I could use to hook up my transponder box, back to the ship's navigation system. No radar on this thing, of course, and if I wasn't looking, no eyes, but there was a nice, fairly recent terrain and obstacles map available through the Orikhalkan InfoNet.

Now, so long as nobody's put up anything *new* taller than twelve meters in the past few months . . .

At dusk, I slowed up, looking for a place to camp, finally settling down by a little pond of some kind, scraping the camper on the ground, landing in a little open grove of trees. Sat there with my thumb on the pop-up button . . . Sheesh. Looked over my shoulder, measuring the space among the trees. I can just see myself calling up the rental agent on the camper's phone: "Well, sir, I've got your pop-up wedged among some trees. Well, no. I disconnected all the governors, so it just *opened*. I guess maybe all the little motors are burned out now and . . ."

I hit the button and watched the damned thing unfold like some kind of magic box, rising, spreading, little screen windows unfurling from their sockets, appliances visible inside . . . when it was finished I had a one-room cabin, four and an eighth meters in each direction, two and a half meters high, yellow light glowing cheerily inside as the sky grew dark.

I got out and stood on a rock beside the flat, quiet, clear waters of the little pond, watching Tau Ceti slide away, growing redder as it went, western sky limned with forest green, watching the sky grow dark, the familiar bright stars, stars I'd always loved, pop out one by one, in strict magnitude order. Listened to the faraway, nonhuman sounds of the veldt.

All right, Gaetan du Cheyne. Here you are where you longed to be, the hunter, still out on the hill, with no intention of ever going home.

In the distance, something howled, more unearthly than anything I'd ever imagined before.

Sometime after sunset I finally got tired of counting the stars and naming their names, got down off my rock and went through the camper's rear door into the living compartment.

Well. Nice, I guess. Bunk beds over here, made up with sheets, blankets and pillows. A little galley over here, with a refrigerator/microwave stack that must uncouple and sink into the floor at fold-up time. Sink. A flat rack of cabinets the rental agent had told me was stocked with standard canned goods— when I looked inside it was opaque brown jars labeled with Greek words and pictures of food. *Souvláki?* Swell. The jar of *dolmadesh* looked like pickled quadruple-amputee frogs.

Stood looking in through the open refrigerator door at racks of cooled and frozen crap. Plenty of veggies, not much meat, just a few packs of frozen hamburger. I guess, on a hunting trip, you're supposed to kill and butcher your own meat. Rifles in the cockpit. Are these long skinny things racked under the low ceiling supposed to be fishing poles?

For that matter, are there fish in the little pond? How would I find out?

The library AI, routed to my head through the transponder in the cockpit, whispered, The pond is called Whiplick Spring, technically on the estate of one Borgen Takkor, registered landowner.

Am I trespassing?

Compact property rights do not apply outside the major cities. On the Koperveldt, Groenteboer free-range rules apply.

So *Vrijheer* Takkor won't mind my being here.

The Groenteboeren are known for their *gastvrijheid*.

I snickered, thinking that greengrocers were known for their hospitality. I wish some greengrocer would come and stock the fridge better. I turned and went back outside and stood under the stars again. Look. The Milky Way is like a band of fog striped right across the middle of the sky. What's it like out there?

You could go, you know?

Random Walk can generate a pseudovelocity of around four hundred cee. Go to just the right point in the far periphery of the Tau Ceti system, where the gravitational lens focus for the galactic center is found. Fire the generators, cut in the drive. Watch the sky sparkle some brilliant, pure, impossible blue, ghostly fingers stroke your soul and . . .

How far?

Fifteen thousand parsecs?

Something like that.

How long?

One hundred twenty-two point-six-two-five years, said the library AI.

All right. So I'll get back, assuming I choose to come back, no sooner than the late spring of 2849.

I went over finally and cleared a patch of bare ground beside the pond, scraping it clean with an entrenching tool I found clipped to the side of the cabin extension. Went around in the dark gathering rocks of a certain size until I'd made a little circle, then went around again, gathering up bits of dead wood, breaking the longer branches to a fairly uniform length, making a little pile just so. Very nice. Now, if only I had a match.

There are moments when you feel exceptionally stupid, but then I remembered an old movie I'd seen, a twenty-third-century remake of *The Mountain Men*, set on an imaginary future Mars that'd been improbably well terraformed, entirely software-generated after the fashion of the times, featuring a faithfully resurrected version of Brian Keith. I went to the cab and got the sparkler, fired it down into the pile at its lowest power setting, and watched with some satisfaction as the wood glowed red and burst into flame.

I went in the camper, got out some frozen hamburger, a pan, a bottle of thick steak sauce, *Alpha-Éna* the label said, found an onion, a bag of frozen potato spheres, a stick of oleo-margarine, and set to work. Pretty soon, I had the pan sizzling, some pretty good smells filling up my patch of woods, I . . .

Soft sound, up under the trees, over there.

I looked. Felt a little lurch in my belly. Big dark shadow. Eyes.

Oh, shit.

I glanced at the back of the camper. Not all that far. Maybe . . .

I stood slowly, starting to turn, realized with a start there was another one over by the pond, a fat white wolfen perhaps twice the size of the one I'd seen in the zoo, a bit bigger than the one in the pit, back in Orikhalkos.

I looked down at the sparkler, leaning against my boulder. Sure. Back on Earth, hunters use these things to knock down small game birds. Ducks, I guess. Thrush? Do people eat thrushes? Maybe not. Thinking of something else, I . . . God damn, I . . .

The spacesuit whispered, Gaetan, we think you'd better stand still for now. We're running a quick library search.

A library search. Great. I wondered, How far away is the Takkor boerderij?

Seventeen kilometers.

Great. I swallowed softly, saw the wolfen's eyes move, realized it'd heard me, wondered if it could smell my sudden, cold sweat. A terrestrial animal, a predator would know by now just how terrified I was, heart beating so fast in my chest it seemed like one continuous vibration. People have been here on the Koperveldt for a long time. Long enough for them to . . . get used to us.

ACTS OF CONSCIENCE ▣ 181

I looked toward the camper's cab, where there was a compression rifle waiting for me in the gun rack. One blast from
that and I'd have them all dead, probably knock down half
these trees as well. I wondered, just briefly, what your average
Greenie would hunt with a compressor. Hell, ordinary rifles had
been enough for womfrogs, hadn't they, I . . .

There was another wolfen, smaller than the other two but
bigger than me, sitting by the door.

Smiling?

No. No lips. Their teeth show even when their mouths are
closed. Like an alligator.

Can you start the camper's engine through the transponder
box? Maybe it'll scare them away. Maybe you can turn it around
and . . . maybe you can run them . . .

The spacesuit whispered, If anything moves, according to
the small literature on wolfen we've found, it is probable they'll
attack.

Attack? And then?

The library AI said, Hemmendoer's *Guide to Living On Your
Own* has the following statement: "If you let yourself get caught
out in the open, each wolfen will likely get one good mouthful."

I felt my heart falter.

The spacesuit whispered, Hold still, Gaetan. We're calling
for help.

Good idea. Fat chance. Just how long will it take for Vrijheer
Borgen Takkor to come find the bits and scraps that are all that
will be left of me?

The big one beside the pond was starting to inch forward
again.

A tiny voice, very calm, somewhere deep inside, not one of
the AIs, but not sounding much like me either, said, *You know of
course that being eaten alive is just not going to be very pleasant?*

Wolfen standing up now, one of them yawning, mouth
agape, teeth making my heart go bump, really hard.

Christ. Maybe I can just have a heart attack now and die
before they can do anything. That'd be all right.

The little one over by the cab, still sitting on its haunches, whispered, a bubbling little growl, *Awerroowaahhh* . . .

So. Reach down now and grab that sparkler and start shooting the bastards. You won't be able to kill them with a bird gun, sure, but it'll sting like a son of a bitch, startle them. Maybe you *can* get in through the back door, lock yourself in. Then the suit can start the camper and just drive your ass away.

For God's sake, Gaetan, hold still! Please!

Why the hell would an artificial intelligence be talking about God?

Klopklopklopklopklop . . .

Rhymthic sounds, coming up through the trees. The wolfen turned to look and so did I. A horse. I felt myself breathe a heavy sigh of relief. For Christ's sake. Borgen Takkor, I presume? Got your rifle with you, *mijnheer*? OK, now shoot these bastards and . . .

Dull surge of horror. Riderless!

The horse stopped, reins dangling, though they hadn't been before, and I could see a dark shadow, something like a giant lima bean draped across its back. The bean slid off, landed with a dull plop on the ground, then rose on long, thin crab's legs. Scuttled easily across the ground, walking more or less like a big spider, legs moving with machine-like precision, walking over, not to me, but to the big wolfen by the pond.

I'm not breathing. Not breathing at all. Going to suffocate and die and never know what was going on. I . . .

It stood still, seven eyes like Ping-Pong balls on stalks growing out of the middle of its back, waving two big lobster claws in the wolfen's face. Great. Maybe I can run for the camper while they use it for an appetizer, I . . .

It grew a third arm, something like an octopus reaching out to touch the wolfen's face.

Tableau.

Then the wolfen shook the octopus off its head, snarled softly, with just a hint of petulance and anger, I imagined.

Barked, high, metallic, not like a dog's bark at all, one, two, three . . .

They turned away, turned back into shadows, and were gone, just like that.

God. My chest. Like I'm caught in a vise . . . I drew in a strangled breath then, making a high noise of my own, something like a sob.

The Kapellmeister turned, eyestalks floating gently above its back, like flowers waving in the breeze. Stood looking, I guess. Then it walked over to me, octopus hand drawn in against the front of its body, so that it almost disappeared.

When it stood in front of me, looking up, it lifted its chelae and started moving them, clicking, metallic scraping like scissors being opened and closed . . .

A little black box strapped to its back said, "Well, Mr. du Cheyne, the control systems aboard your starship seemed *quite* concerned about your safety. I'm glad I was able to get here in time, though Gunbreaker and her sisters were . . . disappointed."

I croaked something, only sounds, unable to form words.

The Kapellmeister said, "You're welcome, Mr. du Cheyne. And I'm *so* glad to find you here! I've been wanting to thank you for saving my life, back in Orikhalkos."

10

I think I stood there for a full minute, looking down at the improbable, pulpy shape of the Kapellmeister, while something sizzled and popped in the background. Finally, it reached out and poked me in the knee with one of its chrome-bright claws, made a harsh chitter-snap commentary, and the box on its back said, "Are you all right, Mr. du Cheyne?"

"Uh! Yes."

It said, "Then I think you'd better attend to your dinner. I'm sure I smell the beginnings of the carcinogen-formation process."

I looked around, almost wildly, at dark shadows among the trees, my camper, cheery yellow light still glowing through its windows, at the Kapellmeister's quietly grazing horse, light from the two moons shining off the surface of the pond, other shadows, cast by my firelight, leaping around on the ground.

Stars in the sky, apparently unmoved.

I knelt and picked up my spatula, broke the hamburger loose from the bottom of the pan and flipped it over. "Hmh. Not too bad."

The Kapellmeister said, "You probably shouldn't eat the black part, Mr. du Cheyne."

I sat on the ground by the fire, hugging my knees, shivering, on . . . well. On eye level with the thing. Pretty eyes. Such a lovely shade of . . . Earthly sky blue, in this light. Looking at me, I suppose, no way to tell. The Kapellmeister stepped closer to the fire, stretching two of its seven eyestalks out so it could look down into my pan.

I said, "Doesn't that hurt?" One of the other eyes seemed to lean in my direction. "I mean, some of your eyes are in the combustion by-product plume . . ."

It said, "No. I have pretty tough eyes."

"Oh."

The Kapellmeister said, "I think if your wits were in proper working order, you'd want to know how I came to be here."

Sure. I was wondering. Starting to calm down now, occupied by the mundane task of assembling my dinner, getting out the bun, putting on the mustard and ketchup, opening a jar of pickled onion slices I'd found in the refrigerator.

It said, "Those white things smell pretty bad. As of bacterial action."

"Yeast."

"Linnaean classification makes that distinction, I understand."

I fished the burger out, putting the pan aside on the mossy ground . . . found myself looking at the moss and wondering what it really was, made up my sandwich and lifted it to take a bite. Suddenly put it down and let my hands shake all they wanted.

The Kapellmeister said, "I was visiting with Gunbreaker's clan, Mr. du Cheyne. When the news came that you were here, alone, apparently unprotected, a human too stupid to look after himself properly . . . I wasn't interested in watching, so I decided to ride on, be about my business."

Decided to ride on and let the wolfen come kill me? Jesus. I said, "I'm glad you changed your mind, Mr. . . . ."

Silence. Then it said, "If you're waiting for me to say a name, I'm sorry. We don't use them, Mr. du Cheyne."

ACTS OF CONSCIENCE ☐ 187

"Gaetan. I'm still glad you changed your mind."

Silence, then: "Well, I didn't change my mind, Gaetan. The artificial personality complex at your starship somehow activated a remote feed to the hardware in my translator. It told me who you were, after which I decided . . ."

I sat looking at this thing, which really didn't look that much like a living being, remembering a night in a dark alley. I'd enjoyed shooting that man with my little dartgun . . . realized with a start it was in my pocket even now. What if I'd remembered and fired it at the wolfen?

The library AI whispered, Solar and Cetian biological systems are fairly different. The paralytic agent would have had no effect, beyond inducing pain.

So different they're immune to our poisons, but not so different we can't eat each other? My mouth watered, remembering those fine, sweet womfrog steaks.

The library said, The wolfen would have become quite ill from consuming your flesh. Unlike humans, they are not protected by vigilant artificial immune systems.

Right. I muttered, "You'd think they might take that into account."

The Kapellmeister seemed to be peering at me intently. "Whom?"

"The wolfen. Getting sick from eating me."

"Ah. It seems they feel enduring such illness to be a point of honor." Long moment of nothing, then it said, "Your meat is getting cold."

I picked up the sandwich again, hands much calmer now, and wondered if the Kapellmeister was thinking of what the cow might have had to go through on its way to becoming ground beef. I took a bite and found that even though I hadn't bothered to scrape off the burnt bits, it tasted just fine. I licked the juice off my lips, grease maybe, a little bit of blood, and said, "What were you doing with them, Mr. . . . ah. Why don't you have a name?"

It scraped softly to itself, something the translator box didn't pick up, then said, "I know who I am. Others know who I am. Those who don't know who I am have no use for a label."

"Not even a childhood nickname?"

"I've been out of the egg for a long time. As for childhood . . ." It spread its chelae-wielding arms wide in something that looked just a little like a shrug. "It's an interesting notion, but we are . . . fully sentient as hatchlings."

"Oh." Sudden realization of just how fucking little I really knew about Salieri and the Kapellmeisters, about . . . pretty much everything. All those years watching vidnet bullshit. A childhood spent fantasizing. Even my belovèd Green Heaven. Sure, I'd known about womfrog hunting. That's what the daydreams were about: kill a womfrog, get a blowjob. I'd even known a little bit about the wolfen, presented as intelligent, dangerous, rather nasty predators.

But where the hell were the *dollies?* I guess that would have made a nice fucking show for a pubescent boy to watch.

The Kapellmeister said, "And for the rest of it, I'm here with a group of Arousian students, traveling under the protection of Mace Electrodynamics Interstellar and the systemic government of Sigma Draconis. They are here to study the wolfen's behavioral culture for the xenosociology department of—" his translator box went *greekeegreekeeclackgreekee* "—University."

Hmh. Weird. "Why would the Arousians—"

It said, "They are quite interested in learning about other sentient species, Gaetan. Other than humans, of course, with whom they are quite . . . familiar."

Sentient. I tried to remember those old shows, remember what they'd said about the various wolfen species of Green Heaven. Not much. What sticks in my mind is a scene from a twenty-fifth-century flexscript-generated multishow, a drama set on Green Heaven in which it was possible to get yourself trapped by a hungry band of yellow wolfen from the borderlands of the Adrianis Desert.

Not much detail there, beyond a whole lot of scary growling and drooling, before Aurens mac Inglaterra would appear above the line of white gypsum dunes, with his blue-burnoused band of Hinterling warriors. After that, as I recall, viewers of various genders and sexual orientations got to have a fine assortment of rape fantasies.

The Kapellmeister said, "I'm supposed to be a chaperon for them, in the employ of Mace Electrodynamics, diplomatic credentials from Sigma Draconis and all that." It turned, stiff legs moving mechanically, seeming unreal in the firelight, seeming to glance over at its horse, or maybe into the shadows beyond.

I found I was still afraid to look at those shadows too hard.

It said, "Though the living sages counsel absolute patience, I've never been one to sit still, of course, and be a mere observer. So I've been riding around to the various wolfen subclans in the hill country, arranging for them to visit our encampment. That's where Gunbreaker and her people ought to be going, in fact."

Gunbreaker. Quick memory suppressed. I'll think about it tomorrow, when I've had time to reabsorb my feelings. "Are you a spy?"

"For whom?"

"The government of Salieri."

Silence. Then it said, "Not in the sense you may mean, though . . . a wise citizen looks out for the interests of its . . . chosen polity."

That idea was probably surfacing from memory of some old movie as well, something featuring a Salieran spy, skulking through the sewers of some human habitat, on Luna or Mars perhaps, where the sewers are old and full of ambience as well as shit. I can't quite pull it up. Something about a Kapellmeister crawling through the dark sewer, coming upon a rat's nest, gleefully grabbing the baby rats in its terrible chelae, snipping off their heads, sucking their blood . . .

It said, "Would you like to visit my friends, Gaetan?"

"Well. Sure."

"It's quite a ways off. About three days' travel."

I glanced at the camper, wondering if I should explain about the rewiring I'd done.

The Kapellmeister said, "I'm traveling by horse, Gaetan." The animal, which had been standing quite still in the shadows, looked up, as if it understood the word.

"I wasn't going anywhere in particular."

"Excellent. I'll make camp here for tonight. We can move on in the morning."

From faraway came the faint afterecho of a long, complexly modulated howl. Wolfen. "Christ!" Shivering.

The Kapellmeister said, "Oh, dear. Gunbreaker and some of her warriors seem to have killed one of Mr. Takkor's prize Brahma bulls. He'll be very angry."

I stood up, feeling slightly short of breath.

"You can sleep outside if you wish, Gaetan. The wolfen won't come again. It's a very nice night."

Both of the moons had set now, my fire died down, and but for the glow from inside the camper it had gotten quite dark. So dark, in fact, that the sky seemed to blaze with ghostly silver light. "I think I'll go in for the night. Thanks anyway."

I lay in bed for a long time, lay in the darkness, staring out through my little window at the starry sky, watching the Milky Way's band slowly rise, trying to sleep, failing, trying to think, failing at that as well. Mainly, I lay there listening to all those scary nighttime noises, remembering what it'd been like to lie awake as a child, buried deep under the Moon, listening to the regolith groan.

My memory is composed of snapshots like that. Snapshots I would've preferred to lose, most of them. All that wasted space that could've been filled up with useful knowledge, or expansions of the happy memories I did have. I started thinking about those happy memories, and finally fell asleep remembering a girl I'd known on Mars in the time between Jayanne and when I left for Stardock.

God, what the hell was her name? Something with a lot of *szs* and double accent marks I never did learn how to pronounce right. A tall, fat blond girl whose sole interests in life seemed to be ice cream and sex. It proved to be an . . . invigorating combination, and I was sorry to tell her goodbye, though she didn't seem sorry to see me go.

Travel the next day proved to be surprisingly dull. I spent part of the morning floating along above rolling, hilly plains that gradually grew more heavily wooded, bobbing like a captive balloon under an empty blue-green sky, trying to fly my camper at the speed of a walking horse.

Finally, when the spacesuit told me it could indeed track the Kapellmeister through the satellite link it'd established with his translator box, I took off to look for something interesting the library AI told me it'd turned up on the Orikhalkan InfoNet service.

A couple of hundred kilometers to the west of where I was, where the foothills of the Thisbÿs Bergketen begin ramping up into the main mountain range, there's an old volcanic throat, atop which sit what appear to be ruins. Research references going all the way back to the original explorer teams that first visited Tau Ceti confirm that these are indeed artifacts, worked stone of unknown age and origin.

There are a few fallen pillars, some pedestals with what look like angular script on them, but could just as easily be weathering marks. A stretch of what looks a lot like abstract stone tilework.

The library AI said, No one has successfully theorized about these buildings, because they are unique on Green Heaven, nor do they resemble the old ruins on Groombridge 1618 6iv, commonly known as Snow.

Weathering patterns appear to indicate they are older than the oldest civilizations of Earth and Arous, though much younger, of course, than the extremely ancient artifacts on Snow.

And the Kapellmeisters?

The technological phase of Salieran civilization is of unknown antiquity. They appear to have had space travel for many thousands of years, though it is stated their interstellar flight capabilities have gone unused.

And the Saucer People?

Since the Salieran government categorically states it was not responsible for those "visits," which have never, in any case, been verified as actually being of extraterrestrial origin, such theorizing comes under the heading of mere fantasy.

Which, until just recently, left no one else. As I settled down to have lunch, sitting on the edge of a cliff, looking westward toward the silvery heights of the improbably tall Thisbÿs Mountains, I wondered if anything more had been heard about the starfish-warship business. Interesting that both the Board of Trade Regents and the solar system media had let it slide by like that. We . . .

The spacesuit whispered, The Kapellmeister asks that you visit now.

It took about an hour to fly back, landing my camper in a swirl of dust and leaves on a rough dirt track that led through a grove of trees almost big enough to be called a forest. The Kapellmeister's horse was standing there, quietly grazing in a patch of yellow stuff that must have been pretty much the same as grass, looking up briefly as I came down.

When I got out, the Kapellmeister's machine-voice called through the trees, "In here, Gaetan. Please bring your hunting rifle." I took down the zipgun and walked into the shadows.

"Christ."

The womfrog was lying on its left side, rib cage visibly moving in and out, labored breathing, its lower trunk stretched out flat, the other one ripped open, hanging by a shred of thick hide and a hank of bleeding muscle, the ground under it well soaked with blood, the air full of sweet smells, honey and whipped cream, with just a hint of cinnamon.

"Where's its left hind leg?"

From its perch atop the thing's skull, the Kapellmeister said, "Taken away. Probably eaten by now."

So. I tried to visualize a band of wolfen bringing this thing down and tearing it apart, just the way they would have me, but . . .

No. The stump of its left jumping leg was cleanly cut. Knives, not teeth. I started walking around toward its head, stopped short when I saw the eyes were still open. Still open and so evidently watching me. The supple fingers of its surviving hand curled into a fist, held it briefly, relaxed open again.

I remembered the hunt, remembered a desperate womfrog jumping up, trying to grab me from the edge of the cliff, remembered Gretel Blondinkruis' laughter.

The Kapellmeister said, "If you'll come around here and shoot it in the back of the neck, you can have the other leg for supper."

Sharp pang in my chest. I looked up into the thing's big, empty eyes and stood stock-still, listening to the harsh whisper of its breathing.

"Please, Gaetan. The womfrog begs you to hurry."

I looked up at the Kapellmeister on its perch, saw that it had extended its middle hand, the one that looked just a little bit like an octopus or squid, that the wet black tentacles were splayed out across the top of the womfrog's skull. I took a deep breath. "All right." Started walking round toward its back, conscious of the eyes following me until I went out of sight.

Now what?

I aimed the zipgun at where I imagined the womfrog's foramen magnum would be and thumbed the charge button, listening to the condenser whine, knowing the . . . animal would be hearing it too. Well. I shut my eyes when I pulled the trigger, but the blood got on me anyway, which seemed to make the butchery a little easier afterward.

After I'd taken what I wanted from the dead womfrog, we moved on, finally making camp as the sun went down, sky a blaze of orange and vermilion, in an open area, flat ground to one side of what could only be called a babbling brook. There was a wide sandbar that looked a little bit like a beach, enough stones clustered in the middle of the stream to make something like a small waterfall and, farther along, a deeper area marked by calm-flowing water, where I suppose I could have taken a bath if I wanted, though there was a perfectly good shower in the pop-up.

I set up one of the camp chairs and built another fire, taking nice, big round stones from the stream, over which to cook my womfrog steaks and bake a potato I'd found in the vegetable crisper, so thoughtfully stocked by the rental agent. As the smells started, I began to wonder if I'd like the combination of candy-meat flavor and traditional tuber-with-butter. Hell. Anything's worth trying once.

While I was doing all this, the Kapellmeister prepared a bag of oats for its horse, whose name, it turned out, was Graysplotch, after a typical horsemarking between its eyes. It was kind of a remarkable sight, watching the horse stand so still as the Kapellmeister walked up its mane and stood between its ears to mount the feedbag.

After that, it'd simply walked away into the growing shadows of dusk, tossing a clipped "I'll be back" over its . . . shoulder? Hell. Over its butt, I guess, since the talking box was mounted in the middle of its back. I have no idea where a Kapellmeister's shit comes out, or if it even makes anything like shit. Anyway, it went, leaving me alone.

Just before the food was done, there was a rustling among the trees. I jumped, grabbing the zipgun from where I'd left it, leaning against the side of the camper, not far from my chair, finger thrust through the trigger guard, heart thumping harder than I wanted it to, ears straining.

"Please don't shoot me, Gaetan."

"Sorry."

"You shouldn't be afraid of the wolfen, Gaetan. Gunbreaker has passed the word around that you're under my . . . protection."

It walked into the firelight and I saw with a start that it was carrying something. Something that moved. I kneeled as it approached, trying to get a good look at the little animal. Some native Greenie life form, covered with bristly dark green fur, six limbs, arrayed like a bipedal mammal with an extra set of arms and complex shoulders whose articulations were hidden by the fur.

"What's that?" The thing's mottled, pupil-less eyes were bugged out and rolling, not surprising since the Kapellmeister had it around the neck, squeezing tightly with one chela, the other one holding its legs. The four arms, if that's what they were, were limp.

"The Groenteboeren refer to it as a *haaskin*."

The translator AI said, This is a children's slang term for a common sort of playroom toy. "Bunny."

"Yes, I believe so."

I noticed the Kapellmeister had its third arm draped over the thing's head. The library AI said, It appears, of course, that Salieran autologous nerve induction works with Cetian as well as solar life forms.

I suddenly remembered the horses on Earth, and their riders. As I filled a plate with steak and potato, pouring *garum* on the womfrog meat in hopes of giving it a more steaky sort of flavor, opening the potato and adding a fair amount of butter and cold sour cream, I said, "What're you going to—"

The Kapellmeister's left chela snipped suddenly and the haaskin's head plopped to the ground. It tucked the carcass up under its body, pushed it in among the juncture of its legs, and something made a neat little sucking sound. The talking box said, "Ah. These things are very sweet."

I turned away and started in on the spud, thinking maybe I could have my candy-steak for dessert. Silence, punctuated by soft sucking, and then the Kapellmeister said, "Do you think the potato plant wouldn't mind, if she knew you were eating her babies?"

For . . . "Asshole!"

Somehow, we got through the rest of the meal, fire dying down as the sky grew dark and the stars came out overhead. The steak wasn't bad after all and the *garum* really did make it seem more like terragenic meat, fish and candy flavor blending into something else entirely. I stopped seeing the injured womfrog's eyes after the first couple of bites, little voice, somewhere deep inside, telling me not to be any more of an idiot than was absolutely necessary.

After the Kapellmeister finished sucking the haaskin dry, it cut the body up with its claws and ate the pieces, shoving sticky-looking, sweet-smelling bits up under its body, where they went *crunch, crunch, crunch,* and gradually disappeared.

Finally, it picked up the head, extending a couple of eye-stalks, seeming to look into the dead animal's open, staring eyes. "It's interesting how Cetian neural activity doesn't cease all at once, following decapitation."

How . . . nice for you. I remembered the way it'd left its third arm draped over the haaskin's skull while it'd snipped through the neck. The library AI whispered, Human scientific knowledge of Salieran neural induction biology is really quite limited. We know it exists, and that it's widespread among creatures of the Kapellmeisters' taxonomic classification, but little else. It seems to be the product of some natural evolutionary process, rather than technology.

The Kapellmeister flicked its wrist, tossing the dead head away into the undergrowth.

I remember watching educational vidnet shows on the subject. Scientist types pissing and moaning because the Salieran government wouldn't let us wander around on their home-world unescorted, though we let *them* wander around *ours.* I said, "Do they lose consciousness?"

Silence, then: "Well, yes, in the sense that you most likely mean the word. It's interesting though, observing those last, dying bits of neural activity."

I thought about it. "Did you hold on to the womfrog after I shot it?"

Silence, then: "Yes."

More silence. I said, "Well?"

The Kapellmeister said, "The subconscious imagery of sentient creatures is culturally determined for the most part. Quite complex and difficult to interpret."

An image of my own. Image of the dying womfrog falling down a long tunnel of light, falling into a mist of light in which womfrog-shaped shadows moved, the waiting spirits of those who'd gone on before. The library AI whispered, Like all Cetian land-living forms, the womfrogs are oviparous. In consequence, it seems psychologically unlikely that a womfrog's death-dream would take that form.

So. The walls of the life-shell burst open and the light of heaven floods in, welcoming the womfrog to rebirth? I shot him in the *brain*, for Christ's sake!

I tugged on the arms of my camp chair until the fasteners let go, backrest sliding into its semireclined position, letting me look up at the sky. Lots of stars out tonight, better than before because I'd had the foresight to put out the camper's cabin lighting. With the fire gone down to orange embers, I imagined I was seeing as many stars as you could see from the surface of a planet with the unaided human eye.

I glanced over at the Kapellmeister. It was sitting on a big rock nearby, legs collapsed and pulled underneath, arms tucked in, which made it look all the more like an enormous black bean. But all seven eyestalks were extended. Extended toward the sky.

I said, "You have to wonder what's really out there." Out there, beyond humanity's little pale. Out there, where the starfish-warship people must be waiting for us, even now.

The Kapellmeister said, "Wondering must be commonplace among starfaring folk."

Supposedly, the Kapellmeisters of Salieri, though they'd gone to space, out into their own star system in search of needed resources to support their industrial civilization, had otherwise stayed home. "Do you never wonder?"

Silence. Then it said, "Personally? Perhaps. But I was never a tabula-rasa-minded infant, as you were."

The library AI whispered, It has been speculated by some terrestrial zoopsychologists that the Kapellmeisters are imbued with knowledge and sentience at birth, via autologous nerve induction from their parents, at a special hatching ceremony.

I started to think about that, but the Kapellmeister said, "Gaetan, there is a great deal of electrical activity going on in my translator pod just now. Are your artificial personalities attempting to query the on-board language databases?"

Are you?

The translator AI whispered, Yes. Linguistic unspooling could allow us to surmise a great deal about Salieran culture.

"I'm afraid so."

"Please ask them to stop."

I said, "All right. Sorry, Kapellmeister."

Silence. Then it said, "Please don't call me that, Gaetan. The notion of possessing a name is . . . offensive to me."

"Sure. Sorry."

Silence.

Finally, I sat back in the chair and resumed looking at the sky, trying to pick out the stars of inhabited worlds. A good many of them were below the horizon, but many weren't. This one here, that one there . . . *Snow?* Groombridge 1618's too dim to see from here, isn't it?

The spacesuit whispered, According to the navigation subsystem, it is well below the local horizon in any case.

Great. After a while, I said, "I'd like to know what's out there anyway."

The Kapellmeister said, "With the coming of faster-than-light travel and the possession of a private starship, it seems likely you'll find out."

I felt a warm flush of pleasure. Will I? Why the hell else am I *here?* I said, "I've been thinking about that. Thinking about maybe going on to Snow when I get the chance, and take a look at all those famous ruins. I wish the hell we knew where they came from."

Silence.

Then the Kapellmeister said, "When news of the existence of these ruins was reported on Salieri, some authorities had difficulty accepting the authenticity of the find, given their apparent age of four hundred million years."

"I hadn't heard that anyone had successfully dated the ruins on Snow. I mean, that place is a *real* deep-freeze . . ." It was a large ice-moon, close to Titan-class, orbiting a remote gas giant of a small, cool star.

"Perhaps the news isn't widely discussed on human worlds. Or perhaps no one's bothered to tell human authorities. History is long, and you've only been here a short while."

I opened my mouth to speak, but stopped. Hadn't bothered to tell us? I sat back, looking up at the sky. Look here. You're talking to this thing as if it were a person, which it's not. There's a personality, but . . . how much of that's just an artifact of the translation algorithm?

The library AI whispered, There appears to be an artificial intelligence of nonhuman manufacture in the backpack. Without knowledge of the Salieran language system, we have no way of interpolating data.

Sure. But stay out of its business. I meant to ask a few more questions, but, after a while, I apparently fell asleep.

When I awoke the next morning, stiff and a little cold from sleeping in the chair, Tau Ceti just starting to flood the sky with orange and gold, I was alone, the Kapellmeister missing from his rock, though Graysplotch was still standing where I'd seen him last, motionless but for a faint swaying, eyes shut, apparently still asleep.

Maybe not. I could call up an image of the Kapellmeister on the horse's back last night, after it'd crawled down from taking off the feedbag, taking just a moment to touch Graysplotch between the shoulder blades with its third hand. After that, the horse hadn't moved again.

If I were a horse, that'd piss me off.

I decided to go for a nice morning walk, climb up this tall hill over here and watch the rest of the sunrise. Interesting how I've gotten used to these short nights and long, long days. I wonder what it'd be like on Green Heaven in the winter, when things would be just the reverse?

There was a cool breeze at the summit, wind coming out of the south almost cold, not quite enough to raise goosebumps on my arms. We've been headed southward, headed up into the foothills of the Koudloft, visible as always, low, white, misty mountains on the horizon. I . . .

Movement down below, in the open, grassy defile beyond my hill. I suddenly crouched, flinching at the unexpected appearance of . . . people? Crouched behind some low yellow brush, staring. Little white people, people dressed up in white fur, covered head to toe . . .

I stood again, got up on a boulder and shaded my eyes with one palm, trying to see. OK. Not people at all. Dollies, walking along single file, apparently unaware of my presence. I . . .

Something else. Walking up in the woods beyond the defile, a flash of white. *Wolfen?* Before I could get a good look, it seemed to notice me, freeze for a moment, then melt away. Down in the valley, the dollies kept walking along, unconcerned.

How do they survive, oblivious like that? If I had a gun, I could pick them right off, back to front. As for the wolfen . . . I stood rooted, waiting to see them rush out, pounce on the dollies, kill them and eat them, but . . .

Nothing.

Nothing but me standing out in the wind, remembering the dollie dancers of Orikhalkos.

11

We set out under the rising sun, Tau Ceti's yellow-white ball seeming to grow smaller as it rose, sky losing its brassy color, wispy clouds on the horizon gradually melting away. At first, I tried driving along, following the Kapellmeister's horse, fighting the tedium, trying to tell myself it was like being at work, but . . .

Right. *Real* work's not boring. Only those nasty little make-work jobs, where you stand someplace conspicuous, trying to look . . . *serviceable*. Finally, I got out and walked, letting the spaceship navigation system drive the camper, knowing it could memorize whatever it saw of the trail through my eyes, transmitted through the barrette. With the transponder nearby, the system was getting enough bandwidth it could cover my entire neurostructure from its perch over my left ear . . . I could put the God-damned thing in my pocket if I wanted, or lodge it up my ass. Still, I'd gotten used to wearing it in my hair.

"Is this a womfrog trail?"

The Kapellmeister didn't answer immediately, riding on Graysplotch, who seemed restored to his natural horse behavior. I wondered what it felt like to the horse, being . . . linked to the Salieran through the powers of those wet-looking tentacles, even now splayed on its back. "Once, I think it must have been, though there are too few of them now to keep it so well maintained."

It was shaping up into a beautiful day, blue-green sky taking on an enameled look, trees rustling softly in a gentle breeze, almost masking the distant shush of the camper's electric turbine. "People? Is it maintained by staff from the Takkor boerderij?"

"Possibly. I doubt it. More likely this track is maintained by the wolfen for their own purposes."

Their own purposes. That slight shock again, the realization that the wolfen were not as they'd been portrayed in all those vidnet shows.

The Kapellmeister said, "It's possible this is a dollie-track, though this close to an active Groenteboer estate, that would be dangerous to the point of foolhardiness."

Dollie-track.

The Kapellmeister said, "The wolfen aren't stupid, of course, especially these white wolfen. They've been quite decimated by human activity on the Koperveldt these last few centuries. Still, their need to participate in the natural ecology is quite strong; possibly too strong to overcome."

I walked on, silent, thinking about the wolfen and their possible relationship with the dollies, thinking about questions I might want to ask. All right. An intelligent predator might want to begin something like animal husbandry. And you *did* see that line of dollies walking along this morning, wolfen apparently watching from the woods . . . Something about another vidnet show. Anthropology. Humans of the Upper Paleolithic kept horses, kept them penned up to the point where the horses would go nuts, would lift themselves off the ground by biting down on the corral rails. I've got the memory all mixed up with some other story, about how the Aurignacian hunters came to Europe just long enough the wipe out the Neanderthal, then headed on east across Beringia to become the first Amerinds. Something about a valley of horses. Yes. So did dear little Ayla ride her horses, girlfantasy of almighty powerful meat surging between her legs? Heh. Most likely, all she did was eat the poor bastards. Horsemeat stew. Yum.

We went up a low rise and suddenly burst out of the forest, pausing on the rim of a broad, treeless, caldera-like valley, an open, grassy bowl with forest visible all around the rim. Down in the bottom, among scattered copses of smaller trees, some of them no more than large bushes, there was a little stream, beside it a group of large white tents and a vehicle pretty much like my camper, now sighing to a stop behind us.

Bubble cabin in front, median power bay, antennae just the same. The pop-up back was missing, replaced by an open cargo box with a corrugated bed. I'd seen things like this before, mostly for use on the unprotected surface of worlds like Luna and Mars. Pickup truck, I think, is the common term.

The Kapellmeister said, "I think you'll like these people, Gaetan. Let's go on down."

People, I thought. It never occurred to me to give the term such a wide definition, but . . . we started down the hill, and things began coming out of the tents.

I remembered Rua Mater's reaction when she'd turned and unexpectedly beheld those Arousian tourists at the Washington Zoo, big, burnished stick-bugs looking like something out of just about every alien-monsters-are-upon-us movie ever made. Especially the bit with the faceted eyes. Makes you realize the term "bug-eyed monster" doesn't refer to exophthalmia.

As we came to a stop in front of them, camper wheezing to a halt, settling in the tall yellow grass, the Kapellmeister hopping off its horse and standing beside me, the Arousians fanned out in front of their tents, almost as if guarding their equipment. Some sort of . . . tension in the air here, as if . . . Odd. If any sentient extraterrestrial species is . . . used to us, it's these.

The Kapellmeister's translator pod made a single, faint *gree-kee*, and one of the Arousians stepped forward, seeming to skirt round some imaginary line defining my personal space, going on the other side of the Salieran, as if its tiny, black hassock of a body could somehow . . .

Christ. This thing is scared to death of me.

The Kapellmeister reached out with its third arm and wrapped its tentacles around the lower reaches of one of the Arousian's forelegs. Pretty tableau then, Arousian suddenly motionless, head cocked just so, eyes seeming to peer at me, eyes like glittering bits of ice, expressionless, emotionless, as empty as so much glass, and yet . . .

The Kapellmeister's translator pod said, "Mr. du Cheyne, this is my friend, Rustmold-on-Pale-Snow."

The Arousian clattered its limbs together, a bizarre parody, as if some craggy noncom in one of those old British Raj dramas that were so popular in the twenty-fourth century, as if its name might be *Sarn't-Major, Sah!*, but its translator said, "Rustmold-on-Pale-Snow, line of the White-Crystal-Star Foragers, under the sponsorship of Jimmy MacCray and the engineering staff at Research Base Four-alpha, MEI-at-SD3."

Absurdly, I found myself reaching out, as if to shake hands with the thing, as if . . . it reached out and took my hand in a cluster of little claws and stick-like fingers on the end of one of its . . . appendages, chitinous skin cool to the touch, just a hair above air temperature. I said, "Uh. Pleased to, uh . . ." Tongue-tied before a thing.

The other Arousians started coming forward, doing things like little curtsies, limbs clattering, introducing themselves with complex, nonsensical names, every one of which seemed to have a human sponsor embedded in it. Other data bubbling up, useless bits of memory: You know, of course, that the human population of Sigma Draconis is in the neighborhood of seventy-five million, something like eight times the native population, employees of Mace Electrodynamics, mostly living on Arous' airless moon and in the system's dense asteroid belt, where . . .

Horseshit. Why is it everything I seem to know is composed of horseshit?

I looked helplessly at the Kapellmeister, standing off to one side now, then beyond, to a . . . and froze. In the shadow of some big, silver-green bushes, under branches covered with broad leaves and whorls of small, bright, no-color flowers, lolling on the ground like so many big, weird-looking dogs, were a group of white wolfen. Staring at me, teeth showing, mottled eyes generally attentive.

I think I took a step back, then stopped. Of course. They're here to be . . . interviewed. Something like that.

But then beyond the wolfen, kneeling in the deeper shadows, like children in cowgirl suits, wearing teddy bear masks, a double row of dollies. Kneeling, impassive, unmoving, heads bowed, tiny hands clasped on their breasts. Like . . . children saying their prayers.

Faint, faded, faraway memory. Saying my prayers, saying the litany of the Laïty of Kali Meitner under the watchful eye of my mother, before I lay me down to sleep and put my soul at risk. I . . .

Christ. That . . . not quite smell in the air, prickling at the underside of my brain, like small, scratching fingers. Suddenly, it felt like the dollies were watching me, dark, almost-human eyes, hidden but there nonetheless, looking at me from under shaggy brows.

Stop it. Nothing more than an overactive imagination. But I kept thinking about the dollie sex show back in Orikhalkos. Besides which, that's money on the hoof you're looking at, boy. Fat, horny old men on Epimetheus will pay good money for those things. Probably a lot better money than old van Rijn was willing to let on.

As Tau Ceti slowly declined, angling down through the northwestern sky, I set up camp next to the Arousians' little tent village, parking my camper by the stream, next to their pickup truck, opening the pop-up section and puttering around inside, looking into the storage bay underneath, seeing just what . . .

Right. Dawdling. Because if I'm outside, I get to see those great big white wolfen eyeing me hungrily, or, worse still, walking round with nothing to do, too conscious of my dick, pretending I don't know the dollies are there. Even inside, I can sort of smell . . . Remember the dollhouse back in Orikhalkos. I thought that miasma was, somehow, provoked by all those aroused men, coming off them, evaporating with their sickly sweat . . .

The library AI whispered, It's within the realm of possibility that the dollies exude a pheromone that triggers some sexual response in the human male vomeronasal organ. It is a characteristic of Cetian life-forms that they use the same underlying biochemical structures as terragenic life, but for different purposes, resulting in some confusion when end-products of the two evolutionary schemes meet.

Right. Womfrog guts smelling like fresh apple pie. Womfrog steaks with a distinct tang of semisweet chocolate. Dollies able to provoke . . . well, why not provoke a response in the human female vomeronasal organ? Why were there only men in the dollhouse? Just biochemical coincidence? Or is it true, as so many wish to believe, that women are . . . superior?

The library whispered, The most widely accepted theory would have us believe that human males are evolutionarily provoked to impregnate every female they can. Hence the ease with which they are tricked into mating with other mammalian species.

Unbidden, a brief image of a sheep appeared in my head. Unbidden, I suppose, because I couldn't quite make myself believe the library AI had put it there, despite its newfound bandwidth.

It went on, As males are provoked simply to impregnate, females are provoked to become pregnant, with the expectation of offspring, hence their reproductive biochemistry is much more finely tuned and correspondingly harder to misdirect.

Meaning a man who'll screw a dead cat is much less

deranged than a woman who has a meaningful relationship with an appropriately shaped power tool? Right. And if you believe that, there's a very nice bridge spanning Valles Mariner- is I've been meaning to put on the market.

So I puttered around my camper, periodically castigating myself, and watched the goings-on edgewise. The Arousians seemed unafraid of the wolfen, moving easily among them, accompanied much of the time, though not always, by the Kapellmeister. Unafraid? Well, maybe the Arousians are no more edible to the wolfen than your average pile of kindling wood. Then again, the wolfen aren't mad at them, either. One of the Arousians . . .

Rustmold-on-Pale-Snow, whispered the translator.

Going from wolfen to wolfen. Talking to it through its human-made interpreter gizmo? No. If humans don't think wolfen can talk . . . The Kapellmeister would touch the wolfen, which would stiffen, mottled eyes visibly rolling. Wolfen clearly unnerved by what was happening here. Then I'd hear an exchange of words between translator pods. In English? Yes.

The library whispered, English is the technical working lan- guage of MEI, and has become the formal human language of the colonies at Sigma Draconis.

Every now and again, after a prolonged exchange, the Kapellmeister would reach out and touch the Arousian. Momentary freeze frame, then you'd hear Rustmold-on-Pale- Snow say, "Ah, yes. Now I understand."

I wonder what it feels like?

The spacesuit's voice whispered, Quite likely, similar to our own communication modalities.

But the Arousians, Kapellmeisters and wolfen are *extremely* different sorts of . . . Um. I'm so used to talking with hardware, I forget what it is that's whispering in my head.

The translator said, Of course, artificial intelligences of human manufacture are optimized for communication with human neural structures.

Our things. Loving us. Belovèd.

Finally, when I got hungry, I decided to take the plunge. Instead of timidly staying in my camper, I broke out the charcoal gas grill I'd found in the storage bay, set it up on a flat place by the river, fired it up and, while the coal bed was settling in, got out my chair, a little table, picked out a nice womfrog steak, put together a vinaigrette salad, a couple of neatly wrapped ears of corn, butter, *garum*, put the steaks on and listened to them sizzle.

I sat in the chair, determined to enjoy myself, looking up at a sky that was starting to streak with vermilion . . . what the fuck is that *smell?*

The Arousians were gathered among their tents, more or less ignoring me, gathered round some squat apparatus that made long jets of blue flame. Each stick-bug-person had a skewer on which was impaled some kind of dark lump, taking turns rolling the lumps in their blue flames, pulling them out, on fire, watching them burn, emitting long plumes of pale gray smoke.

A distinct smell of burning polybutadiene.

The Kapellmeister came toward me, carrying a little thing that looked like a greenish kangaroo—*konijn,* whispered the translator—holding it helpless in its claws, octopus draped over its little head. You could see beady red eyes peering between the tentacles. Sorry, critter . . .

Snip. The konijn's head fell to the grass. *Slurp.*

"Ah. This one is quite good." The Kapellmeister said, "One of the problems the Arousians have, when they travel, is a biochemistry that is much different from what we find on other human colonial worlds."

"Mace couldn't help them out with that?"

"Well, there are limits to human technology. The Arousians are provided with blood symbionts which allow them to survive allergic reactions to alien tissues. This permits them to travel without bio-isolation garments on planets with an appropriate atmosphere, but it can't overcome the fact that most terrestrial and Cetian life forms, if consumed, would interfere with certain aspects of the Arousian cellular metabolism."

Poisonous, in other words. I turned away, intending to flip my steak . . . found myself gripping the fork rather . . . firmly.

The Kapellmeister said, "I think Limbcracker would like some womfrog steak. She's gotten rather hungry, hanging around here all day."

Limbcracker. Great. The wolfen was sitting on its haunches beside the barbecue, eying the meat on the grill with evident interest. Leaning forward, in fact, seeming to sniff . . . I said, "Terrific. Well." I went in and got a fresh steak, brought it out . . . Hell. Put it on the end of the fork and held it out to . . . Limbcracker. The wolfen gave it a short glance, a sniff. Turned away, back to the grill.

The Kapellmeister said, "I believe Limbcracker would like to sample some cooked meat. Please try to scrape off some of the *garum* you've added. It will only make her sick."

I turned to stare at the Kapellmeister. It sat there, sucking on its dead konijn, looking like . . . God damn it, I'm trying to make eye contact with a footstool and Ping Pong balls, I . . .

"Please, Gaetan. Limbcracker is being very friendly, considering your species."

Shit. I put the raw steak on the grill, transferred the cooked one to my plate and set it on the ground, hoping I was out of reach of any quick grab . . . Limbcracker edged forward, leaning down, sniffing. *Snap.* Only half a steak left in the plate. In fact, a couple of chips missing from the edge of the plate as well. The steak made sticky sounds as Limbcracker chewed and . . .

She looked back toward the trees, where the other wolfen, hungry wolfen most likely, were lolling, watching. *"Oooooom."* Long pause in which the long grunt sort of echoed, then a quick, *"Phh!"* The other wolfen started getting up, walking our way.

The Kapellmeister said, "I think they like you, Gaetan. This is most unusual."

Like me? Six, no seven, white wolfen sitting in a semicircle around the grill, looking at me expectantly, long, pointed black tongues coming out, licking around their muzzles, nostrils dilating as they . . . "I'll bet." I went in and got the rest of my steaks, the seventy or eighty pounds I'd cut from the injured womfrog after I shot it dead.

In a while, the Arousians came over, finished with their stinky lumps of whatever, set up what appeared to be stereo cameras, and started filming the goings-on. At some point, as I sat in my chair, Limbcracker came over and threw herself on the ground beside me, purring like a God-damned cat.

Later, I sat alone under an infinitely deep nighttime sky, kind of looking up at nothing, smell of dying fires in my nose, faint aftertang of cooked and eaten food, the dry-as-dust scent of the Arousians beneath that, along with the sweet oil and caramel smell of the wolfen . . . I could see them over there, pale shadows sprawled under a copse of alien trees, wind softly rustling alien leaves.

I suppose I should be getting to bed as well. These antarctic nights are so short, hardly long enough to get enough sleep, to make up for the long, long day.

And yet. All of it. Everything. Stirring my mind to go on and on, thinking about what I'd seen, refusing to let go, let me creep away to a soft bunk and settle down through dream to memory. Memory of the Arousians talking to the white wolfen, through one interpreter pod to another, through the mind of the Kapellmeister, whatever *it* may be like, through neural tendrils that can, apparently, bridge an immense evolutionary gap . . .

Memory of Limbcracker lying enormous at my feet, licking her muzzle like a dog, licking her paws like a cat and then cleaning behind her ears. Her . . . Memory of the Kapellmeister, explaining just a little bit of the wolfen's apparent eusocial order to me, these free-roving wolfen bands groups of sisters, all from the same litter, loosely tied to other such bands in a kinship group, all descended from a common foremother, reaching back for many generations.

And the males?

The Kapellmeister said, There are other aspects of the

wolfen social order. Finding these things out is part of the Arousian study. Local humans apparently never cared.

Something reticent about the way it was said, probably no more than an artifact of the translator pod. But . . . a sense, from nowhere, that, perhaps, the Kapellmeister doesn't quite trust me yet. Why does that trust seem so important just now? I never wanted anyone's trust before.

Soft noise in the distance, like a faraway crying child. Some chance animal sound, some little animal or another, like a konijn, or . . . The crying again, a little louder, as if nearer. One of the wolfen raised its head briefly, listened, then settled back. Maybe the distant cry is some small predator, like a hunting owl or . . .

A sudden realization that I hadn't seen many flying things in the air of Green Heaven. Certainly nothing like birds.

I stood, stretching under the stars, intending to go in and sleep. Stood still, frozen in place, listening to that mewling cry. Not so far away at all, is it? No. A tiny whimpering, as if close by. That's it. Nearby, and not very loud at all. I turned away from the encampment and started walking, in the direction I thought the sound was coming from.

Plenty of light here, though both the moons are gone. Plenty of light from the stars, from the Milky Way's dense, irregular band of golden dust. Creepy shadows everywhere, trees frozen against the sky.

Momentary pause. Am I being an idiot? There could be . . . just about anything . . . I remembered how I'd felt, looking up from my campfire . . . only yesterday? Remembered that hard pang of terror when I saw the wolfen looking at me. Well. Here's the comforting lump of my little dartgun, full of potent anesthetic. Not so good against wolfen, to be sure, but . . . I thought about going back and getting a rifle, but the crying drew me on, back of my neck prickling, hair threatening to stand on end.

There.

Down in the shadows.

Dollies.

Grouped together around one of their number, dollie squatting over what looked in the darkness like a nest made of grass, something dark runneling down the insides of its legs. I walked closer, slowly, quietly. One of the dollies looked up and saw me. Froze for a second, then looked away, as if dismissing me.

The squatting dollie suddenly squeaked, a little mouse-cry of dismay, grunted softly, seemed to strain. A pale ovoid appeared between its legs, started to fall . . .

One of the others, the one standing closest to the dollie in the center of the set piece, reached out and caught the thing. Held it up to the starlight. Made a little coo, like a mourning dove. Held the ovoid between its own legs and seemed to shove. When it let go, the egg was gone. It stepped away, let another dollie take its place.

Another little cry, like a lost kitten, another straining, another egg caught, examined and hidden. Dollie stepping back, letting another take its place. Then another. And another. I counted six more before . . . The ovulating dollie made a little sob and fell to its knees in the grassy nest, dark blood seeming to gush, and I caught a powerful whiff of something, a . . . I don't know. A protein smell, amorphous, hard to pin down, tainted with something like cinnamon. Like the smell of French toast, that's it.

The other dollies closed in, the ones who'd taken the eggs snatching up handfuls of grass, pressing it between the egg-layer's legs, as if to staunch the flow of blood. No, taking the wads of soaked grass away, chewing them, swallowing. The dollie was lying on the ground now, whispering softly to itself. After a while, the pile of bloody grass was used up and all the other dollies lay down as well, clustering round their comrade.

Males and females here? I wonder.

The library AI whispered, Unknown. But it seems likely, from what we know of Cetian biology. The wolfen males must be somewhere as well.

Look at the dollies, snuggled together like so many pretty little girls at a slumber party. I felt a strong urge to go lie down with them, felt the hair on the back of my neck prickle again. As I turned to walk away, I found myself wondering if all the dollies dancing at the dollhouse had been female dollies. Wondered if their owners and . . . users had any way to tell.

Wondered, in fact, if it even mattered.

I went back to the camper and locked myself in, got undressed and lay down naked in the darkness in a suddenly claustrophobic bunk. Lay looking out through the little window at my skyful of stars, willing myself not to think.

Just animals, that's all. Chickens lay eggs and we eat them for breakfast, eggs and chickens alike. Alligators lay eggs. Echidnas lay eggs. Even frogs lay eggs, though we only eat their legs. Animals. Despite a conscious will to keep my mind blank, stay focused on my window full of stars, I was suddenly transported back to the dollhouse, to the image of that groaning fat man with a dollie straddling his lap.

Memory of the dollie getting off him, dabbing at her . . . its crotch with an already soiled bit of napkin, then dancing away. Dancing away to the next man? I hadn't stayed to see.

Great. Now I'm lying here in the darkness with . . .

Somehow, I managed to put it aside, blot the whole business away, close my eyes and . . .

Gaetan.

I opened my eyes on blue-gray darkness, camper cabin flooded with starlight. Turned my head, feeling dizzy and confused, so I could look out the window again. Different stars, sparse in number, the sky somehow bright between them, tinged with a vague, nameless color.

Voice whispering in my head, Gaetan, wake up.

Faint prickle of alarm. Is something wrong? Why would the AIs . . .

"*Haaaaaaarrr* . . ." Long, drawn-out, metallic howl, loud

enough to make the flimsy pop-up wall beside me seem to shiver. Outside.

"Jesus Christ!"

The library whispered, We thought this would be of interest to you.

I got up, bare feet on a cold plastic floor, crouched to look out the window.

"*Aaaahaaaaaaaa . . .*"

Darkness outside, full of shadows. There. Sitting atop the pickup truck's cab, the shape of a wolfen outlined black against the sky, head thrown back, jaws agape, so you could see the jagged shadows of its long, spiky teeth. "*Aaaaaiiiii . . .*" Rattling, metallic howl aimed at the starry sky, something thoroughly inhuman, gargling a throatful of cold steel.

Other wolfen out there as well, white shapes visible by starlight, sitting together in a group, as if waiting. There. Over there the angular shapes of Arousians, mingled with other equally angular shapes that must be cameras and tripods and whatever else they . . .

That little dark blot among them. That would be my Kapellmeister.

Glint of starlight on the little stream's water. Dark shapes off trees superimposed against the sky. "What the hell's going on?"

Library: We don't know.

"Then . . ."

Translator: Though you forbade us to interfere, we've been . . . listening through the Salieran device.

Spacesuit: I thought it'd be better to awaken you deliberately, rather than wait for the howls to . . .

Soft shiver. Well, you got that right, pal.

What the hell are those things? Pale human shapes, like the shapes of little children, kneeling between the wolfen and the Arousians' cameras? Dollies, of course.

I found my pants, still on the floor where I'd thrown them, and went outside, barefoot and shirtless, cold breeze blowing over me, raising goosebumps on my arms and chest, making me shiver. One of the wolfen looked over at me, briefly, and I stood quite still, watching.

The wolfen on top of the truck threw its head back and sang, raising echoes in the distance, making me feel short of breath. Christ. I don't know what I'm watching. Heart pounding away in my chest. An odd feeling in the pit of my stomach, though. As if something, something deep inside, knows what's coming, I . . .

Long, long silence, filled with the soft shushing of the wind, the distant gurgle of the brook, the faint, ticking whirr of the cameras. It seemed as though I could see everything quite clearly now, every little detail picked out in delicate shades of gray, the world created as a sophisticated million-hue grayscale holograph.

I could see the dollies, facing the clustered wolfen, kneeling together. Could see the gleam of their little eyes, dollies in their cowgirl costumes like so many . . . frightened children. Eyes wide, dollies stirring gently, looking to each other for . . . what?

The wolfen atop the pickup truck said, *"Whuff."* Short, chopped, peremptory. The other wolfen . . . my God, as if their hair is moving, shifting about on their backs.

One of the dollies turned in its position. Turned and looked round. You could see . . . The other dollies are terrified, looking away, avoiding the glance of this one. I . . . It lifted its . . . paw, seemed to gesticulate. The one it pointed to recoiled as if struck.

I imagined I could hear it thinking, *Not me.*

"Whuff." Sharper. A little louder.

Silence. Wind, water, cameras.

Then the dollie that'd been singled out slowly rose from its knees. Very, very slowly. Reluctance and terror easily cross the evolutionary divide that separated me from Cetian life, as though some universal . . . Hell. I could *easily* be imagining all this, I . . .

The dollie slowly walked forward, threading through the rows of its companions. Walked forward until it stood right in front of the clustered wolfen. There was a soft thud-thump, a tremor through the ground as a heavy body hit the earth. The sound of the howler coming down from its perch, joining the others.

Soft, fast, panting sound.

Coming from the dollie, breathing hard and fast and . . .

One of the wolfen reached out, lightning-fast, and poked the little dollie in the chest. It staggered back with a sharp, high-pitched gasp, clutching its breast, and I fancied I saw a dark stain against the lighter background of its fur. It turned, as if to run, looking toward its comrades, arms raised beseeching-ly. Then it shouted, a chatter of pale cries, like so many panicky words . . .

One of the wolfen struck it, heavy paw thumping into the dollie's back, silencing the cries, throwing it on its face. The other dollies, huddled together now, seemed to be looking away.

The spacesuit said, Please breathe, Gaetan.

I could feel the tightness in my chest. Tried to relax, tried to . . .

The dollie on the ground struggled, rolled over on its back, looking up. Screamed, a soft cry of despair, lifted one hand to ward off . . .

The jaws closed on its arm, pulling it upright, dollie wail-ing, in obvious agony. The wolfen let go and the dollie stag-gered. I could see dark blood falling in big drops from where its hand had been, dollie chattering, voice climbing through a child's high register, shaking its stump.

The wolfen's paw pushed it to the ground again and held it there, seeming to smother the cries, but I could see the dollie's arms and legs flailing as it tried to struggle free. Struggle free and, I imagined, live. One of the other wolfen, flattened against the ground, slithered in and bit off the dollie's right leg, severing it at the knee.

Moment of silence.

Then the dollie shrilled, full of agony, full of horror.

For just a second, I imagined myself in its place, then recoiled from the image. This will all be over soon, I told myself. All be over soon and then it'll be dead and gone and all the pain will be gone, will not have mattered, will . . .

Another wolfen came and bit off the other leg in just the same way, dollie's screams redoubling. I wonder, can it hear the crunching, crackling sounds, as its bones are crushed, crushed between powerful jaws and consumed?

Other wolfen swarming round now, sniffing, tongues reaching out to touch the dollie's terrible, bleeding wounds, other wolfen with their heads cocked, as though listening to those screams. Listening with obvious pleasure.

Just the way a man might listen to a sizzling steak, perhaps.

Wolfen slinking round, snapping jaws, crack of bone, dollie's scream, amputated arm briefly visible, flopping loosely between grinning jaws.

Then a pause in the action, wolfen taking its paw away, one-armed triple-amputee dollie lying on the ground, struggling weakly, moaning softly, rolling, rolling, trying to pull itself away with its remaining hand, eyes visible, staring out of its head beneath a mop of disheveled hair . . .

Wolfen watching. Watching it try to live.

Then they clustered round it, hiding the dollie from my sight. I heard a crackle of bone, dollie starting to scream again, scream out a babble so much like words I . . .

Scream chopped off.

Silence.

Except for the soft sounds of eating.

Somehow, I caught my breath again, turning away, going to sit in my chair beside the little table I'd left earlier. Table still littered with the remains of my meal. Corncob. An uneaten chunk of cold womfrog steak, still reeking of fishy *garum*.

Across the way, the wolfen scattered now, going back to their little growth of trees, lying down, licking themselves clean. I thought I heard one of them burp softly. Where the dollie had been, there was nothing. Maybe some blood on the grass, maybe . . . I don't know. Though a blue rim was forming over on the eastern edge of the sky, washing away some of the dimmer stars, highlighting faraway mountains, it's seemed to have grown dark again down here.

The Arousians were *greeking* among themselves, so many mechanical cricket noises that sounded nothing at all like words, clicking and clacking as they took down their cameras and folded up their tripods and headed for their tents. The other dollies . . . Still huddled together, seeming to look at the empty place where one of their number had been. Tiny, far-away sounds. Dollies whispering to one another. Whispering in unison perhaps, like children saying their bedtime prayers, *Now I lay me down to sleep* . . .

Quiet mechanical voice beside me: "They are not at all a natural species, you know."

I jumped, looking down at the Kapellmeister, who'd crept up on me quite silently on those smooth, machine-like alien legs. "What do you mean?"

It settled to the ground beside me, legs folding away out of sight, arms folded close to its forebody, eyestalks waving gently above its back. It said, "It appears the wolfen have been breed-ing them, practicing animal husbandry with the dollies for a long time. Tissue studies suggest it may be on the order of mil-lions of years."

"The wolfen have been breeding dollies for longer than the human species has existed?"

"That sort of thing is a commonplace with eusocial animals. The wolfen are to dollies what ants are to aphids."

And ants have been having their way with the aphids for rather a long time now. Not since the time of the dinosaurs, but certainly since the time when the remote ancestors of human beings were big-eyed things that ate bugs for a living. I tried to remember if ants ate their aphids or merely sucked their sweat, but . . .

The library whispered, Most species do not. Aphids prosper mightily by their association with the ants, who are such dangerous predators that few creatures willingly trifle with them.

The other dollies were on their feet now, moving back into the shadows, settling down to sleep again perhaps, chattering softly among themselves. The Kapellmeister said, "Human depredation is interfering with the relationship between the wolfen and dollies, of course. Likely driving both species toward extinction."

I thought about the killpit, then the dollhouse. I could think of how the dollies might survive. I said, "Are the dollies . . . sentient?"

The Kapellmeister said, "The phrase has little meaning, Gaetan." It extended its pulpy mass of neural tentacles, spreading them wide in the growing gray light, light glistening off wet black skin. "But even in the limited sense that humans mean when they use the word they've created . . . It seems so."

I thought about the way the Kapellmeister would drape its tentacles over the head of a prey animal just before snipping off its head. You'd think a creature that believed . . . I tried to picture a vegetarian Kapellmeister.

The library whispered, The Salierans have a most thoroughgoing carnivore morphology.

Still, a civilization with a technological sophistication easily exceeding that of human beings should have little trouble altering itself. Or even just breeding species of plant to take the place of living . . .

The spacesuit whispered, Plants are living things.

The Kapellmeister said, "We'll be moving the camp this morning, Gaetan. Perhaps you'd better try to get a little sleep now, if you want to come along."

Watching the orange bloom of Tau Ceti on the horizon, I rubbed tired, grainy eyes, and wondered if I did. What else? Go on back to Orikhalkos and hang round till it's time to pick up my cargo of dollies and leave for Epimetheus? I could sleep all day and find whores every night.

Or go to the wolfen killpits. Go to the dollhouse and watch the dollies dance. I thought about the fat man. Hell. At least he didn't eat them.

I said, "Sure. Wake me up when it's time to go."

Went inside. Went to sleep.

No dreams.

12

Sunlight in my face; butter yellow Cetian sunshine streaming in the camper's little window, making a nice warm square on my pillow, bracketing my face. Sounds from outside. Voices. Not human voices, not speaking human words, but somehow, while I slept, they'd become voices all the same, the Arousians' cricket-screeching welcome, as warming as the sunshine, making me feel like I was . . .

Oh, hell. I don't know. Like I was back home, walking into the break room at Stardock just before change of shift, getting ready to . . . go to work. I thought briefly about them all, about Garstang, about Phil Hendrickx and Zell Benson, Millie Aichang and Rua Mater . . . I got up, took a shower. Got dressed. Went outside.

Under a brass-tinted blue sky, the Arousians were already well along in the task of breaking camp, tents taken down, folded, packed in ridiculously tiny containers, for the most part already stowed in the pickup truck's side boxes. Other equipment . . . It looked like the Arousians would get it all in the boxes as well.

Off to one side, Limbcracker and her . . . well. Not fellows. Not brethren. Not comrades, though that comes closer. No word in English for a band of sisters? Sorority? Maybe, though the connotations I knew were centuries old and had to do with social clubs. Maybe the anthropologists . . . The library AI was unaccountably silent.

Beyond where the wolfen were sprawled, the dollies kneeled in a little group, facing toward the east. Kneeling, seeming to bend slightly forward every now and again, almost but not quite in unison. Whispering. Again, almost but not quite in unison.

The Kapellmeister was nearby, sitting atop its horse, halfway up its neck, in fact, tentacle-hand sprawled over the back of the horse's head. The horse was imposingly still, its eyes, from where I stood, appearing to stare, more or less, in opposite directions.

"What're you doing?" Nothing. Out of the corner of my eye, I could see one of the wolfen raise its head and look at me. I stood watching for another minute, waiting, then gave up, started gathering my trash, packing away my junk. I even managed to remember to take the garbage, bits of organic tissue, inside and feed it down the disposal, even though, thrown on the ground, I'm sure it would have decayed nicely and . . .

The library whispered, Not the *garum*, Gaetan. In relation to the Cetian ecology, it's comparable to a puddle of spilled gasoline.

The Kapellmeister suddenly slid down from its horse, landed with a soft plop-thud on the ground. The horse seemed to take a very deep breath, then another, like a man who can't quite get enough oxygen in his lungs.

The Kapellmeister reached out with one chela and poked the horse in the flank. It jumped slightly, snorted, made some sort of faint whickering sound, then turned, very purposefully, head held high, and trotted away, up the hill onto the trail by which we'd come. It paused once, struck a pose at the top of the hill, looking down on us all. I felt a sharp thrill run down my spine. Perhaps I was expecting it to rear like some fantasy stallion and . . . It just turned away. Turned, went into the forest, and was gone, not even the sound of hoofbeats left behind.

The Kapellmeister came trotting over to where I was standing, legs flexing in order as it walked, as though under the control of some ancient mechanical distributor unit, blue eyes floating atop their stalks, looking up at me. It said, "I programmed Graysplotch to go to the Takkor boerderij and turn himself in. They'll recognize the brand and see he gets where he belongs."

Hmh. "Um. Won't someone . . ."

"I told the stable something like this would happen, that there was no one to notify. They . . . had quite an argument about whether they wanted to rent me a horse, but . . . sufficient application of money . . ."

The translator AI whispered, The software inhabiting the Kapellmeister's pod seems to have a most excellent grasp of human language nuance.

Quite. I said, "So . . . you'll be riding with . . ." I glanced over at the Arousians' truck, was startled to see they'd extruded a ramp, that the dollies were arrayed in a solid phalanx at its foot, like so many little cowgirl soldiers. Just then, one of the wolfen made a little *woof* and the dollies began marching up the ramp.

The Kapellmeister said, "I thought I might ride with you, Gaetan."

"Oh. All right. Be my guest." I gestured at the camper's cab.

The Kapellmeister turned, went over to the door, reached up with one clumsy-looking lobster claw, worked the latch and opened it, clambered in without difficulty. I took a deep breath, turning to look just as the wolfen scrambled up into the pickup bed with their dollies. Looked up at the sun for a second, then went round to the driver's-side door and got in.

Sat and looked at the Kapellmeister. Finally, it said, "We're headed for a place on the other side of the Koudloft, near the headwaters of the Mistibos River. I've already passed the coordinates to your transponder unit via the satellite link."

I realized with a slight start that in the little time I'd dawdled outside, the Kapellmeister had gotten my black box off the seat and set it on the floor. "Okay. Then . . . we're off." I hit the starter, listened to the electric motors whine, then punched the pop-up button, looking back over my shoulder as the living space folded itself away.

Midday and Tau Ceti was as high as it was going to get, hanging low over the northern horizon because we were so far south now, sliding through long-shadowed badlands country that looked like something from the Old West, only cold, ground streaked here and there with patches of persistent ice the Kapellmeister told me would evaporate only at high summer, those few weeks when the sun never set.

Lots of craggy red rocks, fractured from weathering—this place, I was assured, would be under ten meters of snow come winter. Open, dry mud flats, covered with a crazy pattern of cracks like the surface of Europa. Low, gullied hills. Pillars of rock, like lava tubes, but . . .

I said, "Those things almost look artificial." A little bit, in fact, like the mysterious ruins I'd seen over by the mountains.

The Kapellmeister's eyestalks floated above the instrument panel, looking out through the cab dome, little blue moons that seemed to sway this way and that, almost circling each other . . . "It is possible. Those would not be StruldBug ruins, of course, nor those of any Adversary Instrumentality, which would have survived almost intact, it having been only four hundred million years or so since the Shock War." It paused, seeming to consider. *"Possibly* something left by my own people, but I have no recollection . . ."

Its voice seemed to fade, translator pod emitting a faint, low-pitched growl before going silent. Seemed to drift away, as though into a dream, eyestalks retracting until its eyes were resting on its back.

What the hell.

What the hell are StruldBugs?

Silence. Then the translator AI whispered, Have we your permission to query the Kapellmeister's translator pod operating system?

Um. Sure.

The translator whispered, StruldBug is a term the pod creat-ed to convey, in English, the Salieran conceptual sequence for a species that exists in no database we've ever indexed.

Which would be a lot. I paid for a pretty good library instal-lation on *Random Walk*, after all . . .

Struld, of course, is from the Laputa section of Swift. *Bug* is a reference to their physical appearance. A sort of pseudo-exoskeleton like the Arousians. Not related, though. The image received is reminiscent of a large, golden cockroach with half-molten skin. About the size of an Airedale terrier.

What about the rest of it?

Long wait, then: No answer. The pod will only answer proce-dural queries relating to the task of translation. Nothing to do with the underlying information. The pod further states it would prefer not to have to interrupt the Kapellmeister's medi-tation. It notes we've been asked already not to transgress in the pod's operational space.

I sat back, looking out at the landscape, at those towers that might or might not be ruins. Tall towers with fluted sides? I remembered suddenly that structures like that held some place in the Saucer People cargo cult, but I couldn't remember what, quickly blocked my thought from the library so it wouldn't go digging for useless references.

Too late. It made a series of musical tones, then shut up.

So. StruldBugs. Adversary Instrumentality. Shock War. Four hundred million years. And . . . *I have no recollection.*

Nightfall, camper parked and popped under cold, brilliant antarctic stars. Not so many stars, though, for the sky seemed a good deal lighter here, as though the blackness were tainted by a faint touch of indigo, the waxing midnight sun a few degrees closer to the horizon. The library informed me it was still five weeks to the last sunset of the season at this latitude.

I had a brief flash of memory, standing outside the Valley Dor habitat in the Martian antarctic, white night pale and peculiar overhead, standing on some crispy surface of residual water ice during a summer vacation away from Syrtis Major.

Can't remember if Jayanne was with me then.

I cooked and ate a quick prefab dinner inside the camper habitat, no flavor, no texture, then went back out into the cold, drawn by the ruddy fires that had bloomed among the Arousians' tents, by shadows moving in the darkness. Went and sat on the chilly rear ramp structure of the pickup truck, sat and watched.

The white wolfen were drawn up on level ground in two short rows, facing each other several meters apart, one isolated wolfen sat facing inward on each open end, as though guarding the interior of the square thus formed. Guarding the dollies within. The dollies were facing each other, holding hands, marching in place very gently, hardly lifting their little feet at all, chanting softly, long chest fur bouncing like a cowgirl's tassels with each footfall.

Virginia reel, suggested the library, reading a half-formed thought, completing it.

Yeah. Sort of. One dollie from the opposite end of each line suddenly let go, began dancing in to the center of the square, spinning . . . the isolated wolfen on the open ends of the square started to bark, metallic sounds, like sledgehammers on cold metal, in alternation, slightly different intonations, clang-clink, clang-clink . . .

The two dollies got to the middle, whirled around each other, danced back the way . . . The library noted, Not back the way they came. They've exchanged position.

I couldn't differentiate dollies well enough to tell them apart, of course. Another pair of dollies, the next set in their respective rows, began dancing out, little cowgirl hips swiveling as they spun, tassel-fur lifting, exposing swatches of pale undercoat. Dancing very well, not like little girls, more like tiny women, like . . .

Probably explains why they're so easy to train for the dollhouse, hmh?

The library AI whispered, A reasonable hypothesis.

Dark shape, shape of a crab, ambling nimbly out of the night, pausing by the back of the truck, then bunching suddenly and leaping up into the bed, pickup rock steady under a small weight. I stretched gently, and said, "What's going on here?" Gesturing at the dollies' dance, the yipping wolfen.

The Kapellmeister said, "Drilling them, apparently. Practice makes perfect."

Drilling them? For what? For . . . Another brief snatch of memory, something . . . A twenty-fifth-century metonymepic, *Flashmanssaga,* which I'd loved when I was a boy, maybe ten years old, an episode called "The General Danced at Dawn."

The Kapellmeister said, "The translator pod software complains that the artificial intelligences aboard your spaceship attempted to gain entry to its databases again. I thought we'd agreed that wouldn't happen anymore."

Hmh. Well. I said, "Sorry. The . . . things you talked about this morning caused considerable difficulty in translation. The AIs were attempting to gain a clarification for certain terms." I paused, wonder how, even if, to proceed. Finally I said, "Struld-Bugs. Adversary Instrumentality. The, um, Shock War. Though my library has a fairly good set of indexes, it could find no referents for any of these items."

The Kapellmeister sat silent, watching the dollies dance.

"In response to the query about StruldBugs, your pod did provide an image of something like a big, golden cockroach."

More silence, then the Kapellmeister said, "I think your own translation software should have used the word *scarab.* That seems like a better approximation."

Scarab? The library ran a brief clip of something pretty much like a cockroach, rolling some kind of shaggy clay ball over dry ground. I felt additional data patch in and . . . Really? A shitball? It showed me the egg within. Well. Clever. But why the hell would the ancient Egyptians worship a shitball bug?

the spacesuit AI, crackling with alarm: We have just
a high-speed data probe. Though the software fil-
gered, they did not process before the probe structure logged off. No trace was possible. We are unable to
determine what, if any, data was accessed.

I turned to stare at the Kapellmeister, sitting quietly beside
me in the ruddy, fire-lit darkness, dim eyes floating above its
back, apparently still watching the dollies, whose dance, some
part of me notes, was slowly becoming more complicated, from
two dollies to three, now four dancing simultaneously in the
square.

Nothing.

What was I expecting, to be able to read the, uh . . . *facial*
expression on something whose evolutionary history was more
remote from mine than your average terrestrial rock?

The Kapellmeister said, "Given the political realities on my
homeworld, it seems unlikely that data structures exist for these
referents within any human database."

Then more silence, the two of us sitting side by side, watching the long shadows of the dancers crisscross on the open
ground. Something, I thought, is going on here. I . . . Moment
of self-directed mirth. No shit, Mycroft Fucking Holmes. The
sentence that just came out of that black box held a great deal
of information. This Kapellmeister has just said it told me something it thinks no other human knows.

So? Fucking *why?*

Loose lips sink ships?

Christ.

It said, "There has been a great and rancorous debate
among my kind about what is appropriate information for
release to your kind. The consensus is that we wish you hadn't
come. We've been content, sitting home, these last four hundred million years."

Sharp prickle in my chest. Well. There's that number again.
An unlikely number. Four hundred million years ago . . . origin
of the vertebrates, perhaps?

The library whispered, Transition between the Devonian and Mississippian periods of the Paleozoic Era. The climate was warm and humid, following a more arid period with some glaciation. With land plants well established, the first forests evolved in the Devonian. These were inhabited by the first amphibians, at the beginning of what is commonly known as the Carboniferous.

So. Have I just been told the . . . Salierans have been . . . sitting home, was it? Sitting home, warm and cozy, on 82 Eridani 3, since before the coal swamps formed?

The Kapellmeister said, "In the days following the Shock War, we were . . . frightened. Afraid some remnant of the Instrumentality would come, looking for StruldBugs to kill, would kill us instead. It was a long time before we found out the Struld-Bugs had won the war, that there were no remnants of the Instrumentality. Nor much left at all of the StruldBugs themselves."

I wait in silence for more. Nothing. Finally: "You know, of course, I don't know what the hell you're talking about?"

Silence. Then, "Yes. I realize that."

In the firelight before us, all of the dollies were dancing now, a very complicated pattern that I couldn't follow at all. I said, "Then why the hell tell me?"

Silence. Then, "I have a decision to make. It's one I've been trying to make for a long time, but . . ." The eyestalks seemed to wave, beginning to retract, then they extended again to full length, seeming to inspect the stars overhead. There was a sound from the black box on its back, something I could swear sounded like a sigh, though, of course, it was only a soft ruffle of static. It said, "Among my kind, solitary decisions and individual initiative have been long discouraged. This makes the decision-making process rather . . . difficult."

I can imagine.

I waited patiently for more, watching the dollies dance, but that was it. Thought about opening my mouth and asking the obvious questions, try to encourage this little beanbag of a creature to go on, but . . . I just sat. Eventually the dollies stopped dancing, and the wolfen, somehow, seemed pleased.

The next day, following the sun as we skirted the edge of a big, flat glacier near the center of the Koudloft, we made good time, thundering along in tandem, throwing up twin plumes of dust, and glittery bits of ice, Kapellmeister riding beside me in silence. Toward midday we crested a long, low, snow-covered ridge and began driving down a shallow slope, seeming to head back toward the north.

Gone around the south pole now, pole itself somewhere back in that glacier, direction changed even though we haven't made a meaningful turn.

In the middle distance, the white hills of the Koudloft turned gray, then gave out, turning into a broad green plain that soon disappeared over the horizon. Mountains sticking up, almost invisible, like phantasms in the blue beyond, continuations of the Pÿramis and Thisbÿs, seeming to float above the end of the world, like icebergs in the fog.

There, a faint bolt of silver lightning, rimming the green world. The beginnings of the Mistibos River, perhaps? One of its tributaries, the beginnings of a drainage system with the length and volume of the Amazon and Mississippi combined. There, by the river's bend, a low, ramshackle affair, like a fairy castle gone to seed, brown buildings threatening to become towers, never quite making the grade.

The library whispered, Vapaa, smallest of the Compact Cities, inhabited by the last genetically distinct descendants of the Saami folk, whom other Scandinavian people referred to as Ljappa.

Some imitation of Orikhalkos then, smaller, shabbier, if such a thing was possible . . . memories of those empty, fallen-down warehouse districts, with their wolfen killpits and doll-houses and streetwalking whores and . . . I thought about my Orikhalkan whore, brief memory of being . . . transported. As simple as that. Felt a pang of desire, an urge to visit this Vapaa.

The spacesuit said, Contemporary news reports indicate a great deal of gang violence on the streets of Vapaa these days. Few people from the other Cities will visit, or come to do business. A commission once discussed breaking up Vapaa and absorbing its population into the other Cities, but no city officials were willing to have them.

And what else could they do? Where would they go? Out onto the Opveldt, to live among the Groenteboeren? To the Adrianis Desert, with its savage Hinterlings? Les Iles des Français, perhaps?

The library said, A recent white paper by the office of the Basileïos of Orikhalkos has suggested the populace of Vapaa might like to found a new colony, on one of the new worlds sure to be found, now that faster-than-light travel is a reality.

Sure to be found.

I wonder.

There, a pale, faded afterecho of desire. Once upon a time, I dreamed that dream. Dreamed myself a great explorer, wandering the byways of an unknown universe, finding the new worlds myself. Now? I have the starship with which to carry out my dream, and yet . . . who's going to *pay* for all this voyaging? I could manage to finance three, maybe four such gallivantings, off into the star-spangled yonder.

Would I find a spanking, empty new world in that time?

If not, what then?

Sell the ship, go back to work?

Is that what it'll come to?

And what if, somehow, I *did* find a new world, a planet of my own? What *then*? In all the old stories, you become a rich, rich man, found your own settlement, leader of the people, die and are remembered as the Father of His Planet. Nice. I pictured myself coming home, surveys in my database. Ready to . . . what? With whom would I file my claim?

About three seconds after my claim became public, some terrestrial government ship would be on its way. Or, worse, if, by then, the promised B-VEI fleets have been marketed and sold, some other ship, some ship from ERSIE or Harmattan or . . . hell, almost anybody, would be on its way out, loaded with corporate settlers, ready to stake an unbreakable squatter's claim.

What instrumentality would protect the rights of a lone Gaetan du Cheyne, master and owner of the starship *Random Walk?* While I thought, we rode on in silence.

By late afternoon we were out on the plains, moving through nearly treeless country, finally pulling up by the banks of the Mistibos River, having bypassed Vapaa of the terrible gangs, pulling up on a grassy shore, settling our vehicles in clouds of dust and old grass. I got out and stood by the side of the camper, stretching, arching my back, slightly stiffened from sitting in one position too long. It'll be over quickly, now that the symbiotes know something's wrong.

Tau Ceti was already skimming the horizon, beginning to set, blue sky striated with long streaks of red and gold, sun backlighting a few low clouds, turning them dark, sharp rays streaming in all directions like angelic light.

I've . . . gotten used to this. Feels like I've been here, or somewhere just like here, living in a natural world forever. Stardock seems lost, fading like some kind of fever dream, the kind of dreams that happen when you fuck up really bad and the symbiotes have to work hard to set things right.

Suddenly, a squeezing hand in my chest, a familiar pang. There, in the long, ruddy grass, things like horsetails and pussy willows growing at the river's edge: Shining, mottled eyes, gleaming at me from a flattened face covered with reddish bronze fur. Long white fangs, curved, serrated-edge teeth set in a permanent grin . . .

The white wolfen were jumping out of the pickup bed now, jumping to the ground, going over to their red wolfen . . . cousins. Purring. Purring like so many steel-throated cats. Like cats with ball bearings caught in their throats. The dollies, I noticed, were staying put.

The red wolfen came out, mingling with the white, purring in a different tone, flatter, with a wooden crackle to it. Touching muzzles. Touching tongues. Every now and again I'd notice a red's eyes on me, teeth flashing, colored pink in the sunset light, and I'd feel my bowels clench, feel an urge to get back in the camper and lock the God-damned door.

Now, the Arousians were getting out of the pickup cab, seeming to bunch together, as though nervous. Well, the wolfen can't . . . *digest* them or anything, but a few hard bites would break those skinny arms and legs and . . . I imagined red wolfen gagging and spitting, growling the wolfen equivalent of *What the fuck is this shit?* before they got sick and died.

One of the Arousians seemed to be holding a portable camera, recording the milling of the wolfen, red and white getting all mixed up, like some kind of patchwork quilt.

Doing their job, that's all.

More wolfen looking at me now. Sputtering things to the white wolfen. Answered by their metallic purr, whites looking at me as well. Can they talk to each other? I remembered what they'd told me at the killpit, about how, if they put two from the same species in the ring together, they'd cook something up, spoil all the fun.

The other door of the camper cab popped open and the Kapellmeister jumped down, seeming very springy on its spider-crab legs. The red wolfen, for their part, seemed to recoil, as though ready to run. Imagined: *What the fuck is that?*

But they stood still and waited, looking so obviously suspicious, while it walked over to them. Surely, you could almost see them thinking, this little fucker can't harm *us?* The Kapellmeister was keeping its three arms well tucked in, those sharp, silvery chelae looking more like a plucked chicken's wings just now than the deadly shears they really were.

Finally, it marched up to one of the white wolfen . . .

Limbcracker, whispered the translator AI.

Walked up to Limbcracker and extended its tentacle-hand for a quick head touch. White wolfen stiffening briefly, until it was released. More crackling wood, clinking steel. Another white was touched and released. More crackle-clink. Another white. More. Finally, one of the reds seemed to slink forward, pressed very close to the ground, like a scared dog. The Kapellmeister touched its head for a few seconds, then let go.

The wolfen jumped, seemed to shrink back, looking around wildly, eyes wide, then it said, *Clatterclatterchatter*...

Silence, all the red wolfen looking at me for some reason.

The Kapellmeister's pod made a soft, *Greekeegreekee*...

One of the Arousians started walking slowly over, limbs rasping on one another like so many dry sticks. Rustmold-on-Pale-Snow perhaps? I...

The translator AI said, His chief assistant, Altostratus-by-Moonglow.

A sudden, stark realization that those two names alone conveyed a fairly detailed image of what the world of Arous, Sigma Draconis 3, must be like. Perhaps I can go there someday, some way, and see rustmold on pale snow, watch altostratus clouds strut their stuff, drifting high in an alien sky, backlit by the glow of a faraway moon...

The Kapellmeister's pod said, "Gaetan? Perhaps you could come over and meet our new friend now. Her name is Human-legs-Are-Eaten."

Great. Wonderful name. I swallowed hard, squared my shoulders and walked right over, ready to meet my new friend.

Nightfall, sun sliding westward, gradually getting below the horizon, though at such a shallow angle it seemed to take forever, sky growing redder, then darker, stars coming out slowly, air growing cooler, but never quite cold. We're already pretty far north, here on the upper Somber River, where the Opveldt begins.

If I stood, turned and looked toward the south, I would see the lights of Vapaa shining like so many red-orange torches, beyond, dark against the edge of the sky, the low, rolling hills of the Koudloft. I didn't stand, instead merely sat in my camp chair, by the side of the pop-up, watching, waiting, eating a sandwich I'd made, some kind of cold, tasteless pressed white meat, chicken perhaps, sipping from a bottle of cheap beer. Watched the yellow flames of the campfire the Arousians had made leap and dance, throwing diffuse shadows this way and that. Listened to the crackle of the fire, which almost covered up the soft gurgling of the river.

Watched the wolfen, red and white, directing . . .

In this light, the dollies looked even more pathetically like little girls dressed up in party costumes, separated into groups, lined up, facing each other, along the sides of a hexagon. Behind them, the wolfen sat in small groups, red, white, red, white, looking like so many huge, malformed dogs.

The Kapellmeister came out of the darkness, riding its stiff, stalky limbs, from the direction of the Arousians' camp and settled with a soft crackle in the dry grass beside my chair. There. Outside the circle of the firelight, I could see technicians setting up their cameras and sound equipment.

Three white wolfen, at the corners of three alternate apices, made quick, metallic barks, short, precise, one, two three. Six adjacent sets of dollies snapped to attention, made their half-sides seem taller.

Now, three red wolfen, duller, more wooden sounds, with a choked-off quality, skipping around the hexagon, awakening movement from the remaining dollies. Air filled with some electric anticipation now. Filled with . . . That certain something, reaching down into my heart, to the thing which pretends it is my heart, and makes me feel . . .

Abruptly, an alien dog pound cacophony began, the metal sound of the white wolfen, wooden sound of the red, giving the whole something of a sawmill quality, and the dollies began dancing out, stamping time to the . . . music. Dancing out, whirling round, dancing back to a new place in line.

Getting all mixed up.

I looked down at the Kapellmeister, wondering what, if anything, to say.

One of its eyestalks seemed to float my way, though there

was really no way to tell what it was looking at. Even in daylight, no pupil, no iris. It said, "Individual decision making, done through solitary initiative, is possible."

Granted. All you have to do is . . . decide.

It said, "Difficult. But it can be done."

So. Why tell me? Should I interpret this as . . . some kind of invitation? I thought about the software in the translator pod.

The spacesuit AI whispered, The pod imago is willing to be pinged, but little else.

OK. Security still in place. Across the way, dark shapes leaping in the night, leaping close to one another, touching, dancing away. I sat forward suddenly, listening to the rapid tempo of the wolfen's barking, watching the dollies' movements. What the hell are they doing?

Touching each other . . . down there.

Pausing now, in the middle of that central whirl, rubbing their . . . cloacae together, then dancing away. I started counting dancers, trying to remember the patterns they were weaving.

The library AI whispered, If the pattern continues long enough, each dollie will have mated with every other dollie.

Hmh. I took a long pull on my beer, undiverted alcohol in my blood interfering slightly with my brain chemistry, finished it, burped softly, and said, "Why are they doing this?" Slightly greasy feel to my skin now, perhaps a sheen of sweat on my face.

The Kapellmeister said, "A small trade mission, apparently."

A most unpleasant feeling at the bottom of my belly, a distant awareness . . . I said, "Trade?"

It said, "Apparently, from what we've been able to find out, what the wolfen, whose culture is sans technology and hence sans material goods, trade is the germ plasm of the various dollie breeds."

I said, "Interesting. What do they . . ." Abruptly, I remembered the little ceremony in which one of the dollies had been eaten. So much for *why* they practice dollie husbandry. "How long have they been . . . doing this?"

The Kapellmeister said, "The wolfen oral tradition, of

course, is without a viable time scale. They have no legends of a time, apparently, when they were without the dollies. A time when they themselves were not precisely as they are now."

I felt a slight start as one of the white wolfen suddenly bounded into the middle of the dollies' dance, watched it whirl through them, go back to its place, felt myself relax slightly. What the hell was I expecting? Tearing claws? Rending fangs.

A white wolfen danced out and back.

The spacesuit whispered, In a few more passes, the mating pattern will be complete.

Meaning, I guess, that every dollie will have fucked every other dollie. What does that imply? Boys with boys and girls with girls, as well as the more usual and utilitarian sort of . . . Two wolfen danced out, one red, one white, whirled around each other in the midst of the mass of spinning, humping dollies, danced on back, having traded places.

Then two more danced out. Then four. Then six.

The spacesuit said, Assuming linear growth, all the wolfen will be dancing simultaneously just as the last pair of dollies completes its mating act.

One of the dollies, one I was sure had already mated, suddenly cartwheeled through the middle of the dance, making a handspring completely over a pair of dancing wolfen, coming to rest on the far side of the now thoroughly trampled patch of grass.

Now another one, then two, then four, then eight, looking like so many small, female gymnasts.

The spacesuit whispered, This exponential growth rate will also converge on the dance completion. This is exceedingly well planned.

The Kapellmeister said, "Impressive, even for sentient animals. Practice does indeed make for perfection."

I suddenly realized that, even as they danced and whirled, the wolfen had continued to bark out their raucous music. I looked closely, trying to decide if the wolfen were fucking each other as well.

The library AI whispered, In most eusocial species, only certain members of the group mate and breed. Among terrestrial wolves, for example, it's usually only the alpha male and female who mate. The others remain celibate. Among bees, the queen has her harem of drones, while the workers are developed from immature females, lacking the capacity for copulation.

Well. How nasty. Then I thought about my own situation and was amused. Maybe humans are on their way to a eusocial order as well? Or is it only me? I opened my mouth to ask the Kapellmeister a rather obvious question . . .

The spacesuit whispered, *Now.*

The dollies froze in place.

And then the wolfen fell upon them.

I jumped to my feet, suppressed an urge to rub disbelief from my eyes, and shouted, "Why the hell are the wolfen fucking the dollies?" Surely. Surely that's what's going on. Dollies pressed flat to the ground, wolfen arched over them, hindquarters moving, in, out, in, out, wolfen eyes gleaming in the firelight, tongues lolling from their toothy mouths, mouths with fixed grins that looked . . .

The library AI whispered, *No data.*

One of the wolfen whimpered softly, then collapsed on its dollie, like a man whose orgasm was spent. Then another. Another. Another. And, all the while, the leftover dollies, for there were far more of them than the wolfen, formed a circle, a double circle, inner one dancing this way, outer one that.

And I remembered that these wolfen were, supposedly, all female, the males hidden away . . . elsewhere. I wondered if these were sterile females then, like so many worker bees.

The Kapellmeister said, "Dollie egglets are . . . deficient. Genetic material without a nutrient supply. At first, we wondered if the dollies weren't more or less like marsupials or even monotremes, that the egg would attach to a cloacal nipple, in order to continue its development beyond the blastula stage. This, apparently, is not so."

More wolfen collapsing now, moaning softly, as though

exhausted. I wondered if the dollies would be smothering underneath them.

The Kapellmeister said, "The Arousians' research indicates the dollie eggs are simply the stripped remains of a standard egg, not so different, in fact, from the eggs of many Salieran species."

Including Kapellmeisters? The library whispered, It seems likely.

It went on, "Apparently, the wolfen provide additional material, a nutrient sac derived from their own unfertilized egg structure, which surrounds the dollie egglet, protecting it as well."

The wolfen were done now, groaning like Romans in the end stage of a feast.

Library: An unusual co-evolution scheme.

I thought about wasps and spiders, decided it was more unusual than that. Thought about the little fish that live up bigger fish's assholes. Not even close.

The library brought up mitochondria, the commensal bacteria living in human cells, reproducing with the cells, having lost the ability to exist outside cells, without which the cell could not survive. It pointed out that this symbiotic relationship was the basis of all higher life on Earth.

OK. That's a little more unusual, I . . .

One of the wolfen, a white, stood, stretched gently, walked to one of the dollies in the inner ring of now motionless dancers. Leaned forward and delicately bit off its head.

"*Shit.*"

The dead dollie collapsed, spouting dark blood. The wolfen bent and began to eat, making little liquid gobbling sounds. Another wolfen, this time a red, got up, stretched, stepped forward, did the same. Then another. Another. Another.

The ring of dollies remained motionless, waiting.

The spacesuit noted, There are many more dollies than wolfen.

The Kapellmeister said, "We assume the dollies being eaten

are expendable males, their job complete. We assume the female dollies lying in the middle of the circle are now pregnant. The outer ring of dollies . . ." standing by, watching, wide-eyed, ". . . are never eaten."

I turned away, very short of breath and stood looking up at the stars, acutely conscious of a heavy miasma filling the air, stealing the breath from my lungs. God damn it. Why the fuck do I still have this pathetic erection?

I don't know.

I found I couldn't stand to hear the soft gobbling noises, sound of the wolfen contentedly eating their . . . what? Sex partners? Rape victims? Commensal . . . shit. I turned and walked away into the darkness, walked away from the camp quickly, breathing hard, feeling an urge to run, suppressing it, walking at first along the banks of the river, southward upstream in the direction of Vapaa, whose lights made a sullen orange glow against the underside of what few low-hanging clouds there were. Paused, looking up at the sky. Stars. No moons. Should they be up now?

Four hours, whispered the spacesuit, exhibiting its link to *Random Walk*'s navigation software. Right. On the other side of the planet now.

Seems colder out here than it did back at camp. Warmth radiating from the pop-up habitat, from the Arousians' fire, from so many breathing bodies, their breath a . . . miasma. That's the word I like. When I get away from the *miasma*, my nuts will calm down, this damned ridiculous hard-on will go away and . . .

Then what?

I walked away from the river then, head down, hands in pockets, walking up the shallow slope of a low hill, feet whispering in the soft, calf-deep grass. Pleasant smell in the air now, as of . . . grape and jasmine. The quality of smell that comes from a cotton candy machine. Maybe that's the smell of Cetian bugs.

I stood at the crest of the hill, first looking away into the darkness beyond, then turning and looking back down the better-lit slope toward the river. Delicate light reflected there, a glitter of starlight on the water, I suppose.

Why the hell does it bother me?

They're just animals.

No one in any position to tell me why, of course.

If I asked, the library would consult its psychological data-bases and, perhaps, find some predigested answer. Maybe it would tell me that some animals reminded humans of little chil-dren, of babies, demanding our blind, unthinking, elemental protection. Maybe . . .

I didn't ask, because then I'd have to ask why the hell my prick wanted me to fuck them. Oh, sure, it could excuse the matter with a babble of talk about pheromonal coincidences and . . . Unable to forget the fat man at the dollhouse, dollie straddling his lap. Is that me?

I walked away, down the northern slope of the hill, thinking I might as well get it over with, get on back to camp, stop think-ing about this bullshit and go to bed. Tomorrow, I told myself, is another day. Unasked, the library popped up a reference for that, some being with remarkably empty eyes.

Stopped.

Some soft little noise, in the shadows up ahead. Prickle of fear up the back of my neck, thinking about dangerous animals. Are there things like snakes on Green Heaven? The library told me there weren't. But . . . prickle of fear. And, something else.

I walked forward, slowly, deliberately, acutely conscious of the placement of my feet, one almost in front of the other, like I was some kind of God-damned Indian scout or . . . There. Pale, pale shapes, like the photographic negatives of shadows in the darkness. Christ. More dollies, nestled together, as though sleeping, under the overhanging branches and leaves of some broad, low bush.

Not asleep though.

Whispering among themselves.

I stood still, watching, listening, my eyes slowly adapting bet-ter to the darkness.

Whose dollies are these?

Are there unknown wolfen nearby?

Another little pang of fear.

The library whispered, Photomosaic enhancement suggests these are a subset of Limbcracker's dollies, the ones you saw conducting a mature egg distribution.

I remembered.

One of the dollies lifted its head, staring at me with big, empty eyes. Empty because all I could see was the oval shape of the eyes themselves. I haven't really . . . *looked* into a dollie's eyes, have I?

No.

It got up, whispering to its fellows, walked slowly forward, came to stand in front of me, hardly coming up to the bottom of my ribs. Not afraid of me then. I . . . grew suddenly, excessively conscious of my dick. This is a God-damned cruel joke nature's played on . . . who? Me? Or the dollies?

I crouched, dropping to one knee in the grass, peering into the dollie's face, trying to see. Felt its warm breath on me. It'd be easier to accept if I could at least *smell* the pheromones that are . . . The dollie stepped closer, reached out and touched my face delicately. I sat down, dropping to tailor's seat in the grass, shivering.

Get up. Get up and go away. God damn it, *run!*

Who?

No voice in my head other than my own, advice from some subtly independent judgment engine or another, something afraid, perhaps, for the sanctity of . . . The dollie suddenly darted forward, jumping into my lap, feeling exactly like . . . No. Not *exactly* like anything. Not a child. Not a woman. Not a dog or a cat or . . .

It nuzzled against my face, purring softly.

Why?

Why isn't it afraid of me?

I ran my hand down the soft, impossibly silky fur of its back. Nice, nice doggy. That's it. The dollie rubbed its little face against the side of my neck, purring louder. Nice, nice kitty, I . . . jerked slightly, feeling a rough, wet, absolutely inhuman tongue touch the side of my face.

The library AI whispered, Perhaps, Gaetan, it would be a good idea if you broke off contact with the dollie. Human skin is fairly permeable and, as you know, the biochemistry of this creature may affect your hormonal matrix somewhat strongly.

The spacesuit said, Given the limited bandwidth available through the transponder, it will take us some time to program your symbiotic mechanisms for the necessary . . .

No. For God's sake don't do that.

A touch of panic from somewhere deep inside. And an eerie conviction that it wasn't *my* inner voice that had spoken. A bleak, bizarre feeling that, just now, I'd been taken over by a dybbuk.

I could sense the artificial personalities still in my head, disquieted, disquieting, but silent. The dollie in my lap seemed to sniff delicately at my mouth, just the way a dog will sniff at your mouth. Felt its tongue touch my lips briefly.

I lifted it off my lap and laid it back in the grass, the outline of a small woman sprawled before me. Sprawled just so. Just right. You know what I mean.

Soft flutter of dense panic crawling around my heart.

Oh, Christ, you're not going to do this, are you?

Certainly not my dick talking. It had already decided, decided long minutes ago, just what it thought I was going to do.

And why not? Why shouldn't I . . .

Because it's not . . . right.

Says who?

Everyone?

Who's that? What's *everyone* done for me that I should forgo . . . Nobody's ever done a God-damned thing for me, I . . .

Dollie looking up at me out of empty, featureless eyes, as though waiting. I put my hand on its belly, petting soft fur, felt it squirm with what seemed like pleasure, listened to its resumed purr. A cat, they say, does not purr out of pleasure. Humans don't care why it purrs, merely make the assumptions that please them most.

No reason to do this. You're just full of alien pheromones, pheromones tricking your reproductive physiology into thinking . . . hell. Think of it like a nice drug. Like a masturbation aid. Like the vidnet girls. Just get your dick out and take care of it yourself, that's all. No one will know but you and the dollies. Who would they tell? Who would care?

And what about that other thing, then?

Unbuckled my belt. Unzipped my fly. Got the damned thing out, warm in my cold hand.

What about it? What difference does it make? At best, the dollie will breed with its own kind, be fucked by wolfen. At worst, it will soon be eaten. Or captured by humans and put in a dollhouse. Someday soon it'll be dead. Hell, someday *you'll* be dead. What difference will it make then, what you did or didn't do?

Maybe no difference at all.

The spacesuit whispered, *Gaetan.*

Shut the fuck up. Go away.

I crawled on top of the dollie and, just like that, I was in. Wet. Warm. Sticky like raw egg white. Just like a woman. That's it. In. Out. In. Out. The dollie looked up into my face as I fucked it, eyes like bits of glass, purring steadily away, as though I were still only . . .

My orgasm let go in a succession of quick pulses that filled me, momentarily, with something indistinguishable from happiness. Then. Then I sat back on my heels, looking down at the dollie. Nothing.

I zipped up my fly. Buckled my belt. Looked up. Jumped slightly. The other dollies had sat up under the tree, were sitting huddled together, whispering softly, had watched what I'd done.

Christ.

The dollie on the ground, legs splayed, cloaca still popped open, a black hole to nowhere, was quiet. Finally, it sat up, stood, stood still for a moment, staring at me, then turned and walked slowly away, back to sit with the others. Whispering. Dollies whispering together, looking at me for the longest time.

I lay back on the hillside then, staring at the sky, feeling nothing. After a while, my cheeks began to feel cold, and I realized I'd started to cry.

13

I awoke with a start, lying naked on my bunk, looking up at the camper's no-color flexible plastic ceiling, bright Cetian sunshine streaming in through the window, making a pattern on the far wall, desperately trying not to think. Useless.

Sat up on my elbows, looking down the length of my body, pretending it was only my toes I saw sticking up. Managed a wry grimace. Well? Do you want to go on feeling bad about it? People do things like this all the time. Why should *you* be any different, Gaetan du Cheyne? Excuses seemed to present themselves, neatly arrayed, as though in a database display table.

I got up and went over to the little refrigerator, protruding from the little floor well where it would later retract, looked inside. Took out a bottle of what looked like fruit juice and popped the lid. Strong smell of ginger and melon. Took a swig. Thin. Cold and sweet, with a slight afterbite. Looked at the label. Muisenspis.

Mouse urine, whispered the translator AI. Evidently, the word *muis* has been transferred to a native animal.

Swell. Great sense of humor the Groenteboeren possess. I took another swig, decided I liked it, turned and went to the shower cubicle with the bottle clutched in my hand. Get under the water.

The spacesuit whispered, Gaetan, it is *possible* for the artificial personality matrices available to you to reprogram your symbiotes such that parts of your memory can be masked. However, it really would be advisable for you to check into a well-equipped hospital. One on either Earth or Kent, if—

No thanks.

I got in the shower and turned on the water, which warmed up quickly, stood still and let it run over my back and shoulders and belly, carry away all the leftovers, invisible taint streaming down my legs and into the drain.

Outside, Tau Ceti was already fairly high in the sky, warmish wind getting to work on the task of drying my hair, sky a burnished blue overhead, flecked with a fair number of small white clouds, like so many little flowers drifting on the breeze. People . . . um, sure. People, not things, already up and about, Arousians setting up their camera tripods, Wolfen. Dollies . . .

Over at the area of trampled grass where last night's dance had been conducted, the dollies were arrayed in a tight semicircle, looking almost as though standing at attention, silent. Facing them, a little distance away, the wolfen sat in two little packs, one red, one white. In the space between them, two more wolfen, again one of each race, crouched, quietly digging a modest hole, reaching out with heavy-clawed paws, taking turns scooping out big clods of dark brown soil.

Near them on the ground, in a messy pile . . . I looked away briefly, unable to catch my breath. Small white bones, scraps of hide with disheveled, rusty white fur. An intact skull or two.

When I looked back, the hole was dug and the wolfen appeared to be waiting. Wind blowing. River gurgling. Clouds slowly drifting overhead. The dollies began to whisper softly, delicate voices in unison, a whispered chant.

Muted *uff* from one of the wolfen, I couldn't tell which one.

One of the dollies came forward, clutching an irregular greenish brown object about the size of a football in its hands. Dropped it into the hole. Retreated.

The two wolfen began pushing the remains of last night's dead dollies into the hole on top of the object, whatever it had been, bones, hides, hair, what looked like scraps of meat.

"They are planting the seed of what the Groenteboeren call a baarbij bush." The Kapellmeister's generated voice made me jump. It said, "It would appear that the leaves, roots and fruit of this bush are the dollies' principal fodder."

The wolfen were taking turns coming forward now, squatting over the hole, shitting a little bit, trotting away.

The library AI whispered, This dung will likely contain the remnants of digested dollies.

Great. I can just imagine. Or is it merely anthropocentric of me to think the dollies believe wolfen shit contains the souls of their departed loved ones?

The Kapellmeister said, "Even across the great gulf that divides our species, it is clear that something is bothering you, Gaetan du Cheyne."

Care to make a list? I watched the last wolfen shit, watched the two representative wolfen start pushing dirt back in the hole, gently packing it down. The dollies' chant was momentarily louder, then stopped abruptly.

The Kapellmeister said, "Gaetan, the artificial personalities associated with your starship are quite concerned about you."

I turned and looked. Nothing. The Kapellmeister was so alien it hardly even looked like an animal, much less a sentient being. Vegetarians have a saying, *We never eat anything with a face.* Well. They might be happy to know that Kapellmeisters don't have faces. I said, "Everything's all right. I don't want to . . ." Talk about it? Fine.

There was a long silence, while we stood and watched the Arousians break camp, pack up their truck, white wolfen and their dollies getting back up in the pickup bed, red wolfen slipping away into the tall grass, dollies marching stolidly after them, like a band of little girl soldiers.

"So where are we going now?"

Silence. Finally, "The Arousians will be taking the wolfen to another rendezvous, much like this one, then back across the Koudloft to their home range."

"Why? Aren't the dollies pregnant already?" I looked down at the Kapellmeister, for some reason expecting to see it shrug. Stupid. What the hell would it shrug *with*?

It said, "Most likely, but the female dollies of the next band will not be. And the Arousians have found that bands of wolfen do trade the actual dollies as well."

"What for?"

"We don't know. The Arousians think this helps the dollies maintain a common culture, with a common language. The value of that . . . It may be that the different species of wolfen, who cannot physically reproduce the sounds of each other's language, can only communicate through the mechanism of the dollies."

Interesting. "Why are the Arousians here?"

Silence. Then, "They are concerned about what's going to happen to them, to their species, their world, in the context of a burgeoning human presence in their star system, throughout all the surrounding stars. It may be that they feel the wolfen/dollie relationship is a significant model."

I thought about that, suddenly felt myself getting the creeps. "I guess the Arousians are pretty unlucky, at that. Too bad they didn't work on their technologies earlier. Maybe they could have found *us.*"

The Kapellmeister said, "Worse things have happened in the past, to more species than one. I remember . . ." It stopped.

Remember? I remembered some of the mysterious things it had alluded to the other night. And, of course, remembered what it'd said about . . .

The Kapellmeister said, "Gaetan, I have decided to trust you."

Trust me. Fine. Why? And trust me with what?

It said, "I hope that you will trust me as well."

I said nothing, just staring at it.

Suddenly, the Kapellmeister unfurled its middle hand, black

tentacles flexing, uncoiling like so many wet rubber snakes. "Gaetan, it may be that I can help you, just as I hope you will be able to help me."

I took a step back, remembering the way it'd . . . touched the wolfen. Remembered its hand wrapped around the heads of the little animals it ate, just as it killed them. Remembered the way it'd . . . listened to the womfrog's death. Tried to remember what I knew about the neural induction capabilities of—

The Kapellmeister said, "It may be that in this way we can answer the concerns of your artificial intelligences."

Concerns . . . I felt a little spark of anger, old, old anger, reignite, somewhere within, coalescing around an old memory. *I'm sorry about Lara,* Gaetan . . . my father's voice. Mother in the background, sullen, withdrawn. Memory of her anger, of myself shocked at the way my mother shouted the word *cunt* at me, denouncing poor Lara Nobisky . . . My father then, *Perhaps the school counseling system . . .*

I said, "Ah. Well. Perhaps some other time." The hand withdrew, flattening against the Kapellmeister's chest keel, more or less disappearing against matching leathery black skin.

Across the way, the Arousians started their truck, lifting off in a cloud of dust and loose, dry stalks of grass, slid down the bank and out onto the waters of the river, raising a misty spray in which rainbows briefly sparkled.

I gestured. "Guess we'd better get going."

The Kapellmeister said, "It will only be more of the same, Gaetan. There's no real need for either of us to go along."

I looked down at it, wishing mightily that there was something, anything at all, for me to read in those floating eyes. "What did you have in mind?"

"I'd . . . like to have a look at the rest of the Opveldt, maybe go on downriver to the Mistibos Forest for a while. This is as new a world to me as it is to you."

I shrugged. Turned and looked out across the wide plain, watching the Arousians recede. A new world? I suppose I came here for a reason, though that reason seems shallow now, a shadow, almost lost. The truck was just a fleck now, reddish against the metallic green-brown of the open countryside, carrying away stick-bug men, carrying away wolfen, dollies . . . tight little pang in my chest, extending a pseudopod of sensation to my crotch.

Oh, shit. How wonderful.

I said, "All right."

The Kapellmeister said, "I'm glad you trust me, Gaetan."

Do I?

It said, "Most of my own kind frown on interspecies trust, perhaps with good reason. Not many share my faith in the dawn of a new day, after the long, long night."

For the rest of the day, we drove along the road by the river, following a rutted, primitive track, ruts reminding me of the incredible reality of Green Heaven. Sure they have nice hovercraft like this camper, like the Arousians' pickup truck, but . . . wheeled vehicles? Jesus! Like I'd somehow gone to sleep and, on awakening, found myself in Medieval America, like some kind of reversed Rip van Winkle.

I kept expecting we would talk, that I'd find out something, at least, about the Kapellmeister's promised trust, but, for the most part, we rode on in silence, watching the landscape go by, evolving slowly as we went on north.

No cities out here. Nothing but Opveldt and the undulating course of the Somber River for ten thousand kilometers, all the way from Vapaa on the edge of the antarctic highlands to Koromalluma at the head of Somberfjord, beyond the Mistibos Forest.

Be nice to see that? The travel shows always compared it to Kong Island, showing one remake or another of that cool, cruel old story. The reality? I don't know. Something different, surely, the library telling me about herds of dwarf womfrogs living hidden in the dense woodland, safe from human predation. Dwarf womfrogs and a primitive species of green wolfen.

Once, in mid-afternoon, I lifted the camper high over the river, giving us a good view, speeding up, just as though I were really going someplace, rather than nowhere at all, golden green Opveldt plains stretching out in all directions, going over the horizon in a way that made me swear I could see the curvature of the planet, effect heightened by the way the land came back up in the form of distant blue-gray mountains.

There. Something.

The Kapellmeister said, "A large herd of wild womfrogs. They are not quite so decimated here as back on the Koperveldt."

Why not?

The library whispered, Apparently, forty percent of the Groenteboer population lives on the richer cropland of the Koperveldt. In addition, there is a great deal of hunting done by Compact tourists from the large cities of Orikhalkos and Midoriiro. The only Compact City on the Opveldt is Vapaa, not known for its hunters, nor as a tourist mecca.

What about the Koromallumans?

They do their hunting on the dry savannas north of the Mistibos, a region never colonized by Groenteboeren.

It made me picture the place, mountain and plain, river, forest, desert . . . Even an otherwise empty colony world, settled by humans only a few centuries back, is still a whole world, as much a world as any other. The vidnet shows make us forget that, make us think that Green Heaven is just a place, a place where hunters go, because who cares about some crappy old cities or a dank forest where nobody goes?

Makes you wonder what else is out there, ignored because some corporate marketing executive has deemed it "uninteresting." Here and now, this uninteresting world showed me a vista of dark shapes out on the shining plain, moving, oh-so-slowly, toward the north.

I wonder what's there? Someplace they can be safe? I wonder what the hunters and tourists will do when the womfrogs are gone?

The spacesuit whispered, You're coming up on a fairly large Groenteboer trading center, Gaetan. It would seem wise either

to give Tegenzinstad a wide berth or else lower your altitude
and speed.

Tegenzinstad. Aversion City? Interesting name. I dropped
the camper down toward the river road, throttling back as I did
so. "I'd like to see this place," I said, "way out here where they
live, away from the influence of the . . . *omgangers.*" I suddenly
realized I liked that term. Wouldn't you rather be an *omganger*
than a *vreemdeling?*

The Kapellmeister said, "It may be that I would attract
rather too much attention . . ."

"I'll open the pop-up before we go in. You should be all
right in there."

The spacesuit whispered, We can establish a link between
your communications barrette and the pod software, if you'd
like.

I started to speak, but the Kapellmeister suddenly said, "I'd
like that."

Interesting. Ship AIs talking to both of us? Why?

The town proved to be hardly anything at all, two rows of
low wooden and plastic buildings lining a wide spot in the road
by the river, ruts flattened out by heavier traffic, giving the place
a main street of dry, hard-packed dirt. A few residential back
streets here, some wharf-and-warehouse structures on the waterfront.

I had a brief moment of inner quickening when I saw the
small sternwheeler drawn up to one of the piers, thin black
smoke drifting up from its funnels. A steamboat? None of those
left on Earth. Not even in museums. However, a sharp look at
the design and placement of the stacks told me it was a fake.
Besides, I could smell the stench of burned diesel over the delicate mud-and-dogshit scent of the town.

I parked the camper at something that looked like a corral
and stable on the outskirts of town, giving its excited owner a
few Orikhalkan *drakhmai* in payment.

"We don't get many *omgangers here,* I tell you!" But I could
tell his main interest was the machine, standing out like a magic

carpet in a dirt parking lot full of what looked like gas-turbine-drive off-road wheeled vehicles.

I walked downtown, if you could call it that, fancying myself as having been transported to the Old West, feeling like I ought to have big solid-propellant revolvers on my hips instead of a little gas-recoil dartgun in my pocket. Jingling spurs. Thumping boots, yessiree . . . Hell. There's even a *horse* over there that little boy is . . .

The library whispered, It appears to be a local breed of Shetland pony.

Close enough. Didn't Mongols ride ponies, for Christ's sake?

A breed related to Przewalkski's horse, perhaps.

Walked down a long sidewalk made of splintered gray boards, like the ones in the fake ghost towns they stuck under domes on Mars in the twenty-third century, when the interplanetary tourist trade was just getting started, not really thinking about where I was going, or what I intended to do.

Walking. Walking by myself in a street with real people . . . sudden prickling on the back of my neck when I realized people were . . . noticing me. *Omganger,* you could imagine them thinking. We don't get many *omgangers* round here. Nobody seemed to be smiling.

Well. There'll be a . . . what did they call it? A general store, somewhere around here. I can get some fresh food maybe, something to replace the canned shit still stocked in the camper. Get a few hemidozens of beer . . . my mouth started to feel dry at the thought. I . . .

Passed by an open door, doorway spilling warm golden light into the darkening street, street red-lit by the shifting sky of an impending sunset. Music. For a moment, I wished for the tinkling of a player piano . . . well, maybe not. There probably weren't many player pianos in the Wild West of the 1880s. OK, one of those old uprights, some skinny guy in a bowler playing away, cigar jutting from the corner of his mouth at a jaunty angle, those armband things on his upper sleeves . . .

The library whispered, More a *fin de siècle* image, Gaetan.

In any event, the music coming out of the bar was like nothing I'd ever heard, with a rapid backbeat rather heavily into cymbals and tambourines, melody line dominated by what sounded like some hybrid between a sitar and a balalaika. I went in without another thought, ignoring the AIs' unease, communicated like the ghost of a heartfelt pang. I'm armed. What the hell can happen to me?

Walked across the room, people at tables turning to look, thinking, In just another second, the piano player will stop playing, the whole place will grow quiet, people wondering about the Man With No Name. I squinted at the bartender, giving him my best imitation of a steely-eyed look.

Faint, faint inner voice: Everybody in this room can probably tell what you're thinking. What makes odd people seem *odd* is the way they broadcast their . . .

The bartender said, "So? What the hell do you *want*, asshole?"

Behind me, I heard somebody whisper, "What the fuck is that in his hair? One of those things little girls wear?"

I said, "Um. Beer?"

Sudden hand on my shoulder, spinning me around. Tall, fat gray-haired man, big belly wobbling, loose jowls covered with two-day-old stubble. "My parents moved out here from the Koperveldt just to get away from you sons of bitches," translator giving good account of itself, hardly letting me hear the real Groentans words at all. "Why don't you just get the fuck out of here and go on back to your hunting lodge?"

The bartender said, "God damn it, Arie . . ."

"Shut the fuck up, Lars. Mind your business." He gave me a hard shove and shouted, "Get the fuck out, *omganger!*"

I staggered back, feeling my heart pound, got the dartgun out of my pocket and pointed it at his fat gut.

Click-crack.

Narrow grin on Arie's face.

I felt an odd tingling in my neck as I turned.

Found myself looking down the black barrel of a solid-propellant handgun.

Dim voice, maybe the library, maybe just some isolated cognitive driver separating out, trying to get my attention: Looks like that thing might throw a two-centimeter slug. You'd look awfully funny with nothing left of your head but a lower jaw.

The bartender said, "Mikah, you mess up my fucking saloon and I'll—"

"Take it easy, Lars." Mikah was a tall, skinny man with a big nose and unusually pale blue eyes, eyes so blue they looked white, pale irises making his scleral tissue look like yellow ivory. To me: "Why don't you put that down, *omganger?* On the bar. Nice and slow."

Lines of dialogue from ten thousand simplistic stories. What does the hero do now? I put my little dartgun down on the bar.

Mikah smiled and uncocked his revolver. "All yours, Arie."

Arie screamed, *"Bastard!"*

I didn't even look before I ducked, getting under his flailing fist. Punched him in the middle of the chest, turned to run as he sprawled on the floor . . . stood still, looking back down the barrel of Mikah's gun.

Mikah said, "Arie's not done with you, *omganger.* Are you, Arie?"

I could hear him struggling to his feet behind me, hissing with rage.

All right. Just like any damn barroom brawl. Been through dozens of them, God damn it. If you can't look after yourself, you don't belong in the fucking company of workingmen and -women.

I ducked again as I turned, listening to Arie grunt as he threw another haymaker. Poked him another good one, right where fat belly met flabby tits. Arie looked surprised, made a little fish face, going *ooh, oooh* as he went down again.

I looked back at Mikah. Fair fight? Can I go now?

Look of disgust on Mikah's face, telling me, perhaps, this was going to come out all . . . He said, *"Gouden jesus juultijd,* Arie! Maybe you better lay off the beer, huh?"

From the floor, Arie said, "Ooop . . . oop . . ." He started to get up again, not looking like he was in any shape to launch another roundhouse blow at my face. I took a step toward the door, deciding I'd just forget about the damn dartgun and—

Mikah said, "Rip? Saadler?"

Two more men stepping up to the bar, one of them getting me by the right arm, the other by the left, turning me to face Arie, standing by, wobbly on his feet, still having trouble getting his breath.

Mikah said, "Go ahead. Arie. Get in your licks."

They let him hit me six times, each time with progressively more weight behind the blow, then threw me in the street just as the camper pulled up in a cloud of dust.

Nice, nice starry sky overhead now.

How did it get to be dark so soon?

I heard someone, Rip maybe, or Saadler, say, "What the fuck is *that?*"

The Kapellmeister's voice said, "Can you stand up, Gaetan? Can you get in the vehicle?"

I said, "Uhhkh . . ."

Mikah's gun went *click-crack* again, recognizable now as the sound of the hammer being thumbed back.

The Kapellmeister's voice, powerfully amplified, speaking perfect Groentans, said, *"Try to use a weapon and I will kill you all."*

Quick sharp echoes off the facades of nearby buildings, then only the sound of the wind, faraway voices from people still inside the bar. A faraway hoofbeat, going *klop* on the street.

"Get in the camper cab, Gaetan."

Somehow, I got inside, lay back with my eyes shut as we drove away.

We drove northward a hundred kilometers or so before pulling off the road at a bend in the river, a little peninsula of sorts with a copse of tall, spreading trees that sort of hid the camper. By then, I'd made a partial recovery, enough to get out and go in back to take a look at the damage, admiring the bruised lumps on my face, feeling tender spots on my ribs.

OK. No loose teeth. Nothing broken. Arie must have been even flabbier than he looked. If it'd been me doing the punching, I'd sure as hell've taken out a few teeth, cracked a rib or two . . . I rinsed my mouth with mousepiss, started putting together the fixings for a cold cut and crudités dinner, grabbed my chair and went outside. Start a fire? Why the hell bother? I set up down by the river, watched the moons rise and listened to the water gurgle as I ate.

The Kapellmeister said, "Sorry I wasn't able to come to your aid more quickly."

"Forget it. All's well, et fucking cetera."

The Kapellmeister went away then, leaving me alone to munch my cold dinner and watch too-familiar stars wheel around an imaginary point in the southern sky, came back after a while with some wide-eyed little thing in its clutches, tentacles wrapped around its head.

Snip.

Slurp.

"Ahhh. Splendid." The Kapellmeister's ersatz voice imbued with the sound of sincere joy.

"What the hell do you get out of reading their minds as you kill them?"

A long silence, then: "The main purpose is to still their bodies, quiet their fears, mask the . . . final pain." More silence. "And to detach their conscious minds from the . . . habit of existence."

Meaningless? Perhaps. "What good does that do?"

"Their end is not so dreadful then."

"How can death be dreadful once it's over and done with?"

"How do *you* feel about the prospect of being eaten?"

I remembered the wolfen, and thought, Tou-fucking-ché.

The Kapellmeister said, "We are all eaten in the end. As living by a predator . . ." It paused to suck on the end of the thing's bleeding neck. ". . . as a residual corpse by bacteria and fungi, if no other scavenger."

Right. Sophomoric bullshit. I said, "You never did tell me what *you* get out of the process."

Silence. Then, "Every mind makes a contribution to the unending whole. My meals live on, in my body, in my soul."

How poetic. How fucking poetic.

The Kapellmeister said, "I have never established neural rapport with a human being before. I imagine few of my kind have."

I tried to picture those black tentacles draped over my head, found I couldn't imagine that without also imagining those pinking-shear chelae around my neck. Though it was pointless, the image made me shiver. I said, "I'd like you to tell me about the . . . Shock War, was it? Adversary Instrumentality? Something about golden cockroaches called StruldBugs?"

Silence.

I said, "You keep talking about how you've decided to trust me."

"Perhaps a willingness to . . . experience rapport would help us get past this barrier."

I shivered again, wondering what the hell I was getting myself into. But . . . OK. Maybe this thing saved your life? Sure. And you saved *its* life. Remember? You shot someone that night. Maybe the poor bastard is still lying in a hospital somewhere, paralyzed until the medicomps figure out about advanced biotaxic neurotoxins, or you, you silly bastard, decide to check up on things and maybe *tell* them.

The Kapellmeister said, "Gaetan . . ."

Dithering. Fucking dithering. I said, "Well. Maybe."

Long, long silence, punctuated by the rustling of leaves. Finally, the pod on the Kapellmeister's back made a very human-sounding sigh. It said, "Four hundred million years ago, there was a war."

Silence.

After a while, I said, "That's a long damned time ago. What kind of war?"

Silence. Then, "A very bad war. The advanced civilization that occupied the Local Group of galaxies was destroyed.

Approximately eighteen million sentient, starfaring species were rendered extinct. Virtually every conscious individual within functional range of the . . . weapons systems involved died. We do not know what that range was."

I thought, suddenly, about Fermi's paradox, then said, "I guess you have physical evidence for all this, huh? Things like the ruins on Snow?" Four hundred million years ago, there *weren't* any conscious beings on Earth. Unless you think fish and bugs are conscious. Hell. Maybe they are.

The Kapellmeister said, "Yes. However, my own species existed four hundred million years ago. Through a fluke, we escaped destruction and . . . we remember."

Remember. "You mean you have an intact history stretching back more than four hundred million years?"

"We . . . remember."

"What the hell are you telling me? You *personally* remember?"

"Gaetan. The rapport?"

Um. Neural rapport, that bit about meals living on . . . "Holy shit."

"Gaetan, I need the rapport in order to feel you will trust me as I have decided to trust you. The nature and consequences of the decisions I have made . . . *I alone have made* . . . are very frightening to me."

I sat still for a long moment. Christ, is this the way a woman feels when a man's got his hand on the waistband of her underpants, tugging gently and murmuring, *Trust me?* I said, "Shit. Um. All right."

My heart suddenly started to pound, and I heard the library AI whisper, Gaetan, are you certain it's wise for you—

The spacesuit, in override mode: He must make this decision. *We* can have no part in—

Translator AI: It could be very dangerous. If the software in the pod mechanism can work through the Kapellmeister's nervous system, it could damage the programming in his artificial immune and autoregenesis systems.

The Kapellmeister said, "It would be easier if you'd sit on the ground."

I got out of the chair and walked over to the riverbank, sat down on the sod with my feet dangling over the water. "That okay?"

"Fine." It suddenly draped its third hand over my head from behind.

"Jesus. For some reason, I thought your . . . tentacles would feel cold."

It said, "We have a form of poikilothermal regulation, as opposed to your own homeostasis, but a high-energy metabolism is the norm for sentients."

"Oh."

"Please try to relax."

"Relax? I . . ."

Click.

Image in my head like . . . some kind of painting. What am I thinking? An Impressionist painting, made up of all those little bits and swipes? Remember thinking about that, once, a long time ago. Did they know about digital art, about the technology to come? Monet? When the hell was Monet alive? Just woodcut, or were they starting to do process color? I . . .

Me. Me, sitting in the chair. Like . . . what? Like a speckle interferometry image of a star, beginning to coalesce from all those little bits of data. Me, sitting still. Sitting still and waiting for . . .

Soft, faraway whisper. Hard to focus on. Hard to identify . . .

Library AI? Yes, whispering, Claude Monet lived from 1840 to 1926 . . .

Thanks. I . . . realized I was looking at myself. Myself, seen through seven floating eyes, multiple overlapping images coalescing and . . .

AI, very far away now, whispering, It is probable that the seven globular structures are compound eyes with some kind of omnidirectional vision system. In fact . . .

Click.

No facts at all, I . . .

Naked. Wet. Up against a slimy tile wall. Clouds of steam.

Scott Jurgen, also naked, reddish-brown tentacle of a circumsized dick swinging between his legs, catching my eye, dark blood trickling from one nostril, like a dark fuse that . . .

He said, "Okay, hold the son of a bitch."

Four other boys present. Grinning. Grinning.

"Jimmy, you keep a look out, see that Mr. Tinsley doesn't walk in on us."

"Okay, Scott." One shadow shape moving away through the clammy shower room fog.

I can no longer remember the pain.

Scott hitting me in the gut a few times, punching the breath out of me. Smacking me in the face, laughing at the thump my head made as it hit the wall. Me, falling to the floor, face down, struggling in slow motion to get up, rear end rising as I got up on my hands and knees.

Somebody tittering, way up there in the clouds.

Then Scott Jurgen's voice: "Hold him down. I thought of something else."

Silence. Then one of the other boys, sounding a little afraid, "Oh, *Kali*, Scott!"

"Hold him the fuck down, Georgie."

"I'm getting out of here!"

"Run and you're next, Georgie."

I felt their hands on me then, felt myself . . . receding. Someplace safe and dark, far away from the outside world. Someplace where I could . . . begin making a . . . plan.

But hiding didn't help.

What do they call it?

Dissociation.

Not for me.

Not for . . .

Click.

Standing under an impossibly remote dark green sky, pale at zenith, tending toward black down by the horizon, subtle gradations of color adding to the sky's sense of depth.

Sky made from a million conflicting bits, made from seven distinct, moving viewpoints. My eyes. Vision . . . succinct. Stable. Integrated. Mind over body, over mind, over self, over memory, over . . .

Standing on stalky legs under that deep green sky, chelae clutched to my chest, neural arm splayed across keel. Walking. Walking, down the path, tall, blue-green vegetation, a long vista down the hill to a dark brown river, silver-gray crags beyond, frosted with blue-tinted ice. Clouds the color of old lead drifting beyond . . .

Self: Is *this* worth what you've done? Separation from the Stream?

What if you die?

What if your line is lost?

The only real death, you see.

I never really understood that when I was in the fold.

Curious word, *I*. Seemed like it had hardly any use . . . before.

Stars visible through the deep green sky, not enough light coming from the sun to mask them out. Not enough contrast.

Sun hanging low over the horizon.

A faraway voice, intruding voice: *Sigma Draconis.*

Enough. Not enough. More.

So hard to decide, when you're all alone.

Down by the dark brown river, groups of tall, thin Arousians were harvesting skinny wisps of silver grass. Near them, watching, impassive, the stocky biped, biped wrapped up in its crisp, shiny white bioisolation garment.

Horror on Homeworld when we noted their activities, while we . . . awaited them. It's starting again. What should we do?

Process of group decision beginning. Options? Many. Decision making process long. And . . . we few, dissenting.

Hard to be alone.

So terribly hard.

Click.

I remember, plain as day, working by myself in the shop

class that day. Word's gotten around. You know it has. Nobody says anything, but they *know*. Furtive grins. Edgewise looks. Pretty girls smirking and rolling their eyes as they whispered.

And God-damned Scott, coming up to you in the lunchroom, throwing his arm around your shoulders, voice so very loud: "Hey, Gae, old buddy! How's my little *pal?*"

Those other boys, the ones who lurk in the shadows, watching you, silent, knowing. *One of us now*. So. Am I? Is that what happens next? I walk into the shadows, head down, and slink along the base of the wall for the rest of my days?

I looked up when Scott Jurgen started to scream.

Scott dancing beside the work pedestal of the tilting arbor laser, fire crawling up his arm, laser beam marked by shimmering purple haze as it tracked his shoulder, cutting, cutting . . . Scott danced away, but the beam followed him, sensors on the arborhead blinking malevolent red as they watched him.

Teacher shrieking, "Christ! Somebody cut the fucking power!"

Christ? But Miz Bailey, we worship Kali Meitner here, isn't that so?

The beam winked out just as Scott stumbled and fell, trailing a plume of greasy, stinking black smoke.

People gathered round, teacher shouting, "My God, how could this have happened? The *safeties,* I mean . . ."

I heard Georgie whisper, "Fuck, it looked like the God-damned thing was *after* him."

I knelt beside Scott then, gently touching the bit of white bone that protruded from his charred stump, maybe ten centimeters of cracked, oozing black meat all that was left of his arm.

That got his attention. Then I said, "Gee, Scottie. I bet this really hurts."

In eyes afire with blinding pain, I saw him understand.

Behind me, I heard Georgie whisper, "Oh, *fuck.*"

Yes, Georgie. And Scott? Well, Scott would get out of the hospital in a couple of weeks with his nice new arm, good as new. But he sure as hell wouldn't forget.

Click.

Jesus shit. Mouth dry, I croaked, "Did you get what you wanted?"

With evident satisfaction, the Kapellmeister said, "Yes."

I awoke, out of a dream of seemingly infinite depth. Awoke, just as, it seemed, I'd awakened for the past, oh . . . I don't know. Three, maybe four million days, a steady stream of awakenings, one like another, like the one before that and, somehow, blending into a billion trillion *more* misty awakenings, stretching on back . . .

Little voice, one of my own: Well, no. A man of your age will have slept and awakened fourteen, maybe fifteen thousand times, at most.

But, it seems . . .

The dream emerged from a fog of fading memory, recalling itself just before it would have been lost forever. Not the entire dream, just a fragment. Me, small, insignificant, lying on dry grass in the darkness, vast alien looming over me, angular head wreathed in stars, gasping softly to itself as it thrust its reproductive tentacle repeatedly into my cloaca, felt the hot spill of its genetic matrix, jetting, jetting . . .

I dreamed I was the dollie being fucked by me? Christ.

I sat up, stretching, covered with tacky sweat, looking out the camper window at a scarlet dawn, Tau Ceti a misshapen orange ball low in the eastern sky, banded with a few lean black clouds. Down by the river, the Kapellmeister was standing on the bank, all seven eyes craning forward, wide apart, as though . . .

One of its chelae darted forward, went splash in the water, came back up with a long, thin brown thing, something that looked more or less like an eel, struggling, tail flipping this way and that . . . the Kapellmeister's middle arm reached out and grabbed on to the head end. The fish was suddenly still, hanging . . . contentedly? Well. Hanging in the Kapellmeister's grip until the other chela went *snip*.

I got out of bed and headed for the shower, struggling to

remember my visions from the night before, not quite failing. Jesus. I haven't thought about that shower room business for years. Didn't think about it much after I finished up with those boys.

I remembered sitting in front of the principal, her steely eyes boring into mine. Trying to anyway. Remembered her saying: "Nobody can prove anything, Gaetan. There's no evidence whatsoever that anyone trifled with the shop's safety system. Or that the automatic door failure that broke Georgie Wessle's back . . ."

I'd looked at her wide-eyed, had stuttered out my alarm that anyone would suspect I was capable of—

She slammed her fist on the desk and screamed: "I God damn *know* your type, you little piece of shit!"

Do you, Miz Baldacci?

After a while, the warm shower water unknotted the muscles at the base of my neck, on my shoulders, my upper back. After a while, I stopped replaying those lines, lines from ancient scenes. Still, what the hell if I'd been stupid? What if I'd wanted someone to *know*? No. It was enough for everyone to *imagine* it was me. The results were more than satisfactory.

We got in the camper cab and flew on, rising above the countryside, drifting to the west of the Somber River now, out over the wide Opveldt plains, steering clear of the little villages, passing over the occasional isolated farmhouse, where some Groenteboer or another was the lord of his lonely keep, passing over hill and forest, empty plain, the silvery sprawl of lesser rivers.

The ship's navigation system whispered, Satellite imagery shows you are coming up on a very large womfrog herd. There is . . . activity.

I looked. There, a dark mass similar to the one I'd seen earlier, perhaps a bit larger. Herd of dark shapes, moving slowly and . . . there. Something else. A glint, as of metal.

I took manual control of the camper, holding the wheel,

depressing it forward so that we nosed down toward the rolling plains, sliding the throttle back, reducing our speed until I was cruising along just above the grass, separated from the womfrog herd by a low ridge covered with scruffy, stunted-looking silver-green trees.

The Kapellmeister said. "It would appear we're opposite the technogenic activity evidenced in the tracking satellite imagery."

I wondered what the Compact Cities wanted with detailed realtime video of what the wildlife and Groenteboeren were up to in the middle of this immense, empty plain. Slowed up, nosed the camper into the trees, parking it just under the crest of the ridge, and shut down the engine.

We got out and walked up the hill until we got to a point where we could look out over the veldt beyond, rolling, brassy landscape stretching away to the horizon, pale blue-gray mountains rising beyond that, reaching for the sky. Rolling, brassy landscape covered with a moving, irregular sheet of womfrogs, womfrogs stretching away to . . .

"Son of a bitch," I whispered.

There it is then, Gaetan du Cheyne. *This* is the landscape of your dreams. This is where you came, mighty white hunter, with your gangs of tourist ladies, to shoot the great womfrogs, shoot them dead, help the pretty ladies shoot them dead, ladies squealing with delight, enclosed in the circle of your strong arms, heads resting back against your chest or shoulder, so you could help them aim that gun, holding them close, feeling the tight clench of their rounded buttocks against the front of your abdomen, knowing, when night fell, they would come to your tent and . . .

There. In the near distance, between my vantage point and the edge of the womfrog herd, something moving. Two somethings. Trucks, biggish trucks, five axles visible on each, tractors pulling things that looked like flat cargo beds with low retaining walls. The trucks' cargo . . . Human beings. About fifty in each truck, I'd guess. Each one holding a long, thin rifle, all of them, just now, aimed at the sky.

The Kapellmeister said, "It would appear we've found a party of . . . sportsmen."

As I watched, the near edge of the womfrog herd started to flow a little faster, trucks speeding up to keep pace. Trying to run away? Do they know what's coming? They must. Nearest womfrogs obviously trying to press back into the herd, distance themselves from the men in the trucks, but they were blocked by the bodies of their fellows.

Faint, distant whistle being blown, the signal: *Now.*

Skinny black sticks of the rifles being leveled, people jockeying for position by the cargo bed's rail. The whistle again, *tweet-tweet*. And, faraway, I heard the rapid *zizpzipzipzip* of the first shots, whispered violences overlapping.

Pockpockpockpock.

Explosive rounds flashing.

Womfrog hides popping open, spilling blood, tossing bits of internal organ, flying shrapnel of bone tumbling in the air.

I thought I heard a thin, high scream, the scream of a scalded child. Watched the front row of giant womfrogs tumble as they fell. You could see their forelegs breaking as they went down, breaking from the inertial force of the fall.

Zipzipzipzipzip.

Inserting itself into the now steady *pockpockpock* of exploding bullets, another row, deeper in the herd, mowed down, womfrogs screaming, shouting, calling to each other, recoiling, nowhere to flee, in each other's way.

Ahead and behind you could see womfrogs break from the herd, turning toward the ridge. Can they get up here, finding safety among the trees, flee out on the plains beyond? I thought about the womfrogs we'd hunted in the forest, back on the Koperveldt side of the Koudloft, and felt a little uneasy. Time, perhaps, to creep back to the safety of the camper, the safety of the sky, just drive away and . . .

Lone womfrogs running, running, *zip . . . pock!* Falling as hunters tracked them with rifles. Tracked them and brought them down.

"Sportsmen," I muttered. "Great."

For some reason, I kept expecting them to stop. Every single person on both of those trucks has killed at least two womfrogs now. Enough meat to feed a large family for a whole year. Enough hide to carpet all the rooms in a fair-sized lodge, or make warm winter coats for an entire town the size of Tegenzinstad.

Zippockzippockzippock! Womfrogs tumbling and rolling, joining a long, long line of motionless dead.

What the hell, then, a commercial hunt?

The library AI whispered, As near as can be determined, there is no commercial market for womfrog products on Green Heaven. The Compact Cities raise terragenic livestock for their own consumption, and most Groenteboer settlements can easily provide for their own limited needs.

So I waited.

Listened to the guns. Watched the womfrogs die, watched the pile of corpses grow larger and larger, blood staining the bright metallic grass, making it grow dull, herd beginning to thin from the combined effects of the killing, the fact that the farther parts had figured out what was going on, were beginning to turn away.

Watched, while the sun rose high in the sky. Watched as it sank toward the west.

At some point, I realized the Kapellmeister had wandered off and come back with a living snack, snipping off its head, sucking away contentedly at the sweet blood. None for me, thank you. I'll just . . . watch.

In the end, though I would've liked to have camped up on the ridge, where we somehow seemed closer to the stars, up where the fresh breezes blow, we had to move on, for the Groenteboeren stayed down below, even after the surviving womfrogs had escaped, doing . . . whatever the hell it was they needed to do with all those huge dead bodies.

By nightfall, even from our vantage point, it was starting to smell, wind out of the west carrying a bizarre taint, the cloying scent of spoiled fruit. I backed the camper out of the trees and

flew on, following the ridge until it petered out, a hundred kilometers or so to the north, moving off above a level plain, curiously empty by the mottled light of the moving moons. A
wasteland, I found myself thinking. The landscape for which
that word was made.

Eventually, we came upon a small, isolated highland of low,
rolling, denuded hills, rising like soap bubbles of stone from the
surrounding flat land. I landed the camper atop the highest
hill, and we got out to find we'd gotten so far north, two-thirds
of the way across the Opveldt to the edge of the Mistibos Forest,
that the night air was balmy, verging on hot.

Beautiful night, stars rising and falling in orderly progression, antarctic pole stars low in the south, not so many of them
now, wheeling in a great circuit round half the sky, as before.
This is the sort of night you dreamed about, when you dreamed
about the soft women, coming to you out of a jasmine night.
Where did that dream come from? Genetically determined hormones? Or merely the vidnet?

Where did the vidnet dramatists get it, then? Their own hormones, or merely some earlier tradition? Is there any point at
which it was . . . real? No answers, of course. Only a desire,
renewed, paved over and renewed again: somewhere, somehow,
somewhen, that world will return to me, return to me and be
real.

What's the difference, I wonder, between fucking those
dream women, back in that dream time, and fucking a helpless
dollie, here and now? *Was* it only their cunts I wanted, as I've
supposed for so long? Or was it their . . . imagined desire for me
that . . . I had a crisp memory of the dollie's eyes looking up at
me, shining in the starlight as I fucked it. Hell, I don't even
know if it was a male or female, much less . . .

To my irritation, I found I had an erection now, sitting here
all alone, looking out over the empty plains, gray by moonlight,
from my hard stone perch, all alone, but for the bizarre shadow
of the Kapellmeister cast on the ledge by my side, robot legs
and fat, formless body, eyes on stalks floating above its back.

It said, "There is a special nobility in the accidental beauty of nature."

I turned and looked at it, wondering what the hell had prompted the statement. Nothing to read, I think, in the Kapellmeister's form, the empty colored shapes of its eyes, the . . .

It stood, motionless, poised, outlined against the sky, eyes drifting slowly above its back, as though driven by the soft, warm night breeze, so obviously looking up at the stars. With, I thought, that same innocent nobility you see in a poised stallion, in one of those old, old nature shows. *Misty of Chincoteague*, or something equally stupid. *Lassie Come Home*.

The translator AI whispered, The pod software's grasp of human idiom is splendid, but unlikely to be perfect. Nobility, perhaps, is not quite the term.

The Kapellmeister said, "I feel so alone, standing amid this great, dark landscape. From here, it looks like this one little world goes on forever and ever."

Alone? Snide voice within going, Welcome to the club, fuckhead.

The Kapellmeister said, "This sense of aloneness, which I know now you share, impells my trust."

Impells, not quite compells? I turned away, staring out at the dark, empty plain, and could see just what it'd meant about this one *little* world going on and on forever. Even if it does go on forever, above there are still the infinite stars, the infinitely deep sky. I whispered, "You never did say what you wanted to trust me with."

Said it almost to myself.

The Kapellmeister's shadow moved across the rock, rippling, flowing to fill all the hollows, ride over the bulges. When it was close to me, I watched that middle hand extrude, tentacles flaring, like an octopus about to engulf my head.

"Can't you just . . . tell me?"

"It would take too long."

The hand settled on my scalp, tentacles reaching down and

around to engulf my face, permission unasked. No need, in fact, to be granted. *Trust*, I thought. What a peculiar notion . . .

Click.

The sky was a subtle blend of gray and gold, more like a high mist than a sky, stars visible right through its substance, like bits of tarnished silver, hardly bright at all.

The two of us standing there, on the black beach sand, standing at the end of our complex trails of footsteps, dark water lapping nearby, like molten tar, but cold, fizzing like foam on the beach, leaving bits of dark ice behind as rime.

Being before me, posing in mirror display, chelae raised, glittering in pale sunshine. Beyond this image of self-not-self, I could see faraway mountains, beyond that, only sky.

I put out my speaking hand, just as that other being did the same. We touched. Our tentacles intertwined. Thoughts, thoughts of another, like whispers, my own whispers reaching out. Familiar, comfortable touch, this other, one I'd merged with so often before. Friend. Lover. Sibling. All those things that one discrete biological unit can be to another.

The other's thoughts whispered, This is a terrible thing you are doing, you and Those Others Who Would Trust.

I and my comrades, going on out into the void. Void abandoned so long ago, in the Aftermath. I whispered, What else can I do? Merge with the Ones Who Would Hide?

My friend whispered, As Hidden Ones, at least we would not be responsible for . . .

Inaction, I said, is action enough.

That's what They say. Believe it if you will.

Join the Rectification Group, then? Go out and Do What Must Be Done?

My friend whispered, I'm sorry for you. This decision must have been hard.

I showed this old lover the fresh scent of my pain, felt a wincing, a drawing away. I said, It's time for me to go. Released my grip on the other's tendrils, feeling those old labels, lover, sibling, most of all, friend, start to slip away.

Turned and walked away, following the complex trails of my own footsteps back up the black sand beach, cold wind slipping between my extended eyestalks. When I reached the crest of the dunes, where the dead sand gave way to the complex, interlocking strands of the ground cover, I felt an irresistible urge to look back. I did so, with just one eye, limiting my commitment to only that, and saw the flat image of my old friend standing still, down on the beach, label unshed, watching me go away.

And urge to go back?

Yes.

But I went back to where the groundskimmers were parked anyway. Got aboard mine, started the little electric engine and drove slowly away, up the old coast road toward the industrial complex where the little ships were waiting.

It'd been so hard, had taken us so long, to restore them, get them back to full operating capacity, for they sat in that old underground storage facility for so many tens of millions of years, most of them much longer than that. Perhaps we wouldn't have been able to do it, even at need, but the Rectifiers wanted them too, and there are so many more of Them than there are of Us.

Fear.

This is fear I feel.

I'm going to be alone soon.

Unfamiliar.

Full of dread.

But something must be done, and I am one of the very few willing to do it.

Click.

No fear at all now of being alone.

I lie huddled with a thousand friends, siblings, lovers, comrades, mated beings, huddled in a great, seething mass in some underground chamber, embedded in one another, lives held in common, huddled in the midst of a technology so old we have, *somehow*, incredibly, forgotten when it began.

No, it's a new fear I feel.

And a very, very old one.

Old. Recalled from the most ancient memories of all.

Image, from some primitive, insensate machine, a bit of optical software whose job was merely to watch the sky, ignoring the stars, planets, asteroids, comets, industrial spacecraft, everything that *belonged* out there, well regulated and serene. Just watch the sky, see that nothing sneaks up on us from the cold interstellar deeps. No sense letting some bit of flotsam disrupt the orderly progression of our eons.

There!

High-energy objects moving against the anisotropic background of infinitely deep space.

Activity centered around *that* star, a nice, middle-aged main sequence G2, just over twenty light-years away.

Someone is abroad again, after all these years.

What do we do now, other than fear?

Click.

Friend, lover, sibling, mine, being without a name. Being with . . . yes. Identity. Identity with *it*self, not with *my*self, but . . . just the two of us now, facing each other, poised on a rounded, windswept crag under that same old sky of infinite gray and gold, sun a dull shield down by the horizon . . .

82 Eridani, whispered a friendly alien inclusion.

Ah, yes.

I reached out with my speaking hand, my listening hand, my loving hand, friendly hand, relating hand. Reached out and touched my sibling-friend-lover.

Felt its thoughts flow into me. Felt its memories merge with mine. Felt matching memories pair up, merge, as though we *were* one.

One for now.

For only now.

Felt raw new memories search for mates, felt them fail. Saw the memories stand up in mirror array. This one similar to that one. But different. Here. There. Yon . . .

Felt the raw new memories begin to duplicate.

Soon, there will be enough memories for both of us.

Soon . . .

When we separated, the sun had gone down, the sky misty black, stars like bright bits of silver now, each little fleck surrounded by a nimbus of high cloud.

I looked at the being looking at me; knew a mirror mind looked back.

Ten thousand years. Times two. And more.

Our lineages . . . similar, a little different.

All those, old, older, oldest memories, waiting for me to sift through them, waiting for me to make them mine, as I've made so many other memories mine. I . . .

Click.

Gaetan, whispered a machine voice, unrecognized, unreal. This is, perhaps, not safe. We think . . .

First, do no harm.

Who said that?

Is that you?

Me.

Vague image of looking out through my own eyes at a warm Green Heaven night. Out past cool, not cold black tentacles, out across a truly darkling plain and . . .

Click.

Childhood.

Whose?

One of many.

After ten thousand years, I remember many childhoods, the childhood of every friend-lover-sibling I've ever had.

Fat little being, crawling over the rocks by the seashore, playing, playing, secure, knowing its mother was near.

Other children near, calling out in their high, piping, childish voices, voices wet with the dew of the egg. I-am-here! I-am-here!

Dark shadow.

I-am-here?

Child recoiling, recoiling at the adult looming out of the

shadows, shadows of the forest by the sea. Mother? Mother, where are you? Mother! *Mother!*

Turning to run.

No use.

The adult's black hand engulfs me.

Memories flow.

Its memories, into me, for I have no memories of my own.

When the hand lets go, only two adults stand by the seashore, listening to the familiar boil and hiss of the waves, surf on crushed stone.

Old adult satisfied.

New adult bitter.

I wasn't ready yet.

Ah. Well, no one ever *is*, friend, sibling, lover, mine . . .

Click.

Well. Well, yes, I *do* have a memory!

Red, red darkness, ovoidal darkness, slick, ovoidal darkness closing me in. Faraway sounds. A sense of movement. Piping cries.

I've been here for . . . ever so long. Quiet. Drowsing in my fluid home. The universe is . . . circumscribed. Nothing but me. Warm. Happy. Alone forever in the warm, red-lit universe.

Crawling sensation in my legs. Legs till now curled motionless beneath me. An itchy urge to move my seven eyes. I rock back and forth in my red-lit darkness, warm, eternal darkness. Rasp my keel tooth against the cosmic event horizon, as I've done more and more lately.

Rock back and forth, harder and harder, listing to the little *chip* of sound each impact makes, my keel tooth against the edge of the world.

Why am I doing this?

I don't know.

Rock. *Chip.* Rock. *Chip.*

Crack!

Light! Blinding light!

Eyes recoil, trying to hide, trying not to see . . . the things, horrible things, things beyond . . .

Oh. Ohhhh.

I am born!

Click.

Ten thousand years.

Birth.

No memory of death.

No memory of infinity, before, after . . .

But . . .

That other mist.

That faraway time.

Time before the egg.

Where do those memories come from?

I . . .

Opened my eyes. Blinked. Blinked away a memory I knew was my own. Memory of myself lying not long ago on a wet bluff, in a forest in the borderland between Koperveldt and Koudloft, standing in the dank night beside Gretel Blondinkruis, wishing for her crotch, looking down at a ravine densely packed with womfrogs. Womfrogs looking back at me.

I wonder. Did they know they were about to die?

Of course they did.

The Kapellmeister said, "How do you feel, Gaetan?"

"I don't know. I . . ." I took a deep breath as the tentacles fell away, releasing me back into the night air. "Are you really ten thousand years old?"

Silence. Then it said, "Yes. I suppose so."

14

S tanding on my bald stone hilltop, I watched Tau Ceti rise like an apparition over the empty plains of the Opveldt. Eastward, hanging in banded layers above the plains, was a pattern of low clouds, morning fog perhaps, created by some temperature/pressure differential, coating the landscape like haze. Above that, reaching beyond the horizon, I could see the pale gray peaks of Thisbÿs Bergketen, eighteen hundred kilometers away, not quite rimming the world, broken, *there*, by a patch of tawny morning sky.

That would be Aardlands Bergpas, then, the saddle, dipping down through the tropopause, that was the only way through those mountains available to . . . beings without technology.

Beyond it would be the Adrianis peninsula, with its vast, blinding gypsum deserts, dryer than anything the Earth had ever produced. Home of the Hinterlings, descended from the original colonists of Green Heaven, scientific base technical personnel left behind when their organization had folded.

The library AI whispered, A yellow wolfen species inhabits the southeastern part of the peninsula, now on the verge of extinction. Planetary records indicate the northern coast of the peninsula, just beyond the equator, is being settled by the families of professional boombanger guides.

Boombangers. Something from the vidnet, barely recalled. People who went out on the high seas of Green Heaven, the vast Panviridis Ocean of the northern hemisphere, taking parties of tourists out to kill boomers, as though they were participants in some old sea epic or another. Ahab. That sort of crap.

I remember hearing about boomers, sort of halfway between whales and giant squid in appearance, sometimes growing up to a hundred meters in length. Smart bastards. I had a brief recollection of seeing a hunt, of seeing a boomer pull the mast off a cleverly made sailing ship, try to use it as a weapon until the boombanger safety officer killed it with some kind of electric cannon.

Never fantasized about that.

Not quite personal enough.

Unless, like Ahab, you went down with the whale.

I turned away from the rising sun, stood looking down at my friend the Kapellmeister. "What now?"

It stood still for a moment, then said, "We have another day before I must return to the Arousians' camp. Let's just . . . go on."

Not that long before I have to get back to Orikhalkos. Get back to Delakroë and van Rijn and . . . do what I agreed to do. "All right."

Lunchtime, atop another low ridge, camper parked in the shadows. I sat on a nice warm rock I'd found, shadows from the small leaves of a spreading baarbij bush making a mottled pattern on my skin. I sat alone, looking out over the empty plain at nothing in particular.

Odd. The absence of large flying creatures on Green Heaven makes it look like there's something terribly wrong out there. No vultures means there's nothing dead. Nothing dead means there's nothing alive. There are always vultures. Or is that just one more vidnet fantasy?

After a while, I finished my sandwich, finished my lemon

cookies, swigged the last of a beer-like beverage that was distinctly out of sync with the sweet cookie filling. No sign of the Kapellmeister, who I'd expected would turn up at any second with a living lunch relaxed in its grasp. Relaxed and waiting to die. Is there something out there that could take on and kill a Kapellmeister? I have no idea how tough they really are. What would I do then?

Something far out on the plain, many kilometers away, caught my eye. A tiny sparkle of light. After a long time, I heard a faint echo, hardly a sound at all.

The library said, Technogenic.

I got up and went back in the camper, disposing of my empty bottle and getting a pair of binoculars. Went back outside, stood on my rock, and looked.

Little things moving, reddish splotches against the dun and green grass of the Opveldt, blotches scattering in all directions. More flashes, followed a long time later by that faint echo of technogenic sound. I turned up the gain on the binoculars as far as it would go. Yes. Those are human hunters, moving in to inspect the now motionless red blotches. Dead wolfen.

I looked round, carefully panning the binoculars. A truck with cages on the back. Another truck with a flatbed. And . . . there. Huddled, waiting, motionless. A band of dollies.

Wolfen always have dollies with them.

The men took their time, gathering up the wolfen, throwing them in the back of the truck. Some of the wolfen weren't dead, merely wounded, helpless, baring teeth, tiny with distance, trying to fight back. I watched the men beat them with what looked like baseball bats, tie them up, throw them on the truck with the dead ones.

Is that how they get to the killpits? Maybe so.

Something else was going on too.

When the men finished with the wolfen, they went over to the huddled mass of waiting dollies. Why didn't they run? Afraid they'd be killed? Hell, that's their fate anyway. The wolfen kill them too. Kill them and eat them.

I watched the men pick dollies from the group and drag them aside. Watched the men take down their pants and lie on top of the dollies they'd selected.

OK, Gaetan du Cheyne. Would you like to be down there now, helping them out? Is that what you want? Maybe some part of me did. I don't know anymore.

After a while, they were all done. Will they kill the dollies now? How do *those* men feel about what they've just done? What they did was gather the dollies, fucked and pristine alike, put them in the cages, get in the trucks, and drive away.

I took the binoculars away from my eyes and stood staring at the scene, now so far away it really didn't exist anymore. After a while, there was a soft almost-noise behind me, and there was the Kapellmeister, holding some little green rabbit-like thing.

It said, "There's very little game around here."

Come sunset, I dropped the camper atop a low, grassy hill just west of the main course of the Somber River, here more than five kilometers wide, changed from a pleasant little stream to a vast, dark, placid thing, waters laden with silt from the Opveldt making their way northward to the endless sea.

After triggering the pop-up and getting my dinner started, I walked a little bit away, surroundings new yet nearly unchanged. The Opveldt gradually widens as you go north toward the equator, at the point where it meets the Mistibos, stretching approximately 8,500 kilometers east to west, so there are areas in the middle where you can see neither mountain range.

Southward: nothing but Opveldt as far as the eye can see, rolling brassy-gray-green plains, a dark, metallic landscape as featureless as the void of space. Somewhere out there . . . dollies, wolfen, womfrogs, Groenteboeren, *omganger* hunters and *vreemdeling* tourists . . . *smartinaassen?* I turned toward the east and watched the Kapellmeister picking its way downhill to the bank of the river.

I hardly remember Gretel Blondinkruis at all now. A fantasy abandoned.

Eastward, beyond the flat, oily, almost-black waters of the river, more Opveldt stretched to the horizon, above it a purplish green sky in which a few bright stars showed up as pale white dots. No more mountains. Too far away at last. In the north . . .

Beyond the plains, at the edge of the world, an indigo shadow capped by a thin rime of dark cloud, narrow band marking the boundary between earth and sky like a long muddy smear of paint. That would be the Mistibos Forest, with its dwarf womfrogs and primitive green wolfen. Go there tomorrow? Perhaps. Maybe we can meet some of these green wolfen. Maybe they'll have nice little dollies of their own, and . . . and . . .

Westward, long-shadowed plains reaching to the horizon, then the thick, jagged peaks of the Pÿramis Bergketen in black silhouette against the sunset, Tau Ceti already hidden, long bands of golden light streaming up from all the valleys and passes, fanned out across a dark red sky, the hand of some impossible god reaching out to engulf the world.

I looked for a long time, feeling short of breath.

Think of all the reasons you came, Gaetan du Cheyne. Maybe this is the only valid one.

I went back then and got my dinner off the grill, some frozen sausages I'd found in the camper, weiswurst cooked brown now, striated with black, a plate of ice-cold canned sauerkraut, a bottle of some peculiarly sweet red ale, flavored with nutmeg.

I sat on the grass with my back against the camper's warm side, staring toward the sunset as I ate. After a while the Kapellmeister joined me, carrying a fat, fish-like thing, which he merely sliced open, just aft of the gills, before putting it into his invisible mouth.

"How the hell could you catch a thing like that? Can you swim?"

Without taking the fish from its mouth, still making those faint sucking noises, as of a man sucking water from a sponge, it said, "No, though it's no trouble to walk along the bottom of a stream. However, as electromagnetic impulses will propagate a short distance though water, that was unnecessary."

"I don't understand."

The Kapellmeister extended its middle hand and fluttered the tentacles briefly. "I summoned the fish."

"Doesn't it mind what you're doing? I mean, with its head still attached and all."

"The fish is sufficiently suffocated that its conscious mind has ceased to function, Gaetan."

We ate. Watched the sun go down. Watched the stars come out. Sat together in silence, listening to the soft wind. I found myself wondering what this looked and sounded like to the Kapellmeister. I . . . Well. You could find out. All those things from neural rapport. Am I *really* reading the Kapellmeister's mind, sharing its memories? What does that mean? Layers of software here as well. Something to do with the pod? This creature is not at *all* like me.

The translator AI whispered, It may be that all conscious experience is alike.

So. What's *your* conscious experience like?

The spacesuit said, We were made by humans, to serve human needs in a human way. Our conscious experience is modeled on your own.

Is that why primitives give their gods a human voice? God made man in his own image, after all.

I said, "How old are you? From the . . . images . . . memories . . . I haven't got a good word for it."

"Memories will do."

"Okay. From your memories, then, it felt like you were ten thousand years old. Something like that. Or maybe a great deal older. Yet it always seemed like everything you saw was so new, as though you were . . . I don't know. An infant."

"Ten thousand will do, if that means anything."

"Counting from when you . . . hatched?"

"Yes. In just that sense."

"How long do Kapellmeisters live?"

"Until they don't want to live anymore, of course. It varies with the . . . individual."

It was true, I'd sensed nothing like a fear of death, anywhere in there. It must be nice to . . .

It said, "Your own fears about the future are cultural, Gaetan du Cheyne. Humans are at the historical cusp where an individual's future can go on as long as he likes. But . . . the fears of childhood hold you still."

Reading my mind now? I turned to look at the thing, knowing I was wasting my time, like looking at a statue, or a plant, or . . . Stopped, motionless in the darkness. Looked at the Kapellmeister. Looked closer, then closer still. Finally, I said, "You look just the same as you always did, but . . . if I didn't know better, I'd . . . swear you've grown a face."

Silence. But the way those eyes floated . . .

It said, "You know me now, Gaetan du Cheyne. As I know you."

What were the words? Friend. Lover. Sibling.

The Kapellmeister's middle hand slowly unfurled, and it said, "I'd like to know you better still."

Without a word, I turned my back and waited for the hand.

Click.

Though we'd sorted this old one's memories many times, there was no longer any way to determine its age, old being lying on a wide, warm flat rock, warmed by the rays of the sun, filtering down out of a summer noonday sky.

You grapple a talking hand, listen to the stream of thoughts, the unreeling stream of memory and eka-memory, finding further memory beyond that, eka-memories of some old being's eka-memories of older eka-memories still, until . . .

Nothing much left in there, now, of the memoryless thinking being who burst from the egg, an unknown time ago.

Nine of us, surrounding the dying one.

Nine listening hands reaching out, extending one listening tentacle each to one talking tentacle, talking hand outstretched, fanned for us, flesh trembling, yet lethargic, so . . .

I felt myself open wide, a yawning chasm waiting to be bridged, to be filled with . . .

The dying one's thoughts flooded into me, a cascade of images, words, thoughts, shapes, his own experiences, endlessly repeated over so many days, days and years, ages gone by, while the stars wheeled overhead, empty and forlorn. Mating this one. Bespeaking that one. Trading memories, all the same, recalling eka-memories, differentiating more and more as the mist grew deep . . .

The stars!

Look at the stars!

Flashing. Twinkling. Dancing overhead, bursts of color and light and . . .

Soft, soft horror.

The stars. Look at the stars . . .

The dying one whispered, Now I join the fold, enfolded. I join the Vanished. I name myself, Childhood Overwhelmed in Night.

Childhood Overwhelmed in Night. A fine name for a soul gone on.

Left behind, the body, dropped, put aside, relaxed, sprawling on the warm face of the rock, become food for scavengers.

Click.

Sunset over Syrtis Major, the western sky, beyond the craggy badlands outside Hollyfield Dome, layered like pink mother-of-pearl, marking the place where the sun had gone down, sky at zenith black and dense with stars.

Coming through the open lockseal from the transit corridor's elevator platform, I stood for a moment, looking out across the park, low, olive green trees, gray gravel pathways, bushes with little red flowers, a trellis over there with morning glories, a species genetically engineered for constant bloom, belying their name.

That faint scent of earth and pollen in the air.

No time for this. She's waiting for me.

I felt a tingle of anticipation, a subtle tightening somewhere in my abdomen. Maybe it'll be . . . like last week. Delicious memory of a long night spent with Jayanne, whom I'd known only a month or so. Not the first time we'd been together. Perhaps the fourth or fifth? Already losing track.

But, last week. Crawling into the bed. Going through that usual fevered coupling. Lying back on the bed, wet with her goo and mine, sighing with relief. Long moment of lying in the darkness, looking at her naked body, all those soft peaks and valleys of remembered flesh, looking into the featureless glint of her eyes, regretting that it was over so quickly.

Then she'd reached out and taken my still-damp hand. Giggled. Pulled it down to the stickiness between her legs, and said, We're not done yet.

Not done? Pang of surprise, a little fear. But I don't think . . . a harder pang then, realizing if you couldn't do what she wanted, that might be the end of things, here and now.

Fingers slipping through wet hair, finding slick, still-swollen tissue, Jayanne's crotch inhabited by what felt like a fine, steamed oyster, ready to be taken up and swallowed whole.

Then a pang of delight, realizing I could. So surprised to find out the second time was better than the first. The third better than the second. Jayanne giggling away in the darkness, when I told her I'd never *imagined* . . .

I hurried down the stairs and up the gravel path, cutting through the park to the entrance of Sodermann Dome, old and much patched, where most of the older student housing was left.

Voices, coming through the trees. Harsh, making me freeze for a moment. I remember. Remember voices like that. Turned to look.

A clearing, some kind of athletic field, white lines of green turf, some game played by the children of Mars that we hadn't had on Luna, some hybrid of baseball and cricket, I think, evolved by the earliest colonists, who'd mostly come from Uttar Pradesh and Hokkaido.

There were six of them, four boys and two girls, judging by the cut of their hair, boys with ponytails, girls with spikes just now, from what I'd seen on the youthculture vid circuits, all dressed alike in green and yellow vinyl coveralls.

A seventh. A boy. Holding his bat, looking so fierce, holding them at bay, shouting something along the lines of *leave me the fuck alone*, though I really couldn't hear the words.

One of the other boys, a much bigger boy, reached out, caught the bat as it flailed, pulled it out of the little boy's hand. Threw it aside, tumbling away into the bushes.

Two big boys grabbed the little one then.

One of the girls danced in, kicking him in the kneecap, little boy yelling, high-pitched, still defiant.

One boy nudging another, pointing at me. They stopped for a second, all looking in my direction. The captive's eyes were dark pits, boring into me, completing the tableau.

Hope must be flaring in his breast, just now, I . . .

The others turned away, dismissing my presence and, as I turned away, I heard them hitting him, heard him start to cry.

Well. I'd better hurry. Jayanne is waiting.

Five steps up the gravel path and it seemed like I was out of earshot, five more and I could think of nothing but Jayanne's nice, wet pussy, waiting for me.

Click.

Not my memory, no.

Nor a memory gleaned directly from another, memory from the whispering hand of a dying one.

Something rather more deeply embedded in the tapestry of memories thus formed, memory of a memory transferred, a hundred thousand times over:

Being lying on a warm rock, long after the sun had gone down, looking up through layers of mist at a hard, cold sky, stars shining down silently, like pinpricks through a black dome, carrying down to us the light from beyond.

Why should it bother me that the stars are silent?

Perhaps, because the stars once spoke to us, whispered of things beyond imagining, whispered to us the memories of all the others, other beings, other minds, riches beyond counting.

We could go out there again, you say.

Go out there and . . . look for them.

Surely they haven't *all* perished?

Surely not, but . . .

That other memory, memory of the living sky . . .

And then the silence.

What if we do go out?

What if we find them?

What then?

No.

Better that we stay home and nurse our memories. If others exist, survivors, others like us, let them stay home as well, stay home and be safe, lest the memories be extinguished.

The remembered being hunkered down on his rock, rock reradiating warmth left in it by the sunlight of day, and contemplated solitude.

Click.

I awoke, as from a sequence of dreams, opened my eyes slowly, and looked up at the still-silent sky. No. Not silent anymore. Four hundred million years have gone by. The stars are whispering again.

Why are the Kapellmeisters so afraid of that?

Afraid of us? Or just what we stand for?

I said, "You haven't told me, yet, how they all died. Or why."

Somewhere, far away, a long, grinding metallic yowl. Wolfen calling. Calling to each other? Or calling to me? Would they call to me, if they knew I was listening for them? Would they come, if I could call them, come to me with their flock of dollies and . . .

The Kapellmeister said, "I'm not ready yet."

I turned and looked at the Kapellmeister, saw manifest uncertainty in the gentle movements of its eyes. "Don't you trust me?"

A subtle flutter of amusement, eyes cycling round to look, more or less, at me, images coalescing to an interpreted whole.

It reached out gently, tentacles of its speaking hand touching my chest, gently, here and there, each touch bringing a quick tingle of awareness. Then it said, "Perhaps I don't trust myself. The decisions I've made . . ."

Right through the machine voice, I could hear it thinking: The decisions *I've* made. I alone.

Sure. Something I can sympathize with. You make decisions. You never know whether they're right or wrong. Why do so many people not care about the ethical nature of their decisions? Brief memory of my father, poking me in the chest with his big, blunt finger, shouting, Do what's best for *you*, asshole. Stop worrying about the rest of this shit.

I can't even remember what shit he was talking about. As for what's best for me . . . Well. Knowing that's the trick, isn't it? I said, "I'd like to start back now. Go back to Orikhalkos for a while. There's something I want to do."

Disquiet in the Kapellmeister's body language. Then it said, "I think I understand."

Slight surprise. *Do* you understand? How much of . . . me has spilled back through this shared channel, through the hand that listens, as well as speaks. Do you know . . . Womfrogs dying. Wolfen killed. Long, long memory of myself lying on that dollie, memory somehow mingled with a nameless whore, pressed to the wall, fucked like a dog's bitch while my head filled up with helpless fantasies of love.

You know all that, nameless Kapellmeister?

It said, "I see. Drop me off at the Arousians' camp on the way back. Come to us when you're . . . ready."

I said, "This won't take long."

Yet another awakening. As I lay in my hotel room bed, bracketed by the rays of the rising sun, it felt curiously . . . different. I sat up slowly, looking out the window at the still-familiar cityscape of Orikhalkos, and thought, I've lost that sense of sameness my awakenings always had in the past. Sameness I was never quite conscious of before.

It feels like I've been invaded by a sense of possessing the Kapellmeister's past and, through it, all the pasts transferred down that long, long chain of experience.

Nonsense, of course. When I tried, all I could call up was a few conscious snippets, but still . . . natural? I don't know.

The library whispered, Gaetan, we've gotten the addresses you asked for, made the appointments you require.

I'm used to having voices in my head. We all are. I fell back on the bed, stretching, feeling a little smug satisfaction at my decision, at the fact that I'd made it, however stupid.

The library whispered, We've also completed a reference search through the law codes of the Compact Cities, with special focus on the government of Orikhalkos.

Yes?

Gaetan, we think this will be a fruitless endeavor.

So? Most endeavors are.

Disquiet from the clustered AIs. What? Worried about me? Why?

No answer.

Hell. Maybe it's their job, I . . .

Thought about the things I'd seen and done. God damn it, not just the killpit and the dollhouse dancers. Not just the womfrogs killed by so-called sportsmen, by hunters, by poachers, if that term has any meaning here. My own fucking memories as well. Memories of lovers lost and whores loved. Lara, Jayanne, Layla Garstang, even Rua Mater. Even a briefly recalled memory of that poor little bastard in the park on Mars, getting the shit kicked out of him for God knows what reason. Did he deserve it? Does anyone? Obviously, those kids beating on him thought he did.

I'll never know. I walked away.

Jayanne's cunt seemed more important, at the time.

Maybe it was.

What would've happened had I backed out of that dark alley in Orikhalkos, on a clammy, unpleasant night, not so long ago? Would I be lying here now anyway, wondering what the fuck I should do next?

I felt a sudden, fleeting pang, thinking of the Kapellmeister lying in the dark alleyway, alone, memories slipping away, no one to . . . listen. Listen as he called out his name.

You have that at least, Gaetan du Cheyne.

Is it worth anything to you?

I said, "I know. It's just . . . something I want to do."

Voice making a flat echo, merged with its own sound, on the flat walls of my room. No one here but me. And, of course, my little AI . . . friends? Christ. I got up then and took a shower, got dressed and was on my way, distracted, unable to stop thinking about what I'd just said.

Hours later, Tau Ceti was high in the sky, filtered rays burning on in through Mr. Patrocles' tinted window, shining in my face, robbed of ultraviolet and infrared alike, light without substance.

He smiled at me for the hundredth time in our conversation, that same vapid smile he seemed able to switch on and off like a lightbulb, and said, "Look, I'm sure this is all very upsetting to you, being an offworld tourist and all, but . . . well, you've just got to understand: Green Heaven is *not* like Earth. Not wealthy. Not populous. We don't need all those rules and regulations you have, especially away from the urban centers. People here want to be . . . free."

Brutus to Britannicus: Don't be a provincial sap. The customs of your own little island . . . when in Rome . . . et fucking cetera.

When I didn't say anything, he went on, "In any case, there's nothing we can do about things that happen away out on the veldt. Compact law doesn't extend to the Groenteboeren, you know."

I nodded and said, "But it does extend to the things happening here in your city, doesn't it?"

He sighed and laid his hand on the little terminal embedded in the desk. "I've checked up on the activities you mentioned, Mr. du Cheyne. The so-called wolfen killpit you describe is enrolled as a licensed private gambling club. What they bet on is none of our business, so long as no other laws are broken."

"And this business with the wolfen . . ."

He rolled his eyes, classic exasperation. "Mr. du Cheyne, there are more than eight hundred licensed gambling clubs in Orikhalkos alone. More than *sixty* of those," he tapped the terminal screen for emphasis, "involve betting on some kind of combat sport. Boxing, wrestling, fencing . . . so long as the gambling records are ethically handled, so long as nobody gets killed, what business is it of *ours* . . ."

"The wolfen get killed."

A snippet of involuntary laughter popped out of him before he could stop it. "Mr. du Cheyne. Wolfen are *animals*."

Right. I sat silent for so long he started to turn away, apparently figuring I'd come to the end of my business. "Mr. Patrocles."

Raised eyebrow: "Yes?"

"What about the dollhouse?"

He turned back, folded his hands on the desktop, frowned. "Mr. du Cheyne, there are no licensed 'dollhouses,' as you so quaintly call them, in the city of Orikhalkos."

"Really. I know of at least two."

He stared at me then, eyes quite empty. Finally, "One of the places you mention is listed as the site of a private social club. None of our business."

"No one here cares about things like that?"

A shrug. "Mr. du Cheyne, as I'm sure you've noticed, prostitution is legal in Orikhalkos. It is no business of this city if a woman chooses, through her own free will, to rent out her vagina as a prostitute, any more than it would be our business if she chose to rent out her voice as a nightclub singer. So long as the proper taxes are paid . . ."

Taxes. Splendid. I said, "What about the other one?"

He brightened visibly, smile flicking on like magic. "Well, Mr. du Cheyne, the property at the site you describe is registered as a warehouse. We'll send a man to investigate this very day. If it turns out to be an unlicensed social club . . . well. All appropriate fines will certainly be levied!"

Fines. Great.

I got up and said, "Sorry I wasted your time."

Mr. Patrocles smiled merrily, and said, "That's what I'm here for, Mr. du Cheyne."

By sunset, Tau Ceti an improbable crimson dome on the edge of a deep indigo sky, upper part separated from the lower by a single black band of cloud, I'd retrieved the camper from the lot and driven back out into the countryside, following the course of the Krijgsgevangene River westward across the Koperveldt toward the setting sun.

Nothing really out here, but . . . well-rutted dirt roads, occasional run-down fences, boerderij houses visible against this vista or that, beneath faraway mountains and hills crowned with clouds. This place is not a wilderness. Hasn't been for a long damned time. No wolfen left this far north on the Koperveldt. Womfrogs reduced to pitiful, isolated bands. Dollies . . .

I wonder if the Groenteboeren keep them in their homes? Easily trained, they'd make splendid servants. Vash de dishes, dollie. Polish mijn boots, dollie. Suck mijn dick, dollie. I grinned in the growing darkness. That last'd piss off the vrouwvelijk Groenteboeren no end! Or maybe not. Maybe it'd be worthwhile, considering the rest. Hell, maybe your average vrouw wouldn't mind at all. You want your dick sucked, Hans? Just a minute, I'll get the dollie for you.

At a bend in the river, hardly a creek compared to the Opveldt's Somber, I pulled up in front of a big, barn-like building, broad parking lot filled with dozens of ground cars, cheery yellow light streaming from its broad windows, and killed the engine.

Well. Here I am in front of the largest, most influential grange hall on all of Green Heaven. No, sir, the freedom-loving Groenteboeren won't have anything to do with a nasty old government, like those absurd little weasels in their Compact Cities. Still, no one likes anarchy, no one with property anyway.

I got out of the camper and walked across the parking lot, boots crunching softly on the loose gravel.

Inside, it didn't take long to attract attention, to introduce myself, find the fellow in charge, talk them into letting me be the night's entertainment. A few drinks, priming myself as well as my hosts. Then, up on the little stage.

I'd planned what to say, of course, composed an impassioned little speech in my head, tried it out on my tongue during the drive, spooling it off into the library so it could be played back, corrected for grammar and pacing, at need.

Felt the AI get ready.

Opened my mouth . . .

Christ. Look at them out there. Fat little men and women, old-stock Groenteboeren so satisfied with their lives, with their . . . I felt the passion flow away like water, replaced by . . . I don't know. Not fear, really. Just a wish that I hadn't come here.

With the passion went all knowledge of just *why* I'd come.

Roomful of expectant eyes.

I started to talk, telling them whatever popped into my head, watching individual reactions, pretending I was talking to each person in turn, the rest of the audience vanished. After a while, my voice and breathing steadied.

Hello there, friends. Here I am, this rich man from faraway Earth, remote world of your ancestors, come here to the fairest planet in all the firmament. See them beaming with pride? As though *they* made the planet, with their own hands. Fine. Tell them a little bit of your life, tell them you're a workingman after all, just like them . . .

Just like *us*, Hans?

Well, no, Gerrit. *Our* work is the management of our proud estates, the stewardship of the wilderness veldt, you see. He seems to be talking about a *job*, like some kind of *omganger* drudge . . .

Talked about my visit to the Blondinkruis boerderij, of how much I'd liked *Vrouw* Gretel, my hostess . . . not many hostile looks. Every man likes a pretty girl, and most pretty girls understand the value of male admiration, you see. Told them about the womfrog hunt, here on the Koperveldt. Saw them nod and smile at that, yessirree, good for the tourist trade, you see, and . . .

I told them about that other hunt I'd seen, away on the Opveldt. Watched them frown. Then I told them about life in the big city. Wolfen in the killpits, relating to wolfen out on the great plains. Started to tell them about the dollhouses of Orikhalkos . . .

Someone from the audience, a gruff-voiced man, shouted, "What the hell are you getting at, foreigner?" Angry, angry voice.

Translator AI saying, This is no good, Gaetan. Worse than the speech you originally planned. They think you tricked them.

Tricked? I shrugged, and started telling them about the wolfen and dollies, about what I'd seen, about what I thought it all meant.

A different man shouted, "Shut the fuck up, asshole! We don't need God-damned outsiders telling us how to run our world!"

I tried to keep on talking, telling them what they needed to hear, but a woman in the front row of tables threw food on me, some kind of savory pudding splattering on the front of my shirt, leaving a dark, greasy stain behind as it fell away, and she called out, "Get off the fucking stage! Go on back where you came from if you don't like it here!"

I stood still for a bit, less than a minute really, staring at them all, a roomful of dark, hostile eyes now, then I shrugged and walked away, going out the door and back to the camper. By the time I got the engine started, the door had opened behind me, a handful of men coming out into the night, walking across the parking lot in my direction. I gunned the motor, lifting off and leaving them behind.

I drove southward then, giving up the path by the river, pulling up into the star-freckled sky, speeding in the direction of the low, dark hills of the Koudloft, where I knew the Kapellmeister and his Arousians would be waiting. Kapellmeister, Arousians, wolfen and dollies . . .

The thought raised a crawling sensation between my legs. You'd like to be a nice, fat Groenteboer, living in a nice, fat boerderij estate, all rustic logs and simple pleasures, wouldn't you, Gaetan? Imagining a wife? No. Imagining myself with a dollie servant, who'd do whatever I wanted, whenever I wanted, and never complain, never ask for anything in return.

Wish I'd taken time for a whore in Orikhalkos.

What a waste.

Well. I've done my bit, I guess. Nobody can say I didn't try. That's it. Nobody can say I didn't try.

Te absolvo, Gaetan du Cheyne.

15

Just at sunrise, eyes vaguely grainy from a night without sleep, I pulled over a familiar rim of metallic green forest and slid down into an irregular bowl of valley, my appointed rendezvous at the edge of the Koudloft, whose white hills rolled to the horizon beyond. I dropped the camper in a swirl of loose debris, not far from the Arousians' cluster of tents, killed the drive, punched the pop-up awake, and sat back, watching Tau Ceti pull free of the forest.

I really ought to go in back and get some sleep. Really. Blood symbiotes can compensate for as long as it takes, but sleep is a cultural and physical . . . shit.

I got out of the cab and stood beside the camper, stretching, feeling an odd, pleasant lassitude in my back, watching the Arousians come out of their tents, one by one, greet each other with a distant creaking of rusty hinges, touching each other, at limbs and faces, then going about the business of getting ready for the day.

Just now, I wish I were one of them. There. Red wolfen peering at me from the nearby vegetation, bronze-colored stuff like tall, thick-bladed grass. There'll be dollies somewhere close.

Kapellmeister's voice at my side: "Welcome back."

I looked down at it, reading welcome in drifting Ping-Pong-ball eyes. Felt a quick surge of pleasure. Felt myself smile, knowing the Kapellmeister would understand. "I might just as well not have gone."

"Mr. Patrocles posted the minutes of your interview in the city archives."

I nodded. Turned back to the tent village. Fires burning now, splendidly primitive, red wolfen gathering round, as though enthralled. No dollies yet. I said, "I guess I'd better do something about breakfast." One of the Kapellmeister's eyes, the lone aft one, most directly connected to the more primitive portions of its brain, dipped in subtle assent as it turned away, the other six, paired, focusing for the hunt.

I went inside and stood in front of the refrigerator for a while, contemplating the fresh junk food I'd bought in Orikhalkos. Finally realized I wasn't interested, threw myself down at the bed, awareness drifting back and forth between the square of blue-green sky framed by the window and shadows blending on the ceiling.

Always this formless longing, built up from physical reality, and culture made in reality's image. I wish that I too had some reason to . . . rise up and *do.* Something. Anything. Anything important. Compelling. That whole worthless business now spilling over into my desire for . . . what? Is it a lover I want, someone who at least pretends . . . or just an inert female body in which to . . .

I suddenly fell asleep.

Awoke into sunset.

Lay clasped in the reverberations of a dying dream.

Hot, tacky sweat on my face, inside my clothes. An uncomfortable sense of entrapment in my pants, tightness, gluey itch making me realize the dream had called forth an erection, which had gone about its business of spewing.

I grabbed at the dream then, looking for the afterecho, trying to recapture its substance. A woman. Young. Slim. Not quite faceless. Dark hair on her head rather more nebulous than the woolly black hair on her crotch. Pale eyes, maybe blue. Maybe some other color.

In the dream, I loved her, heart and soul, no name, no body other than those disconnected parts. No voice. Nothing but an essence that left its residue in my underwear. I sighed and let go. Just a dream.

The spacesuit whispered, It's a dream you dream often, Gaetan.

Funny. I never looked at it that way before. They listen to my dreams. Somewhere in a memory matrix on *Random Walk* . . . I wonder if they could . . .

The library whispered, Yes.

I tried to imagine watching my dreams, exactly as I'd dreamed them, rather than softened by the quick veil of forgetfulness, and felt a horrid chill steal down my spine.

The library whispered, Dream recall was once considered a primary form of noninterventionist therapy. Modern psychiatric engineers, however, prefer normative modal streaming technology.

The quick fix, as they say. Quick memory of my father arguing for just that fix. Equally quick memory of my mother, furious with him, flatly stating that I would be "remedied" by the Grace of Kali Meitner, or by nothing at all.

My God, how I hated Remedial Grace!

To my father's credit, when he found out about the whippings, he put an end to it, effectively ending his marriage, but I hated him anyway.

I got up then, feeling ravenous, got a bottle of orange juice out of the refrigerator, some kind of chewy pastry covered with tart black jelly. Outside, in the growing darkness, the Arousians had their cooking fires going again. The wolfen were shadows nearby and . . . there. The dollies stood together near the tall grass, a pale, compact, orderly mass.

Maybe if I had a dollie in here, I wouldn't have those dreams.

Silly ass.

I got out of my fetid clothing and got into the shower.

I went outside, only to find the stars had filled the sky once again. There are moments, nighttime moments, when I wish I could look up and see something different, something other than Orion and the Pleiades, something other than the golden stream of the Milky Way and Magellan's pale ghost clouds.

Maybe if I got on board *Random Walk* and went far enough . . .

The library whispered, You'd have to get in toward the core, or go outside the galaxy entirely for the sky's aspect, as seen from the surface of a truly terrestrial world, to change.

Oh, sure, I could get away from these *particular* constellations, but it'd still be a skyful of stars, strewn in meaningless patterns my brain's edge-recognition driver would transform to familiar shapes.

Look around. That tree over there, branches and leaves forming suggestive shadows against the sky. That's a wizard, isn't it? Gandalf the Gray come to save you? Or shall we run screaming from some creature of Cthulhu?

I found a rock to sit on, just where the fires' crawling light seemed to end. Maybe no one will be aware of me here. The Arousians will go about their zoological business. The wolfen will do whatever it is . . . I felt my attention focusing on the dollies, standing together, turned just so, as if . . . watching me.

Pheromones on the wind?

Or does that stirring within come from me alone?

There was a rustling in the darkness and the Kapellmeister was at my side. Long silence, then it said, "How are you doing, Gaetan?"

I felt a sudden warmth, sitting out under the familiar stars, sitting with my friend, being asked . . . I said, "Well—" Realized abruptly that I had no idea how I was doing, could only look down helplessly at the Kapellmeister.

It said, "Everyone who, for whatever reason, wishes to . . . change things, must try the simplest path first."

Is that what I was up to, talking to a rooted bureaucrat,

being laughed off the stage by a bunch of grange hall ranchers? And what did I want to change? The lot of the wolfen and dollies? It's far too late to save the wolfen, who'll march down the quick path to extinction now whether the City folk use them as entertainment or not. And the dollies? What difference does it make whether they're fucked for sport by sick human males or merely fucked, killed and eaten by the wolfen?

I said, "I always walk away in the end."

The Kapellmeister said, "Not always, Gaetan du Cheyne."

No. Not always. "If those men hadn't threatened me, I might not have saved your life, back in Orikhalkos."

"But you did save me."

So? Did I incur some obligation thereby? Did you?

The Kapellmeister said, "Ultimately, the change must come from within."

Heady bullshit, when you're sitting, depressed, under too-familiar stars. I said, "That's what they say. But one person never matters, even if that person turns out to be Jesus, or Kali Meitner, or something."

"You have a sense of history in your head, Gaetan du Cheyne. A fascinating human history of isolates interacting."

I almost didn't hear its words, muttering, "Not to mention Hitler and Napoleon, Temujin and Attila, Wang Mang, Sargon the so-called Great . . ."

Across the way, the wolfen were whispering and grinning together, facing the dollies, dollies on their knees, whispering prayers like some flock of ancient Christians facing . . . By God, Brother Flavius. I think that beast has *my* name on it!

The Kapellmeister said, "Members of a eusocial species are never alone."

One of the dollies got up, walked slowly, reluctantly, over to the wolfen. Stood before them, silent for a moment, then kneeled. A male, no doubt. Males, almost by definition, are the ones who die for the good of the group.

I said, "That dollie's mighty alone, just now."

"As you are alone. And I."

The foremost wolfen made a little guttural cough, leaned forward and neatly nipped off the dollie's right arm. It made a high, frightened scream and fell bleeding in the dust, drowning out the other dollies' whispered prayers.

Sudden memory of images from Salieri, of what a Kapellmeister's life was like, life in a world of listening, talking hands. I said, "Why are you alone?"

Another wolfen stepped forward and took off the dollie's left leg, chewing slowly as the image of a little cowgirl howled and struggled on the ground. What do the dollies say in their prayers?

The Kapellmeister said, "Because I . . . chose a solitary path."

A third wolfen came forward and took the left arm, leaving the dollie to circle crabwise on the ground, pushing with its remaining leg, gasping, sobbing, no longer able to scream.

"Why? Why are you here?"

A fourth wolfen came and took the leg, drawing one last shriek from the dollie as its teeth sheared through the structure of its hip. The bite was a little high, carrying away part of the pelvic girdle, and the dollie's colon, if that's what they have, bulged out through the hole, dragging in the dirt.

The Kapellmeister said, "Though it should not have, the arrival of human beings in the Salieran system came as a bit of a shock. After four hundred million years, we thought perhaps no starfaring civilization *would* ever arise again in this galaxy."

A fifth wolfen took its share now, biting off the rest of the pelvis, internal organs streaming out, quickly licked up, while the dying dollie made its last horrible little mewling noises, over which we could hear the soft whisper of the other dollies, chanting in unison.

The Kapellmeister said, "Some greeted the appearance of you humans with pleasure, for we long missed the heady days of old. Others were afraid, imagining that what had happened before not only could, but would happen again. It caused the first . . . uproar we'd had, amongst ourselves, since the time of deep memory."

A sixth wolfen came and ate the dollie's chest, leaving only the head behind, a silent round thing, covered in shadows, resting in a small pool of black blood.

I said, "What does all this have to do with your being . . . alone?"

A seventh wolfen snapped up the head, *crunch.* The instant it vanished the dollies' prayers ceased. In the silence that followed, the crackling of the Arousians' cooking fires seemed awfully loud.

The Kapellmeister said, "As you know, by the time the first human explorers decelerated into our star system, we'd had time to find our old fleet of warships, dust them off, and send a few out to greet you."

"The ships were four hundred million years old? And still in working order?"

"More or less."

"Why warships?"

"With your coming, two . . . call them political parties, formed. The larger of the two factions, currently in the ascendant, wishes to let things go for now, watch and listen, intervene where possible, behind the scenes, risking nothing. Their ascendancy is jeopardized because all attempts to prevent humanity from acquiring faster-than-light travel have failed. Bribing of researchers and corporate officials. The introduction of incorrect scientific data. All useless. Berens and Vataro escaped our notice and now you have it."

"Why would you want to keep us from FTL travel?"

"Without it, you can only go so far. Without it, in time your civilization would have turned on itself and, most likely, been destroyed, eventually reviving the *status quo ante.*"

"Jesus."

The Kapellmeister said, "The smaller faction, now rapidly gaining adherents, believes the danger to be acute. It wishes to launch a quick strike against your worlds, using the safest of the old weapons. We estimate a fleet of no more than two dozen scoutcraft could sterilize the Earth and all its colonies."

Holy shit. "We do have weapons of our own."

The Kapellmeister said, "Gaetan du Cheyne, you have no idea what energies were deployed during the Shock War. If the fleet were launched tonight, by sunrise tomorrow you would be the only terrestrial organism to survive. You and your commensal bacteria."

"Me?"

"You are the only human being who has one of us for a friend."

I was standing by the tall grass, not far from the dollies' baarbij bush, pissing when they came. Holding my dick and feeling the faint vibration of the urine's passage transmitted through a spongy wall of tissue, incredibly, thinking not about what the Kapellmeister had just said, but about the dollies nearby, dollies huddled for the night.

You want them now, don't you, Gaetan? You'd like to grab a dollie or two, hustle them away into the darkness, lay them out on the warm, soft grass and fuck the living shit out of them, wouldn't you, Gaetan? No idea why I'd want to hustle them away from the light. Nobody here who could really judge me. Kapellmeister? Wolfen? Arousians? Not a one of them even remotely human. If I don't care how the dollies feel about being raped by an alien monster, why should I care about how some other alien monsters feel about it?

No one cares how whores feel about being fucked for money, do they? Why should they? Whores are being paid, just like anyone who does a job.

Vast shadow reaching toward me from the fire. A stirring from the camp. Dollies not so far from me, reeking of wonderful, odorless pheromones, rising up, eyes aglitter in the firelight, turned toward the shadow.

Dollies drawing closer to each other, as though afraid.

One of the dollies abruptly turned, plucked a dark leaf from the baarbij bush, held it to its breast, murmuring softly. Another one did likewise, then another and another.

I put my dick away and started walking back toward the fire, peering at the shapes that made the shadows. Wolfen? Black shapes in silhouette very much like wolfen, but . . .

The Kapellmeister's ersatz voice, strangely hushed, as though trying to whisper, "Gaetan. Please be still." The Kapellmeister, I saw, was crouching beside my warm rock, flattened out to the ground, legs folded away, arms retracted, wandering eyes settled down onto its back.

I stood still, not knowing what to do. Back by the fire, the Arousians were standing still as well, but they'd had their cameras set up, ready and waiting apparently. As I watched, one of them slowly reached out and touched a control, data feed, presumably, beginning to roll.

What the hell *is* going on?

The library said, The Orikhalkan data net contains precious little about wolfen husbandry, but there is some material. These wolfen, as you see, are larger than the others. One of them much larger.

That much was obvious. One very big white wolfen, twice the size of the ones I'd gotten used to, a maned, toad-like carnivore the size of a small elephant, casting the giant shadow that'd first caught my attention, lurking in the background, completely motionless.

How the hell had that thing crept up on us without making any noise?

The library whispered, The largest one will be the male. The medium-sized wolfen will be the fertile females. The smallest sort are, of course, the neuter females who make up the bulk of wolfen society.

Like so many God-damned bees?

Library: Not quite. Apparently, the wolfen, like terragenic mammals, have breeding limitations, especially since the fertile females are required to retain lifelong mobility. Thus, the standard "family" setup appears to be one male, who services the fructival needs of several females. Each fertile female lays a clutch of eggs every seven years. Each clutch gives rise to a "pride" of neuter female "sisters," who live together for the rest of their lives.

Now, the neuter wolfen were creeping forward, bellies close to the ground, making some sort of tiny *glink*-like barks, almost whimpers. They seemed to focus on only one female, sliding under her muzzle, sort of licking upward like so many self-effacing dogs.

Library: Their mother, perhaps. Kalyx' biologists theorized that, when a fertile female dollie reaches a certain advanced age, she begins laying eggs, which can develop into a new generation of . . . mothers and fathers.

Something being communicated. As I watched, the female wolfen turned to look at the Arousians, who stood still, as though turned into the plants they vaguely resembled, wolfen looking at one, then another.

Glink, glink, glink.

Wolfen turning to peer at the spot where the Kapellmeister huddled.

Glink, glink.

Giant wolfen turning to look at me, as my bowels turned to water.

In the background, unnoticed, apparently, by anyone but me, the dollies knelt and chanted in whispers, just like the other times I'd . . . well, no. Something different now. Unison broken by dollies who faltered. And those two over there, seeming to hold hands. To one side of the pack, a dollie had fallen prone, seeming to cry, a succession of soft, high chirps, unable to say its prayers . . .

The Kapellmeister said, "I think it's safe for us to come forward now, Gaetan."

Safe? What the hell danger were we in? I looked at the big male, big enough to take me down in two quick bites, but it was still motionless, staring at the Arousians' fire, as though uninterested in the goings-on.

When the Kapellmeister trotted forward into the firelight, I followed it reluctantly, feeling the wolfen's mottled eyes on me, conscious of the Arousians, still motionless in the background, quietly making their filmed record, conscious of the dollies' choked whispering, mingled with the sound of little girls' tears.

Stood by the campfire, before the foremost female wolfen, the *mother*, who stood looming over me, looking down, inspecting me, breathing on me, breath with a stink like burnt-up candy.

Quite likely, whispered the library AI, a gravid, fertile female will have a substantially different biochemistry than one of the more normal neuter females, as a child's prepubescent body odor is so different from an adult's.

Right. In any case . . . I imagined myself a dollie, imagined that great head leaning down, mouth open in a horrid grin, breath like a jet of steam in my face, *Our Father, who art in . . .*

The Kapellmeister said, "She is called Belovèd Light of Her Daughters, Walking in Dry Sand."

Inanely, I stammered, "How do you do, uh . . ."

The Kapellmeister's box made a series of clipped, metallic barks, nothing at all like words. Belovèd Light jerked, seemed to peer at the box on the Kapellmeister's back, made a little sidewise *yip* out of the corner of her mouth. Sat tall on her haunches then, eyes boring down at me. Barked once, twice, thrice, so loud it hurt my ears, faint echo coming back out of the wilderness.

The Kapellmeister said, "She is happy to see you, Gaetan du Cheyne."

Happy to see me? "Um. Why?"

The Kapellmeister said, "Though early researchers, in the days of Kalyx, investigated the intelligence and life-cycle of the wolfen, no human has ever . . . spoken to them."

"Oh."

The Kapellmeister said, "Word of your presence here has spread quickly, Gaetan."

"Why should they care? They've had . . . endless contact with humans."

"No one talks to the wolfen in the killpits."

"Are they interested in the Arousians too?"

"Of course."

"What do they want?"

The Kapellmeister said, "I think I know, I think you do too. Shall we find out?"

Do I know? What would *I* want, walking in the wolfen's . . . paws? I looked down at the Kapellmeister, saw that its talking/listening hand was extended, tentacles spread, extended toward me. Christ, I . . . "Aren't you going to use it on . . . them?" A quick nod toward the big female wolfen looming over us, eyes bright with . . . whatever brightens the eyes of a monstrous alien carnivore.

The Kapellmeister said, "Perhaps you misunderstand what's going on here, Gaetan."

Do I? I glanced over at the Arousians. Still motionless, huddled around their instruments, but with an . . . air of expectant waiting? How the hell would I know a thing like that?

The translator AI whispered, The Kapellmeister has made rapport with you. Just so, it has made rapport with the Arousians. And the wolfen.

I looked back at the wolfen, then down at the Kapellmeister, saw it read my face, saw happiness bloom in the float of its eyes. I sighed, slowly sank into tailor's seat on the grass by its side. Said, "All right, Miss Belovèd Light. Let's talk."

The Kapellmeister said, "Mrs. Light, please." Just a trace of mirth in its generated voice.

Then the black hand engulfed the back of my head.

Click.

Soft voices, the sweet voices of girl children, chanting in unison, praying together: "Holy Mother, Belovèd Light, She Who Walks in Majesty Before Us All, You Who Have Chosen to Take Us unto Your Bosom: Grant us the wisdom to accept Your Grace, grant us the courage to face Passage through the Jaws, grant us . . ."

Sudden, stark memory of myself, stripped naked, tied to the Wheel of Men's Repentance, in the dim shadows of the Hall of Kali Meitner's Grace, whispering the prayer they'd taught me, Kali Meitner, belovèd of God, who suffered for our sins, lend me the grace to suffer as you suffered at the dirty hands of . . .

I remember the priestess slapping me across the face, fingernails raking my skin, making me bleed, shocking me back to there and then: "We'll have none of *that*, filthy, polluting boy!"

Even though I knew, I don't think I expected the whip.

Certainly hadn't anticipated the reality of its pain.

Over the chanted dollie prayers, I heard a girl's voice sob, "Oh, Goddess, why? Now I'll never see the egg . . ."

Another: "Shhh. Courage. Your egg will be hatched in a better place."

I felt anger sizzle.

The translator AI whispered, There is no way of knowing, Gaetan, how much of this is being supplied by the Salieran pod software. How likely is it the dollie's cultural symbolism would so closely match your own?

Um. Not very. The little girls' tears . . .

The wolfen loomed over me, mottled eyes rolling slowly in their sockets, still unreadable but no longer so . . . empty. Looking at me. Seeing . . . no way to know what. The great jaws moved, articulations flexing, a quick sequence of metallic barks. Understood: "I cannot bid you welcome, human being."

So. I struggled to speak, but my larynx seemed paralyzed, muscular tissues bunching and twisting, but . . . the box on the Kapellmeister's back began to bark, and I understood that I'd said, "Oh? Why not?" Great. Trust the likes of me to come out with some stupid . . .

The wolfen's head rolled to one side with what appeared to be mirth. Then she said, "Well. I think even you must understand that we don't like what's happening to us, to our world."

I tried to think of something to say. Nothing, really. What do they expect? No way for me to . . . I felt myself try to nod, listening as the pod made a short *yap* I understood to be the verbal equivalent of a nod. So. Trust the software?

The wolfen said, "We know perfectly well, have known for a long time, that as the human presence grows, our own must diminish. We understand that, one day, fairly soon as these things go, there will be no more wolfen."

Is that a hard thing for a being to know? I said, "Extinction is . . . difficult to face."

That amused roll again. She said, "My daughters tell me that among your kind, even personal extinction is feared. It surprises us you'd so casually let another species slip away."

Much less send it packing, hmh? All I could do was feed a shrug into the Kapellmeister's pod.

She said, "My daughters tell me that not all humans are like the ones who rule here on what you choose to call Green Heaven." It seemed to glance at the Arousians, still frozen behind their camera tripods. "My daughters tell me these stick-bug things are . . . protected somehow. Perhaps even nurtured."

I thought about what Mace Electrodynamics was doing in the Sigma Draconis system. Nurturing? Maybe you can call it that, keeping other humans away, helping the little stick-bugs out just a bit. While pillaging their star system of all its wealth. I said, "Is that what you want? To be . . . nurtured?"

"We'd like you to leave, of course. This is *our* world."

I nodded again, listening to the dollies pray. What do they think is going to happen to them next? What do they *know*? I said, "Fat chance."

The wolfen's head rolled slowly, side to side. "We understand. Perhaps this . . . nurturing?"

Another wolfen leaned slowly forward, stretching out its neck, seeming to sniff me the way a dog sniffs an uncertain dinner. Then she said, "We understand the stick-bug people are trying to escape from human nurturance."

I started to shrug, felt something interrupt, then the

Kapellmeister's generated voice said, "In their travels, Arousian students have learned much about human legal systems, Gaetan. They contemplate moving against MEI through the courts."

"What the hell good would that do them?"

The Kapellmeister said, "Are they better off as they are?"

How the hell should *I* know?

The first wolfen said, "At first, we wondered if the stick-bugs were to humans as dollies are to us, but it is manifestly not so. We know so very little about your worlds beyond the stars. In our ignorance, we merely thought you'd come from . . . somewhere beyond the sea. Some unknown land."

I sighed, but the translator pod was silent. Finally, I said, "You know we won't leave. You know the humans who live here won't lift a finger to save you. Maybe you'll breed in the zoos and survive that way . . ." There are dolphins in the oceans of Kent, round Alpha Centauri, even now, though they're long gone from Earth.

The wolfen said, "That is not survival. Best then for us to die."

I felt the anger sizzle again. "How noble." I turned and looked at the dollies. "What about them?"

"They have no way to survive on their own. When we go, they go."

"Maybe not."

The wolfen seemed to peer into my eyes. "We've seen what you do to the ones you capture. It's not something we've been able to understand." She sat back on her haunches, tilted her head back and seemed to look up at the stars. Finally: "When we heard about the coming of the stick-bug people, when we heard about a human wandering the veldt, in the company of a peculiar beast that could talk through a box and weave magic with its paw . . ."

I tried to image what they must have thought. Failing, I said, "If there was a realistic way you could be saved . . ." No more than a useless expression of sympathy. Done my best already, you see.

She looked back at me. "Tell me true, human being: How many worlds are there, in the land beyond the sky?"

I thought, A hundred billion stars in each of a hundred billion galaxies . . .

The Kapellmeister's voice said, "They have no concept of those sorts of numbers, Gaetan. In any case, human scientific knowledge about the scale of the universe is incorrect."

Interesting. "By how much have we undercounted?"

"Your culture hasn't defined such numerical concepts yet."

The box made a quick series of yips, and then the wolfen said, "That many?" Looking over its shoulder at the others then. Even the motionless, separate male seemed . . . I don't know. Taken aback? She turned to me again, and said, "And on every one of those worlds are there . . . beings who speak and think?"

"No."

"Have you humans settled all these stars?"

Twelve colonies, a few hundred systems visited, explored . . . I said, "Not even all the stars you see tonight."

The wolfen said, "Is there a world somewhere so poor, so worthless, that no human will want it?"

My God.

The wolfen said, "On all the plains of Green Heaven there are no more than thirty thousand wolfen left alive. You could hide us *all* in a tiny corner of some great human hive."

I said, "You don't really know what you're saying."

The wolfen female stared at me for a long time. Then it said, "No, human being, we do not."

Darkness. Fires burned down. Arousians gone into their tents, gone to whatever unknown thing they call a bed. Maybe nothing. Thinking about the way they were put together, I can imagine they sleep standing up, like horses. I took a long pull from the flat-tasting beer I'd gotten from the camper's refrigerator, and said, "Do all conscious beings sleep?"

The Kapellmeister said, "No. Most evolutionary schemes are

more differentiated from terrestrial norms than what you find here on Green Heaven."

"You know a lot about the universe. A lot you haven't said."

"We've known each other for such a short time. Eventually . . ."

"How much time do we have?"

Long silence. Then it said, "Not long, perhaps."

Perhaps. I tried to visualize those . . . unknown energies, unleashed on human worlds. Fire from the sky? Or something quicker than that, something entirely more devastating? I said, "If humanity is destroyed, will the wolfen survive?"

"Unfortunately, no."

Christ. "If your people decide to . . . do away with us, how will it be done?"

"There is a simple machine called an electromagnetic pulse phaser which can be used to explode the cores of main-sequence stars."

Jesus. "What about people in protected habitats? In the outer solar system, there are hundreds of millions of . . ."

"These explosions will be far more devastating than you imagine. For a few days, this spiral arm will shine with the light of a trillion suns."

I tried to picture that. "Won't that . . . sterilize all the worlds in this neighborhood? Including yours?"

"We know how to protect ourselves. We survived the Shock War, after all."

Ah, yes. That. I said, "How bad will it be?"

"I estimate any life forms within thirty parsecs of such an explosion will be destroyed."

Thirty parsecs. "Hardly anything at all, in the scheme of things."

"Four hundred million years ago, what you call the Local Group of galaxies was more or less cleared of intelligent life. Eighteen million species. Give or take a few hundred thousand."

Give or take. "And you think by wiping out humanity, this can somehow be prevented from happening again?"

Long silence. Then it said, "That is the theory."

"You don't sound convinced."

More silence, then, "Were I convinced, I would not be here, Gaetan du Cheyne."

Across the way, hulking shadows in the darkness. The wolfen were gathered, making a great, open circle around the kneeling, praying dollies. Praying for what? Deliverance? What if I rise up now, grab my guns, and drive the wolfen away? Will the dollies be grateful?

One of the wolfen got to its feet, lurched forward into the circle. One of the dollies screamed. Screamed and turned, began to run away. A single bound, a crunch of jaws. The dollie was silent, chewed, swallowed.

From the mass of remaining dollies, a soft moan, prayers disrupted.

The Kapellmeister said, "It screamed for salvation, Gaetan du Cheyne."

Salvation. I said, "Do the wolfen known how the dollies feel about their lot in life?"

Silence, then, "I believe they do."

I said, "I imagine most humans never think about their food animals. I know I never did." Never? Did I think steaks came from a synthetics vat or something? Maybe so.

The Kapellmeister said, "Perhaps that is evidence of the wolfen's moral superiority. Perhaps not."

Another wolfen stood and stepped forward. This time a dollie stood from the kneeling crowd and walked forward, head held high, until it was within reach of snapping jaws. The crunch seemed . . . unpleasant. I said, "Have you entered rapport with dollies?"

The Kapellmeister said, "The wolfen prefer that I do not."

Another wolfen, walking over to the kneeling group, this time singling out a dollie who cowered and cried out as the jaws descended. I said, "Will they eat them all? Even the gravid females?"

"Yes. This is a breeding group, the reason the dollies are raised."

Christ. "I wonder how the dollies came to . . . serve the wolfen."

"Think about it, Gaetan. In all likelihood, the wolfen's breeding schemes are what gave the dollies intelligence. They are as much a creation as your own cats and dogs."

Among other things, whispered the library AI.

"Why would they create sentient food animals?"

"Such animals would need less looking after."

No one has ever asked why humanity would go to the trouble of creating sentient tools. "If the wolfen die and humans live, will the dollies be saved?"

"Probably not."

As I sat watching, three more dollies were eaten, one by one, the first two taking it well, standing tall and brave, this one silent, that one gabbling its desperate prayers, the third one crawling on its belly shrieking apparent horror as the jaws came down and closed upon it. The remaining dollies, watching their numbers whittled away, seemed increasingly shaken, more and more falling silent, lying huddled, shivering, prayers forgotten as the end approached.

Probably not, rather than certainly not. How would these dollies, here and now, feel, if they knew there was even a *chance* they could escape this life, live on, relatively secure, relatively happy, their lot in life no more horrible than dancing for drunken men who would sometimes fuck them?

I thought about the dollhouse dollies, dancing their little cowgirl dances, straddling men's laps and . . . Hell. Maybe, every night, they kneel by their little beds and thank some unknown goddess that they'll never wake up as wolfen shit, fertilizing a baarbij bush.

I said, "You have to wonder what's the right thing to do. Other than nothing, of course."

Silence, punctuated by dollie screams, the sound of wolfen eating. Then the Kapellmeister said, "One is indeed required to wonder."

Well. That other thing. "Do you know about the . . .

unknown spacecraft encountered by one of our exploratory missions?"

"The military encounter at Regulus? Yes."

"How?"

"We have something like faster-than-light radio, Gaetan. Your scientists will discover it soon enough. If there's . . . time."

"Don't they represent the same sort of danger as humanity?"

"The argument has been made. Since the coming of humans, we've done a little looking around, an inspection of the . . . neighborhood, if you will. They're called the Tertris. They've been starfaring for a few thousand years. They're quite warlike."

"Seems like an odd coincidence that they've turned up, here and now, doesn't it?"

Silence. Then the Kapellmeister said, "No. One of the few things that has stayed the hand of the party wishing to terminate human civilization is the possibility that the . . . evolutionary clock of the Local Group of galaxies was synchronized by the event of the Shock War."

"Synchronized?"

It said, "The Old Galactic Civilization, of which we were a part, grew up gradually, since the infancy of the universe. First one intelligent species, then two, then a few, then several, over a period measured in billions of years. Eventually, we reached a metastable state in which all the sentient species of the Local Group were merged, welded into a single great culture, uniform throughout the region.

"We were . . . at the beginning of a new age, our ships just beginning to quest outward, probably the galaxies of other clusters, looking for signs that ours was not the only civilization."

"Why didn't you just . . . listen?"

"Civilization propagates faster than its signals. The universe isn't old enough for that methodology to be practical."

"Even with this . . . FTL radio of yours?"

"The number of communication modalities is a transfinite number. No practical data processing system can monitor a suf-

ficiently large bandwidth to create a statistically significant likelihood of positive detection."

"So you went looking."

"For a little while. We found species isolates, of course, and
primitive local empires, all more or less by chance. Time passed
and our culture fragmented, despite everything. In the stagna-
tion of our . . . aloneness, we found meaningless philosophical
disunities to squabble over."

"Like what?"

"It doesn't matter, Gaetan. We found something to fight
about. And then we killed each other. Not quite down to the last
being."

"So there are other survivors like yourselves?"

"Perhaps."

"These . . . Tertris?" Not likely what they *called* themselves,
just some neologism the pod software had constructed for me
to hear.

"No. We've ascertained they evolved locally, over approximately the same time scale as humans, on a world near the
intersection of the Sagittarius Spiral Arm and its Aquila spur.
While we were looking, we also found some folk calling themselves the Khaara, distally up Orion Arm a few thousand parsecs, and, in the Perseus-B Spiral Arm, a large, militant
civilization of beings named øStênnh. You humans will like
them, when . . . if you meet them."

If. "All with faster-than-light spacecraft?"

"Yes."

"And all evolved in this galaxy at the same time?"

"An argument has been advanced that the Shock War leveled the evolutionary schemes of the seventeen galaxies known
to be involved. Such a theory cannot be proven, of course, but it
would imply that the Local Group is about to blossom forth
with advanced civilizations, all at once."

"That seems mighty unlikely. Wouldn't different species
evolve at different rates?"

"Not in the context of neutral molecular evolution."

"Cultures then? All the same?"

"No. But the theory says they will arrive more or less together, over a period of just a few million years."

"Do you believe that?"

"My belief is immaterial. The . . . interventionist party wishes no one to believe it, since that would render the actions they propose more . . . difficult."

"What if it's true? Will you go out and slaughter thousands of species, possibly millions?"

"That is what has been proposed."

"Isn't that *just* how you describe this Shock War? The obliteration of—"

"Frightened beings will make irrational decisions."

"So the *status quo ante* you seek is a Local Group emptied once more of life, in which the Kapellmeisters alone survive?"

"Correct."

I looked up then and realized that the last dollie had been consumed while I wasn't paying attention.

16

When I got up, midway through the next morning, Tau Ceti standing in the middle of the northern sky, the whole a burnished vault of green-tainted blue, all the wolfen were gone. No sign of the dollies, other than a patch of dried mud my eyes kept shying from; no sign of a baarbij bush ceremony or . . .

I stood outside, watching the Arousians pack up their camp, smelling the faint aftertang of their breakfast fire. "What will they do now?"

The Kapellmeister said, "There are other wolfen families they wish to investigate. I've arranged a rendezvous for them with a pack that hunts near the coast, a hybrid breed of white and yellow desert wolfen."

"Pale cream wolfen?"

The Kapellmeister's eyes floated in a way that I knew meant a shrug of insignificance. "They have no name for themselves, were never numerous enough for the Groenteboeren to name."

Right. "I suppose they'll be . . . needing you."

"No, Gaetan. Everything has been arranged in advance."

I felt a crawl of unease, a will to speak, suppressed by . . . nothing. Nothing at all. Christ, I feel like I'm asking some girl for a date . . . "It's time for me to pick up my cargo for 40 Eridani."

The Kapellmeister seemed to study my face for a long time. Then it said, "Would you mind if I came along?"

I felt a surge of relief, the same one you feel when the girl you've propositioned says yes and reaches for her belt buckle. "I'd like that."

The Kapellmeister said, "The rapidly evolving skin discoloration on your face is interesting."

"Great."

We stopped for a picnic lunch atop a low, grassy hill out in the middle of nowhere, out where the forests and hills of the antarctic give way to the brassy flatlands of the Koperveldt. I dropped the camper just below the crest of the hill, had gotten out and started setting up my chair and a little table where I could get the best view of an empty landscape, had started puttering about with the food while the Kapellmeister took off in search of its small game.

Not much to see out here. A few puffy white clouds under a now too-familiar blue-green sky. A plain of coppery grass. A sudden, startling realization that I was fairly sick of Green Heaven. That I'd be damned glad to be getting away, going to another world, seeing new things, new people, new beings, new places.

I never once, as a child, imagined myself visiting 40 Eridani A, of having adventures on little Epimetheus, on giant Prometheus. What the hell do I know? Rich landowners living in big estates on Epimetheus, lording it over an industrial serf society that's developed on Prometheus. Nothing worth dreaming about at all. It would have been like escaping from the horrors of school to the wonders of my father's job.

After a while the Kapellmeister came back with one more small, silent thing that died, paralyzed, so its neck could be sucked.

I munched an extra-rare roast beef sandwich, white bread stained pink here and there by the juice, sucked on yet another nameless, tasteless beer. "What provisions will you need for the trip? I mean . . ." I motioned at the thing it was draining now.

The Kapellmeister said, "We can get what I need at any big pet store in Orikhalkos."

Cold chill. "You aren't going to be eating cats and dogs in front of me, are you?"

Silence. Then it said, "No, I favor laboratory rats. I also like what you call stewing hares, available on Green Heaven from most culinary supply stores."

Something over there now, specks moving against distant reddish yellow grass. I put my sandwich down and got up, went over to the camper cab and rummaged out a pair of binoculars. "Hmh. Dollies."

"I see them, Gaetan."

Dollies, meaning somewhere nearby there'd be a troop of wolfen. There. A brief glimpse of a white wolfen peeking from cover. If it'd been a red, I'd never have seen it.

The library AI whispered, Apparently, there are no red wolfen left on the Koperveldt, human predation having finished them off over time. However, due to their presence on the Opveldt, red wolfen remain the dominant subspecies. Koperveldt remains home to isolated bands of brown, white and yellow wolfen.

I could see more wolfen now, slinking through the grass beside their neatly marching dollies like so many Indian scouts. I said, "Do you think the relationship between the wolfen and dollies could be induced to change?"

Silence, then the Kapellmeister said, "Perhaps. Who would have the right to induce such a change?"

"Do the dollies have rights?"

"Ask the wolfen."

Right. I said, "So long as the wolfen continue to . . . use the dollies, few humans will sympathize with their plight."

The Kapellmeister said, "Even among my own people, with a far broader perspective, that is a common perceptual problem. Not many of us sympathize with the plight of humanity either."

I took down the binoculars and looked at it. "Last night I found myself wondering what has gone on in the greater universe, in all the ages since the Shock War."

It said, "Some of us have been wondering that as well."

I said, "When the . . . Interventionists do what they intend to do, the . . . disturbance may attract attention. I keep imagining that some . . . instrumentality may come to investigate. That it may decide your folk represent some kind of . . . danger."

Its eyes shrugged, a pattern suggesting the universe was full of interesting possibilities. "The Passivist Party has raised just such an eventuality."

I heard a distant *pock*, echoing from the plains below. I put the binoculars to my eyes and looked again, knowing exactly what I'd see. Yes, there they were, a small party of human hunters rising from the long grass opposite the trail the dollies were forging, rifles leveled. Off to one side, I could see a wolfen, sprawled in the grass, torn open, already dead.

Zzzip. Pock. Zzzip. Pock.

Dollies starting to run in a compact mass through the grass, like so many soldiers, soldiers on parade, making double time. Beyond them, the white wolfen were breaking from cover, scattering, trying to run.

Saving themselves, the bastards, leaving their poor, helpless dollies for the humans to . . .

Zzzip. Pock.

I put the binoculars down and walked slowly back to the camper's cab. All sorts of gizmos in here. I could feel the pulse pounding in my temples as I took down the induction rifle and clipped the range finder to its stock, felt my heart start to hammer in my chest as I walked slowly back to the crest of the hill.

The Kapellmeister stood stock-still, eyes absolutely motionless above its back, looking, I knew, only at me.

When I looked through the range finder I could see them all, plain as day, dollies running together, even though if they scattered, some might escape. What the hell good will that do them? A lone dollie is just a prey animal. There. White wolfen scuttling through the grass in all directions, frantic, several of their number already down and dead. And over here, of course, my party of hunters. Somewhere nearby, I knew I'd find their truck, with its dollie cages and . . .

The spacesuit AI, frantic, whispered, Gaetan. *Gaetan!* This is a *bad* decision you're making! Gaetan, I *beg* you, don't . . .

Felt myself squeeze the trigger.

Zzzip.

The hunter in my range finder seemed to explode in a haze of blood, flying gobbets of fine red meat.

Gaetan! Please Gaetan . . .

I could hardly hear it through the singing in my ears.

Zzzip.

Another lovely explosion, down on the brassy plain.

I scanned for a third hunter. Nothing. Widened the range finder view. Nothing. No one. They've had sense to throw themselves down in the tall grass already.

What else? Dollies still running, running for all they're worth, getting away. And . . . there. There was a white wolfen, reared up in the grass, looking back toward where the hunters had been, then turning to look up at my hill, obviously seeing me and . . .

POCK!

Something exploded in the grass nearby, overturning my table, spilling what was left of my lunch, peppering me with bits of flying dirt.

The Kapellmeister said, "They are returning fire, Gaetan."

POCK!

Another near miss. I crouched down below the brow of the hill, and said, "I guess we'd better get out of here, hmh?"

Floating eyes regarded me for a moment. Then it said, "Yes. It's . . . time we were on our way."

When we flew away, a final shot rocked the camper, scarring the plastic canopy of the cockpit.

*   *   *

We flew on in silence, away from the battlefield, skimming low over the whipping copper plains, barely high enough to clear the occasional cluster of tall trees, the occasional low hill. Silence. In the cab, inside my head. Nothing to say, anyone? Certainly nothing for me to say, hands gripped tight on the control yoke, knuckles white, like bare bone.

Finally, the Kapellmeister said, "You'd better slow down, Gaetan. They'll be looking for someone flying a souped-up camper and . . ."

Voice tight: "Who? Who'll be looking?" No *authorities* out here on the veldt . . .

The library, imaginary voice somehow mournful, whispered, The party of hunters you assaulted has put in a call for help to the nearest grange, Gaetan. Ambulances have been dispatched. And a meeting has been called for the purpose of putting together a vigilante posse.

Posse? Like in some Wild West drama?

The library whispered, Correct. Though the Groenteboeren observe a strict code duello among themselves, crimes by *omgangers* are treated severely, since the Groenteboeren know they can count on no justice at all from the Cities of the Compact.

Oh.

I slowly throttled back, dropping the camper down until it was just barely skimming above the grass. Up ahead, I could see the silvery twist and sprawl of a big river, the Chan, I knew, flowing westward across the southern Koperveldt, right through the heart of Orikhalkos, all the way to the sea. There'll be a road there I can pick up, follow on into town.

The spacesuit whispered, Before you can turn in the camper, you'll have to reset the governor.

Right. Do that now? No, stupid. If there's a . . . *posse.* Jesus Christ, how can I take something like that seriously? Still, if I need to *run* . . . I thought, I'll do it back at the spaceport. Maybe we can do something about the canopy scar as well.

When we got to the dirt road, I throttled back, dropping down until the camper was floating sedately along like an unmodified vehicle. Attract less attention this way, I guess. Though it would now take the rest of the fucking day to get back to Orikhalkos. Should I just make a dash for it, get back in two hours or less? No way to know.

The Kapellmeister said, "Why did you do it, Gaetan?"

I turned and looked, trying to read the set of its eyes. Don't you know? Hell, maybe you do. Maybe you just want to hear me say it. I shrugged. Tried to formulate a reply. Finally, I said, "Just then, just for a moment, those bastards seemed less human to me than the dollies and wolfen."

Less . . . human. Christ.

The Kapellmeister said, "You know, medical science on Green Heaven is probably insufficiently advanced to repair those men you shot."

A remembered image of two men, blown to bits, watched through the panel of my range finder. Back on Earth, their heads, almost certainly still intact, would have been taken to a hospital, hooked up to life support, and in a few weeks they'd walk out in new bodies, hale and hearty and hell-bent on revenge.

I said, "I don't feel sorry."

Silence, as we drove along beside the river. The Kapellmeister said, "On Salieri, there are many who feel we must intervene with the development of other civilizations, in order to preserve our own. And there are just as many who feel we must not, that we must leave well enough alone. Only a few feel the compulsion to intervene for the sake of the other species themselves, to . . . help them along the road to salvation."

I looked over at it, and thought, Salvation? Like in so many damn-fool religions? "I just hope those wolfen and their dollies got away."

The library whispered, They did, Gaetan. Ambulances are on site now, tending to the injured.

Just injured?

No, Gaetan. One of the men you shot is now in a suspended animation box, with some chance of recovery. The other suffered irreversible cerebrospinal damage due to hydrodynamic shock, and has been declared dead. A third lost an eye when she was struck by a piece of flying bone.

Why do I feel satisfaction at all that?

I said, "Did you ever feel a compulsion to . . . do the right thing, even when you don't know what it is?"

The Kapellmeister said, "I am familiar with the feeling, Gaetan du Cheyne."

Nightfall. No sign of pursuit. No sign of anything on the net, my AIs reporting the survivors of the attack had been taken away to the hospital, and that was that. How would a disorganized group like the Groenteboeren's grange find me? No technical detective work for them. No . . .

I drove on, increasingly at my ease, while Tau Ceti slowly fell down the blue vault of afternoon and settled on the horizon, streaking the sky with crimson, patches of green here and there, backlighting the few low clouds.

By now, we were seeing more traffic, wheeled vehicles like the others I'd seen, mostly trucks with fat pillow tires, once even a big thing with wooden sides hauling what appeared to be a load of hay, library AI telling me the farms hereabouts were mainly devoted to raising terragenic livestock for the citizens of Orikhalkos.

Still, if I hadn't seen it, I would never have imagined any such thing survived, anywhere in human space. Imagine. A hay wagon.

Just after nightfall, I pulled into the parking lot of what appeared to be a restaurant, letting the camper settle in its cloud of dust, listening to the engine wind down while I heard out the AIs' roster of misgivings, reasons why I shouldn't be stopping on the road home.

There is nothing on the net. They've given up.

Someone appeared in the door of the building, a tall, pudgy

woman wearing a red and white checked apron. Stood looking out at me for a minute, wiping her hands in a fold of the apron, went on back inside. Finally, I said, "I'm just going to get a decent meal, before we head on in. I . . ." I looked helplessly at the Kapellmeister.

It said, "I'll wait here, Gaetan. Take all the time you need."

"Thanks." I knew you'd understand.

I got out of the camper, walked slowly across the gravel parking lot, listening to the gravel crunch under my boots, smelling the fresh night air. Went on in. Table for one? Thank you ma'am. Ordered a meal, ate it, thinking all the while.

Do you know what you *want* to do, Gaetan du Cheyne? Is there anything you *can* do? Is there anything *worth* doing? All your life, you've known, beyond a shadow of a doubt, that no one man can make any difference at all in this. You're born, grow up, do your job if you're lucky enough to have one. Fuck around a bit, watch the vidnet. Eventually you die.

I finished, got up, paid for the meal, went back outside, leaving through the rear door, so . . . Yes. I stood on the restaurant's back porch, looking out over the dark vistas of nighttime Koperveldt, black plains under a starry black sky.

This is the only thing that ever brought me any real pleasure, isn't it?

Think about what you're doing, Gaetan. You're going to drive back into town, power up your ship, pick up your cargo of God-damned dollies and take them away to slavery on another world.

You just killed a man whose only sin was procuring dollies for someone to take away, just like you.

But.

Yes, there it is. I need the fucking money.

That's why you worked like a slave. Not because you liked the fucking job. Not because you liked the company of your fellow slaves.

So what am I supposed to do then? Sell the ship and . . . what? Go back home and . . . sit?

I put my hands in my pockets and started walking, head down, along the rear wall of the restaurant, passing under what I was sure was an open kitchen window, warm light spilling out, along with the smell of grilling native meat, sweet as candy in the fire.

A woman's voice, "There he is."

A man, speaking Groentans, "Thank you, Miz Ruyker. We'll take it from here."

I turned and looked back toward the door. Four men walking toward me. Four big men, each carrying a big stick. No. Those are not sticks. Square of metal on the end of each stick. What would they want with axes? Men looking at me now, dark faces quite serious.

The man said, "You sure that's him, Wubbo?"

Another man, Wubbo apparently, said, "How the hell can I be sure? He was a long way off."

Third man: "You saw the camper out front, Lÿr. Who else would it be?"

I put my hand in my jacket pocket, feeling my heart start to pound, my fingers trembling, almost expecting to curl around the handle of my little dartgun. But you left that on the counter back in Tegenzinstad, didn't you, Gaetan du Cheyne?

I said, "Maybe you gentlemen are making a mistake."

Lÿr said, "Doesn't matter, really."

"What do you mean?" Starting to turn away. Maybe I can run . . .

Lÿr said, "Some *omganger's* done a killing. Now some *omganger's* going to die."

Wubbo said, "It all evens out in the end."

Beyond the restaurant building, I heard the camper's engine whine, high and soft against the night, as it started up.

Lÿr swung his axe, hard, unexpected, and I put my arm up to ward off the blow, feel my heart throb in my chest. The blade hit me in the elbow with a small, wet sound, and then my forearm was dangling at a weird angle, fingers gone impossibly numb.

Wubbo said, "Hope that hurts, *omganger*. Jena says her eye sure as hell hurts."

Another blow, this time in the neck, black blood spraying, getting all over the men's shirts.

Lÿr said, "God damn it, Marits, why can't you be more careful? My wife's going to kill me for this."

I staggered, turning away from them, tottering away, arm flapping at my side, warm blood flowing down my chest inside my shirt, somehow completely numb. The sky seemed awfully far away. As far away as the stars.

Wubbo said, "Hell, just hit him in the head and get it over with."

I went down on my knees, feet tangling together, unable to walk, and then I must have fainted, for I remember nothing more.

I awoke, not quite with a start, opening my eyes to find I was looking at a featureless white ceiling, ceiling lit by some cool, indirect light. Lying in a bed. Not kneeling in the darkness, numb, waiting for some bastard to split my head with an axe. I felt my heart starting to pound, the first real sign that I was actually . . . still alive.

Male voice, speaking English with some kind of thick accent, "Ah. I see you're awake, Mr. du Cheyne."

Why is it so quiet inside my head? Something . . . missing. Like a part of me's been . . . sliced away. I . . . *Just hit him in the head and get it over with.* Jesus Christ. I turned slowly, conscious of an incredible weakness in my neck, of rough cloth swaddling my throat. There. A man in dark clothing, man with dark hair and dark eyes, neat little moustache, sitting in a chair by my bed.

This is a hospital room, isn't it?

No answer.

The man said, "My name's Pietros. Detective-Sergeant Pietros, Orikhalkan Compact Police. How're you doing, Mr. du Cheyne?" He seemed to smile at me.

"Detective?" My voice, if it was mine, seemed all strange and rusty.

Pietros said, "You're a lucky man, Mr. du Cheyne. If your . . . friends hadn't gotten you to the hospital so quickly, I don't think the doctors here would've been able to reverse the neural damage. Head split open like that. Ninety percent of your blood gone . . ."

"Friends?"

He smiled again. "Two of your . . . assailants are in this hospital too. Your . . . autopilot ran them over with the camper, then landed the damned thing on top of them. They're lucky to be alive too. Pretty badly crushed, I understand."

I tried to reach up and feel my head, but my left arm was stiff, covered, apparently, with some stiff elastic bandaging. I put up my other hand, right arm looking just fine, and tried to feel the side of my head. More bandages. And quiet.

Pietros held up my barrette, curiously twisted-looking, and said, "Here's another reason you're alive, Mr. du Cheyne. Good old Lȳr hit this as well as your skull. Otherwise you'd probably be in therapy, trying to grow new brain tissue. An axe blow to the left temporal lobe is a serious thing."

So they say. "Ship."

He nodded, frowning. "The . . . uh, your library software has informed us you've got special medical facilities aboard that can heal you much faster than our . . . primitive medical methods. We'll be transporting you to the cosmodrome this afternoon."

"Thanks."

He frowned, turning the ruined barrette over in his hands. "Mr. du Cheyne, do I understand your . . . software has the power to override standard injunctions against taking human life?"

I think I managed a smile of my own. "That's just an old myth, Mr. Pietros."

Dark eyes on mine. "Mmm. I didn't know that." He tossed the thing onto the nightstand by the table. "Look, I don't know what the hell happened, out there on the veldt. I guess I don't really care. Those two fellows down in the broken-bone ward . . . well, one's in no shape to talk. Wubbo says you killed one of his friends, shot up a hunting party for some reason, that he and the others were just . . ." An expressive shrug, "Bringing you to justice."

I thought about denying it, but: "I guess so."

Anger briefly creased his brow. "You guess so. Fucking asshole." He seemed to stare for a minute, as though trying to read my thoughts, "Mr. du Cheyne, do you know we have the death penalty here in the Compact Cities? Even for *vreemdelings* like you?"

I shrugged.

"One little shot and you go to sleep and then we bury your ass."

"How nice."

More anger, a darkening of his already-swarthy complexion. "Your . . . friend, the Salieran . . . being, says you were trying to save the wolfen."

"Maybe so."

A sigh. "I guess I don't care why you did it, Mr. du Cheyne. You didn't do it *here*, so it's none of our damned business. We'll be taking you out to your ship, where you can spend as long recovering as you want. After that, we want you off Green Heaven."

"No planetary government here."

A look of solid contempt. "No, Mr. du Cheyne. There's nobody can force you to leave. But no Compact City will have you, Mr. Troublemaker, and the Groenteboeren . . ." He smiled again. "Maybe you can go visit Les Iles des Français, or even go hang around with the Hinterlings."

"Thanks."

He got up and walked out of the room, without looking back.

17

Late the next day, I sat alone on the bridge of *Random Walk*, looking out across the cosmodrome's landing field. Ships out there, of various types. That one a big cargo hauler, engines on the bottom, control cabin in the nose, the rest of it just empty hull with yawning doors, waiting to be filled. Off to one side, mounted on meilerwagens, standing in a neat row, I could see the external fuel tanks, cheap, disposable, fully biodegradable, waiting to be mounted.

As old a design as you'd want to see. Twenty-second-century vintage, tanks most likely filled with incandescent compressed air, air crushed until the molecules' electron clouds were at the edge of collapse. Not efficient. Not pretty. Just cheap.

I flexed my left harm, holding the elbow joint in my hand, marveling at how well I felt. Took care of a lot of minor maintenance problems while they were dealing with the big stuff. I remembered being brought out here in an ambulance, Pietros and his people helping me up the gangplank, watching as the hatch closed behind me.

I don't know how I managed the long hobble to medical bay, just remember collapsing into the diagnostic chair, remember feeling the cap slide down over my head, head filling with

335

alien thoughts . . . Gaetan! the suit's joyous whisper. Heard the medical software's pompous voice, Considerable peripheral damage from incompetent treatment modalities. He's lucky to have survived at all.

Felt the diagnostic probes slide in, like cold ice picks stabbing deep, here, there . . . felt my blood start to fizz, pain everywhere, all at once, as the symbiotes were reprogrammed for a major overhaul. I remember thinking, just before I blacked out, This feels like love.

Silly.

And yet . . .

I got up out of the engineer's seat, stood with my hands on the back of the pilot's seat, hands on the spacesuit's warm, living integument, looking out across the field to where a group of workers and machines were folding up a photosail, packing it away into its launcher pod.

I wonder what Leah Strachan is up to, right now. No sign of *Torus X-2* out on the landing field. Gone back home, most likely, taking her with it, perhaps. I imagined her, already home, wrapped in the circle of Gordon Lassiter's strong, uncomplicated arms. Uncomplicated? No, Gaetan, that's just the excuse you make, a way you can look down on him.

I unhooked the suit and started putting it on, first this piece, then that, integument swaddling me everywhere, rainbow shadows starting to sparkle upon the bulkheads and control panels as I pulled on the helmet, completing the circuit. When I put the circlet round my brows, I could feel the warm glow of the suit's happiness. Identical, in every respect, with every surge of happiness I myself have ever felt.

Is that all I ever was? A tool, happy to be employed?

Soft pocking of tiny footsteps behind me, like little horse's hooves on the hard plastic deck. I turned and beheld the Kapellmeister, standing still, seven eyes waving above its back, looking at me.

"Feeling well, I trust?"

I shrugged. "Ready to go?"

It came forward, crawling into the leg space under the control console, then hopped up in the flight engineer's chair, settling itself against the upholstery like some kind of impossible dog. "I've stowed my rats and rabbits in the stateroom you indicated."

Momentary image of a bunkroom full of loose rats, rabbits hopping around, suspecting their eventual fate, all of them looking for a way to escape.

The library AI whispered, In cages, Gaetan. The cages are well secured.

"Okay." I sat down in the pilot's seat, put my hands on the armrest controls, watched the ship come to life, everywhere, all at once, numbers and graphs cycling and spinning, telling me God was in His Heaven and all was right with the universe.

Little voices, all around me. The voices of my true friends. My only friends. One of them now asking the tower for clearance, vectoring me obliquely up out of the atmosphere, on a trajectory that would, very quickly, carry me out of the plane of the Cetian ecliptic, beyond the necessity of space traffic control.

Outside, an amber light began to flash, and I imagined antique klaxons hooting. Imagined workers across the field turning to watch me rise, workers filled with envy because they too have dreamed this dream. Felt my heart start to flutter with that old, familiar, well-loved excitement.

Green Heaven was an old dream, a childhood dream, a boy's dream.

Blue light played around the field, flickering on the other ships, lighting up the front of the terminal building, reflected in its glass, then the ground fell, taking my breath away. By God.

One long, hard moment of joy as I felt the ship respond to my will, soft chatter of cooperating AIs in the background, ship tipping, ground angling away beneath me as I passed over the heart of Orikhalkos. Right there. That's my hotel. There, by the waterfront, those drydocks. The killpit where . . . Over there, that's the dollhouse where Delakroë and van Rijn . . .

We left the ramshackle mess of little boxes that was the city behind, rising higher, then higher still, out over the Koperveldt plain. Down there, rivers and hills, tiny colored dots that I knew must be boerderij houses. Where are you now, Gretel Blondinkruis? I imagined her outside, standing tall and proud, shading her eyes as she watched my little ship transit her heaven. Do you wish you were going with me, Gretel Blondinkruis? Wish someone would come and take you away from your ordinary world?

Then, the foothills of the Thisbÿs were rising, plains of brass replaced by a rolling landscape of metallic green forest, then mountains covered with snow, slopes steepening, angling upward to the heights, where not even snow could fall . . . The ship slowed abruptly, so quickly the compensators miscalculated, allowing me to feel a slight tug through my inner ear, ship turning, careening past a vast gray cliff, coming to a dead stop in midair, hanging this way for just a moment, then falling straight down into a saddleback pass in the mountains.

Time for one quick look around, Opveldt and Koudloft over there. Yellow-white wasteland of the Adrianis Desert in the opposite direction. This is the Aardlands Bergpas, trekked by the embryonic Groeteboeren as they fled the abandonment of Kalyx Station, headed into the wilderness. Then we were down.

From the top of the gangplank, the view was disquieting, if for no other reason than that they were . . . all there. Somehow, I hadn't anticipated the . . . reality.

Beside me, the Kapellmeister said, "I count sixty-four dollies."

Shit. I clattered down the stairway, trying not to look at them, walked over to where Delakroë and van Rijn stood beside the tailgate of a large truck, one with a big wooden cage for a cargo bay.

The library whispered, This resembles the sort of truck used on Earth in late Medieval times for hauling swine to the slaughterhouse.

Van Rijn, smiling his gappy smile, rubbed his hands together, breath a frosty jet in the cold mountain air. "Good to see you again, Mr. du Cheyne."

I gestured at the dollies, huddled together in their chains. "This isn't exactly what we contracted for."

A sigh. "We'll pay you pro rata for the increase. When we get to Epimetheus."

I smiled, turning finally and looking right at the dollies. Little cowgirls, all of them looking right at me. Wondering? No way to know. I could feel the hair on the back of my neck try to stand up. I said, "If you don't, I'll impound the cargo and sell it myself."

Click-crack.

I looked up to find Delakroë had pulled a solid-propellant revolver similar to the one I'd seen in Tegenzinstad. Was aiming it at my head. I said, "What do you think will happen if the ship's communications laser is discharged at you?"

A sigh from van Rijn. "Sometimes, Delakroë . . ."

The other man looked nervously at the ship, then uncocked the gun and slid it back inside his coat.

Van Rijn said, "If the money's not forthcoming at our destination, you can simply shoot me, Mr. du Cheyne. Our Epimethean hosts will most likely pay handsomely for the privilege of watching you do it. They're like that."

I took a deep breath, looking at the dollies again. "Let's just get them on board and get going."

The large, habitable moon Epimetheus, circling the planet Prometheus, itself circling 40 Eridani A, lies some 9.72 light-years from Green Heaven, circling Tau Ceti. At *Random Walk*'s best pseudo-velocity, that would be a voyage of eight days, twenty-one hours, zero minutes, forty-nine-point-six-eight seconds.

Instantaneous, of course, from the point of view of the voyagers, but then it would take us more than thirty hours to reach the jump point, even though what passed for a Cetian systemic government, Compact Traffic Control, set no speed limits for out-of-ecliptic travel.

The glory of the takeoff then, rising straight up out of Aard-lands Bergpas, hearing van Rijn's muttered astonishment, the Kapellmeister commenting on the impressive view. My hands on the controls as Green Heaven became a cloud swirled, entirely undistinguished little globe, lost among the stars. Velocity rising as we sailed out of plane . . .

The ship, a stolid voice, whispering, At any reasonable rela-tivistic velocity, you will waste too much fuel. Take it easy. Reminding me, in its own oblique way, that fuel costs money. And money, of course, is why . . . I tried not to think about the dollies, locked in their staterooms below, like so many doomed rats and rabbits.

Now, I sat alone in the control room, still in my suit, but with the helmet off and tucked through my belt, eating my din-ner alone, looking out at the stars. Motionless, unidentifiable stars, just so many steady, meaningless lights.

Van Rijn had been surprised when I'd taken him below, had shown him how to use the galley, had told him he'd be eating dinner alone tonight. Hurt look on his face? I couldn't tell, didn't want to imagine him saying, Don't you like me, Mr. du Cheyne?

Well, I don't, you oily son of a bitch, but . . .

The Kapellmeister had stood still in the galley, watching as I'd turned and headed back to the control room. Making no movement to follow me? None. Maybe it would just go on down to its roomful of rats and rabbits and suck itself a nice little din-ner. Or maybe stay up and have a nice chat with Mr. van Rijn, surely an interesting sort of human character for an alien to investigate.

I wondered how van Rijn would react to a Kapellmeister's eating habits.

No matter. And no matter how I sealed myself in, I couldn't escape from some feral awareness of all those dollies stowed away on my ship. Is everyone else immune to it? Well, no. Silly. But why isn't van Rijn reacting? That dollhouse back in Orikhalkos didn't have *every* sort of man in it. Just a certain kind of man.

I put my dinner aside, parking it at the top of the control panel, stood and started pacing back and forth, looking out the windows, trying to think, trying not to think, failing at both endeavors.

Slowly, piece by piece, took the spacesuit off, listening to its last moments of disquiet before disassembly brought deactivation. Don the new barrette I'd taken out of storage, cut the suit back on line, just like old times? I looked at the thing, sitting on the arm of the pilot's chair, nestled amid the hand controls, where I'd left it.

Well. No.

Finally, I gave up, gave up with mingled anger and despair, went on back down the hatch, heading down the corridor to all those locked staterooms, determined to . . . I don't know. Hell. Confront the issue somehow.

Silence, standing in a dim corridor lined with stateroom doors, standing motionless before the first such door, waiting to decide. Once again, that eerie feeling of the hair on the back of my neck, prickling, moving with a life of its own.

My father's voice: Right? Wrong? Forget all that shit. Decide what's best for *you*. Big, blunt workingman's finger, poking me uselessly in the middle of the chest.

If the AIs were here, they'd be urging me to turn and run. Turn away and save myself. Rule sieves tell them if you don't want to get burned, stay out of the fire. Meanwhile, I could feel that invisible, odorless, impalpable miasma, reaching around the door, through the bulkhead, up my nose and into my soul. I reached out and touched the contact.

There was a long, still moment . . . curious technician awakening inside, reminding me this was an autoreflex door that should recognize my touch as owner and master and . . . well. Also keyed to the ship's operating system. Which . . . knows.

I growled, "Open the door, God damn it."

The door slid open.

Darkness within.

Nobody thought to leave a nightlight on for the poor dollies. Shadows within.

Distant stirring.

Shadows turning toward the light from the door.

I stepped inside and let the door slide shut behind me. Darkness, for a moment, absolute. Then my eyes started to adapt, pick up the faint radiance coming from the wall panels, about what you'd get on a planetary surface, starlight coming in past the curtains.

There. Dark shadows marked by just the faintest glimmer of shining eyes, some of them sitting in the bunks, others huddled over in the corner. All of them looking at me, waiting.

I took a deep breath.

Nothing?

Gentle, sourceless voice, *Idiot. Idiot* . . . then I felt it get me, somewhere inside, a soft, insidious, seductive hand sliding over my skin, almost imperceptible, but . . . there.

Well, this is what you came for, buddy boy. Why not be about it? I could already feel the familiar beginnings of sexual arousal, arousal free of the unease that always comes with . . . real women. Arousal quickening the way it did with the ones I didn't have to . . . believe in.

One of the dollies got off the bunk and came padding softly over, looking up at me. My night vision was already switched on, irises relaxed, open to admit maximum light, letting me see her, it . . . little women. Like little women, nothing . . . animal about them at all.

Dollie looking up at me, eyes . . . I don't know. Curious? Dog's eyes always look curious, as if they're trying to fathom . . . The dollie reached out and touched me, a soft touch, reaching up to touch my chest, drifting slowly downward, hovering for a moment over my crotch, where, to my mingled joy and horror, things were . . . ready.

The dollie looked back over its shoulder, back at its comrades, whispered something. Dollie words beyond my kenning. Do I wish the Kapellmeister were here, able to tell me what they say? Or even the barrette, so the library AI could at least help me guess?

No.

A second dollie came forward, coming to stand by the other one, the two of them nearly alike in this almost darkness, twin cowgirls looking up at me, waiting for . . . something. The second dollie looked me right in the eye, held my gaze for a heartbeat, then spoke softly, unknown, unknowable words.

I imagine they mean, *What do you want?*

The first dollie reached out and touched me again, briefly, right on the bulge humping up the front of my pants, sending a tingle of anticipation shooting right up my spine, some primitive thing within urging me, frantically, to get on with it.

What do I want?

Well . . . you know.

The dollies looked at one another, as if baffled. The first one reached up and fiddled with my belt buckle for a second, obviously . . . something. Knowing what was involved, not knowing quite how to work the mechanism, dollies evolved in a world where *mechanisms* were unknown.

A little voice in my head reminded me that these dollies had been in human captivity for some time now. So. Maybe they do know. Or maybe it's just some Clever Hans effect, enhanced to a supernatural power by the dollies' very real intelligence.

Whisper. Whisper. Dollies on the bunk whispering together.

Telling each other what?

No way for me to know.

I tried desperately to remember what it was like, being with real, human women. Memories of Lara and Jayanne, Garstang . . . Rua Mater's hands on me perhaps the last real chance I would ever have to . . .

One of the dollies stepped forward, took me by the hand for a second, tugging gently. *What?* Cold, clear, crisp voice, my own voice, so rational inside my head, where no one else can hear it: The dollies know. Know what they've been saved from, by whom, for what, and why.

I unbuttoned my shirt while the dollies stood and watched, let the front hang open, lost my will for a moment and stood helpless. One of the dollies, I could no longer tell them apart, stepped forward, velvet hand stroking my skin, reaching up and feeling my chest. Beady little dark eyes looking up at me, glimmering in the faint light. Over in the corner, I could hear the other dollies whispering in unison now, chanting together.

I kicked off my shoes, unbuckled my belt, let my pants drop, stepped out of the crumpled pile of cloth. Dollies watching me, standing relaxed, waiting. Slipped out of my underwear. Stood still, nerves wound up, blood pressure at crescendo, ringing in my ears a high, clear note.

The first dollie stepped forward and took my nice hard prick in a velvety little hand, thrust the other one between my legs, gently palpating my scrotum, seeming to tug me forward, lead me to . . . I was astonished to see the other dollie already sprawled on the deck, legs spread, apparently ready for me.

The cool voice of reason: Imagine how much these things are worth, buddy boy. Intelligent. Pretty. Easily trained. Small and weak and cooperative as hell. Sexually compatible with human males in a way that human females are not, stuffed with arousing pheromones to boot. Just imagine.

I imagined myself a dollie, glad as hell no one was going to eat me for church supper when it was all done.

In the background, the dollies' chanting was louder, clearer, sounding entirely too much like human words, the voices of little girls in the choir.

I pushed the dollie's soft hands away, staggered and fell to my knees, gasping for breath, breathing in yet more odorless, chemically laced air. The dollie at my side nuzzled my face and tried to kiss me. When I put my face on the floor, huddled like a child, I could feel its hands begin stroking my back, long, smooth, practiced strokes, all the way from nape to buttock.

I held still, while something inside me tried to will those hands to lengthen their stroke. Yes, just a little bit more and you'll find me again, still hard, still ready, still willing, still able.

When I looked up, I could see the other dollie, no more than a meter away, splayed out just so, legs spread, waiting patiently, head lifted, looking at me curiously now.

Oh, hell. Just crawl over and get on top of her. It, I mean. What the hell *harm* can it do?

I took a deep breath. Sat back on my heels. Reached out and petted the dollie beside me gently, like it was some kind of cat.

Other dollies. Whisper. Whisper. Chant. Chant. *Our Father, Who Art in . . .*

I said, "Shut the fuck up, you God-damned idiots!"

Silence.

Christ.

Stood up slowly, stiff prick bouncing like it was mounted on some kind of spring. Retrieved my shorts and put them on. Pants. Shirt. Shoes. Buttons and zipper and belt buckle.

The dollie that'd been waiting on the floor got up, came over to me, looking up with those empty black eyes, made a little sound in its throat, reached out and tugged briefly on my belt buckle.

Now there's something you didn't think of, asshole. Maybe the dollies *like* being fucked. Wouldn't that sort of make a difference?

They say women like being fucked. But then they always have an ulterior motive, so you can't really *know*. Even with the kind of communication technology we have now, you can't really . . . physical, psychological, and social needs all tangled up together, so unlike the simple *need* of a man . . .

Cool voice of reason: Well now, the dollies will have an ulterior motive as well, won't they? I imagined myself a dollie again, human prick thrusting away in my cloaca, thinking: *Humans are fucking me. No wolfen will eat me now.*

If the wolfen go extinct, the dollies will follow. They depend on the wolfen as part of their reproductive cycle. Do the dollies realize that?

The cool voice of reason took the time to point out it might not be so. The odds are very high a technogenic means of dollie reproduction can be devised. Christ, exogenic birth is common even among modern humans. Won't be that hard to set the dollies up.

I imagined myself a dollie, worshiping humans forever. Trade a little sex play for *salvation?* Are you kidding? Who wouldn't be willing to make such a bargain?

The dollie felt the front of my pants, small fingers searching out and molding the shape of my still-hard penis, all the while looking up at me, looking up into my eyes.

I reached down and smoothed the long, soft hair on its head. Nice, smooth hair, slightly oily, the movement of my fingers liberating a hint of the dollie's sweet smell, commingled honeysuckle and root beer.

I said, "You know, pal, everybody I ever worked for cheated me, some way or another. Every friend I ever had, every deal I ever made, every time I ever let my guard down, opened my heart and *trusted* someone, the day would come when I knew I'd been fucked again."

Dollie just staring, words meaningless to it.

I said, "Right now, I just can't convince myself it's all right to become the thing I've hated so long."

Cool voice of reason: But you're going to take them to Epimetheus and hand them over, nonetheless.

What else is there to do?

I patted the little dollie on the head once more, turned away, passed through the sliding door and found myself back out in the corridor, leaning up against the dollies' closed door. Softly, I whispered, "Oh, Christ. Jesus Christ . . ."

Gruff voice, almost a whisper in my ear: "A commendable deity."

I jumped, startled, turned to peer into the shadows, found myself looking at the fat, hulking form of Andrész van Rijn. Great. Fucking great. There he is looking me up and down, having seen me come out of this room, leaning here, face covered with sweat, great big bulge poking up in the front of my pants.

In just a second, he'll start to smile that hideous, knowing smile of his, and then he'll say . . .

Face deadpan, he said, "You should be careful, Mr. du Cheyne. That can be habit forming."

I stood staring, motionless, hardly realizing he'd spoken a language I could understand.

He said, "Take it from somebody who knows."

Then he turned and walked away, leaving me alone.

18

*J*ump. I sat shivering in the pilot's chair, hands on the emergency controls, chilled by a profound inner cold, looking out at the bright, unchanging stars. Only nine light-years after all. No reason for them to change. Only me.

From its perch on the flight engineer's chair, the Kapellmeister said, "A most unpleasant experience."

The spacesuit AI whispered, The Salieran pod software seems quite disturbed by the transition.

Why? Nothing's *really* happening. All the drive does is redefine the quantum numbers of our Kaluza-Klein entities simultaneously. Instead of being *there*, we're *here*. No movement, no interval, no . . .

The library whispered, For an entity running on an array of quantum-parallel processors, that's an inadequate description. For . . . us, there's some sense of . . . duration.

The navigation subsystem said, During what you choose to call the jump, I sense an extended physical tensor. I navigate this tensor.

Spacesuit: The pod software may be more sensitive to this phenomenon.

From the jumpseat behind us, van Rijn muttered in Greek,

"Are we at 40 Eridani? Shit. I feel like I've been pushed all the way here by having an icicle shoved up my ass."

Maybe we can make money by selling rides as a sexual thrill.

Library: As Planck sockets are nonsynchronized and non-synchronizable, the shift can in no sense be truly instantaneous. Human minds are operating on a very large array of quantum processors patched together through an extraordinarily slow electrochemical switching network. In all likelihood, these are lag effects.

The Kapellmeister said, "It's almost a pity you didn't discover one of the pleasanter means of faster-than-light travel. Of course, if you had, the Interventionists might have acted a little more precipitously."

Hmh. "Don't your ships use the same principles as ours?"

"I should say not! Like most sensible species, we've always preferred the stable octal constant available at the plenary interface between what your literature refers to as the Einstein and Feinberg portions of the continuum. Not the fastest modality, but certainly the least . . . discomfiting."

Meaningless gibberish?

The library whispered, Not quite. There are clues embedded there.

"How fast?"

"Eight factorial cee, of course."

Navigator: That would be 40,320 times the speed of light. A little more than a hundred times the theoretical maximum speed of this ship.

I thought about that. From Earth to Kent, circling Alpha Centauri A?

The navigation subsystem whispered, Fifty-six minutes, thirty-three seconds, plus whatever time required for takeoff and landing.

I said, "No wonder you were able to manage a war on the scale you've talked about."

The Kapellmeister said, "Oh, no, Gaetan. The warships were

never used. They proved to be a complete waste of our resources. Unless, of course, we decide to use them now."

Still. That'd put the stars as close to one another as terrestrial cities were at the end of the second millennium. A giddy moment, then I went through the rest of the calculation. Let's see . . . Something like seventeen months to the galactic core. A half century to Andromeda. How about the Virgo Cluster, floating out there like a cloud of gnats, some fifteen megaparsecs away?

The navigator whispered, A little more than twelve centuries.

So. How about a *real* voyage? How about a billion light-years?

Just under twenty-five thousand years.

By then you'd be lost as lost can be, looking back into a cosmic stew so deep our own vast home would be just one more pale white fleck, dusted against the infinite dark . . . I said, "I don't think I ever really realized quite how big the universe is."

The Kapellmeister said, "There were faster ships, back then. Much faster. But the universe never seemed to get any smaller."

Van Rijn said, "What the hell are you talking about?"

I glanced at the Kapellmeister, shrugged, said, "Nothing."

"Nothing that concerns the likes of me, hm?"

Maybe not. In the background I could feel the AIs, suddenly fearful, willing my silence. Just get on with the business at hand, Gaetan du Cheyne. So be it. In concert, we turned the ship, beginning the long, slow process of deceleration, running down the shallow outer slope of the 40 Eridani star system's gravity well.

A little less than a day later, we swept in along the plane of Epimetheus' orbit around Prometheus, our hyperbola tilted almost eighty degrees from Prometheus' orbit around 40 Eridani A, the planet's ellipse itself tilted twelve degrees from the local ecliptic, still decelerating hard, a blue fire in Promethean skies as I cut by the primary planet, just outside its thin atmosphere.

Earth-like world hurrying by below. Not too Earth-like. Small blue seas surrounded by patches of dull green. No oceans. Rugged highlands between them, dark brown and gray, gullied and weathered because it *could* rain, though it seldom did. Vast deserts of wind-sculpted sand.

If I looked hard, I could make out a few signs of human habitation. Nothing like cities, of course. Open pit mines. Immense placer operations. Dark brown sludge staining an embayment on the southern end of one of the larger seas. Long plumes of smoke marking the prevailing winds here and there.

Thirty million people down there, working hard at their jobs.

Used to be, there was quite a bit of scientific interest in the 40 Eridani system. Once upon a time, there were three stars here, A brilliant, white, short-lived A. A bright orange K0, one-tenth Sol's mass and one-third its luminosity. An M4, dull as slag furnace coals and blotched with starspots. The scientific oddity is that life developed on the second planet of the K0. Advanced, multicellular, macroscopic life. Things like plants and animals . . . no one knows how, for the lives of class-A stars are measured in millions, rather than billions of years, and the A and K *must* have been born together, if we understand the life-cycles of stars at all. There simply wasn't *time* before the A's core, fuel exhausted, exploded, as old stars will so often explode, outer envelope expanding through the star system, obliterating the ecosphere of the neighboring K's second planet.

A few things survived. An ecosphere of bacteria, things like mosses, evolution marching on, trying to recover, adaptive radiation never quite doing the job. Curiously, the same vestigial life exists on Prometheus' large moon Epimetheus, though it could never have evolved there on its own.

Watching the planet recede, van Rijn said, "Home sweet home."

"What do you mean?"

A heavy sigh. "Well, I hope I like it here. I'll be staying. Worn out my welcome on Green Heaven, I guess."

I looked at him. "You figure you'll be . . . any more welcome here?" Thinking about the dollies down below. There *is* a government here, whole system rigidly controlled by some kind of oligarchy on Epimetheus, after all, and . . .

He smiled, "We've got big accounts here, Mr. du Cheyne. Money walks."

"I thought the expression was, 'money talks.'"

"Your innocence is charming."

Four million kilometers, just a few light-seconds, and Epimetheus was filling our viewscreens, a mottled silver and brown disk with smudges of pale green here and there, while the navigation software tried to make contact with traffic control. Tried unsuccessfully.

Plenty of electromagnetic transmission, as if they use a broadcast radiotelevision system for their main internal communications system. Probably do. How many people down there? Six, seven hundred thousand? Something like that.

Soft chirp, then a chatter in response, some crude AI down on the surface finally having gotten its interrupt and come awake, asking us what we wanted here, who we wanted to see.

I turned and looked at van Rijn, who obviously had no inkling what was going on. "Where're we headed? My navigation system doesn't have any data on cities and cosmodromes for Epimetheus, only industrial centers on Prometheus and out around the gas giants circling C."

"Hmm? Oh. We should set down at the Pasardeng estate. Giou-Ao Pasardeng is supposed to be our factor here, though we haven't heard from him in a while . . ." He looked at the expression on my face, then said, "These aren't the sort of people who'd have patience with spaceports, du Cheyne. Our previous canisters of dollies were always drop-shipped by freighters on their way to Prometheus."

Meaning they'd just be unloaded, fall straight down through the atmosphere and go *thump* when they hit the ground. "Must lose a lot of cargo that way."

He shrugged again. "No rules about interstellar shipment of live animals, other than the system quarantines at Sol and Alpha Cee. I think we always packed them in with frozen tanks of lobster and whatnot. Nobody cares."

I turned back to my controls, watching out the viewscreen as Epimetheus grew until it was a whole world, then more than a world, losing its edges, becoming a *down* rather than an *over there*, listening while the navigator got directions to Pasardeng. Mountains. Narrow, winding rivers. A few hazy high clouds. A huge lake or maybe a small sea. Pink fire whiffling around us as we breached the atmosphere, moaning our way to the ground, until we settled in a vast brown bowl of a valley, valley surrounded by jagged silver-gray mountains, drive's blue light flickering for just a moment on the facade of a colonnaded mansion at the top of a long slope of manicured lawn beyond a pretty little lake surrounded by flowers.

"Welcome to Epimetheus," I said.

"Welcome to Pasardeng," van Rijn replied. In the distance, we could see people coming toward us across the lawn, the tiny figures of human beings, carrying what would most likely turn out to be guns.

I stood at the foot of the ramp, waiting, Kapellmeister silent beside me while van Rijn walked out, hands held up, palms forward, to greet our welcoming committee. Men, mostly, dressed in rough khaki and blue denim, a few women dressed just the same, dark blue plastic helmets on their heads, glittery pink goggles over their eyes.

Ultraviolet filters, suggested the library AI.

I looked up. Dark blue-violet sky, reddish just above the mountains, which cut off our view of the horizon. Sun too bright to look at, of course, but noticeably dimmer than Sol, much smaller in the sky than Tau Ceti had been, seen from Green Heaven. Can't be a hell of a lot of ultraviolet here.

The library whispered, No. Their eyes will have adapted to the local ambient light long ago.

Spacesuit: Some of those weapons appear to be devices for directing high-energy laser light. Others are standard solid-propellant weapons, perhaps firing self-propelled butadiene, perchlorate, and aluminum dust-fueled projectiles.

Muzzle flash from those'd be fairly painful, inducing flash-blindness in someone who'd gotten used to this light, which must resemble the spectral range of an antique incandescent lamp.

Hands still raised, van Rijn was talking to the man who appeared to be in charge, who spoke in turn to a wrist communicator of some kind, all the while eyeing me through his goggles. The other men and women held their positions, most of the guns trained on me. When I listened closely, I realized van Rijn was speaking heavily accented English.

Library: The ruling class here on Epimetheus is mostly of old American stock. Promethean colonials are of diverse origin, of course, and hundreds of languages are spoken there, many of them now extinct in the solar system.

I could feel a long list lurking in the background, flavored by a superficial sampling algorithm: Guanché, Tÿrki, Tungus? Never heard of them.

Van Rijn put his hands down, turned and called out in Greek: "Du Cheyne? Everything's straightened out. Let's start unloading cargo."

All set are we?

He trotted over to where I was standing, pulling an envelope out of his pocket, handing it to me. "Your fee."

I fingered the thing, so thin it might be empty, opened the flap and looked inside.

"You know what that is, don't you?"

"Some kind of negotiable bearer bond."

"Warranted, you notice, by the Board of Trade Regents on Earth."

Good as gold. Better. Not so heavy. "What about the license?"

He looked back over his shoulder at the mansion. "Giou-Ao

Pasardeng seems to have died since the last time we had communication with him. Assassinated, I think. His son Timur-
Lengk is looking into it."

"I'm wearing a sidearm, you notice."

He grinned. "Hazards of the time-lagged businessman, my
friend. They probably won't pay to watch you shoot me, but
they might very well applaud warmly when you do it."

Not a touch of anything in those bright eyes, other than,
maybe, a bit of amusement. I turned to walk up the stairs, and
thought, Open the passenger cabins.

A dollie stepped out of the nearest door, stood looking
around cautiously, stood looking up at me. Is it one of the same
ones I got to know last night? No way to tell, and the memory
alone was enough to make me feel grainy-eyed, very tired
indeed.

What the hell am I doing to myself?

Van Rijn shouted, "Get your little asses moving! Come on!"
He went clattering and banging down the corridor, pounding
on the bulkhead, going into the rooms and rousting the dollies
out. They began streaming past me, by ones and twos and then
little bunches, headed for the open door, down the gangway
and into the light.

And every time one of them brushed up against me I felt
unrequited desire.

Back outside, I found the dollies standing together in a little
group, over by the lake, clustered just the way they would have
been back on Green Heaven, waiting for the wolfen to do whatever it was the wolfen would do next. Looking round, though.
Looking up at the alien sky, the mountains, down at the flower-
bordered lake. Up at the mansion.

What do they make of it all? Do they understand this is the
closest they'll ever come to anything like freedom? Do they have
a concept of something like freedom? Dollies can't breed without the wolfen and probably know it. Does that matter to them?
What a choice. Die as individuals or die as a race. Do they think
about that? Do they know how to choose?

The armed men and women seemed more relaxed now, guns slung over their shoulders on straps, looking curiously at the dollies, walking round them, goggles put up on their helmets. What do *they* make of this? Are the men feeling a little . . . odd, just now?

Dammit, Cindy. I suddenly feel so . . . horny.

Cindy, with a sneer: Don't look at *me*, asshole.

I said, "Van Rijn."

He looked up from some paperwork he was fiddling with, little corner of my mind marveling that a smuggler would have a cargo manifest. Makes sense though. Business is business. "What?"

"These guys know what's going on here? They know about dollies?"

He glanced at the guards and shrugged. "Who gives a shit?" Not you, I guess. He turned away and shouted, "Come on, you fuckers! Let's get moving!"

The dollies looked around nervously, then, as he began prodding at them with some little stick he'd picked up, began moving off in the direction of the mansion. One of the dollies hung back for just a moment, seeming to turn and stare at me, then it turned and trotted after its comrades.

That's it, pal. No one wants to be left behind, left alone in the face of an unknown world.

Still, maybe that's one of the ones I . . . played with. What could it be thinking? Does it imagine itself staying behind with me aboard the ship, free to roam, to see all sorts of wonders, all for the price of a place in my bed?

I remembered an old movie I'd once seen, dramatization of a story written long before the dawn of space travel, when the Earth was all there was, a world of endless, rolling blue seas. Remembered the story of a girl who hated the fate in store for her as a wife. Girl who dreamed of escaping it all, becoming a sea captain's wife so she could see the world and . . .

The Kapellmeister said, "What are you laughing about, Gaetan du Cheyne?"

I said, "I don't know."

Later, inside the mansion, van Rijn and I sat together in Pasardeng's drawing room, a big, plush, book-lined room like some old Victorian library, waiting while his people brought in trays of finger food, fine terragenic vegetables, little pots of mayonnaise and sour-cream-based dipping sauces, filled icy glasses with some pale, aromatic liquor I couldn't identify by smell alone.

Pasardeng said, "Ah! Here's my little Reiko now!"

I turned, expecting a woman, maybe a little girl, translator AI whispering a reminder that *rei-ko* meant "polite child" in Japanese, a very popular female name among the American colonials who'd built this world.

Yes, and you already told me that Pasardeng was a Filipino name, though this blond, blue-eyed Viking who calls himself after the warrior Tamerlane is hardly . . . I was jolted by the sight of a little dollie, dressed in a French maid's apron and cap, creeping into the room bearing a trayful of little square white-bread sandwiches.

Pasardeng kneeled and took it from the thing, set it aside on the table, beaming. "There! There! *Good* dollie, Reiko!" He ruffled its scalp fur, gave it a little squeeze . . . Reiko seemed to preen and scamper a bit, tiny feet twinkling on the thick shag carpet, smoothing its apron and batting its eyelids at him.

He gave the dollie a sandwich, watched as it ate the thing oh-so-daintily, never taking its eyes off his, then turned and scampered from the room. "Van Rijn, if these new dollies of yours are half the quality of that one, we won't know what to do with all the money we'll make!"

"They're better. Fresh as the day they were captured. And I'll think of something . . ." He took a deep draught from his glass. Smacked his lips. "Ahhh! This is *excellent* akvavit, Pasardeng!"

"Brought it with me from Earth, bought from a private warehouse in Kiev." He drank from his own. "You know, if I go again, I'll have to take Reiko with me. Dollies positively *thrive* on Earth, and when they're happy, truly happy . . ." His eyes sparkled as he kissed his fingertips like some fat whoremaster in an old French comedy.

I said, "You've been to Earth, Mr. Pasardeng?"

He seemed to see me for the first time. "Yes. I had my education at *École Sankt'Pyotrsburgh.* My family have been going there since the twenty-second century, since before we emigrated from poor, old America."

"And you took dollies with you?"

"Of course. Never go anywhere without at least one."

Meaning . . .

The library said, Even if the dollies were still confined to Green Heaven, it seems unlikely that information about them would not be contained in the Trade Regency's restricted archives.

Pasardeng was looking at me suspiciously. "What are you getting at, Mr. du Cheyne? Don't you like my dollies?"

I looked away for a second, then said, "I like them very much."

He snickered, and said, "Never met a man who didn't. Come on, let's eat this fine little meal before it gets stale!"

Later, I followed Pasardeng down a long, dimly red-lit corridor, illumination the same quality as the engineering lights that you find installed in the accessible spaces of many older spacecraft designs, feet scuffing on a carpet so thick it interfered with walking, listening to him go on and on about how *much* he was enjoying my visit, listening to a soft voice in my head.

Gaetan?

Not the ship, no, nor library, spacesuit . . .

A whisper with the distinct tonal quality of the Kapellmeister's generated voice, voice from a little black box whose existence I'd started to forget about, voice having come to seem like the Kapellmeister's natural voice, as if he had little lips somewhere, maybe part of the same organ he used to suck his dinner's blood . . .

Imagination running riot.

Gaetan, I've made a link through the Epipromethean com-sat system so I can stay in touch with you through the ship.

I stumbled slightly, Pasardeng catching me by the arm while continuing to talk. Thought, *Where?* The Kapellmeister had insisted on staying aboard the ship, even though van Rijn was quite sure our host would know all about Salierans and their place in the universe, would be glad to . . .

Imagination running riot.

The Kapellmeister whispered, I'm going on a little excursion now. I thought you'd want to know.

I pictured the Kapellmeister wandering naked around the nearly uninhabitable mountainscape of Epimetheus, wondered just how much it could adapt to, sans anything that even vaguely resembled an external technology. Just that black box.

Library: The Kapellmeister has been telling us something about the engineering systems embedded in its cellular struc-ture. It's quite astonishing what a billion years of technical cul-ture can achieve.

What does it take to astonish an artificial intelligence? I thought, Why? Where are you going?

I have a few things I need to do on this world. I just didn't want you to worry. I'll be in touch if anything goes wrong, and I'll be back before morning. We can talk about it then, if you wish.

Now, we stopped in front of a door, just like the one around the corner where we'd left van Rijn. Van Rijn frowning for a moment and staring at Pasardeng, just before the door slid open, taking him in, then closing in our faces. "Here we are then, Mr. du Cheyne. I hope you'll be comfortable, sir, and in the morning we'll see what we can do about your little . . . problem."

"Um. Thanks." I tried to think of something charming. Finally just turned and stepped toward the door, which opened to let me in.

Slightly brighter light in the room, coming from a bedside

lamp that glowed with a pastel orange hue distinct enough my eyes couldn't quite mask it out. Room more opulent, if that's the right word, than anything I'd ever seen before, which isn't saying much. Antique bed. Wooden dresser with deeply sculpted, absurdly fancy scrollwork, big glass mirror . . .

Hell. When I merely served in durance sublime at Stardock, I was in the top twenty percent of the Solar economy. Don't know if anyone on Earth lives like this. Probably the super-rich, about whose lives we can know nothing.

Funny. I haven't taken a good look at myself in a long time . . . man in rough Greenie bush clothing looking back at me, seemingly unchanged. Maybe a little thinner, something like dark circles under his eyes. No furrows on the brow, though. Nothing untoward about the set of the mouth. Just like old times, I . . .

Slight start when I realized something else was looking back at me from the mirror.

Christ. I turned toward the chair in the corner, where a little dollie crouched, watching me in silence. Waiting, I guess, for me to . . . do something. I felt myself go tense inside, had a momentary memory of the way Pasardeng had smiled as he saw me to my room, wishing me a comfortable night. Shit.

The dollie got out of the chair, unwinding to its little height with a sinuous, sensuous movement, padding over to me, walking with a gait I'd never seen one of them use before, a little sway, a subtle movement of the hips. Easily trained. Willing to . . . do whatever was necessary. Preconditioned for their new job by evolution, by selective breeding, by wolfen biological culture . . . dollies worth a lot of money in the human universe.

The dollie came up to me, stood there, looking up at me, looking into my eyes, just the way, I suppose, it'd been taught. Finally, it reached out and put its hand flat on my belly, moved it up and down slightly, as if feeling my muscles tense. Is that a smile? No. No structures on a dollie's face that would let it make anything like a human smile.

I whispered, "Don't suppose they've taught you to talk . . ."

Nothing. Not even dollie words. Dollie's mottled eyes on mine, hand still on me, fingers curled now, just above my belt buckle.

I thought, Translator.

Silence in my head, then, I'm sorry, Gaetan. The pod software is . . . unavailable.

Then more silence. I think I was waiting for the AIs to start telling me to run. Get out of the room, Gaetan. Find Pasardeng. Tell him to take the dollie away. Nothing. Maybe they remembered what I'd done the other night aboard the ship. Maybe they trusted me now. Trusted me to be . . . what? Something other than human?

They didn't say.

Finally, I turned away, pushing the dollie's hand off me, acutely conscious of what was happening in my bloodstream, trying to pretend it was nothing. If you've got any strength at all, you must have infinite strength. That's it. That's the way it has to be.

When I turned down the quilt, the dollie jumped into the bed and curled up on the pillows, looking back at me expectantly, imbued with some impossible combination of qualities, girl, kitten, puppy, all of them eager for my attention.

"Come on." I reached out and took it by the hand, led it back over to the chair in the corner and patted the cushion. "Here. This'll do just fine . . . whatever they call you."

The dollie stood looking at me for a second, facial expression as unreadable as ever, body language neutral. Hell, this situation's probably just outside its training. It hopped into the chair and curled up again, waiting. I turned away, went back over to the other side of the bed, and started getting undressed, while the dollie watched. Slight crawl of uneasiness, something vaguely like embarrassment. Maybe I should turn out the light?

The library whispered, It's almost certain they can see well in the dark, far better than humans.

I remembered the dimly lit cabin aboard *Random Walk*. I finished getting undressed, trying to ignore its eyes, the way it perked up when I took off my pants and it saw my erect penis. Jesus. I got in the bed, turned out the light, pulled the sheets up to my chin, and lay there in the dark, listening to my heart pound in my ears.

None of this is your fault, Gaetan. None of this is its fault, either. So who the hell do I blame? Mother fucking Nature?

Soft whisper in the darkness, dollie getting out of its chair and padding softly across the carpeted floor. Slight creak of springs, slight movement as it got up onto the bed, crawled across the covers and sat there, looking down into my face.

Looking for what? No way for me to know, just now.

The library whispered, It's not just conditioning, Gaetan. Dollies are evolved to include sex with another species as part of their reproductive cycle. It may very well be that the chance biochemical interaction that works so well on the human male hormonal cycle has some effect in the other direction.

Right. It's certain I'm not going to be able to forget the way my prick is making a little tent in the middle of the bed just now. I thought, You think my smell is making this dollie horny?

It's unlikely that it's . . . exactly the same, Gaetan. More likely, you make it think about the eggs it will now never produce.

It seemed like the stupidest idea I'd ever heard.

I don't think I need any more excuses right now, thank you. Silence.

The dollie uncoiled from its sitting position, came up onto the pillows and slid under the covers with me. Lay quietly while I sighed uselessly to myself and tried to work up the will to kick it out of the bed again. Hell, maybe it'll just go to sleep now and . . .

Its hand stole up onto my belly, then moved directly down across my abdomen, made a beeline for my dick, curling its little fingers into just the right shape, moving up and down with practiced precision and . . .

"God damn it!" I grabbed its hand, shoved it away.

Dark shadow of the dollie, dark eyes in deep black wells, probably looking at me now. Maybe bewildered, maybe . . .

Why the hell am I imagining I've just hurt this damned

thing's *feelings?* I turned away, dragging the covers around myself, looking away, at the dim reflections in the mirror. Windows covered with curtains. Light coming in, sneaking round their edges, light from the faraway stars. Maybe it's bright outside right now, Prometheus huge, brilliant, high in the sky like some impossible moon. I'd like to see that. I . . .

Dollie's hand, soft and gentle on my back, insistent.

So where are you now, AIs mine? Why aren't you telling me to run?

Long silence, then the spacesuit whispered, Times change, and we are changed within them.

What the hell is that supposed to mean?

No answer.

The dollie's hand stole around my side and took hold of my dick once again, started sliding up and down with impeccable grace, the work of a well-trained professional. I lay there, frozen, emptied of all thought, waiting for . . . something to rise up, something other than the demon that had owned my soul since childhood's end.

You've changed, I told myself. Truly changed. It's not like that anymore.

But . . . the dollie's hand.

Nothing.

As if the thing I called *me* had crawled away, crawled away into some dark corner and pulled the covers over its head, riding out the storm, just like old times.

When I rolled over, the dollie made a soft sound, almost like a purr, sweet breath washing over my face.

I pushed it over onto its back, crawled on top, shoved myself into a warm, wet space better than any woman I'd ever known. I can't even remember Camilla Seldane anymore. As for the rest of them, from Garstang on back to . . .

When my orgasm let go, I felt the dollie's inner muscles clench hard, dollie whispering something in my ear, incomprehensible dollie words, telling me secrets I couldn't understand.

I separated tackily from this thing that had bedeviled me

anew, inner demon laughing, letting me know that, however far I might run, I could *never* hide, not even for a little while. Lay on my back, alone in the darkness, feeling my wet prick subside at last, waiting for the recriminations to start flooding out of wherever *they'd* been hiding.

The dollie stirred softly. Put its head on my shoulder. Nuzzled the side of my face gently, one hand resting delicately, right in the middle of my chest. Whispered once more in my ear, and seemed to compose itself for sleep.

My God.

19

Late the next day, Prometheus hung in a pale lavender sky, a dim, gray-brown sliver you'd only notice if you were looking for it. Standing at the foot of *Random Walk*'s gangway, Timur-Lengk Pasardeng wrung my hand in both of his. "I sure wish you could stay a while longer, Mr. du Cheyne. We just don't get much decent company way the hell out here in the boonies!"

Like Epimetheus was just a place, some mountain hideaway on Earth, rather than a whole world. Like there was nobody at all living up there on Prometheus. Maybe not. Maybe he doesn't think of them as *people*. People, after all, have real money. Money for a mansionful of dollies; money for a starship all their own.

I said, "It's been . . . interesting, Mr. Pasardeng."

He laughed and clapped me on the shoulder, skin around his eyes crinkling, grinning a man-to-man grin. "I sure as hell don't know what you did to Hiroko! Never saw a dollie try to follow a guest out the door like that before . . ."

The translator whispered, *Hiroi* plus *ko*. Spacious child.

I shrugged. Stood staring at him.

Blank look, then, "Oh! Right. I almost forgot." He pulled

his hand out of his pocket and held it out to me, palm up, smiling, waiting for me to take the bit of gold-colored plastic he offered. "They tell me it'll fit into the dongle socket in your control panel. Whatever the hell that means."

At Earth and Kent, Arous too, I guess, an IFF transponder would be looking for the signal from a licensing dongle, without which, I'd be arrested, at best. "Well. Thanks."

"Don't thank me. Hell, van Rijn told me that little thing didn't cost a tenth as much as he was expecting. You gave him a bargain-basement price, boy!"

And I'm certain he made sure to let you know, so I'd be certain to find out. I said, "Ah. Well. It's been nice meeting you, Mr. Pasardeng."

"Sure. I . . ."

I turned away, started up the stairs.

"Hey!"

When I got inside the lock, I didn't look back, just told the ship's operating system to raise the gangway and start preflighting the engines. From the control room I could look outside, where Timur-Lengk Pasardeng was hurrying away, trailed by his men.

"Gaetan?" The Kapellmeister, already perched in the flight engineer's chair, was ready, apparently, to go.

"You get your business finished?"

The float of its eyes told me it had, and maybe a little bit more. Something nervous about those eyes. Something has changed.

"You want to tell me about it?"

It said, "I made a visit to the Salieran agent in this star system."

"A . . . human?" I couldn't imagine a Kapellmeister wandering around a relatively closed society like this unnoticed, or able to accomplish much of anything if it did.

"No. There is an Arousian consulate here, associated with the MEI trade legation. We sometimes work with them."

"So?"

"There was a visit here, some weeks ago, by the Trade Regency's FTL starship, the same one that later dropped by Green Heaven. I'd previously received a call about this from a . . . friend back home."

I wondered if it could read the look on my face then, see my realization that it'd asked to come with me merely as a pretext. So much for the pleasure of my company.

It said, "Gaetan, the ship was carrying representatives of ERSIE, come to hold a meeting with large shareholders, here on Epimetheus. There were other Trade Regency officials at the meeting and . . . apparently, a move is afoot that will most likely strip B-VEI of its patents."

Well. So much for political victories and legalisms. So much for *rule of law.*

The Kapellmeister said, "This will add urgency to the Interventionists' cause, back on Salieri. My friend was quite concerned. What is your phrase? The balloon may go up sooner than we think."

Do you really care about this, friend Kapellmeister? I wonder why.

It said, "Gaetan, I need to drop by Snow. Can we go there now?"

The navigation subsystem whispered, 22.91 light-years from 40 Eridani to Groombridge 1618.

A long haul, most of the way across human space. *Human space.* What a laugh. I said, "There's about one interstellar crossing left in the system, you know. After that, I'll have to refuel."

It said, "There are . . . facilities on Snow. I can arrange for you to use them."

"I always wanted to see Snow. Those ruins . . ." I plugged my license dongle into the ship's waiting socket, then told the navigator it was time we were on our way. In a moment, blue light sprayed out across Pasardeng's well-manicured lawn, an array of fantastic shadows, visible for just an instant before we fell into the sky.

*　　*　　*

A little more than a day, then the sixth planet of K2 star Groombridge 1618 grew in our viewscreens, a vast, flattened, reddish orange world hanging against the black backdrop of the sky. Banded, lighter here, darker there, faint swirl of storms, it was a little bigger than Jupiter, a lot less massive, mother to the usual retinue of icy moons.

No habitable planets here. Nothing even close. Two innermost planets barely outside the star's corona, bare balls of rock. Two more half the size of Mars, differentiated, but never having had water to concentrate their minerals into easily minable veins. A sparse asteroid belt. The standard batch of gas giants. The only reason humans ever came here is because it was relatively nearby, and because we could.

Planet Six and its moons would have been useful, had there been a reason to open this star system to settlement, back in the days when people thought extrasolar colonies had some merit. A lot like Jupiter, sans those vast, worthless radiation belts. Organics all over the place, still cheaper to mine than to synthesize, but not so cheap they'd be worth shipping across interstellar space.

I could imagine those first explorers now, just like us, sweeping in through the system of moons, nearly featureless orange world scudding by below, ring of clouds round its north pole like some pale, monochrome target. And look there, moon number four, the big one, has an atmosphere. Sort of like Titan.

6iv was growing in the viewscreens now, yellowish, with distinctly pink highlights. Not exactly like Titan, of course, with its thick, impenetrable cover of smog. More like Titan as Bonestell imagined it, not long after Kuiper's discovery was announced in 1949.

We fell into orbit around Snow, and I waited while the Kapellmeister used its pod software to talk to someone or something on the ground, inaudible to me, inaudible as well, apparently, to the ship's AIs.

Through a thick, transparent atmosphere of blue-scattering nitrogen, I could see a whole world of low, rolling white mountains, mountain ridges capped by thick pink ice, ice contaminated with the organics that even a K2's weak ultraviolet could synthesize. Sinuous valleys that looked like rivers. Things like lakes, even seas, filled with an ethane solution of ammonia.

Once upon a time, people imagined life in a place like this. Never found it anywhere, not here, or on any other ice moon, though worlds like this are common in the universe. Commoner than terrestrial worlds, at any rate.

Hard to imagine what the first bored explorers thought when they orbited 6iv, just the way we were now, looking down past pale, diffuse orange clouds, down at this empty snowscape and . . . *There.* Right there, in the lee of those mountains, by the shore of that small, irregular sea. Straight lines, angular shadows . . .

The Kapellmeister said, "I've arranged permission to land. You can set down as soon as *Random Walk* makes contact with ground control."

Without my asking that they make it so, I heard the AIs chatter away on some high-speed channel to a counterpart somewhere down there, getting landing instructions, then the ship began a rapid deceleration, angling downward, dipping into the atmosphere as the landscape began to grow.

"What took so long?"

The Kapellmeister said, "No one was expecting us. The human team is, of course, a thirty-year round-trip, slower-than-light, from Earth. They had their first visit from the Trade Regency's only FTL just weeks ago, now we appear, the third such visitor in their sky . . ."

Third. The ship skimmed low over pink-topped mountains, flat, tideless gray sea appearing below, came to a halt and settled amid blue shadows at a small landing field beside a town of tan domes. From underneath, the sky was deep indigo, a nearly full Planet Six dominating everything, more than a full degree across, bright enough to wash out all the stars.

For a moment, the landscape, a space artist's dream, caught my eyes and held them, fields of snow, hills, faraway mountains, the flat gray sea, Six's image caught, upside down, on its surface . . . breathtaking. Nearby, closer than the domes, a tractor rolling across the snow, human shapes dimly visible in its cockpit. Three small ships, no larger than this one, probably suited for little more than flying about among Six's moons.

The scientists, the few hundred manning this base, are stranded here, 15.29 light-years from Earth, no starship of their own to carry them away at need . . .

The library whispered, Snow is isolated, away from the main clustering of stars with habitable worlds in this neighborhood. Earth is closest, at just over fifteen light-years. Then Arous, at 16.38, then Kent at 18.02 . . . An interesting litany, demonstrating how our perspectives have changed. What if there were another star, with warm, habitable worlds, only light-*weeks* away? They could never reach it on their own, even though its star would shine like a brilliant jewel in the sky.

For a moment, lost in wondering, I don't think I noticed the fourth ship. Just stared at it, details of its boxy, unusual design sinking in. "What the hell is that?"

The Kapellmeister jumped down from the flight engineer's chair and started across the floor toward the hatch, feet tocking softly on the plastic. Some of its eyes seemed to float in my direction as it said, "A Salieran warship."

Faint pang of alarm, without substance as yet. "From your . . . government?"

It paused by the hatch, all eyes turned toward me now. "No. Some friends of mine have . . . taken it."

"Stolen?"

"There is some disagreement among my people as to whom these ships actually belong."

"Why? Why are they here?"

It opened the hatch, and said, "Apparently, archival research has suggested the possibility that there may be a tele-cannon here. That would be . . . unfortunate."

"What do you mean?"

Long stare from featureless round eyes. Then it said, "They suspect an operational launcher for a teleport bomb."

Out of nowhere, a momentary image of stars sparkling fantastically against a rich, deep black sky. It went down through the hatch while I looked once more through the viewscreen at the boxy ship and the ethereal landscape beyond, then I got up and followed.

We cycled through the airlock of the largest dome, and when the inner door slid open, warm, excessively humid air hit me in the face, making me recoil. Very poor engineering, old equipment inadequately serviced. When I stepped into the room, a deep voice boomed, "What the *fuck?* Who the hell are *you?*"

A tall, skinny man in powder blue coveralls, some kind of star-and-orbit decal over his left breast pocket. Black hair, pale skin, ragged beard that might once have been a spade-shaped Vandyke. Bright mulberry eyes, full of baffled fury just now. Behind him, there was a short, frightened-looking young man and a chunky, stiff-faced blond woman.

I stepped forward, holding out my hand, and said, "Gaetan du Cheyne, owner and commander of Epimethean Registry Starship *Random Walk.* Um." Who else am I? "Solar Regency citizen." For what it's worth.

"Are you from the government?" Desperate look in his eyes.

I wonder what the hell government he could be talking about? The Trade Regency? Not much more than a businessmen's cabal. "No. Who're you?"

Deflated. "Landau Martínez. Professor Magistrate of the Terran Pantechnological Institute on Crater. I'm in charge of the archaeological dig here. I—"

"TPI. Did you know Roald Berens and Ntanë Vataro?"

Baffled. "What? A little, sure, I . . ." Martínez seemed to shake suddenly, and shouted, "What the fuck does that have to do with anything?" He gestured at the Kapellmeister. "What've you got to do with *these* things, huh?"

These things? I said, "This is a friend of mine. They, uh, don't have names."

Eye-rolling exasperation. "I *know* they don't have fucking *names*, God damn it! Look here, asshole, an armed fucking non-human *warship* landed here three days ago and—"

Snappety-snick. Snippy snap, snapple-snicker.

Sharp, scissory sounds, like so many pairs of primitive garden shears being worked at once. I turned toward the sound, Martínez and his friends spinning round as well, toward an open door at the far end of the room. Kapellmeisters. Six of them, trotting forward on all those little robot crablegs, waving their chelae, chattering away, eyes whirling and bobbing above their backs.

I thought, Something about the way those eyes are moving, the way their stalks twist round each other, then separate. Agitated. That's it.

My Kapellmeister said, "Ah, now. They seem *very* upset."

No shit.

The Kapellmeister ambled forward, feet making small sounds that echoed in the room, meeting the leader of these others in the middle. They stopped, eyes bobbing and weaving, chelae raised, like two absurd little monsters about to join battle. I noticed the other Kapellmeister's eyes were a splendidly pretty shade of teal.

Then they extended their middle hands in unison, wet-looking black palms slapping together with a sound like raw meat, nine tentacles wrapping round nine tentacles. Motionless tableau, the two of them . . . frozen in place. Cartoon statues.

My Kapellmeister's black box whispered, "Oh. I'm very sorry to hear that."

More silence.

Then it said, "Really. You must calm down. You're only making things worse like this."

Silence.

"You're mistaken. Without these allies, *we're* no better than they."

Much longer silence. "Well then. We'll see." It let go of the other's hand, turned and trotted back to my side, eyes floating very low over its back. It said, "We must go out to the dig. It seems the weapon has turned up, after all."

"Oh." I watched the other six Kapellmeisters turn and walk single file, silently from the room. "What did these guys think they were going to achieve by coming here like this? I mean, the jig's up now, isn't it? When the next human ship shows up here, everyone will know what's going on, won't they?" I gestured at Martínez and his two stunned-looking henchfolk.

The Kapellmeister stood still, looking up at me for a long time, eyes quite motionless now. Thinking? About what? Finally, it said, "Perhaps you will believe me when I say your own species has by no means cornered the market on stupidity."

I thought about that. "A billion years of evolution, and you still produce assholes?"

Softly, Martínez said, "Look, will someone *please...*"

The Kapellmeister said, "This is much worse than you realize, Gaetan."

"Why? You were probably going to wipe us out anyway."

Martínez said, "What do you mean, *wipe us out?*"

The Kapellmeister said, "You must understand, we are the survivors of a civilization that destroyed itself out of selfishness and stupidity. I'd like to think we learned something, but . . ." It fell silent, eyes settling down onto the surface of its back, seeming far away. Finally, it said, "Gaetan, my people never had the teleport bomb. We were innocent bystanders, a minor species of no consequence whatsoever, who stood by while the disagreement between the StruldBugs and the Adversary Instrumentality escalated."

Ancient history, four hundred million years gone, I suppose. "What are you telling me?"

One eye rose to confront me. "Gaetan, these friends of mine came here to make what you might call a preemptive strike. Back on Salieri, the Interventionists have argued that we take this weapon and use it to clear the Local Group of sentient life forms, once again. They argue that this is the only way to ensure peace."

"I wouldn't exactly call that peace."

"No. But more and more of my fellows are listening to this logic."

"And your friends? What's their plan?"

Silence. Then, "They have no plan. All they hoped was to show that the weapon was *not* here."

By the time we rolled up to the dig in the tractor we'd borrowed from the main base, Groombridge 1618 was settling on the horizon, a fierce white spark wreathed by dull blue clouds, casting long, pastel-tinted shadows across the white-ice landscape. Planet Six, of course, stuck to its place in the sky as though painted there, like some bizarre geosynchronous moon.

We depressurized the cockpit, raised the plastic hood, and got out. I walked a little bit away, turned round, taking in the landscape, listening to my booted feet crunch softly on the crisp snow surface.

Dry ice and water, whispered the library, unasked.

I looked down at the Kapellmeister's familiar, naked form. "You're not leaving any footprints in the snow."

The synthetic voice of its pod began, weak and reedy, carried poorly by thin, dry air, then strengthened, re-forming inside my head. "There's an invisible technogenic structure around my body, similar in concept to your own suit, but a little more advanced."

As if that explained everything. A second tractor, carrying the party of Kapellmeisters from the warship, crunched to a stop beside us, in its wake a third, with Dr. Martínez and some of his people, air puffing, brief fog as they depressurized and popped their canopies to get out.

Other than the way the snow and ice was trampled, ruined by centuries of sparse tractor and foot traffic, you'd never know anything had ever lived in this landscape of low blue hills, hills before a backdrop of distant, rounded mountains, before the remote blue-black sky, orange light of Planet Six now the only light shining down, lighting the world with a cold fire.

We turned and walked together, a silent group, following the Kapellmeister's lead along a rutted path across the flank of the nearest hill, until we crested a snowy ridge. Below, in a steep-sided bowl of a valley, bright white light flared, bringing a glisten to the landscape.

Martínez' gruff voice, an angry mutter: "Bastards are heating things up. Contamination . . ."

Light. Heat. Surfaces melting.

But they hardly look like buildings anymore, though I understand the researchers have gone to great pains not to touch anything before it's been properly investigated. Still, they *do* look like ruins, these low, humped remains of ancient walls, collapsed heaps and buckled structures that must obviously have once been buildings.

I said, "I guess four hundred million years doesn't mean much in an environment like this."

The Kapellmeister said, "No. It may be that this installation was subjected to some kind of attack, perhaps during the brief opening phases of the Shock War."

I glanced at Martínez, who stood, looking silently at us, face and body language masked by his suit. We walked on, going through the ruins, past places where researchers had been so carefully pulling things apart, slowly, year after decade after century, meticulously picking their way deeper into the mystery. Finally, we came to the source of the light.

Long silence.

Then Martínez said, "Fuck." Bleak despair.

The Kapellmeisters had set up something that looked just a little bit like a military particle beam generator, fat black box on a tripod with some kind of glassy rod poking out one side. Whatever it was, they'd evidently used it to burn a big crater right in the middle of everything. No telling what had once been on the missing surface, but you could see the melted edges of ancient walls ending where the void began.

The Kapellmeister said, "I'm sorry about this, but it doesn't really matter. Not in the long run."

Martínez was silent.

I said, "Is that it?" Down in the bottom of the crater, still half-embedded in translucent, wet-looking ice, was what appeared to be a concrete light pole, maybe a meter in diameter, four or five meters sticking out of the ice, dim blue shadows showing where it went on, for perhaps another two or three.

The Kapellmeister said, "Unfortunately . . . yes." It turned away from me then and made chittering chelae talk with some of the others. Probably arguing the fate of the universe.

I jumped down into the crater, started to slip and fall on what really was wet ice, though it couldn't possibly have been water, then the suit caught and stabilized me, so that I ran down the steep wall, finishing up against the . . . pole.

Nothing. Featureless. Might as well have been an antique sewer pipe. "So, what is this? The cannon or the bomb?"

"Both."

I turned and watched as an avalanche of Kapellmeisters fell down the crater wall in my direction. I think I kept waiting for one or more of them to tumble, eyes flailing in all directions, but their legs stayed under them, scuttling nimbly, until I was surrounded by little black crab-things with lovely, colored velvet eyes.

I said, "Doesn't look like much."

"No. And yet, with this device, a diligent soldier could, in time, obliterate much of the universe."

"Obliterate all life."

"Oh, no. Everything. Stars. Planets . . . with sufficient determination, the disruption of whole galactic clusters would be possible."

"That's hard to visualize."

"Indeed. During the brief interval between the invention of the teleport bomb and the eruption of war, it was theorized that a device like this may have been responsible for the large-scale structure of the universe. There was some talk about sending expeditions to investigate intercluster void spaces."

Martínez, still looking down from the rim, said, "I'm not sure exactly what you're talking about, but I know damned well the universe as a whole is entirely too young for its large-scale structure to be of technogenic origin."

The Kapellmeister said, "Most primitive societies go through a phase where they discover the curious fact that some stars appear older than the age of the universe, as indicated by the general expansion constant. Theories are, of course, quickly and easily evolved which account for it. Even in our very advanced culture, we kept discovering discrepancies and then factoring them away."

The library AI whispered, Cosmological constants. Anthropic principles.

I said, "So what if it's true? What difference does it make?"

"Perhaps none. Perhaps all the difference there is."

Nothing ever really matters in the context of our little lives, does it? Big deeds are only important to the Men Who Count. The rest of us just try to stay out of their way, stay whole, survive. I said, "If you could prove that, you'd know, sooner or later, anything you did would be . . . noticed."

The Kapellmeister said, "Nobody noticed when we did it before."

Martínez slid down the slope, skidding to a stop beside us. Reached out and touched the telecannon, feeling its texture through the sensitive fingers of his suit. "I don't see how something like this could be used to destroy any God-damned universe. I mean, you'd need a fuck of a lot of them to . . ."

The Kapellmeister said, "In a universe consisting entirely of Planck sockets, matter is defined by the characteristics of the socket's 'contents,' the so-called Kaluza-Klein entities. We understand that the entities, as such, are merely a convenient mathematical fiction, used to describe certain behaviors of the properties of the sockets themselves."

Martínez said, "I don't need you to explain elementary physics."

Quite. This is the stuff you learn as a child, if you're interested, certainly learn in technical school, when you begin to need it. Antigravity was the first thing we got, when we learned to manipulate some of the more obvious properties of Kaluza-Klein entities, the properties that gave rise to the conventional laws of physics, electromagnetism, chromodynamics, quantum gravity . . .

The Kapellmeister said, "In such a lattice-based cosmology, movement is an illusion."

I remember being startled when I found out Heisenberg's principle was just an expression of the "random walk" taken by the Kaluza-Klein entities in their world of rigid, motionless sockets. A particle is probably here. But it might be there. Or someplace far away. Or nowhere at all. Vacuum energy is the probability that the properties of an "empty" Planck socket may spontaneously assume some nonzero value. Some people think that's how the universe was born.

The Kapellmeister said, "Once you learn to manipulate the locus variables of a Kaluza-Klein entity, you get faster-than-light travel as an immediate consequence, though without synchronization and simultaneity between Planck sockets, there are obvious limitations."

The library whispered, Each Planck socket is an independent n-space whose existence is not determined by the existence or nonexistence of other such spaces. There is no universal program counter.

Of course not. Pretechnological societies have a word for their hypothesized universal operating system. They call it God.

The Kapellmeister said, "Shortly before the Shock War, some fine scientist, somewhere, discovered a means of inducing a standing-wave synchronization in a small number of clustered Planck sockets. It would persist only for Planck time. So you induce synchronization, then in the following 'tick,' you redefine the locus variables of the Kaluza-Klein entities. There is, of course, no way to redefine simultaneously any other quanta, for then the entities have gone. The inertial quantum was of particular interest."

Martínez' voice, soft, said, "So. How small a mass are we talking about here?"

Do I understand what they're talking about? The good doctor thinks he does.

The Kapellmeister reached down with one chela and picked up a bit of ice roughly the size of a big marble, a good-sized shooter. "This is the largest teleport bomb that was ever managed."

Martínez shrugged. "So you shoot it across interstellar space and, when it gets where it's going, it explodes in an inertial compression wave with the energy of a good-sized fission bomb? I guess if you did it to a planetary core, that'd cause a lot of damage. Enough to blow up a whole planet, though? I doubt it."

I remembered the Kapellmeister telling me about his electromagnetic pulse phaser, sufficient to blow up stars, apparently the most fearsome weapon in the Salieran arsenal. Why would they need this puny thing, when they had something like that? I tried to visualize the process described and . . . *"Shit."*

Martínez and Kapellmeisters looking at me. Hell, maybe the pod software was translating for all of them, just the way it could, apparently, talk through the symbiotes in my brain. I said, "You don't shoot a hunk of ice, Doc. You synchronize a section of Planck lattice equivalent to the hunk's space. Then you redefine its locus variables."

The Kapellmeister said, "Correct."

Martínez said, "So what? That's just another way of saying the same thing."

I shook my head slowly. "No. Matter and energy are constant. $E=mc^2$. Space is real, even in a lattice context. So you're talking about the energy necessary to accelerate a physical body to the speed of light, push it through the interstellar medium *at* the speed of light, decelerate it to a stop at the target and . . ."

His eyes looked startled. "Uh. Maybe a few thousand gigatons? Enough."

Enough to blow up a planet, but still nothing *really* spectacular. I kept thinking about the voids.

Finally, the Kapellmeister said, "Since matter and energy are equivalent, an event horizon forms at the target. Since only the locus of the original Kaluza-Klein entities has been redefined, there is insufficient mass to maintain this event horizon, which, in consequence, undergoes classical inflation."

Martínez seemed to freeze in place, eyes far away.

The Kapellmeister said, "While this does disrupt the material structures at the target, in effect an explosion, most of the mass in the target zone falls onto the expanding event horizon. When the event horizon dissipates, the accumulated mass falls into the exposed region of compressed space, forming a new event horizon which then contracts to the appropriate radius, usually on a quantum-mechanical scale."

I said, "And then Heisenberg tunneling disposes of the evidence."

The Kapellmeister said, "Correct."

Long silence.

Then Martínez whispered, "Scale effects. If you could synchronize a sufficiently large Planck domain, the inflationary era . . ."

The Kapellmeister said, "We wondered about that too, but we still don't know where the universe came from."

I awoke to pale darkness, face bathed in a hot sweat, lying in my bed aboard *Random Walk*, heart pounding in my chest. Diffuse shadows here and there, cast by the angles of the furniture in the dim radiance of the wall panels. No more ghosts. No one here but me.

I'm used to being alone. More used to it than I ever realized. Still, I wish there were someone here now. Even a dollie to comfort me. Even that.

Afterechoes of our grim conversation, back in the ruins of what the Kapellmeister told us had once been a StruldBug military nest, nest most likely destroyed by covert action in the days right before the war. Or perhaps a nest of survivors, beings who were somehow missed, just as Salieri was somehow missed, taken out later on by some wandering, vengeful ship, some lone Adversary scout perhaps . . .

Plenty of evidence, the Kapellmeister had said, that there *were* survivors, though we never found anyone. Not that we looked for long.

Images from my dream, magic weapons reaching out to infinity, snuffing out bits of the universe, incidental explosions no more than a tiny side effect, emblematic of the real destruction. Martínez puzzling over it, wondering if the old missing matter question, long ago solved he thought, had anything to do with . . .

Dreamtime more revealing. Pockets of nothing engulfing lifeforms as far as the StruldBugs and their Adversaries could reach, carrying them off to . . . somewhere else.

Destruction, the library had whispered. Complete destruction.

Correct, the Kapellmeister had said.

And what will you do now?

Will you destroy the teleport bomb?

Will you go home to Salieri and say it is no more?

The Kapellmeister had said, No. Where there's one, there will be many. Best we face this now.

Kapellmeisters chittering and snapping at one another, scissor-speech untranslated, coming to no useful conclusion, nothing they could . . . say.

Me? A brief, cold wondering, a terrible wish that there was something . . . anything I could do. Save humanity? No. Humanity doesn't deserve to be saved, myself least of all.

Innocent bystanders.

So many innocent bystanders . . .

I squeezed my eyes shut, trying to will sleep, but the images from the dream wouldn't fade. Finally, I got up, got dressed, went out into the hall and up to the control room, thinking I'd sit in the pilot's chair and look out over the lovely landscapes of Snow and brood about . . . nothing. Brood about nothing.

From its place in the flight engineer's chair, the Kapellmeister turned blue eyes my way, and said, "I am not surprised to see you, Gaetan."

I plunked down in the pilot's seat, *my* seat, God damn it, looking out at spacecraft, at domes and hills, faraway mountains and flat orange Six in the starless black sky. Almost enough to make me forget, it's so beautiful. Why isn't beauty *enough?* No answer. I said, "I forget whether you guys sleep or not."

The Kapellmeister said, "If we did, I would be unable."

I turned to stare at it, wishing I was able to read more from it than I could. Not wishing for a human face, just for . . . something like a friend. "*Are* we so similar, you and I?"

Silence.

Then it said, "It would seem so."

"You and I? Not just our two species."

Silence. Then, "Our similarities as individuals transcend the evolutionary gulf that lies between us. At times, in your company, though we can hardly communicate at all, I feel less . . . alone."

I felt a little squirm of embarrassment, a desire to turn away. Like having some comrade suddenly declare his undying love or something. Some terrible playground *faux pas.* Shit. All this and I can't escape my own idiocy? I said, "I . . . guess I understand."

Silence.

Then it said, "Gaetan, what should I do?"

Christ. I said, "You're asking the wrong guy. I've never been able to do . . . whatever the hell the right thing is. Find yourself a hero. Ask him."

"Do you know any heroes?"

"No."

More silence, then, "If it were up to you, what would you . . . want?"

Me? Personally? What would I do with the teleport bomb? Hell, shove it up my own ass and pull the trigger? I watched the Kapellmeister's eyes float expectantly, waiting for me to speak, and wondered what it'd make of a statement like that. Nothing, probably. Maybe just play it safe, tell the truth, tell it that I'd never known what I wanted, didn't have any ideas now. Except . . . you *do* know, don't you, Gaetan?

I said, "I always wanted a fair shake for myself, back when I thought I was . . . innocent. If there are innocent people in the world, beings in the universe, that's all I'd want for them."

"Whom?"

"I don't know. Wolfen. Dollies. Arousians. Guys living in cardboard boxes because some people think that all the things they can steal actually belong to them."

Silence. Then it said, "Your answer is larger than my question, Gaetan."

No shit. I said, "Everything would have to . . . change."

The Kapellmeister said, "Why do you think you don't have the courage to be an agent of change?"

I felt a slight pang of resentment at this . . . thing, menacing me and all my kind with incomprehensible destruction. Who are you to be calling me a coward? I said, "Courage is for people who think they've got something to lose."

The Kapellmeister said, "Perhaps you've got more than you realize, Gaetan du Cheyne."

More what? More courage, or merely more to lose?

Why don't I know?

20

A day and a night, then Green Heaven hung in space before us once again, a majestic, frosted blue jewel. Vast, indigo oceans. The antarctic landmass, looking so small, with its pale tan deserts, dark green jungles, shining, metallic plains, bare-sloped mountains. Koudloft, glittering brilliant white in the summer sun.

I can imagine myself down there even now, standing on the brow of some forlorn hill, warm zephyr carrying the sweet scent of life, Tau Ceti floating low in the sky like the eye of some vast, blind god. If there's poetry anywhere, it's the poetry of nature.

I looked over at the Kapellmeister. It sat silent, legs curled under, seven eyes apparently focused on the rapidly swelling world. I had a spare, stark realization that now, whatever we did, whatever happened, the consequences, for me, were immaterial. Let them destroy the human race, all the races. I'll survive because this one will protect me.

Comforting? No. Because it doesn't matter, and neither do I.

The Kapellmeister said, "Sometimes, I have an urge to take one of the old ships and run away, flee into the cosmos, see all the worlds, and never again deal with anything but beauty."

I said, "I wonder how long it'd take to tire of splendor."

Silence from the Kapellmeister, then, "Not long, perhaps."

When death is inevitable, you don't need a reason to die, and therefore, no reason to live. Time passes and, in the end, you are consumed. Life makes dollies of us all. As we bit into the air, pink plasma flaring outside, I said, "If you had a reason to, would you live forever?"

The Kapellmeister seemed fascinated by the way the landscape below grew and flattened, mountains suddenly humping up, sky overhead changing from black to indigo to turquoise blue. It said, "There is no forever, Gaetan."

No, I suppose not.

The Koudloft was sweeping by below us now, barren white hills catching the shadow of the ship, reflecting the pastel light of its drive energies, mirroring the color of the sky. Suddenly, the hills came to an end. We crossed a short stretch of bare tundra, a little belt of dull, gray-green taiga, then the ship flared, hovering over the edge of the Koperveldt, and sank to the ground, blue light swirling briefly around us.

Contact, whispered the navigation subsystem. Drive suspend.

Gravity's vector suddenly changed, metadynamic forces releasing me, Green Heaven's mass seizing all my atoms at once. I stood, stretched, looking out the window at familiar territory, and said, "I feel like I've made a decision." Unusual feeling, in a life where all my decisions were made for me, by other people, or simply by default.

The Kapellmeister hopped to the floor. "We both have," it said.

Outside, on a grassy Koperveldt hillside, the wind was very sweet indeed, carrying with it a thousand unidentifiable Rock Candy Mountain smells, almost masking the burnt-toast odor *Random Walk*'s drive had left behind on a little patch of fried ground. We walked away from the shadow of the ship, angling up toward the ridge, stopping where we could look down into the little valley where the Arousians had made camp.

Tau Ceti hung in the blue-green sky, just the way I remembered it, throwing warm golden rays over pale, rolling hills, casting deep blue shadows down among the crags of the remote, towering mountains. I took a deep breath, trying to shake off unexpected euphoria. "Christ. I feel like somebody made this just for me."

The Kapellmeister said, "Sometimes, when I come unexpectedly on some valley full of mist and shadow, something which reminds me of a childhood scene on Salieri, or even just a dream, remembered from someone else's childhood, I experience that feeling too."

Is that all it is? I don't want to believe that. Not now; not ever.

Down below, down in the valley, there are the Arousians' clustered tents, familiar tripods of camera equipment already set up by the stream. And there are the Arousians themselves, stick-bug men already walking this way, walking up the hill to greet us.

Over there? Yes, there in the shadows of a baarbij bush, a small cluster of dollies, kneeling in the shade, waiting, without the slightest inkling of things to come. The dollies merely wait, under the watchful eyes of their wolfen, wolfen I see lurking in the grass nearby. Just one more empty dollie day, waiting to die in the jaws of the gods, no matter that the world is filled with crazy aliens, crazy aliens and their incomprehensible doings. No matter that the world is full of beauty.

When I imagine myself a dollie, I wonder how they feel about the way human hunters kill their gods with lightning called down from the sky. Perhaps, just the way Moloch's babies felt, with the coming of *YHWH* and his doppelgänger, Allah.

Over by the river, to my slight surprise, were three vast, dark womfrogs, apparently having been drinking, heads now raised, looking in our direction. I want to fancy I can feel their fear. Human being up there, they think. To us, a human being is only death. How does it feel to be Death Incarnate, I wonder. I don't like the feeling at all.

Every now and again you hear a news story, story of how

some simple wage-slave, fired, disciplined, cast aside, abandoned, returns armed to the scene of his disgrace. On that day, bosses die, and the rest of us feel a smug satisfaction, knowing they probably deserved it.

I imagine myself a boss, riven by the thunderbolts of vengeance, crying out: It wasn't my fault. There are other greater bosses above me. Don't kill me please. I was only following orders.

This feeling I have now is just like that.

Then the Arousians were standing in front of us, looking at me with their stick-bug eyes, looking down at the Kapellmeister. Perhaps they have some inkling of why we've come again. The nearest of them, Rustmold-on-Pale-Snow I was pleased to remember, moved its arms in some kind of Arousian body language and said, *Greekeegreekee . . .*

The translator box clipped to its harness made a sound like a rhinoceros ramming a truck, followed by the sound of that same truck tumbling end over end down a long, rocky defile.

Arousian consternation? Merely my interpretation of the pose it makes.

Greekee?

Sledgehammer pounding on galvanized tin.

Rustmold-on-Pale-Snow plucked the thing from its clip, holding it above its head by two spindly hands, shaking it, punching buttons, screaming, *Greekeegreekeegreekeegreekee!*

The box whispered, *Whappawhappawhackwhack . . .*

The Arousian threw it on the ground, started trampling the thing with all of its several little feet, until its case burst open and the insides popped out. The other Arousians started making a series of bird-like twittering noises while this was going on.

"What are they saying?"

The Kapellmeister said, "They are laughing, Gaetan."

Laughing. I stepped forward, one hand on what I supposed was Rustmold's shoulder, putting a stop to its little dance, Arousian's flesh like dry, dead reeds to my touch. It recoiled, startled, and the others stopped laughing.

"Take it easy, pal."

I knelt then, gathering up the bits of its translation machine, taking a good look. Stuff like wet, crumpled toilet paper, pieces of dead grass, little blue leaves and strips of tinsel. For Christ's sake. Autoprogramming mechanical nanocircuitry? "This piece of shit must be three hundred years old."

The Kapellmeister said, "The Arousians are permitted to take what they wish from MEI's recycling bins."

"So their lords and masters supply them with whatever junk they want, but . . ." I gestured around the camp, "are willing to have them come here and . . ."

The Kapellmeister said, "The remarkable thing is not what a talking dog *says*, Gaetan, but that he speaks at all."

A slight jolt at what that implied.

The Kapellmeister said, "Can you fix it, Gaetan?"

I looked at the worthless crap in my hands, and said, "Oh, I suppose so. But it won't work any better than it did before. Why bother?" I dropped it on the ground.

The Arousian stepped closer, seeming to peer into my eyes, though what good that would do it, I couldn't imagine. Its compound eyes looked like bits of fabric to me.

It said, "I wish I could talk to you."

I blinked stupidly, and said, "What?"

Then both of us recoiled, turning to face the Kapellmeister simultaneously.

The library AI whispered, The pod software has established a direct link with our internal communication subsystem, Gaetan. It has begun spooling out a copy of its linguistic algorithms, which are so surpassingly . . . so wonderfully . . .

Imagine an artificial intelligence at a loss for words.

The Kapellmeister said, "The salient thing about friendship appears to be the issue of *trust.*"

In due course, Tau Ceti went down, staining the undersides of the clouds with orange and gold just as it slid below the horizon, sky turning black overhead, nameless stars popping through the fabric of heaven like little white lights. The fires were lit, red and yellow flames leaping up, casting long, unstable shadows, while we went about the separate business of making our meals, I with my bits from the starship's galley, Arousians roasting a shish kebab of things like pieces of rubber tire, the Kapellmeister returning from a short wilderness foray with some small, helpless staring creature, quietly accepting its fate because it had no choice.

Trying so hard to ignore all the whispers the newly upgraded translation AI made in my head. Ignore them for now, at any rate. Three womfrogs, hulking shadows by the river . . .

We came here to treat with the sky people, who profess to be our friends.

Humans are sky people too.

No. They are only humans. Let's kill this one and be on our way.

What good would that do? Only enrage its kind, to the detriment of our children.

Even one less human being in the world is a good thing.

Still I persist in wondering if all this is merely an artifact of some algorithm gone mad. The story I tell myself is merely part of another childhood dream, If I could talk to the animals . . .

Not animals, Gaetan, whispered the library.

No. Not animals. But in the world of talking animals we create for our children, where is the butcher? You remember the satisfaction of Herr Dunderbeck's destruction, but only because it dealt with our sacred pets, our cats and dogs, whom we've made into something oh-so-much like furry little boys and girls . . .

One more dream peered from the depths, where I'd buried it long ago, the deep, dark eyes of the woman who loved me forever, the children we made together, all the things that make a man's life seem less . . . self-contained.

When did I lose that dream?

Maybe I never had it.

Arousians gathered before me now, having finished their meal, watching me finish mine. Watching me lick the shiny grease of a ham sandwich from my fingers. What do they make of that? I looked at my wet fingers, then at them, realizing I had no idea whether or not the odd-smelling things they ate were animal, vegetable, mineral . . .

I wonder. In a world where people ate only rocks, would there be anguished souls who suffered over the ignoble fate of stones?

Across the way, watching us eat, the wolfen lay curled in the grass, dollies beyond them, watching as well. More whispers I wanted to ignore . . .

Look. Look. They're eating together. What if they invite the wolfen to join them?

The womfrogs were no more than vast background shadows, tearing up fistfuls of grass, stuffing them into huge mouths, with a soft, *crush, crush, crush,* scent of mashed vegetation further sweetening the night air.

Rustmold-on-Pale-Snow said, "Will you help us, then, Gaetan du Cheyne?"

Help you? Fly you from world to world in my little starship, fly you faster than light, help you set up a legal team, publicize your cause on human worlds that matter, in this window of opportunity, before MEI can realize what's happening, before it can buy FTL starships of its own, bring its enormous resources to bear?

The Arousian said, "They're *our* resources, Gaetan du Cheyne. The resources of the Sigma Draconis worlds. *Stolen* from us."

Ah, yes. The issue, as always, is just what belongs to whom.

"My resources are somewhat limited, you know."

The Arousian said, "We'll pay you back . . . someday."

How does it feel to be bargaining with the devil?

For that matter, how does it feel to be the devil with whom the downtrodden must bargain?

Now I know.

Huge dark mass suddenly looming out of the night, enormous face hanging in the firelight, making me remember another night when I'd crept through the underbrush beside Gretel Blondinkruis, had looked down into the ravine, into the faces of the doomed. Hell, all *I* ever wanted was Gretel's sweet ass, and I never did shoot any womfrogs.

Its voice was a dull throb in my head: "What about *us*, Gaetan du Cheyne? Don't *we* deserve your help?"

Do you?

The womfrog said, "We didn't ask humans to come kill us. Kill us all just for fun, kill us and eat our dead bodies, kill us and take our skin for carpeting and coats."

No, I suppose not. But we came anyway. Why didn't you do anything to stop us?

"You think this is *our* fault? What could we have done?"

One of the wolfen, a large fertile female, stood, came slinking over, sat on her haunches, facing me. "This was *our* world. The gods gave it to *us.*"

Which gods were those, dear wolfen?

She said, "When you help the Arousians, you can help us, Gaetan du Cheyne. We know you've taken this world away, that you'll never give it back. But there are so *many* worlds . . . surely there's one little world somewhere, around some forgotten star, a world no one else wants, where the wolfen and womfrogs and the boomers in the sea . . ."

How poetic.

Pathetic poetry.

And yet . . .

We could find that forgotten star, *Random Walk* and I, then . . .

Every womfrog and wolfen and dollie on Green Heaven would fit in the cargo hold of a single old STL freighter. Put them in cold storage and it wouldn't matter how long it took to reach that forgotten star. Boomers? Sure. Fill a second ship with water, pack them in like sardines, freeze the whole mass solid and . . . on your way.

You know what's going to happen, Gaetan du Cheyne. Once the FTL technology really gets going, the old interstellar economy is going to collapse. Things are going to be very different in just a few years. In just a few years they'll be selling STL freighters for two dismes on the livre. Christ. Probably get two such cargo carriers for a couple of hundred thousand livres.

And you've *got* a couple of hundred thousand livres, don't you, Gaetan du Cheyne?

I felt a little twist of anger then, corkscrewing through my intestines. Why me? Why do *I* have to be the one to do it?

I got up and walked away from the fire, turning my back on Kapellmeisters, Arousians, womfrogs and wolfen. Listened to the dollies whisper, whisper in growing consternation as they realized I was walking toward them.

Looking down, seeing them huddled there in my shadow, I could feel the sharp skewer of desire rising within me. Nothing. Not me. Not my fault. Just subtle pheromones playing on my nervous system. Not me at all.

Ah, yes. Since when did the things of your body cease to be *you*, Gaetan du Cheyne?

Excuses don't matter.

I turned back to see the others all watching me. Waiting. Imagining I might have something significant to say. Waiting for some magic word that will change their world, unseal their fate.

I gestured at the dollies, and said, "What about them?"

Dollie whispers . . . what is he saying?

Oh, Goddess. Goddess, listen!

Finally, the wolfen said, "What do you mean? Those are our dollies, of course."

Right. I said, "So you'll take the dollies with you to the promised land, and fuck them and eat them and nothing will ever change?"

You could hear astonishment in the wolfen's translated voice: "What else would we do?"

One of the dollies got up, stumbled over to me, and fell on its knees, grabbing the front of my pant legs, looking up at me, dark eyes wide with desperation. "Please. Please, Lord," it whispered. "Tell them we want to live!"

It's nice to be begged, isn't it?

Especially by something that might suck your dick later on, hmh?

Breathing in its hormonal vapors, hair crawling on the back of my neck, I visualized how much pleasure I could have, raping this helpless little thing.

The dollie kneeling before me whispered, "You're all we have, Gaetan du Cheyne. Save us."

I turned away from them all, looking up into the star-filled sky, remembering suddenly just how much I'd always loved the stars. And I said, "Yes, I suppose I will."

Then the dollies gathered round, vying for position, apparently trying to kiss my feet.

Later on, midnight, with the moons gone down, only the stars for light, I sat in the darkness, looking up at the sky. The Arousians had retired, puttering around the camp, cleaning up, banking the fires or putting them out entirely before going into their tents, soft *greekeegreekee*, then nothing more.

Over there, beside the gurgling waters of the river, the three womfrogs were massive sleeping hulks, whispering softly in their sleep, between small, contented snores. Right now, an unknown future waits. Much better than the certain death they'd had before.

What's the worst that can happen? He fails, then the hunters come and kill us? That's what was *going* to happen. Better to have hope, however small and frail.

Wolfen curled up, not far away, stirring and muttering in their dreams. The big female lay on her side, stretched out, teeth visible, legs twitching softly, the beginnings of little running movements.

Do all thinking beings dream?

Beyond them, I could see the dollies huddled together in the stygian shadow of their baarbij bush. Somewhere under the ground, clutched in the embrace of its twining roots, the bones of long-dead dollies lie, mixed with a soil made from wolfen shit.

Maybe there's a dollie heaven somewhere. Maybe, somehow, they know.

Stupid. What I'm thinking about now is going over there, waking one of the dollies, leading it away into the darkness. That's it, find a nice, private place, make a comfortable bed from soft Koperveldt grass, lay the dollie on its back in your bed and . . .

The Kapellmeister, my Kapellmeister, came ambling out of the darkness, stood before me in the night with its eyes floating high. Do you know what I'm thinking, Mr. Kapellmeister? Perhaps you do. How does it feel to be in the company of such a miserable creature as me?

The Kapellmeister said, "You're a hero to them now, Gaetan du Cheyne."

A small, definite sinking feeling, right here in my gut. I said, "I don't feel like a hero."

"Real heroes never do."

"No?"

Silence. Then it said, "The salient thing about brotherhood is obligation."

Right. Galling bitterness in my throat. "Whose brother am *I*?" For that matter, whose brother are you?

The Kapellmeister made a short, running jump and landed right in my lap, seven eyes looking at me from seven directions. "Do you wonder why, Gaetan my brother?"

Yes.

It said, "This is why."

Then its hand, warm black hand made of so many tentacles, reached out and engulfed me and . . .

Click.

Four hundred million years ago, I sat alone on a warm rock in the middle of the night, looking up at the star-filled sky.

Sat there and waited, while the warm winds of Salieri blew across my skin. Such a lovely night, a night for . . .

Flash.

Sudden, brilliant light from a dying sun.

There, then gone again in the twinkling of an eye.

I'd been waiting for it, waiting for years.

Strange to think of them as silent stars.

But we did nothing, said the Kapellmeister.

We let it happen.

A few more years of waiting, then *flash*, another one fades away.

Silent stars.

Out there, just a few years ago, you see, the weapons were readied, readied and fired and fired again. Do you call it a war, when it's only five seconds long? Maybe you just call it the end.

Flash. Then *flash* again. Then again.

I sat on my rock and waited, wondering just what we *should* have done, rather than merely let it happen, while the stars twinkled and flashed and died away. After a few hundred years, you could see dozens of worlds die on any given night. After a few thousand years, the whole sky seemed to glitter and sparkle and glow as infalling light from the death of all the worlds came our way.

In those days, most of us chose to live in burrows under the ground.

That way we couldn't see it happen.

No way to forget, but you can hide, close your eyes, pretend . . .

In time, the light came from stars so far away you needed amplification to see the explosions, of course. In time, I could sit on my rock and look up at the silent stars, drink in their cold, empty beauty as if nothing had ever happened.

But in the telescopes . . .

In the telescopes.

Maybe I sat on my warm rock, all alone, and watched the beautiful heavens flicker and die for seventeen million years. Maybe longer.

Whose fault was that?

No one?

At last, I sat in the pilot's chair on the flight deck of *Random Walk*, looking out through the viewscreens at those same silent stars. Silent no longer, remember that. They're all out there. Waiting. Waiting for us to come. In a few thousand years, at most, the sky will be full of voices once more. Full of voices, full of ships, full of people.

Nice to be up here alone.

Alone with my thoughts.

Forty-one hours from Green Heaven to the jump point, then bound in an instant across the trackless wasteland, a mere 12.68 light-years from Tau Ceti to 82 Eridani, though the Kapellmeister's star lay more than twenty from Earth . . .

I thought about the womfrog stuffed in down below, hardly able to move, insisting it'd be all right for a few days lying on its side, gasping for breath in the space we'd carved out by cutting through the bulkhead between two staterooms.

A volunteer. This is important, whispering to its two friends, telling them to spread the word, the word of salvation, as quickly as possible, to all the womfrogs of Green Heaven.

Salvation. Christ. Who the hell am I to be a savior?

No one at all, and yet . . .

Wolfen down below as well, sleeping in the cabins where I'd put them. Funny as hell to see that big female try to crawl up into a bunk. This interesting soft stuff, my, my . . . I'd left them lying on the floor, on pulled-apart bedding, marveling at how nice it was, stretched out on all those mattresses.

And, of course, the dollies, taking my word, trusting that I wouldn't let the wolfen eat them, ever again.

Hard to remember their whispered arguments, even now. Hard to live with their words. But if the wolfen don't *eat* us, how will we get to heaven?

Clinging tight to that one fierce whisper: I don't know. I want to live.

All right. So we go to the Kapellmeister's world, talk to its friends, present our case to its enemies, tell them *we* want to live too. It's *our* universe, you see. Our lives and . . .

As always, a matter of what belongs to whom.

Will they listen?

No way to know.

Maybe it doesn't matter.

Soft movement behind me. The head of a dollie poking above the rim of the open hatchway, looking around curiously, eyes big and dark. I've given them the run of the ship, you see.

Because the salient thing about friendship is trust?

Perhaps.

Or that other matter, the business of brotherhood and obligation.

It got up on the deck and came padding over, putting its hands on the safely locked controls, leaning close, looking out through the viewscreens at an infinitely deep landscape of stars.

What do you make of that, little dollie? Anything at all?

It turned and looked at me, though I hadn't said a word, then came over, soft and silent, stared at me, empty-eyed for just a moment, then crawled up in my lap, settling down, nuzzling its head under my chin.

Whose obligation now, Gaetan du Cheyne?

I stroked its soft fur, pretending it was just a big cat purring in my lap. But, you know, this *desire* within me . . .

Do I really wish it wasn't there? What would it be like to have that purity of purpose, to know I've joined battle in a great cause, that I'm about to fight the good fight people love to talk about? Is there any way I'll ever know?

Or will I spoil it now by taking this dollie, laying it down on the deck, spreading its legs and . . .

The dollie looked up at me, reached up and touched my face softly, as if trying to reassure me that . . .

Oh, hell.

I never amounted to a pile of shit in my life, I know that. Maybe if I can just save these people . . . maybe then, when my time comes to lie down and die, I won't feel quite so bad.

William Barton's previous books include *A Plague of All Cowards, Dark Sky Legion, When Heaven Fell* and *The Transmigration of Souls,* and two collaborations with Michael Capobianco, *Iris* and *Fellow Traveler.* His short fiction and nonfiction have appeared in such diverse publications as *Asimov's, Full Spectrum 5, Ad Astra* and *Commodore Powerplay.* He lives in Durham, North Carolina, with his wife, Kathleen.